BRINK

MIKEL PARRY

Mikel Parry Publishing, Salt Lake City, UT

Copyright 2019 Mikel Parry

ISBN 978-0-9976383-3-2

Cover Design: Lindsey Parry

Editor: Joe Spring

BRINK

MIKEL PARRY

TABLE OF CONTENTS

ABYSSOPELAGIC

"Aardvark . . . it's aardvark."

A man sat sprawled out on a long leather couch, slowly closing and opening his eyes. He was an average sized man with an average sized build. His green, beady eyes snaked this way and that, examining every detail of the odd word. His exposed hair resembled a short, trimmed hedge line. His ears perked up upon hearing a response. Immediately his face took on a distasteful look, as if he were swishing vinegar.

"Are you *sure* it's aardvark? That doesn't seem right."

He was speaking to a slender, professionally dressed woman, slouched down in a large arm chair. Her long, pampered hair fell loosely, and was made even more stunning by her deep, brown eyes. She was carelessly holding a dictionary in one hand while working on a crossword puzzle in the other. Her demeanor expressed the obvious—she was both annoyed and bored.

"Thomas, it's always been aardvark. Why would *aardvark* come after *alligator* in the dictionary? And besides that, there's got to be a million words between them."

Thomas sat up slightly in his chair, his face adorned with a cheesy grin. His mind was crafting a playful jab of sarcasm.

"It's not the order that matters; what matters is that it's *there*."

Barb put down her crossword puzzle slightly. She gave him a look of complete annoyance. Her eyes danced up and down while her brain continued to process the ridiculous remark.

"Honestly, why do you come in here? You know this place costs a fortune, just for you to play games. But yet, here you are, week after week. I just don't know what you want from me, Thomas."

Thomas looked out the window by the plush leather couch. He saw two small boys running down the street without a care, streaming two hovering balloons in the air behind them. He felt introspective, but just not enough to care.

"I don't know . . . just trying to figure myself out. Figure out why my tick doesn't tock. And my girlfriend says it helps level me out."

Barb rolled her eyes. The crossword was now sitting in her lap of finely sewn linen.

"Level you out?"

Thomas glanced back at the sudden spark of interest that had pried its way free.

"Yeah, she says I'm more bearable after I come in here—whatever that means. I guess it just is what it is."

"That's putting it lightly."

The heavy handed remark struck dead on. Without hesitation, a look of concern etched its way across Thomas' face.

"Hey, you're supposed to be on my side. What am I paying you for here?"

Barb flung her head back and took a deep breath. Her professionalism was fading into a pit of childish indulgences. She was done playing nice but knew that monetary constraints contractually obligated her to behave civilly and they tightened around her like an anaconda.

"Oh, I don't know . . . to *help* you . . . help you discover the inner you that's just dying to get out."

Her comment had bin dipped in a viscous vat of sarcasm. The poison apple had been delivered; now she was just waiting for Thomas to bite.

"You know I'm getting engaged, right?"

Suddenly, Barb's sarcastic facade was crumbled by the sheer force of her insatiable feminine curiosity.

"You're getting *engaged*? To an actual living, breathing *woman*?"

Thomas stood up and adjusted his finely pressed suit. Inside his pocket his badge shifted loose, slightly peeking itself over the brim of his pocket. He quickly put it back inside.

Abyssopelagic

"You know, maybe it's *you* that should be in this chair sometime. Those claws are razor sharp."

"That's great, Thomas! This could be a real breakthrough for you. This could help you overcome the trust barrier we've been . . . *I've* been talking about."

Thomas looked lost in thought. In his mind, he was sucking in all of the interesting details of the room, one-by-one. So many oddities that his mind just couldn't let go. With lightning speed, he was dissecting each thing with surgical precision.

"What happened to your little boy toy? I don't see any of his pictures, and you have a bunch of things missing that I'm assuming were memoirs of good times. I really miss that picture of you two and the cat. That was a really fat cat. You know . . . they can have heart attacks too, right?"

Barb got off her couch and crossed her arms.

"Thomas, seriously—I don't think that is any of your business."

Thomas paced around in small circles. His brain was doing it again; there didn't seem to be an off switch. There were so many questions that needed to be explored logically. The details of the room were all fighting for prominence in his queue of thought.

"You're right—I apologize—I know I can be difficult."

Barb took a deep, meditative breath and sat back down in her chair.

"I just don't understand why you come here wanting help but then just spend your time autopsying my room while memorizing a dictionary."

"Room I can't help; the dictionary is to level me out. If I can target something then it calms me down. Plus it's just good practice."

Barb crossed her legs before adjusting her tight skirt around her waist. Her long legs gleamed in the room's carefully directed light. She let out a tiny sliver of a grin at his comment.

"Well, you suck at it. At least you can't seem to put things in order. But it would be more advantageous, if you will, to actually focus on your real issues from time-to-time, don't you think? I mean, look at some of these words in here—aardwolf, abbozzo, abyssopelagic—what does that even *mean*?"

Thomas raised an eyebrow as if it was obvious.

"Page twenty six—abyssopelagic— of, like, or pertaining to the

3

depths of the ocean . . ."

Barb looked slightly impressed by the absurd answer, but she quickly dismissed it as she had long ago become accustomed to his circus act.

"Why on earth would you remember that?"

Again, Thomas conveyed with body language his disbelief.

"Abyss, the movie, I loved that movie. That's how I remember that page, word, and definition amongst the others. It's just a simple relation. Eidetic correlation is what they call it. Just has to stick out."

As he stood still pondering all of the other words and their attached definitions, he couldn't help but feel a weird sense of being. Just what exactly was his problem? Years of living with his freakish ability had led him to be both praised and ostracized. But what else could he be? The answer would have to wait. His phone was ringing.

"Oh, no... we were just starting to connect," Barb said sarcastically.

Thomas gave her a snappy look of annoyance. He couldn't help that he was the way he was. Slithering his phone from his pants pocket, he answered.

"Tommy, you know that place down on second Ave., the big office building that smells like old donuts?"

Now this was his language. He was horrible with directions, found them to be completely boring. But a giant building that smelled of old donuts was a clear map.

"Yup . . ."

The phone clicked and went to a harmonious chime.

"You leaving so soon?" probed Barb, twirling her pen in her hand and now sitting comfortably back in her chair, working on her crossword puzzle.

"It's a dog-eat-dog world out there, Barb. Men like me just can't get any breaks. Besides, those crossword puzzles aren't going to finish themselves."

Barb rolled her eyes before sinking even further back into her cushy chair. She stuck one hand high up into the air and gave a firm goodbye wave.

"Good luck on your engagement. I'm sure it'll be the most romantic bucket of banter I've ever heard come next time."

"Barb, you're far too sentimental. You've got a legal battle on your hands, anyways. I hope you get that porpoise feline back."

Barb's eyes narrowed. She refused to look up but it was obvious the comment had struck a nerve.

"I'd ask how you figured that out, but I know it's pointless. Just know your special aptitude has a way of especially pissing me off."

"It's in the details, Barb . . . always is."

Thomas walked out of the office looking down at his watch. Thirty five minutes and thirty five seconds. Thirty five, thirty five—he'd done it. The brief moment of complex pleasure created a moment of reprieve. What a silly thing to care about; matching minutes to seconds. But he was jubilant in the moment. Now it was time to be normal; normal enough to get to the old donut building. To do this he'd need to put his cluttered brain noise on mute. And then there was the driving. He hated driving, passing so many interesting things without stopping to delve a bit further. It was torture.

Heading to the office, his phone buzzed again. This time it was a simple text message that had come from his girlfriend.

C U Later LUV U

The simplicity of the message was beautiful in its apathy. So much time had been saved by merely using the correct letters. The brain could do the rest—one C, three U's, one L, and just one coherent word—there was so little and yet so much.

"Hey! Watch out, moron!" screamed a man jumping out of the way of his car.

Thomas shook his head. Had he really just lost his focus to a text message? Looking back, he saw the man give him a furious gesture of approval while standing dead center in a cross walk. This came as a bitter realization that made him cringe.

Seriously, Tommy, a text message, it's just a stupid text message. What's wrong with me?

A small dose of adrenaline hit his head from the close encounter, jostling his brain a bit. He needed to stay focused. He was now on the job and heading to what undoubtedly would be another heinous crime. He needed to get it together. He needed to make a phone call. Letting his phone dangle near his ear as he struggled to navigate through the

crowded streets of the city, he pressed the call button and waited.
"Tommy, I'm already at the door. You want to carpool this one?"
"Like always, I'll pick you up, you drive."
He clicked the phone shut and threw it down onto the car seat.
Within a few moments he arrived at the doors of a large office
building. There standing in front was his partner. He wore a fine,
pressed suit that was much like the man who wore it. His hair was
carefully groomed, as was every other detail about him. He frowned
upon seeing the front of the car. Quickly, Thomas got out, taking a
deep breath in an attempt to shed himself of all the anxiety he'd built
up on the way there.
"What's this? You ding my car, Tommy? You've got to be kidding me."
Thomas looked at the front of the car and suddenly remembered
the tragic demise of a metal trash can that he had sent barreling into
a dark alley when he failed to stop soon enough. He had been caught
up in thought, trying to understand why some of the sidewalk slabs
appeared to be equally spaced while others weren't. Was there a reason
for this? What was it trying to tell him? The trash can's fate at that
point was text book.
"Oh, that . . . I don't know what that is . . . wasn't it like that before?"
The man circled over and snatched the keys from his hands.
"You know, there are two hundred and six bones in the human
body, but we've only got one car. Maybe it's only fair I break one of
those bones every time you screw things up!"
Thomas ground his teeth, realizing that the impact left a scar far
worse than he'd expected. Why did they make trash cans so hefty?
"Your right shoelace is coming undone. I've seen it slip ever since
you started moving. And it's good to see you too, *Vaun*."
Vaun got into the car, as did Thomas. Vaun looked completely
frustrated. Unable to resist the temptation any longer, he glanced
down. Sure enough, his right shoelace was on the brink of coming
undone. He hated the awkward feeling of realizing that such a
minute detail had escaped him. But when working with someone like
Thomas, it was an everyday occurrence.
"You know, they should lock people like you up; just amazing to me
that you even get out of bed without counting the threads of your sheets."
Thomas began to respond but was cut off by a sharp, pointed finger.

Abyssopelagic

The answer to that was obvious, as was the feather count of his pillow. This and many other useless details came flooding into his mind.

"Shut up. I don't want to hear it."

The two of them sped off towards the predefined location to fulfill their professional obligations. As they drove, Vaun began to rant about his day thus far. The politics in the force had driven him to confide in the least likely candidate to care. But he needed to vent somewhere. He smelled of a mixture of spearmint and coffee, with a hint of cheap deodorant. Screeching the car to a sudden stop, he abruptly stepped out, and began walking into a large building.

Smells just like old donuts. Actually, come to think of it, when have I smelled old donuts? thought Thomas.

He followed Vaun's lead, trailing him up a short flight of stairs into the edifice. Once inside, they were greeted by a vibrant, bright-eyed young officer. Both he and Vaun flashed their credentials before the man spoke.

"They're upstairs. It looks pretty nasty. Hope you're okay with blood."

Instantly, Thomas cringed. The thought of blood made his toes curl; such a thick liquid that held so many intimate details. It was a gross understatement to say that it didn't repulse him. He'd always hated having to deal with it, and it was severe irony that now he had to deal with it almost all the time.

"Blood, you hear that, Tommy? Hope you brought your mittens."

Thomas shot Vaun a nauseated look. He was going to be fine. He would just deal with things, articulately.

"I'll be fine, let's just get this over with."

Into the elevator they went. Once inside, Thomas watched Vaun push the number twenty-three. In his mind the number's relevance began to grow and grow like a snowball as it rolled around in all the sticky correlations. By the time the doors chimed and slid open, he had sapped every bit of information available from the elevator's seemingly meaningless role.

"Twenty-three like MJ, the angel number twenty-three, or the axis of the earth which is twenty-three point five degrees. But the point five seems off."

Vaun looked down at his gun then back at Thomas.

"I have enough bullets, should I do you or me first?"

He then shook his head and pressed forward into a room filled with commotion. Investigators darted this way and that, all burying their heads in paperwork and deep thought. All seemed blissfully unaware of the others' presence.

"Just let me do the talking, like always. You can alienate everybody later. For now, we at least need to know what's going on."

Thomas rolled his eyes. He started to respond with his own witty remark when his eyes scanned over a trail of blood that had deeply stained the fibrous white carpet. The blood had been there for quite some time, its darkened color divulging its timeline to a trained eye. From there it led towards the center of the hustle and bustle that shrouded the remainder of the clues in mystery.

"Detectives, it's good to see that you both made it safe and sound."

Out from the midst of the crowded room, came the towering figure of a very heavy set man. His oversized body breached many points of his undersized shirt exposing the skin below. He came at them quickly, stuffing a chunk of his shirt clumsily into his pants.

"Pete—Pete Boggan—still have no clue how a guy like that hit the top of the food chain around here," mumbled Vaun.

Thomas remained silent. He was looking over Pete in great detail. He looked well fed, as usual, as well as rested and uppity. His skin was slightly tanned and he had actually added a few extra pounds to his already abundant figure. The jiggling movement of his gut mesmerized Thomas. How many fat cells were in there? Had Pete always been so jiggly?

"As I live and breathe, Vaun Josey and the legend Tommy Gun."

As his decree bellowed through the room due to his powerful voice, he looked at Thomas strangely, who was still staring at his stomach.

"My face is up here; you like the package so much you're going to have to sign."

Vaun elbowed Thomas in the side. Immediately he came back into the moment feeling very embarrassed.

"It's Thomas Ghune—the g is silent—I got it from my great granddad. So it's actually Thomas *Hune*, or *Hoon*, I guess."

Pete looked perplexed by the pointless correction of pronunciation. Of course he knew that his real name wasn't Tommy *Gun*. But Tommy Gun stuck. It brought to him nostalgic memories of a time long since passed. Shrugging it off, he continued.

"Got a real busted watermelon over there . . . I suggest you keep yourselves near a trash can; especially you, Tommy."

Thomas waived the comment off.

"I'll be fine; I'm working on my gag reflex."

"Right, whatever, but really guys, this one is looking to be your standard popped top. Big cat on Wall Street poised to make it big suddenly tanks, is my bet. Then, *Pow*! Puts one right through the temple door."

Pete made the motion of a pistol being pressed up against the head using his thumb and forefinger.

"We've got this place pretty scrubbed, but as always, it awaits some of your *special* feedback."

As Pete spoke, he locked his gaze upon Thomas. Without saying the actual word he had just called him a freak.

"Feel free to roam. I'll do my best to clear a path."

Pete clapped his hands and turned. As he did, the chunk of tucked-in shirt fell loose and began dangling in the air.

"With his paycheck you think he could afford to buy a shirt that fits," said Vaun, rolling his eyes.

"Yeah, well, we can't all look as good as you in a five dollar suit," retorted Thomas, sneaking past him.

He immediately began to scrutinize the room in its entirety. A large corner office filled with never been touched books and pretentious nick-knacks, the ideal dwelling place for a money-hungry up and comer. The room was perfectly organized. Every little item had its own place, all meticulously organized to the highest degree.

Where to start?

Now his mind's cogs and gears were spinning. This is what he lived for. The nonstop prompting and begging of his brain for an audience was gloriously hushed and content. Things were just starting to pick up. Walking towards the center of the room he immediately caught a glimpse of the bloodied corpse. The hollowed out fragments of what once was the man's head sat like a thousand pieces to a puzzle strewn about the floor. Without warning, he was on the verge of throwing up.

"Trash can, where's a trash can?"

He plowed his way towards what appeared to be a trash can and let it all loose. The purge brought a wave of relief. Taking a few deep breaths, he got back up onto his feet.

"Tommy, you just puked in a vase!" yelled Pete, shaking his head.

"Sorry, must have been something in the air. I'm good now."

A group of officers gave him a very concerned look before shaking their own heads while mumbling streams of obscenities. It was clear that they would much rather have him incarcerated than to be allowed to freely roam their precious crime scenes.

Looking up from the vase, he followed a row of books that were randomly spaced apart. His eyes darted back and forth, taking in all the interesting details. There were history, law, medicine, and finance books, all carefully bound in rustic looking leather. *What a waste.* Their order was categorized carefully, their orientation all the same. All the same except for one—a law book detailing investment legalities. It was out of order sitting in finance; perhaps placed there by mistake, but in lieu of the painstaking order of everything else, it seemed odd.

"Tommy, you going to come take a look at this guy, or not?"

Thomas closed his eyes. He knew it was going to be difficult to keep from spewing his anxiety. But he had a job to do. Gathering himself up, he stepped up to the dead man's body. Instantly, he could feel the sea of apprehension locked in his bowels begin to swish around. Swallowing a tennis ball-sized lump in his throat, he began investigating the scene.

A man in his forties, dressed to kill. His perfectly polished shoes gleamed against the room's light. Everything else appeared to be, much like the room, in perfect order, with the obvious exception of the chaos that was his head. Words could not adequately describe the carnage that a well-placed bullet had inflicted.

"Weapon; where's the weapon?"

A man came forward holding a plastic bag gingerly. He put it in front of Thomas to view. It was a beautifully designed pistol, most likely custom. A large bored-out hole on the gun divulged the powerful caliber that it was equipped for, a weapon that had some serious fire power.

"How many shots?"

For a moment the man fumbled around as if trying to ask the gun how many bullets it had left. But then his memory brought back the answer.

"One, just one—in fact, the clip only had one bullet—must have kept it empty except for the one that did him in."

Thomas shook his head. Something seemed off about that description. Why was he keeping his gun empty up until now? Most guns held some sort of protective purpose; what purpose did an empty gun have? Perhaps it was more decorative than purposeful. A lot of ideas were beginning to pool in his head, drowning out the commotion around him. Standing back up, he walked around to the desk. The man had shot himself in front of it, or so it would seem. On the desk were piles of papers, notices, fancy pens, staplers, and a computer. It was the computer that peaked his interest. Looking down at the keyboard he shifted his head slightly to let the light reflect at an acute angle. Most of the keys were gleaming with reflected light, but some were heavily fudged from repetitive use by a human hand. And a few looked to be recently wiped. The oily residue was pressed all about, leaving a strange, texture less pattern

Good ol' QWERTY never lies.

On the screen was a log in prompt. It stared back at him defiantly, daring him to find the right password to unlock its secrets. Again he looked back at the papers. They all appeared to be neatly stacked, all organized into distinct piles. Without hesitation, his hand wiggled its way down to one of the top drawers.

A man this organized probably keeps the good stuff inside.

He tugged on a few drawers only to find them locked. Out of frustration, he grabbed hold of one tightly and began to bang it back and forth. A few of the men in the room turned to face the calamity.

"Hey, careful buddy; this is a crime scene, not your apartment."

Thomas pretended to smile at the ill intent expressed in the comment. One day they'd just shut up and let him work. As his hand crept to one final drawer, he tugged and miraculously it came open. Looking inside he could see a sloppy, messy, pile of paper and objects. All were completely out of order, obviously disturbed. Letters, legal documents, stat sheets, and account ledgers created the sea of sharp edges he was now captivated by.

Hello there, Mr. Wall Street. What have we been up to?

He reached towards the drawer, and then stopped. It suddenly hit him. His brain had brought back a stream of relationships that it was tying together on its own. He didn't need to look inside. Instead, he shut it and returned to the dead body.

"Married, significant other?"

This time another onlooker glanced up to see him.

"Are you talking to me?"

Thomas shrugged.

"I'm talking to anyone."

"Forgive my partner—he's a little off today," said Vaun, suddenly rushing to Thomas's side.

"I thought I said let me do the talking . . . didn't I say that?"

Thomas stuck his tongue in his cheek. He was trying to prevent all of his logical vomit from pouring out. He had so much to say, but needed just a few more things.

"Was this fat cat in some sort of relationship? That's all I was asking, seems pretty tame."

Vaun put his eyes back in his head. It was clear that he thought it was anything but, coming from such a human oddity as Thomas.

"No idea. Let me check on that. And please, for the love of sanity, just keep quiet until I get back."

Thomas nodded, but it was just an automated response. His eyes had caught something else—the man's ring finger. An indentation of skin creased up in two spots making a subtle valley of flesh. The spacing was adequate enough to fit what most would call a band of devotion, a ring. But the ring was missing. It seemed odd that someone so meticulously put together would forget such an emblem of conviction. Or had it been purposeful?

Now why did you go and take that off?

It was now becoming quite clear, at least to his relentless mind. He rose up just in time to have his partner cue in some additional details.

"Married, and happily from the sounds of it. At least that's the story his mortified wife is giving."

"Or at least that's what it looks like" added Thomas.

Thomas dug his fingers inside the dead man's pants. Everyone in the room froze. Their jaws dropped to the floor in disgust. Gasps could be heard throughout the room. Here they were professionally piecing together a case and Thomas appeared to be busy fondling a deceased man's private area.

"Detective Ghune, just what do you think you're doing!?" screamed Pete, barely able to catch his breath from the shock.

Ignoring everyone else, Thomas reached down around the inner line of the man's pockets—and there it was. It was slender, unobtrusive, and well hidden; a nicely sewn in pocket to keep anyone who might be interested guessing. A pocket put there with a tight-lipped purpose. As Thomas ripped his hand free from the deceased man's pants, he threw it out into the open, elated.

"Gotcha! I knew it would be there!"

One of the men in the room braced himself against the wall, looking poised to faint. The lack of professionalism on full display was overwhelming. Many looked away, trying to shed themselves of all the awkwardness that filled the room like a sweltering, hot air balloon. Doing his best to take a diplomatic approach towards Thomas, Vaun whispered into Thomas's ear.

"And just what did you find there, crazy man? The rest of us would like to know seeing that you just groped a dead man."

Thomas looked down at his hand and cringed, realizing just where it had been. But his mind was locked on its target and wasn't about to let go. Like a streaming torpedo, he moved about the room as all looked on.

"This wasn't a suicide. This man was murdered."

Instantly the room began to buzz with commotion. Questions and angry remarks flew through the air like fiery arrows. Vaun grabbed Thomas by the collar and drug him over towards the door. There they were joined by a wide eyed Pete who was wheezing frantically.

"You boys sure know how to throw a party. I'm assuming you can back some of that up?"

Vaun hurled his hands into the air and moaned.

"Talk to the freak—I need to sit down."

Pete looked at Thomas with a shocked expression imprinted on his face. One of his juicy, fat lips drooped slightly open to one side. He spoke with a patient drawl, trying to bring himself back together.

"Okay, Thomas, let's hear it before somebody gets burned at the stake."

Thomas lifted up the ring. His eyes narrowed in on it making him practically go cross-eyed.

"It's the ring. I found it in one of those inside pockets that I've never understood why they exist. That with the books, computer, desk, position of the body—it's pretty obvious really."

Pete slapped a hand to his face. Thomas' banter had lost him completely.

"Tommy, you've got to explain it to us humans, alright?"

Thomas rolled his eyes. He was frustrated with the slow progress around him. He carefully explained his reasoning to Pete in an attempt to free himself of the sticky attention he'd gained.

"The books are all in order except for one; a book on investment law. No surprise there. This guy had investments . . . a lot of them. But he wouldn't have put it back there. He would have put it back in its place. Everything here has a place—even his stupid pens and staplers. Someone else had obviously put it back. But that wasn't all; there was the position of the body. Why leave his desk, his comfort zone, to do something very, very uncomfortable? Easy—he was led there by a very seductive, habitual routine. Then there was the computer. People use certain keystrokes over and over again, leaving a tiny layer of residue behind. Nothing special about that apart from the few keys that had been smudged. I found it odd that they were smudged, which to me meant one thing—a glove. But why would someone need to wear a glove? Because that someone didn't want to be found, of course. Then I looked into the drawers; all locked except for one broken drawer at the bottom that had been forcefully opened. A mess of papers, someone had been searching for something. Then, of course, this resolved the question I had about the gun—a decorative gun that blasted just one single bullet? I don't think so. This thing was planted. It's probably got more of his prints on it than his toothbrush. And then last but not least was the ring. It really came down to that. The indentations on his finger were subtle, but present. This guy was happy—happily cheating on his wife. Why else would he need to take it off? Who was he hiding it from? But I wanted to see it for myself. Once I did, this thing was old news. His lover dropped him like a bad habit. She came in ready to do the job under the cover of another one of their late night visits. Only she hadn't thought it all out. Had he erased all of their emails? What else held a memory of her in his desk? I have no doubts that his cell phone is probably missing as well. She must have thought she had cleaned up every shred of evidence and removed her gloves, but she had forgotten one thing; one damned book. Out of habit, she had picked it up and put it back without thinking. She knew him well, well enough to form such a habit. He'd probably asked her to do it a million times. This means she's close—any attractive secretaries in this place? You'll probably find her prints on the book."

Everyone within earshot sat quietly. The long winded explanation had them dumbstruck. No one was quite sure what to say; the logic seemed sound enough, but the amount of information that Thomas had gathered so quickly was staggering. After a few minutes of uncomfortable silence, Pete finally resumed being himself.

"You heard the man, scrub! I got to do everything around here?"

The room erupted back into a flurry of movement. People looked both upset and yet impressed at the same time. Pete grabbed Thomas by the shoulders and looked at him smugly.

"That's my boy. You're worth that stupid high grade paycheck we give you every month—every penny. Just one thing I don't understand. Why did she do it? What was she aiming to get out of this?"

Thomas put on a prideful smirk. He responded boldly.

"I don't know. That's not what I do. Do I look like some freak that can somehow understand these psychos? You're barking up the wrong tree. I look at the details and facts—that's it. Figuring out the motive and all that sentimental crap is your job."

Pete looked surprised for a moment, but came back warmly. The entire event had excited him so much that beads of sweat had formed and were plopping down his round face. He dabbed at them with a small neckerchief.

"Well, I'm glad you do what you do. Sure speeds things up. Why don't we meet up later, drinks on me?"

Thomas shook his head.

"Can't—got a big night planned— finally going to pop the question."

"You're really going to do it? I still can't believe that you found someone that you think will say yes. You didn't mail order her, did you?" interjected Vaun, encroaching on them.

Thomas curled one of his lips up in annoyance. He didn't like anyone talking that way about the woman he would soon be asking to marry. But he knew Vaun and knew that he liked to push buttons. Vaun behaved, at times, like a two year old on a piano; mashing all the keys together just trying to get the biggest reaction out of it.

"Have a good one. Let me know how this goes and if I nailed it. Also, let me know who the woman was. I live vicariously through these people."

Vaun shook his head but gave Pete a silent nod. He followed behind Thomas on his way out the door.

"Couldn't you just tell me first and let me take a little credit once in a while? As of right now I just feel like your glorified baby sitter. Half those guys in there probably hate me just for being around you."

Tommy felt a part of him spring the urge to retaliate. But he didn't care, his mind was elsewhere. All that mattered was getting home to the one thing pure in his messed up life; his love, his purpose, his soon-to-be wife.

LOVE FAILETH

A crowded street with narrow sidewalks moved like a pulsing river through the city center. Everyone appeared to be heading somewhere with purpose. They were all caught up in their own world, including Thomas. He floated around like a half-filled balloon. His movement was light and playful. He hadn't felt this happy at any point in his overly complicated life. It came as a blessing that for once his mind agreed—it could only focus on one thing—his plans for the night. He was poised to sweep her off her feet. She wouldn't know what hit her. His refined suave would wrap itself around her practically forcing her to beg for a higher commitment. But he would tease, tantalize, and then satiate. He wanted it to be memorable. Plunging into a local flower shop he drank it all in. He was going to do this.

I can't believe it's finally happening.

They had been together for years and been friends even longer. All of his greatest joys and failures had been shared with his kindred spirit of the opposite sex. She was his rock, his safe place. Despite his nervousness, he knew it was all going to work out. Looking around the flower shop, he was amazed at the sheer variety of plants present. He'd never seen so many shapes and sizes mixed with such vibrant colors. Perhaps the grey drab of the big city had finally made him colorblind. But there amongst it all was a particular pot of flowers that drew him in with its lingering scent. It looked to be a mixture of plants with some sort of tropical theme. The smell they put off was as sweet as nectar. Without thinking, he grabbed the pot, picked it up and sniffed.

That's amazing. I didn't know things could smell like that. How many smells are in this room? Why are the flowers all so distinctly colored?

"Can I help you, sir?"

Broken from his short-lived infatuation, he looked up. There he saw the thick brimmed glasses and curly hair of a woman giving him a very concerned look. He hadn't realized it, but his face had plunged inside a wonderful bouquet, leaving a headless torso behind.

"I like these; what are they?"

The lady quickly adjusted her front-heavy glasses to focus in on the strange man.

"That would be the birds of paradise bouquet. It's one of our best sellers."

Smelling the exotic medley, he could no longer resist the impulse.

"I'll take them. I especially enjoy all the stimulation these provide. Is there a reason that they do that? Why are there so many different colors?"

The woman opened her mouth but paused, after which she turned and began to walk away, muttering a few lines about how awkward it was.

"I'll ring you up over there; if, of course, you're done being stimulated."

Thomas put on a pouty face. It was a legitimate question, wasn't it? But it didn't matter. All that mattered was he had found the right flowers. Ringing them up at the cash register, he had them carefully wrapped then boxed. He needed to take care of his soon-to-be proposition. Nothing set the mood like a bouquet of tropical flora. As normally as he could he walked out onto the street where he began the walk to his apartment. He weaved his way through the dense evening crowds, practically tap dancing around them. He was still feeling a sense of euphoria running through him. So many things were complicated in his life, but this was so simple, so pure. He loved seeing her bright eyes, her radiant face. She made him feel whole again no matter how many pieces he had been shattered into during the day. This day was going to go down in history.

What's this?

His honed mind suddenly faltered just for a moment. He had

seen something interesting that had conjured up a magical wave of curiosity in him. It was a hat shop. Nothing was very special about that, except for one hat in particular. Its creased crown ran down towards a wide brim, an aged fedora. On its side was a bright red splotch stuck against the velvety black in deep contrast. The splotch was that of a tiny feather that had been carefully stuck into a belt-like wrap that went around the midriff of the bizarre hat. It sucked him in like a funnel. He couldn't help but entertain the idea of buying it. Tommy Gun, the mobster, the gangster, the slick man every woman swooned for. His imagination was getting away from him. But he didn't care. This was a time for indulging; he need not give heed to his prohibitions tonight. Stepping inside the shop he had to ask.

"Excuse me, how much is the hat?"

A man came out from somewhere in the back to see him. He was an older man whose skin looked dry and leathered. He wiped one of his hands over his balding head. It appeared he wasn't sure what to say.

"That one, I didn't even know we had that one. Let me take a look at it."

Pulling it down from its rack, he perused its fine details. It was obvious that the hat had long been out of sight and out of mind. But the inner salesman was always ready to strike a deal.

"A hundred bucks, cash—it's a nice hat."

Thomas gave him a look of annoyance. His eyes narrowed in as he analyzed every obvious failing of the sentence.

"You can't be serious. You didn't even know you had this hat until a minute ago. Thing's probably been up there for decades."

The man shifted the hat around in his hands, puckering up his bottom lip, while letting his eyes wander.

"It's a good hat, good material, handmade—I'll go ninety-five, but that's as low as I go."

Instinctively Thomas reached into his pockets and pulled out his wallet. He fumbled through it as if pretending to count.

"I'll go ninety because I don't like the color. And let's be honest; you think you're ever going to sell that ugly thing?"

The man flicked the tiny red feather in the hat's side. He closed one eye as if aiming a rifle.

"Ninety-three and it's a deal."

Thomas sighed before he pulled out his credit card. He didn't have the time or energy to argue with the staunchly bantering shop owner.

"I said cash only on this; your hearing not so good?"

"You kidding me? What kind of a shop is this?"

Reluctantly, Thomas put down his flowers to begin sifting through his wallet for the cash. As he did, he also placed his credit card down, negligently in full view.

"You're a real ball buster, you know that? I'm going to propose to my girlfriend tonight and this is how you want my night to start?"

The shop owner crossed his arms and shrugged.

"It's a nice hat."

Thomas rolled his eyes but bit his lashing tongue. It didn't matter. He'd just consider it a sunk cost for the memories he'd be making. Pulling out a crisp one hundred dollar bill, he shoved it defiantly towards the shop owner.

"There's a hundred—keep the change—looks like you need it."

Seven dollars had bought him the much needed retaliation for the moment. He let out a rather impish smile before turning to pick his things up. Just as he did, a flash of hand snatched his exposed credit card and bolted. Instantly, the urge to chase came on, but was quickly pacified by his utter exhaustion. It was just a credit card; he'd call in and cancel it and move on in his life. It wasn't worth the energy.

"Hey! That man just took your card!"

Thomas turned and shrugged.

"Good thing I've got more of them. I'll just cancel it."

The shop keeper looked disgusted with the show of apathy, but receded back into his dark lair somewhere behind the counter. Thomas gathered his things and left. He contacted his credit card company and canceled the card. The only true annoyance would be the time it would take to issue him another one. Why couldn't people just live and let live? Here he had just haggled a stingy shop owner into give him what he'd wanted in the first place, only to get robbed. At least it was just a flimsy piece of plastic at this point. No need to feel discouraged there.

Where was I? Oh, yes . . .

Putting a slight skip in his step, he was again on his way. He had the flowers, the hat, and the ring. Well, at least he thought he did.

Love Faileth

Where had he put it? For all the detail about things he held in his brain with impeccable correctness, he often struggled to remember some of the most basic things. A traditional placement of a small, metal circle encrusted with shiny rocks. To be honest, it was quite boring. Fishing around in his suit pockets, he was relieved to find it there. It was a gorgeous piece of romance that he'd spared no expense on. He wanted to blow her mind. It was well worth the hefty price, of that he was sure. Putting it carefully back, he went home.

Standing outside of his apartment, he took a couple of deep breaths. He knew she was inside, probably fixing up one of their routine dinners after a long day at work. She would no doubt have the urge to address every shallow-rooted issue of the day with him over a warm meal. Normally, he loved it when she would do so. She had a way with words, expressions, and unseen vibes that mesmerized him. It was like the world went quiet, finally making some real sense.

Okay, Tommy . . . Don't screw this up.

Opening the door slowly, he did his best to quickly conceal the box of exotic flowers and the hat behind his back. He examined the house to find everything in its place. And he knew this right down to the location of the remote to the television. In his mind, he could pick the room apart to such obscene levels of detail that it would drive a normal person mad. But to him it was normal. It was just how things were. Now, if he could only remember to refill the toilet paper or put the seat back down.

"Tommy, you're home! Where in this cockroach infested city have you been? Dinner's going to be cold."

He knew where he had been and why. He also knew what day it was—leap day. The only day that happened only once every four years; years that were divisible by four. A day from the Gregorian calendar that was closely linked to the Julian calendar, introduced by none other than Julius Caesar in 45 BC. But to him it would be the special day he asked his one-and-only to be his wife, a day that would be forever changed throughout all time. Slowly he shut the door. His smile was now pressing into places he had never thought possible. He had never been so happy. He knew she had no idea. Being such a ridiculously good detective came with its perks. He had set things up meticulously to assure that the world immediately around her would divulge nothing.

"Just out and about, had a long day at the office . . ."

He gazed around the corner to see her in the kitchen rummaging through the open fridge.

"Didn't we have a rutabaga? I swear we had a rutabaga in here. The recipe calls for one and I'm not seeing any. This fridge is like a graveyard of leftovers, Tommy. How many times have I told you to take your meal with you? Is this my eggplant parm right here? It is! I slaved over that one for hours!"

Thomas would normally slyly try to escape the conversation by voicing a couple of cleverly crafted, flattering nuances. But he had something better this time.

"Yeah, about all that . . . I feel just awful, you know. Maybe after dinner we could talk about it."

Placing the items down on the couch he skulked his way into the kitchen. There he could finally see her. She had dressed down into her comfort zone. She had a stained, white apron draped around her shoulders. As she emerged from the fridge she gave him a rather peculiar look.

"You look happy. You see that dog with three legs again?"

He shook his head.

"No, he only comes around on Sundays at the park. But that's not the point. I'm just really glad to see you today."

Practically lunging across the kitchen, he picked her up and kissed her. He could smell her faded perfume of the day mixed with all of her natural essence. It was purely intoxicating. Her warm, soft lips immediately turned all of his testosterone-powered switches on.

"My, my, a man of law and order being so disorderly—there's something up with you—I can tell."

Thomas put her down gently. He gave her another long, passionate kiss before turning away.

"You're looking way too deep into this. You need to relax."

The comment immediately resulted in a soft oven mitten being smacked into the back of his head.

"Says the guy who incessantly harassed me about all the similarities you noticed between me and my mother down to the genetic level.

Love Faileth

Your hours of banter . . . the TV volume couldn't go high enough!"

He smiled. It was true. He was very difficult to get along with at times. But for some reason she put up with it. Perhaps it was true that opposites attract? Whatever it was, it was working. Taking his place at the table, he watched as she brought in both of the artistically formed plates. Her attention to detail in certain areas was marvelous. But it was her lack thereof in other areas that also created a strange attraction that even he couldn't understand.

"That looks amazing. I've never seen so much color on one plate."

She smiled as she placed the steaming food in front of him.

"Well, I always like to try something new. And let's be honest; I'm way too lazy to come up with all this stuff on my own. I nabbed this recipe off the internet."

The two had in a wonderful dinner, easily falling back into their comfort zones. Each expressed their daily frustrations along with their minor triumphs. He was elated to tell her of the hoped for success of the case from he'd worked earlier. He then confessed that Vaun had changed his cologne at least three to four times in the past weeks. This made it obvious to Thomas that he was back into the dating scene and had finally broken up with his long-term girlfriend. It also explained Vaun's more than sour mood as of late.

"So, I've got a surprise for you."

Jen looked up from her plate where she was finishing off the last few bites of her meal.

"Oh, do tell."

"Not here—in the other room. I think you'll really like it."

Intrigued by the proposition, she nodded subtly.

"A man of mystery . . . or . . . have I been naughty? I think I like where this is going."

Thomas wiped his mouth and then grabbed an unused napkin.

"Put this around your eyes. I want some suspense for this."

Jen obliged by putting it around her head and tying it loosely in the back.

"A blindfold, surprise, suspense—oh, Tommy, you're going all out—and it's just a weekday!"

He was smiling both inside and out. He could no longer contain all the joy that was overflowing his emotional cup. It manifested as completely giddy, school boy behavior. As he escorted her into the other room, he allowed his fingers to wander down the small of her back. The tender touch of affection was well received as Jen was practically purring in delight. Once arriving at a spot that seemed adequate, he continued with his romantic gesture.

"Stay right there and don't peek! I want to see the look on your face; I want to remember this perfectly."

"Tommy, you remember almost *everything* perfectly. Stop toying with me; the suspense is killing me!"

Quickly, he seized the flowers and took them out of the box. He then carefully placed the hat on top of his head. It fit surprisingly well. He put on his most devilish charm. His eyes gleamed with delight. He struggled to find the right pose. He tried on a few before he realized that he was making a fool of himself.

"Tommy!"

"Alright, alright, you can take the blindfold off."

In the blink of an eye, the slender piece of cloth flew through the air. Once it was out of the way, her eyes widened into two emotional beach balls. She couldn't believe what she was seeing; a large exotic bouquet of flowers being presented by a man in a silly, yet charming, hat. There was something about it that she adored deeply.

"Tommy, I don't know what to say? You did this for me?"

Thomas nodded. He approached her slowly, keeping his eyes locked deeply on hers. His love for her was growing with every beat of his heart. The tiny ring in his pocket now felt like a large brick. Was now the right time to ask? This was the part he had so feared. His timing when dealing with normal things was usually off. But he desperately wanted to get this right. Once again, he swept in on her and kissed her. He wrapped his hands around her back, clutching the flowers tightly. He held her with every molecule of energy that his soul could muster. He never wanted to let her go. He could have remained in this state of mind for an eternity. Could life get any better than a moment of heaven laboriously created by fate's sweet graces? He didn't think it could, but was willing to find out. Stepping back, he took a deep breath.

"Baby, there's something I want to ask you. I'm afraid if I don't do it now I might not get the chance."

Love Faileth

Tears formed in Jen's eyes. It was beginning to hit her. She had been caught completely off guard. Her lips trembled in anticipation. Dropping down to one knee, he did his best to reproduce all of the cinematic formalities that he had seen throughout his life. He imagined himself as the knight in shining armor finally coming home after slaying the dragon. With fervent eyes of desire, he mustered up the will to ask the most important question of his life—four simple words that would begin a lifetime of beautiful complications. He carefully pulled the ring from his pocket.

"Jen . . . will you marry me?"

Jen practically collapsed to the floor. Her shaky knees wobbled back and forth like two rubbery noodles. But with a flash of movement she threw herself at him. She jumped on top of him, letting the flowers burst apart. The petals fell like a colorful rain on their bodies.

"Yes, yes, a thousand times, yes! I thought you'd never ask, Thomas Ghune!"

They grabbed each other in a warm embrace. They clumsily knocked over some of the furniture as they rolled around releasing all the built up tension and suspense. Thomas struggled to get the ring on the finger of the probing hand of Jena. But as he did, she paused, letting the brilliant sparkle of the diamonds illuminate her eyes. Her heart had grown tenfold. Her love for him was now perfectly sealed in a meaningful verse of their love song that she would sing silently in her heart forever. Her little piece of heaven had arrived and she was gorging on it.

"Should I take the hat off?" questioned Thomas.

Jen smiled a deep, warm smile.

"No, I love it. I want to remember you like this forever—my suave detective, my lover and soon-to-be husband—don't you dare take it off!"

She glanced over towards the discarded napkin sitting a few footsteps away.

"Should I get the blindfold?"

Thomas put on a mischievous smile before affectionately placing another round of kisses on her inviting lips. He started to respond when there was a knock at the door.

"Expecting someone?"

Thomas shook his head. He had made sure no one would bother them; not tonight.

"No, let's leave it be. They'll probably just go away."

They resumed their romantic tango when suddenly the pounding at the door resumed.

"Are you kidding me? Can't this idiot take a hint?" scowled Jen.

Thomas let out an incredibly long sigh of frustration. Why was life always like this? Why couldn't it be more fairytale? Why did it have to be so real?

"I'll tell whoever it is to go away. You hang tight—and get that blindfold."

Jen forced a smile, but it was apparent that she was disturbed by the aggravating interruption. Thomas got up, showing signs of his obvious anger as well. He was poised to let whoever it was at the door have it. Walking quickly, he swung the door wide open.

"Look, buddy, can't you take a hint? Is it really so important that you just couldn't wait?"

The man at the door looked vaguely familiar. His slender body was covered in scars and track marks. His dark, beady eyes shook wildly about. He wore a long trench coat with a hat that covered most of his features. It didn't take long to realize the obvious. But it was too late. In the man's shaky hand was a pistol. It was aimed directly at Thomas' chest.

"I believe that it can't wait."

Jen shot up instantly and began to shriek. The man put his other finger up to his mouth as he worked his way in the door, shutting it behind him.

"Keep it down or I blast Romeo away!"

Putting her hands over her mouth she muffled her cries of terror. Tears poured out of her eyes and streamed down her delicate face.

"Whoa, buddy, let's just be calm here, alright? What do you want? You've got to want something, so what is it? You need money? Here— take my wallet."

Thomas removed his wallet and plopped it on the floor in front of the man. But the man paid no attention to it. Instead, he was locked onto the unnerved Jen. He was searching her over for something.

"I don't need your damn wallet. I already swiped your card, or don't

26

you remember? How do you think I found your place, idiot?"

Then it hit him. In a love stupor, he had been careless and dumb. The scene at the hat shop came back in full view. The credit card had been carelessly left in the open. His intentions for the night obviously placed on full display. The man had followed his electronic trail back to his home address. How had he been so stupid? It was completely obvious to him now what the target was.

"Look just take it, it's just a ring."

The man's body shook violently as if he was losing control. The effects of his vice were clouding his judgment, inhibiting his mind.

"You get it. I want to see your hands the whole time! You bring it to me!"

Thomas nodded and did as he was told. Approaching Jen, he put his hand out.

"Give me the ring baby . . . everything's going to be alright."

Jen was coming apart. She could barely muster the courage to move. But Thomas' reassuring voice powered her forward. Wriggling the ring off of her finger, she dropped it into Thomas' outreached hand. Calmly, he turned back towards the maniac hovering near the door.

"Here—I've got it —I'm going to bring it to you, alright? Just relax; nothing's going to happen."

Thomas cautiously stepped towards the man one nerve-racking step at a time. His heart was doing somersaults as he got closer, but he was doing his best to remain at ease. It was clear that the man was strung out; more than likely, high out of his mind. The last thing he needed to do was to give him a reason to react harshly.

"Hands where I can see them!"

"They are, buddy, don't worry. I just don't want to drop the ring, is all."

The man's face twitched as his nerves continued to fray.

"I can't see them, I'll shoot!"

Thomas instantly opened the hand that was holding on to the ring. As he did, it fell to the ground, rumbling round and round to a stop. The sudden movement propelled the man up a notch in his insanity.

"You threw it! You were going to throw it at me!"

"It just fell; relax. I'll pick it up. It's no big deal."

The muffled cries from Jena penetrated Thomas' heart. He wanted to soothe her, be next to her, holding her. But because of the psycho he'd led to their home, he couldn't. He was stuck in a subservient game of hostage.

"It's right here, see? It just fell down . . . no big deal."

Thomas crouched down and gently began to pick up the ring. Just as he did, something shifted in his pocket and with a clang his badge hit the floor. It rattled around on the ground before coming to a stop, face up.

"What's that? You a *cop* or something? You didn't tell me you were a cop!"

"Look—I'm not *really* a cop—I'm something different. Its fine, I'll let you walk out of here. Let's not do anything crazy."

"I'm never going back! You hear me! Never! You can't make me go back!"

It all happened so fast. The man raised the gun and pointed it directly at Thomas' chest. As he tried to aim his shaking hand dipped and bobbed the gun around in all directions. Then, a fiery, soul-piercing, blast muted everything except the mind-numbing scream from Jena. The smell of the fired round filled the room with its horrific odor.

"NO!"

Thomas screamed at the top of his lungs. He awaited the sharp, intense pain that would accompany his mortal wound. But nothing came. He watched helplessly as the man grabbed the shiny ring and ran, leaving him alone and confused. Running his hand down his body, he was miraculously unscathed. But this brought forward a harrowing detail that was now becoming more and more pronounced—Jena. She was silent. Her painful whimpers and cries had vanished. His mind was a torrential storm of all the data around him. Everything was blasting into his conscious like a fiery maelstrom conjured out of the very depths of hell.

"Jena! NO!!!"

Turning around, his convictions solidified. The love of his life lay motionless on the floor. Immediately, he collapsed to her side and began searching for the wound. He found it, just a few inches below her left breast. A crimson river of life-giving essence was spilling out of her onto the floor. He watched as it ran over his helpless hand which was desperately trying to seal the wound. He was now begging for her life. His pleas for help echoed in the room. He sobbed uncontrollably. His heart was being torn apart, every piece of his soul bursting free in unbearable pain.

"Please, baby, not now! Please, baby, get back up!"

He felt himself falling into a pit of despair with no hope of ever getting back out. He had lost the only true thing in his life. She had been taken from him. Her still, lifeless body was a testament to the vile act. On the night that they were supposed to begin their lives together, their bond had been ripped apart. Letting out a guttural, inhuman scream of anguish, he collapsed to the floor next to her. His mind had fallen apart; his physical and emotional selves had been overwhelmed.

3

DARK PLUNGE

Walking in the dark Thomas felt a part of him linger on the shadows. It was a strange, yet interesting detail that the absence of light could create another realm of existence. Everything changes in the dark. A seemingly innocent alleyway can hide the malevolent eyes of a killer, rapist, or worse. The dark could drown out all logic and feeling, leaving only the numb nothing behind. It was this he felt now more than ever. It had been weeks since Jena had been murdered. Weeks since he last felt her tender touch, heard her gentle voice. His heart ached with such pain he was almost positive it should have exploded, giving him the release he so desired. The pain had consumed his life, leaving nothing behind. His work on the force had all but disappeared. The few friends he had were now distant, removed. He had broken himself out of reality. He was just a shell of his former self, a walking dead man.

Why didn't I do something? Why was I so stupid?

He had taken a plunge into the darkness of his own soul and drowned. Thoughts of suicide followed him from one cursed day to another. His mind was relentless—it wouldn't let him forget—it wouldn't let him forgive. There was only one option for him and he had finally mustered up the courage to do it. He was going to end it. He couldn't possibly live out the rest of his life alone. Jena had been the only human being who truly understood him. And now she was buried beneath a mound of dirt. Reflections of their time together, her murder and funeral, streamed around inside his mind like a tornado. He no longer had a purpose. He no longer had a reason.

He picked out the bridge and time well. He knew no one would be around. He wanted to do this alone. The height would be adequate to kill him upon impact. The cold river water would then drag him out to sea where he would be eviscerated; forgotten and finally at rest. Stopping at the midpoint of the bridge, he took a deep breath. It was late, the air chilled. This was poetic, really. His death would end up as just a statistic, another psycho taken off the streets. The same streets he had worked so diligently to protect and keep clean. He ran his hands over the smooth surface of the bridge fence. This would be his spot. Slowly, he climbed up its edge until he was standing fully exposed to the dark depths below. There the water churned wildly about. The powerful currents were in full view. But there was something else. Amidst his extreme, torturous suffering, he had the odd feeling he was being watched. But this was impossible' he'd checked. But yet, there it was—someone was there. He decided to satisfy his curiosity, but was caught completely off guard by a voice.

"Weird night to go for a swim, don't you think?"

Glancing behind him, he saw a man standing in the shadows watching him, his face shrouded in the darkness.

"Who says I'm going to swim?"

The man emerged from the shadows. His thick grey hair parted to one side and he had piercing, almost gleaming, green eyes that locked on to Thomas directly.

"Well, you won't mind if I watch then . . . been a long time since I've seen a dive from this high up."

Thomas felt his insides shift around in anger. He didn't want to be interrupted. He didn't want to play any games.

"Look, buddy, I don't know who you are or how you found me, but this has nothing to do with you or anyone else. It's literally none of your business."

The man confidently strode to the edge of the bridge and looked over. He momentarily contemplated the swirling water thrashing about.

"I don't think it matters who I am. All that matters is who you are, Tommy."

Thomas paused. How did this guy know his name? A man he had never seen before in his entire life, of that he was sure.

"I don't care what you think you know about me. You have no idea what I've been through!"

Thomas edged his feet a little further over the edge. The pull of gravity choreographed his every movement.

"Oh, I wouldn't say that. You'd be surprised at the things I've seen and done, Tommy. Or is it, 'Tommy Gun, the legendary crime solver turned glorified high diver?'"

"Stop calling me *Tommy*! And none of that matters now. It wasn't good enough."

The man turned around, leaned on the fence, and gazed the other way. He appeared to be lost in thought for a moment or two.

"And you suppose this is the way to deal with that? Just because you couldn't save her means you shouldn't try and save yourself?"

At the mere mention of his lost love, Thomas spewed his fuming rage.

"Don't you *ever* bring her up! She meant *everything* to me, and now she's *gone*! I can't ever have her back! I don't care what you think I'm supposed to do—I'm done with this—I'm done with all of this!"

Thomas let his feet drag a few inches further forward. As he did, the man leaning up against the fence suddenly stood up. He clapped his hands together and frowned.

"I was hoping it wouldn't have to be this way. Things like this tend to get very messy. But have it your way. I'm just here for the show after all—*remember*? No point in trying to talk sense into someone who's obviously lost who he is and what he stands for. Just remember to take a big breath right before you hit. The water's real cold down there so it'll knock the wind right out of you."

The man then took his place back in the shadows. He stood silently waiting for Thomas to make good on his claim.

I'm going to do this! What does he know? I don't even know who he is! He's just another psychopath looking to ruin my life. I hate my life!

Thomas dangled one of his feet over the edge, finally feeling the bitter reality sink in. One more step and he'd be beyond the point of return. One more step and all of his pain would finally end, as would he.

"Are we going to do this tonight? I've never seen such a convincing set-up, just to see someone bail out. Please, if you would be so kind."

The man's comments were all that he needed to push himself forward. But right as he did he felt a part of himself doubt his selfish actions. Perhaps the man was right. Had he truly forgotten who he was and what he stood for? But with a loud squeak from the wet surface slipping his shoe loose, it was too late. In a heartbeat, he found himself flailing through the air on his way to an untimely demise. Unable to control his sudden fear, he began to scream aloud. The cold air wisped passed him at break neck velocity. Below, the dastardly waters waited to forever imprison him in their depths. But all that he could focus on now was the memory of Jena, his sweet Jena that had been taken away. Picturing her now was as painful as it had ever been. Perhaps he was weak. Perhaps he wasn't who he once thought himself to be; the proud knight in shining armor coming home to sweep his princess off her feet. But he was no knight—he was a bastard child of the world. A freak, an outcast, someone no one any longer understood. This was his moment of vindication. He closed his eyes. Soon it would all be over.

His eyes remained closed for what seemed like minutes on end before he finally opened them. The swift, blasting motion of the fall had disappeared. He now felt stable and calm. But this couldn't be. He had just jumped off a giant bridge. His body should have been utterly wrecked against the incontestable strength of the waves below. And yet he was standing.

"Back so soon? I didn't even hear the splash."

Thomas spun around to see the man emerging from the shadows once more. The mysterious man had a rather cheesy grin on his face. He looked to be amused by everything that had just transpired. Thomas, however, was far from it.

"What just happened? How am I back here?"

The man walked up to the edge and took a deep breath. He was mumbling his annoyance with the probing question.

"*Back* here? You never left. So I guess there is no *back* here. Besides, this isn't my realm anyways. I'm not here to explain. I'm here to tell."

Thomas felt completely confounded by the man's odd answer. He could feel his doubt swelling up inside and yet he was still curious. He wanted to know more.

"What is this? What are you trying to pull here?"

The man shook his head. His impatience was growing.

"I just don't have time to entertain those questions at the moment.

Let's just say I have an offer for you."

Thomas could feel frustration festering inside him. The man had answered nothing. A man he knew nothing about who had seemingly interrupted his poetic end.

"An *offer*? Are you *serious*? Just a minute ago I was taking the high dive and now you have an *offer*? Look, buddy, I'm just not interested. I don't play that way."

The man stood up and gazed down at his watch. He closed his eyes and sighed.

"This just gets harder every time. What happened to the good old days of just going with it?" he mumbled.

"What did you say?"

"This is a one-time deal. You have but two choices. Come take a walk with me and hear what I've got to say. Or, you can try your luck again on the high dive. Either way, I need to know soon; I don't have time to play mitigator any longer."

Thomas walked cautiously over to the edge of the bridge. He ran his hands over the smooth surface. It was the very same smooth surface he had just felt moments ago, and yet it seemed distant and fuzzy. Below was the frothy, dark water, awaiting his decision.

What's it going to be Tommy? Take the plunge into madness or jump off the bridge?

"Mr. Ghune, I can't stress enough that my time is short. Are we going to take this walk or not?"

Thomas' mind lit up like a bonfire. He was dissecting every piece of what had happened. No matter how hard he scrutinized each detail, he found no satisfying answer. He was caught up in something supernatural. But something seemed to ring true; if he jumped again there would be no reset button. Perhaps by jumping already, that part of him that had wanted the simple release of death had died.

"Mr. Ghune, last call."

Thomas turned around slowly. He let his eyes pan back and forth like a typewriter as his mind relentlessly continued to bombard him with information.

"I'll take a walk, but that's it. I'm still going to jump off this bridge."

The man smiled, turned, and began walking away. His dark trench coat made him look like some sort of ghostly apparition in the night.

Dark Plunge

Reluctantly, Thomas followed. He swallowed a nervous lump that seemed to be choking the air out of him.

"By the time I'm finished, you'll wish you had."

The man spoke clearly and succinctly. He had obviously come to the bridge with a purpose. It was this purpose that Thomas had to understand. With a short burst of speed, he raced to the man's side. From there he could see more of the fine details; a dark colored suit, red tie, and a white shirt. The man looked aged and yet gave off the vibrant glow of life. Then something else caught Tommy's attention. A strange looking pendant attached to the shirt inside the suit. Three triangles locked together. Perhaps it was a symbol? Whatever it was, he had never seen anything like it. The two pressed on in silence, wandering aimlessly around in the dark, before he finally spoke.

"So you're awfully quiet for a guy who said he's hard pressed for time."

The man stopped on the spot and turned.

"Time, Mr. Ghune. That's something none of us ever seem to have enough of."

Thomas rolled his eyes. Riddles and mindless banter—could this night get any worse?

"I give. You've got me. Now, can we move forward with this, please, and lose the games?"

This made the man chuckle. He glanced down at his watch again.

"Why only forward? So many other directions one can move. But I digress. Simple things deserve simple explanations. You've raised some interest in the people I work for. Let's just say they like what they see. You have a gift, Mr. Ghune—a gift that has a place and purpose. It's the purpose I think you've lost. I'm here to give it back to you."

The man's eyes carefully examined Thomas' reaction. He looked intent, fully anticipating the answer.

"Just what are you talking about here?"

The man held his hand out in front of him; within it he clenched something tightly.

"Why don't I show you? Take it or leave it."

Thomas couldn't believe what he was hearing. Was this for real? A part of him wanted to head back to the bridge; at least there things had made sense. Now he was caught up in the chaotic clamor of nonsensical details screaming at him from inside his skull. None of it made any sense. But he found himself curious despite himself; curious to see just what the man had to offer. Maybe he could entertain the idea, even if only for a night, to see where his mind was come morning. Hesitantly, he put his hand out in front of him, opening it palm to the sky, ready to receive whatever was coming his way. The man smiled at the gesture and slammed a small card into it.

"I knew this wasn't a waste of time . . . always got to keep a positive outlook on things."

The man turned and began walking away. As he did, Thomas' eyes perused the details on the thin piece of paper. A simple address was all that was there. Looking for further direction, he looked back up. The man was gone. It was almost as if the shadows had devoured him whole. There wasn't so much as a trace of him left.

"Can I at least get a name?"

I need to get some sleep.

Walking away from what he had thought would be his final resting place, he could feel his nerves rattle about. Whatever he had just gotten into was completely outlandish. What was going to become of him?

4

LAUNDROMAT HEIST

Thomas woke up feeling completely fatigued. He had spent most of the night staring at the tiny piece of paper with the address on it. The memories of his past had plagued him like a cloud of locusts, suffocating him. And yet, now suddenly, there was something inside of him that wanted to fight. There was something that wanted to press onward even deeper into the unknown. Perhaps he truly had lost his mind. But there was one thing for sure; he knew it bothered him to no end. He was still alive. He knew without a shadow of doubt that he had plunged over the bridge's edge. And yet, here he was, still breathing, lying comfortably in his bed. Obviously, there had to have been some tricks involved with that show. A show so perfectly sewn together that not so much as one loose thread could be tugged free by his analytic mind.

"What have I gotten myself into?" he mumbled.

Rolling out of bed, he looked across to his closet. His clothes and shoes were meticulously organized, everything sitting in pure conformity. The closet held so much worthless detail and yet he could recant it all like the alphabet. He needed to get his mind back under control. He needed a puzzle to solve. After getting dressed, he looked at himself in the mirror. The scruffy looking man staring back at him appeared to be foreign. It was as if he no longer even knew himself. He truly had slid down the metaphorical slippery-slope. Suddenly something in the closet caught his eye and blasted his heart with bolts of energy—his fedora hat. The bright red feather gleamed amongst the sea of proper attire.

I almost forgot you.

His eyes watered with the release of held-back memories that the hat wielded. His heart burned with ardent flames that had once been extinguished. His love was still as strong as ever for her. But she wasn't coming back. Even if she wasn't coming back, he didn't want to let go, he couldn't. Walking slowly up to the closet, he grabbed the hat tenderly. He ran his fingers over its suave surface. The last words she had spoken rang in his ears.

"Don't you dare take it off," he whispered quietly.

It seemed illogical, if not downright silly, to indulge in his nostalgia. But he didn't care. The hat held more meaning for him now. He saw it as a symbol of devotion; a commitment that he had whole heartedly accepted but had been robbed of. Taking it down from the closet, he slid it on top of his matted hair. It fit perfectly, as it always had. Looking back in the mirror he saw someone different staring back. Maybe he could find his purpose again. Maybe he could still make her proud. But first he needed to clean up. If he was going to work, he needed all the familiar details taken care of. It seemed like ages since he had truly resembled his former self. But the hat seemed to empower him. It helped make him feel whole, and not so alone. He was ready to try and face the world he had left behind.

Tracking down the address was easy. The location was as innocuous as any, a laundromat. In fact, it was the location that bothered him the most. Why would someone so secretive want to meet at a laundromat? It made absolutely no sense. Then again, what did at this point? That didn't matter, though; he was just looking for answers. Walking into the building, a few people gave him some very curious looks. His antiquated hat seemed to be driving the unwanted attention. But in the city where attention spans had the lifecycle of a spark, they were quick to dismiss it. Inside, there was the typically wide spectrum of people one would expect, all of whom were deeply involved with some sort of distraction. As far as he could tell, there was no sign of the man of mystery.

Great . . . this idiot's a no-show. I should have known better.

Feeling frustrated, he took a seat near the back of the laundromat.

Laundromat Heist

He slumped heavily into his chair. He stared at the jostling mixture of clothes and bubbles. Round and round they went, over and over in an almost mesmerizing fashion. It felt strangely therapeutic to let his mind focus on the mundane activity.

"It's a funny thing, a washing machine. You see the clothes start at one point, slosh around in a circle, and then come right back to the starting point again. Over and over they go until *bam*, the thing buzzes and you pop in another quarter."

Thomas cringed. He knew that voice well. Peering out the very edge of his eye he could see him. The man was sitting in a chair, grinning smugly. It was apparent that he was enjoying himself and the game he was playing.

"You like being such a creep all the time?"

The man's smile faded slightly.

"I see you've taken me up on my offer . . . had me a little worried back there on the bridge."

"I've taken no offer. I'm just here trying to understand some things, that's all."

"Look, the only thing that I can tell you is that I'm willing to give you a fresh start. I'm willing to bring you in on something really special, something that would be for the greater good."

"The *greater good*? You can't be serious! You can drop the hyped-up semantics. All I want to know is, what happened to me back there? And what do you want from me? And let's not forget a name. I'm tired of all this cloak and dagger stuff."

The man looked up at Thomas' hat. His cheeks rose up, squeezing his eyes together.

"That's an interesting hat, Mr. Ghune. Can't help but wonder what it means to you. The name's Roslin—Roslin Tanner. And what happened to you back there is none of your business unless we move forward. I personally don't want anything from you. But there are those that do. A skillset like yours is highly desirable in our line of work."

Roslin's eyes went back to following the tumbling laundry in the washer.

"There it goes again. Back to the same position; same place, but not the same time. At least not the same instance."

Thomas blinked his eyes rapidly as he tried to process it all.

"What skillset are we talking about here? And can we please stop talking about laundry for just a second?"

Roslin rolled his eyes and glanced down at his watch.

"You think with all your attention to detail you could see what I'm trying to say here. But that's fine. We have people for that. Detail, Mr. Ghune, that's really what this is about. You have a certain affinity towards it—unlike anyone we've ever seen—you can gut open a crime scene in mere minutes when it would take a regular team months to do it. And in my line of work, time truly is of the essence."

"So, you want me because I can find Waldo?"

"Who's Waldo? Look, Mr. Ghune, this is where you take the plunge. You either take me up on the offer or we both just walk out of here never to see each other again."

"You promise?" said Thomas sarcastically.

Roslin shook his head and got up. He turned and began walking away.

"Alright, alright, I'm game. But if I suspect one thing is out of line I'll bail on this. Is that understood?"

Roslin backed up and dropped a bag of coins in his lap.

"Here . . . you're going to need these."

Without another word, Roslin was out the door and gone, leaving a bewildered Thomas behind with a large bag of coins. Did he want him to do his laundry or something? Why couldn't something happen that made even a shred of logic? His meandering thoughts were disrupted by a sudden burst of commotion that poured in through the laundromat's front doors.

"Freeze! Put your hands up in the air!"

Thomas panicked. His eyes darted around like a pinball trying to understand what was happening. A group of policemen were encroaching on him with their weapons at the ready. Each locked in on him with their eyes. Many of the onlookers let out a shriek of panic and ran out from the building, covering their heads.

You've got to be kidding me.

"Sir, put the bag down! We don't want to hurt you!"

Thomas looked down at his lap and cringed. What a beautifully crafted prop. If he ever saw Roslin again he'd give him a piece of his mind he wouldn't forget.

"Put the bag down and step away, sir! I won't ask again!"

Laundromat Heist

Not one to disagree with a lawfully armed mob, Thomas obeyed. He slithered out and away from the seat, letting the bag of coins plop into the seat. He put his hands instinctively up in the air. It was now more than ever that he wished he could pull his credentials out, and then blast them for such harassment. But those days were long gone now. His woeful pity had all but burnt that bridge to ash. Once his hands were up, the cops rushed in on him and plowed him to the floor, his face pressed like putty against its cold surface.

"Easy, buddy! I'm going peacefully!"

On came the handcuffs. They were adjusted tightly around his wrists. Then with a few quick pulls and tugs, they escorted him out of the laundromat into an awaiting car, leaving a completely shocked crowd of spectators behind.

Inside the car, a soft black bag was suddenly produced by one of the officers. Without asking, he placed it over Thomas' head, shrouding his eyes completely.

"What's this? Am I being kidnapped? What kind of cops are you?"

There was no answer. Then, with a slam of the door, they were moving. As they drove, Thomas' brain was soaking in everything it could. The bag was soft and reeked of some sort of cheap fabric softener. Apart from that, there were details about the officers who appeared to be kidnapping him to consider. There was something off about it all. They had even forgotten to read him his rights, not like it mattered, anyway. As corrupt as the court system seemed to be, it never seemed to be that important. How many of his cases had been held stagnate by some self-righteous lawyer?

"Where are we going?"

Again the men in the car said nothing. It was becoming more obvious that this was no traditional arrest. He hadn't been ready for something like this. These types of methods were bothersome. Impersonating an officer was a legal offense. Just who were these people? Who was he dealing with? As the car blazed down the road, he knew that his questioning would ultimately get him nowhere. He'd struck a deal with the devil and now had to live with the consequences. But if he was going to play their game, he at least wanted to know who was involved and why. Why all the pointless build up and secrecy? Well, he had his own game to play. His brilliant mind was already laying the pieces down. It had taken in enough beforehand to draw out a moving map in his head. All he had to do was sit back and enjoy the ride.

The car came to an abrupt stop, and with a whoosh of air, the door nearest to him came swinging open. Walls of muscle created by the escorting officers yanked him out of the car and removed the bag. He was left there to his own, in a dark alleyway between two large buildings. The only thing that appeared obviously placed in his path was a small set of stairs leading up to an unmarked door.

Could this be anymore cliché?

Scanning behind him, he watched as the men in the car sped off without a trace. Again, no instructions had been given to him. Whoever ran this organization apparently frowned on such frivolous things. This would take some getting used to for someone as well organized as him. Cautiously, he approached the unmarked door and loomed for just a moment. Was he really going to do this? This was absolutely ridiculous. At one point in his life he had been at the top of the totem pole. Widely respected, even revered, as being the best at what he did. Now he was some no name washout standing in an alleyway afraid to tap on a door. Just how had he come to this point? With a stern fist, he thumped the door briefly and waited.

"Hello! The guy with the weird hat is here!"

His scream echoed down the alleyway. Nothing remarkable about the location; in truth, it just appeared to be as filthy and disorganized as any. But something about the city resonated with him. Maybe it was the never-ending ocean of interesting details, people, and places that helped keep him whole. The thought of anything slower for his racetrack mind seemed like torture. He let his eyes wander a bit, plowing through it all.

"It's good to see you, Mr. Ghune. Glad you found your way to the back door. Of course, you've no doubt tracked yourself here, so I'll kindly ask that you keep everything to yourself. If you can't, we can aid you with that problem."

The voice was a mixed concoction of thick pride and sarcasm. The identity of its owner was obvious—Roslin Tanner. At least who he had been told was Roslin Tanner. For all he knew, that was a lie. But he didn't have the interest to dig any deeper there. At least not until something presented itself worthy of doing so.

"What is it with you and sneaking up on people? You'd think for a guy who wears such fancy suits you could afford a better office . . . especially on this side of town."

Roslin stepped out into full view. Surprisingly, he looked unamused with the situation in its entirety. There was obviously something troubling him. Thomas was tempted to delve further, but realized that a man like Roslin would remain impervious to such curious gestures.

"Why don't you come inside and we'll see how you feel after seeing just what it is we do here."

He put out an arm beckoning for Thomas to move forward. The door that had once been closed was now gaping wide open. Inside the door was a long white hallway. There was nothing particularly unusual about it.

"Your little show back there, was it really necessary? Is that your version of tactful subtlety?"

"We orchestrate certain things to assure that certain other things work. It's really quite simple. You'll get used to it."

Orchestrate? What have you gotten into, Tommy?

Reluctantly, Thomas moved to the inside of the door, and Roslin promptly closed it behind them. Once inside, Roslin took the lead. Again, he had said nothing. It was almost as if he expected Thomas to understand his implied command. Roslin was a man who was obviously used to getting his way—this fact lead to another curious question—what was a man like Roslin willing to do to get his way?

"Follow me closely, if you please. One can get lost in this place quickly without the right directions."

The once ambiguous hallway was now filled with activity. Men and women, all scrupulously dressed in professional attire, darted about with some sort of genuine purpose, each keeping to themselves, hiding their secrets.

"What is this place? Are you guys the FBI or something?"

Roslin's pace remained constant. Without missing a beat he responded.

"We're many things. FBI could be considered one of them. But that doesn't really concern you at all, I'm afraid."

Roslin glanced down at his watch and frowned. He appeared to be flustered by some sort of time constraint he had in his schedule.

"I'm going to introduce you to someone I'd like you to meet. He'll be able to straighten some things out for you. He's one of our best agents. Someone I've known for a long time now."

Suddenly taking an abrupt turn, Roslin disappeared around a corner. As he did, Thomas' eyes caught something interesting—a man sitting casually in a chair—his dark blue eyes staring blankly out into nothing. He looked extremely jaded, disjointed, and removed. So many questions came to Thomas' mind making him want to dive further into the details. But his thoughts were interrupted by a quick tug on his shoulder.

"I said stick close. You don't have the luxury of wandering."

Thomas shook his head. It was a difficult thing to do to break his mind free once it had locked onto a target. There always seemed to be something that would linger and tantalize him to take another peek.

"Sorry . . . it just happens sometimes."

Roslin shook his head. Behind him was a large door adorned with an array of security devices. He took his time to carefully administer the credentials needed, in the right order, before the door beeped allowing them both inside.

"Pardon all of the security, but to be honest, I still feel like it's not enough" said Roslin.

Stepping inside, he pointed towards a chair and a long slender table. The verbal direction again never came. But the intent was obvious. Doing his best to keep his poise, he proudly walked over towards the chair and stood.

"I think I'll stand."

One of Roslin's eyebrows crept upwards but then quickly came back down.

"Can I interest you in some water?"

"Who would want water at a time like this? Let's just get this over with, alright?"

Roslin smiled. He popped out of the room, closing a door behind him. *What is that guy's problem?*

Sitting alone in what he could now see was an almost blindingly white room, he began pacing. He felt like a caged tiger. He'd come all this way just to be left in some hospital style waiting room? Is this how little they respected him? His looming questions were put on hold when the door to the room hissed open again. He watched as another finely suited man stepped inside. His partially greyed, auburn hair was carefully combed to one side with only a few hairs sprouted loose. He had intense, light blue eyes that appeared almost grey. He moved with purpose. His features were that of a very introspective man. He walked over to the table and took one of the open chairs and sat down.

"Have a seat, Mr. Ghune. We've got some talking to do."

Thomas lingered just a bit longer. He was trying to prove that he was no dog on a leash receiving barking orders. In his own distinct way he was showing his resilience towards the process.

"Mr. Ghune, please."

Finally giving in to the polite command, Thomas screeched a chair across the perfectly white floor and sat down.

"I suppose this time is as good as any for introductions. My name is Agent Mathers; Banks Mathers to those who know me best. I've been a part of this organization for quite some time and have been monitoring your progress. You have a rather impressive ability, Mr. Ghune. In fact, I've never seen anything like it."

"Look, guy, I've already received the patronage. Let's just move things along so I can get back to my life."

The man's eyes narrowed, but his courteous behavior continued.

"Your life, as I understand, was literally on the brink. But then again, whose life really isn't? At any time, any little thing could end any one of us. All it takes is being in the right place at the right time."

Thomas leaned forward in his chair, making sure to catch Banks's eye.

"What is it with you people and time? All I've heard so far are lousy parables and riddles. When is anyone going to actually explain anything?"

He examined the details of the man quickly. There didn't seem to be anything obviously noteworthy there, except for one thing that gleamed like a star in the night sky—a watch. It was a watch whose craftsmanship and design was beyond comprehension. He'd never seen anything like it. His brain raced through every dendrite hitting an abrupt dead-end out of desperation to link it to something. But there was nothing.

"What do you know about closed time curves, the theory of relativity, or paradoxes?"

Thomas' eyes glazed over. Practically every word that Banks had uttered had somehow cornered him into a defensive state of insecurity.

"I know enough to not care."

Banks rolled his eyes. Thomas' arrogant attitude was already pushing his buttons.

"I'll spare you all the technical nausea and just keep it simple. We've figured out how to access points in time. That's it. That's as watered down as it's going to get."

Thomas slumped back in his chair, letting out a roar of laughter.

"Are you out of your mind? You weirdos drag me here to pretend to be some sort of time travelers? What's next? You got some phone booth we need to step into?"

The complete and utter disrespect from Thomas was continuing to poke at the nerves of Banks. He took a couple of deep breaths before continuing on.

"It's far more complicated than just traveling. And call it whatever you'd like, but it's what we do."

Thomas looked up at the ceiling. It, much like everything else, was a perfect hue of bright white. In his mind he was satirically acting out the part of time traveler. But then it hit him. The bridge, his jump, and everything Roslin had hinted towards. But it was impossible! Nobody could break the infinite constraints of time. He'd never heard of such a ludicrous statement. How could it possibly be done? Why hadn't he heard of it before? But looking at the tightly secured door that was his only means of escape, he realized he'd have to indulge his almost childlike curiosity.

"Fine, let's say you can do what you claim. Great—good job—I'm so impressed. But that comes with some serious implications. If someone could just run around the fabric of time, doing whatever they wanted, all hell would break loose. And what does any of that have to do with me?"

"Exactly! I'm glad you're finally understanding this."

Banks got out of his chair and put his wrist forward. He placed his hand over the top of his watch. Immediately, a small holographic projection erupted into the air. Thomas' jaw dropped to the floor. He was speechless. In the projection were what seemed like an endless mesh of lines, all streaming across like waves moving through the ocean. It was on these lines that Banks focused.

"You see the fabric of time flows like all energy. It carries a pattern and a response. When seen from the top level down, it's far too convoluted to be analyzed—but each object, every molecule, carries its own energy—its own pattern, if you will. It's these patterns that we can isolate and examine. Throughout all time, we've each left an instance of ourselves behind. Using our technology, we can access these instances and take a glimpse back into that moment."

Thomas' head felt like a jumbling ball pit. With each of his efforts to logically piece what he was hearing together, he merely sunk further into the chaos.

"What do you mean *glimpse*? Like we go take a peek at old me sitting on the toilet? What's the point if it's already happened?"

Banks shrugged.

"Believe me, I wish I could explain this better. I'll introduce you to the man behind the curtain later. I guess *glimpse* is a rather misleading word. It's just what we call it. As far as I understand it, your *now* would temporarily exist *then*, but only in a small portion of time. The energy required to do it is astronomical. So it's brief—*limited*, if you will . . ."

"So, you guys go back to a limited point in time and do *what*? There's literally an unlimited amount of points there. You go back and try to end some assassination or something?"

Banks suddenly shot a finger directly at Thomas' head.

"Exactly, we can't! We can't change things that drastically. Their energy is far too strong. For me to try and redirect a flying bullet would be almost completely impossible in that moment. It would require far too much energy to do so. At that point we could only observe. But if you began the process years before, changing small, seemingly insignificant things, it becomes much easier. If you but nudge the target just slightly off course at the beginning, it ends up being a mile away later."

Suddenly Thomas' analytic mind was piecing apart the information. It was complicated, obscenely ridiculous, and yet something about it was drawing him in. He had to know more.

"So, what you're telling me is that something like a presidential assassination could be set up years before?"

"It's as simple as him taking the wrong bus because his alarm didn't go off when it should have. I just wish it was always that straight forward."

Thomas shook his head.

"So what, you guys have this all on lock-down, from what I see. Did some chicken fly the coop?"

Banks suddenly looked deeply sorrowful.

"It seems no one is beyond temptation."

Banks walked over to one of the walls and braced himself against it.

"Our job was and is to monitor any ripples. These ripples signify changes in time. Meaning, someone altered its course, even if ever so slightly. They are incredibly difficult to track, but have recently been occurring more and more often. Up until now it was only a textbook problem."

"So, why not just stop the ripples? Just go back and straighten things out."

"That's the problem. Our time is limited and we have no idea where to start. The changes are subtle, and once altered are almost unstoppable at a later stage. We don't have the time or resources to continually throw darts at the board hoping we get it right. We needed someone who could piece apart an entire scene within minutes, if not seconds. We needed *you*."

Thomas' eyes bulged open. He swallowed down a salty, pool of acid that had formed in his mouth. Although the explanation had been long and complicated, the gist of it was simple. Stop someone from altering time, someone who would brilliantly change minute levels of detail, to eventually lead to a catastrophic tragedy. It was the puzzle of a lifetime.

"So why would you suddenly care? There are billions of people on earth, all carrying some sort of potential disaster. I can't possibly comprehend that you'd be safeguarding each and every one of them."

Banks sunk his head into his chest.

"We believe that these ripples being made are targeted. They aren't just happening at random. Whoever has broken into our secret technology has a purpose in mind."

"Targeted? What do you mean?"

Laundromat Heist

Banks pushed off the wall and approached Thomas head on. On closer inspection, his eyes told the story of horrific loss and the tragedy he had experienced.

"Our agents are the targets. The very ones we use to watchdog this whole process are disappearing one-by-one. Soon, if something doesn't happen, we'll all be gone."

"But if you know it's coming, why not just *stop* it? It seems like a simple solution."

"Because we don't know what's coming. Whoever is doing this is good—beyond good. Without the right eyes on this, we're completely blind. But if whoever this is succeeds, there would be nothing to stop them from piecing this world apart. And the real irony of it all is, we'd never know."

Thomas let out a long puff of air. Although it was beginning to make sense, a part of him felt lost at sea, floating amongst wave after wave of complex questions that wanted answers. But the puzzle was calling him in. Its deviant nature wanted a worthy opponent. If he was going to do this, it would take everything he had to win. But what would be the price of winning?

"I need some time to think about this. This is way too much to take in right now. And to be honest, I still don't buy it."

Banks nodded before heading towards the door.

"I understand. Things like this can be incredibly complicated. Just know that you'd be saving lives, real lives that matter. Your work would be of the upmost importance. And remember, we'll be watching."

As Thomas walked down the hall leading towards the door that he now wished he had never come in through, his mind exploded with a million different radiant fireworks; so many ideas, possibilities, and outcomes. He needed to understand it more. He needed to master the craft to become the perfect tool. As he walked, a strange man who looked completely out of place amongst the sea of pretentious suits caught his eye. The man was wiry and awkward, wearing an old worn-out suit and tattered shoes. His curly, messy hair looked like a pile of jet-black worms wriggling around as he walked. The man glanced at him for just a brief moment as they passed.

Looks like they'll let anybody in here; even the homeless . . . what a freak.

During his last moments inside, he debated taking the easy route off the bridge one more time. But something had changed. In all of Roslin's seemingly mindless banter, a truth had been chiseled free. It radiated in his mind like a pristine diamond, encouraging him on. He had found a purpose.

5

NERVOUS TICKS

Sitting outside the all-too-familiar door, Thomas closed his eyes.
It had been so long since this place had meant something to him. It
used to be a wonderful retreat away from the world. He could say
anything, be anything he wanted to be, inside. But now, after all that
had happened, it was foreign. Just how much of himself had he lost
since then? Would things ever be the same? Forgoing all other doubts,
he tapped softly on the solid oak door. He watched as the tiny,
office-door name plate, with an old friend's name printed on it, shook
around in its holder. He put a hand up to adjust it back to its former
state. Just as he did, the door opened.

"Thomas, is that really you?"

Looking down, there was the same old face he remembered; only
he'd never seen it in such shock. But despite it all, he felt glad to
finally see someone he had once known so well.

"Barb—it's good to see you."

Barb opened the door cautiously. It was clear that she was processing a wide array of emotions.

"It's been awhile, Thomas . . . more than awhile. I'm not sure what
to say right now."

Thomas bit his lip nervously. He wasn't good at properly addressing
his emotions. It seemed that his out-of-control brain would prevent
any of the proper lines to connect. Things always seemed to come out
wrong.

"Can I come in? I just need someone to talk to."

Barb looked flustered for a moment. She had evidently not expected such a visit. But slowly her normal self began to return.

"Sure, Thomas; I've got a minute or two. But I do charge by the hour."

Thomas smiled. It was a fake smile he had learned to put on. It's what normal people did. In reality, however, he was still lost within the beehive of his own mind. The deafening buzz calling for his attention seemed to be growing by the minute.

"You look great, Barb. Glad to see time hasn't dulled your sharp claws."

She responded by throwing a handful of her shimmering hair behind her head as she smirked.

"Glad to see your sarcasm is still fully intact. You've got some explaining to do; not to mention, some outstanding bills to pay."

"I've been in a rough patch, ever since . . ."

"Don't—I understand. I was just giving you a hard time. I wouldn't be me if I didn't. Go take your seat and let's chat."

Thomas walked over to the polished leather couch. How many hours had he spent there doubting, pondering, and dwelling? All of his nonsensical banter had found a place here. Maybe he could find it again. Stretching out on the couch, he felt something different. He no longer was the cocky, carefree, ace detective. Now he was far more complicated. Life had dealt him a blow that left an indelible print in his life.

"I missed the smells here, and pondering your random organization of things. I've missed you, Barb."

Thomas glanced over to see her crossing her smooth, pampered legs. She quickly adjusted her short skirt before she began chewing on the end of her pen.

"I've missed you too, Thomas. My other clients aren't quite as interesting as you are. They also don't remind me of the exact amount of time it's been since I changed perfumes."

"I guess I need to do some talking here. A lot has happened since I was here last."

Barb frowned.

"Thomas, you don't need to walk me down that path. It's too soon. Stuff like this takes time."

Thomas felt his heart begin to ache. His mind was playing its games again. The on button had been pressed.

"It's more than that. I've spent my whole life feeling like an outcast. No matter how hard I tried, how many cases I solved, I was never just *normal*. Jena changed that. She made me feel whole. She made me feel . . . human."

Barb sat straight up in her chair. She had never heard such succinct speech come out of Thomas' lips. She urged him to continue.

"I was going to kill myself, Barb. I was at the bridge and I jumped. I, I don't know why, it just seemed right."

"Thomas, don't you ever associate *right* with killing yourself! How many times have I told you that it's never just about you? You'd be leaving a void behind that no one could fill."

Thomas sulked up and gazed out the window. The street was empty. He recalled the free floating balloon being dragged by the children. Such a simple thing, and yet it was so desired.

"It took me taking the plunge to realize that. Only I'm not sure if I did take the plunge. In fact, I have no idea what happened."

Barb looked deeply perplexed. Once again she was gnawing on the end of the pen she was holding.

"I don't understand what you're trying to say."

Thomas looked across the room into her eyes. Immediately, his mind reflected on every shade of eyeshadow she had ever worn. But there was something else. The look in her eyes ushered in something new. He'd never seen a look like that. In some miraculous way, Barb really cared about him.

"What if I were to tell you that I've gotten into something deep? Something that even I still can't piece together. And yet I feel myself drawn to it as if it's giving me purpose again."

Barb uncrossed her legs and leaned over. As she did, thick curls of her hair fell down around her shoulders. It was obvious that she was trying to come to her own conclusions.

"Thomas, that's what it's always been about—*purpose*—you've always said that's what Jena gave you. And to be honest, that's what she'd want you to have."

A few stinging tears made their way into Thomas' eyes. He quickly rubbed them away, doing his best to conceal his emotion.

"I guess I just don't know what to believe anymore. I've felt so empty since she's been gone. My life has always been about details and conclusions. But now I don't see my life having a happy conclusion anymore. What's the point of me? What's my *new* conclusion?"

Barb jostled around in her chair a bit nervously. The question had burrowed its way into her emotional self. She was quick to respond.

"Maybe the point isn't you. Maybe it's never been about you. You've got a gift, Thomas. The rest of us can only speculate as to what it's like to be in your head. Maybe the conclusion shouldn't be about you at all, but about those you help. Great people rarely ever live happily ever after. But they assure that the rest of us can."

The finely sewn tapestry, woven of both compliments and reality checks, resonated with him. Barb had never stuck her allegorical sword of investigation so deep. It had found his heart. For once, all seemed quiet, if only for a second in time. Maybe she was right. All these years he had spent worrying about himself and his curse. Perhaps it was time to change that. But Jena's image would not leave him. He couldn't let her go. Despite his courageous, open-hearted conversation, his memory of her remained. But he had to try.

"Barb, what's it like? What's it like to just be normal? I usually can't sit for even a minute without the world funneling into my mind. It's hell at times."

She shook her head and grinned.

"Normal isn't so great. Us normal people sit and babble about mundane aspects of life day-after-day. We normal people look at people like you and it gives us hope that we can be something more. To be frank with you, Thomas, being normal is boring. If I have to talk to one more supposedly repressed spouse into sticking out their marriage, I'll go bonkers. I need a weirdo like you to level me out."

When she was finished, Barb winked at Thomas, who blushed slightly. A display of emotion threatened to rush out in a river of awkwardness. He quickly dismissed it though, as his electric mind was humming once more.

"Barb, you're an angel, always have been. Maybe one of these days you and I could take a yoga class together and really hammer out your nervous ticks. I'm sure the graveyard of pens and pencils would thank you."

She looked down, realizing that she had again taken up chewing on her pen. She quickly shoved it out of sight and glared.

Nervous Ticks

"I'm the psychiatrist here, not you! I don't have any nervous ticks!" Thomas began to respond with the precise number of times he had seen her put the pen in and out of her mouth, but decided against it. He wanted to focus on the new awareness that he felt more confident. More confident than when he had walked in the door. He now had something to work on. Even though he still felt sick to his stomach for having engaged with the mysterious organization, it did give him some purpose. If that was all he had left in his overly complicated life, then so be it. He got up swiftly and began heading towards the door. As he did he noticed the small picture of Barb's cat had been moved slightly. This gave him pause for just a moment. He wanted to ask but refrained. Now wasn't the time.

"He comes and he goes, a real man of mystery. I'll have to watch myself to avoid swooning to death."

Barb smiled at Thomas, who caught it out of the corner of his eye.

"Until next time, Barb; and *this* time, there will be a next time a little sooner."

6

ONE DOWN

Thomas strode down the street, digging his hands deep into his pockets. He could feel the unusual heat being generated by his ecstatic mind sweltering under his hat. But the hat was going to stay. It had slowly grown on him. In truth, he actually liked it a lot. It was symbolic and odd.

Viewing the street in its entirety, he flashed back to the time before. He had been walking on clouds that day, literally floating with glee. But it had to be that night. It just had to be that store. Out of all the stores in the throbbing city, he'd found the one that accepted cash only. What with all of his mindless, romantic intentions, he'd made one critical mistake—one that he had analyzed at least a million times. He could have stopped it. If he had changed just one detail of how it all had come together that night, she'd still be alive. And then there it was—the hat shop.

Taking a deep breath, he ducked inside. He wanted to revisit the location where the downward spiral of Jena's and his life together had begun. He wanted to see how time had changed its intricate pieces. Looking around, he was greatly disappointed. Nothing had really changed; just a few new hats, but nothing else. After a few moments of silent stupor the shop owner emerged from somewhere in the back.

"Can I help you?"

Thomas did his best to come back to reality.

"Just looking around, seeing what you've got in stock."

The man gave Thomas an odd look before putting on a cheesy smile.

One Down

"Wait . . . I remember you! I never forget a hat. You were the strange man who wanted a special hat for a special night?"

Thomas nodded his head. The oblivious looking shopkeeper apparently wasn't so oblivious after all.

"I see you've taken a liking to it. As you should; it's a fine hat."

The shop keeper's smiled widened before suddenly disappearing.

"You were robbed here. I also remember that well. I'm so sorry that it happened in my store. You can never trust anyone on these filthy streets."

Thomas put on his own cheesy smile, fighting back the sudden rush of painful memories. Then his eyes caught something he hadn't seen before; a small, slender box connected to a wire running behind the counter.

"I thought you said this was cash only?"

The man followed Thomas' eye line to the tiny machine. He shrugged.

"Must have been broken . . . what kind of shop can't do credit cards?"

These details were alluring to Thomas' proactive mind. The shop was in a rather worse-for-wear condition. And judging by the slow turnover of product, things likely took three times as long to get done.

"So are you going to buy something, or just sit and stare?"

Thomas grinned briefly. He glared at the clerk in annoyance but moved on. This wasn't about the past; it was about the present. He was trying to make amends with himself. If he was going to go all in, he needed to be all of himself. Sarcastically, he pointed up at his own hat as he walked away.

"Already got one . . ."

The shopkeeper puckered his lips and snarled before receding back into the depths of his store. Thomas took a deep breath. The memories were bombarding him like mortar fire. They wanted him to dwell, relive, and suffer. Maybe he had made the wrong choice by coming down to the shop, retracing his steps. Why was he doing this to himself? Turning towards the street, he stumbled past a woman walking her dog. The small dog barked furiously on its puny leash. The distraction disorientated him for a brief moment. He quickly regained his bearings at the edge of the sidewalk balancing on the curb. There a large bus whizzed past his body missing him by mere inches. Instantly his heart jumped up into his throat. Just one more step and he could have been flattened out like a pancake.

Seriously, Tommy, get it together.

He took a deep breath, trying to compose himself. It was the city; people almost get hit every day. He didn't need to make mountains out of mole hills. It was nothing.

"Thomas Ghune? What are the odds?"

Thomas looked up to see a face he hadn't seen in ages—his old partner.

"You crazy SOB! What are you doing out here?"

Vaun approached Thomas quickly and gave him a playful shove in the shoulder.

"Hey, Vaun, it's good to see you."

Vaun shook his head at the comment.

"Oh, come on, Tommy. That's all you've got for your old partner?"

Thomas forced a fake smile. He had been wallowing in his own self-pity for so long that the mouth muscles he was forced to use felt exhausted.

"Let's go grab a drink or something, catch up. I know I need one; maybe two."

"Maybe another time. I'm kind of caught up in something right now."

Vaun cocked his head. He placed one of his hands on Thomas' shoulder gingerly.

"Look, buddy . . . I get it. Stuff happens and it sucks. And for that I'm sorry. But you can't keep carrying this around, Tommy. It'll destroy you. Just let it go for now and have some drinks with an old friend."

Reluctantly, Thomas agreed, although he often considered Vaun to be anything but a friend. Their time together had been mildly noxious at best.

"Okay, just a few, and then I've got to get going. A lot of things have changed."

"You can say that again. The office hasn't been the same without you. And I'll be the first to admit our case solving is purely academic at this point; all by the book, for the book. Makes me miss the good old days where we'd storm a scene pistols blaring. Tommy, it's good to see you."

Thomas could smell the tinge of alcohol on Vaun's breath. It appeared that the party had already started for him some time before. But what else was he going to do at this point? So what if he spent a moment or two with his old partner? Isn't that what normal people do? Followings Vaun's lead, he scurried along down the crowded streets. There he remembered all of the smells and sensations he had experienced that night. It was a succinct moment of euphoric reprieve. What he would give to relive every moment that he held so dear with Jena. If only he could have just one more day with her—a day without distractions where they could finally just be themselves— the thought was heavenly.

"Here's my place. Best booze in town. It'll wipe anything that ails ya clean."

"I'll just spectate tonight if that's alright with you. Not feeling the need to drink anymore."

Vaun gave Thomas a befuddled look. But not one to press the point, he just shrugged.

"Suit yourself. But just know that I don't plan on getting any further than the street corner before I take a nap. It's been one of those weeks."

The pair stepped into the bar. The smell of stale liquor and cigarettes filled the air in a low hanging haze. Immediately, Thomas felt slightly dizzy. Bars had never really been his scene. They would often get too loud and obnoxious causing him a surprising level of anxiety. But it was a customary gesture to join a friend at the old watering hole.

"I've got a spot there in the back that's nice and cozy. Are you sure you're not going to sip tonight, Tommy?"

Thomas nodded his head while looking around the room. Men of all shapes and sizes sat about, letting out raspy bouts of laughter. Televisions streamed all of the latest big games of every sport imaginable, while an indifferent bartender tended to the counter. But there was something else, an anomaly that he had not seen before, but that was now coming at him like a meteor.

"Tommy Gun, as I live and breathe!"

"Pete? Why is Pete here? I thought he never came here," Vaun mumbled under his breath.

Pete approached holding a large cup of inebriation. Its foamy top sloshed around with each clumsy step he took. His shirt was untucked; his tie loosened. It was undeniable that he was letting loose.

"I haven't seen you in ages boy, how you been?"

Thomas again put on his mask of forgery. He felt like he was getting better at it.

"Pete, it's good to see you. Just happen to be on this side of town?"

Pete took a swig of his alcoholic concoction then closed his eyes. His savory moment ended when his face drew back covered with a frothy mustache.

"I go to any bar that lets me in! Besides, I was hoping some day you might turn up . . . you never know."

"Pete, you look amazing," Vaun commented, furling up his upper lip.

"Oh, Vaun, you ain't got a lick of sympathy in that tight wad body of yours. Come take a chair with me over here with some of the boys."

Pete turned and began staggering his way towards a table filled with off-duty officers. Once there, he plopped his mug down and struggled to get into his tiny chair.

"Well, we've never really said no to Pete before; why start now?" questioned Thomas.

Vaun put on his own cheesy smile before he let out a tasteless hiccup.

"It's just so good to see you, Tommy. It's just like the old days."

Only it wasn't. Nothing was. The whole scenario had changed. Maybe to Vaun and Pete the memories they had were enough to constitute such a belief. But for Thomas it was anything but. Everything had changed; he had changed. Pete directed Thomas to a chair next to him. Once he'd sat down, he received a massive slap on the back.

"Tommy, I'm soaring over the moon just seeing you. Don't let Vaun tell you any different. We've missed you downtown."

Thomas looked down at the table. There were thirty eight scratch marks of all different size and variation. In a weird way, it was artistic. That's what it used to be about—art. He was the artist and the malevolent world his canvass. Now it was more, it was personal.

"Missed you too, Pete. Haven't had to cover my ears in a while. Glad to see you're healthy."

Pete let out a bellowing laugh that thundered. His aptitude for the obnoxious was being even more refined by his drunken state.

"So what have you been up to? I mean, sooner or later you've got to come back. Bills don't just pay themselves."

Thomas turned to a waitress and asked for water. He took a gulp of the contaminated air.

One Down

"Just piecing my life back together, trying to figure something out . . ."

Pete's face suddenly drooped. The many layers of it reminded Thomas of a topological map; so many contours, depths and shapes.

"Look there, Tommy. I'm sorry about all that. I got the word sometime after but the sting was still there. If there's anything I can do for you, just let me know."

Thomas shrugged.

"What's done is done—no reason to dwell on it—things just take time."

"I'll spare the weird hat comment then. I'm sure you were put up to that somehow."

Thomas shook his head. He placed a finger up on the hat's front and ran it over its edge.

"This? I like this. Not sure I'll ever take it off."

Pete's eyes scrunched together before he let out a loud burp.

"You always were an odd one, Tommy!"

Pete let out another roar of laughter before turning to engage himself in conversation with the rest of the table. Thomas received a few honorable mentions and goodwill during but he still felt largely removed. Nothing swimming in the pool of shallow conversation intrigued him. But there was something that did; a man sitting at the opposite corner who had been staring at him. Thomas was no behavioral analyst, but he knew that something was up. He watched carefully out of the corner of his eye as the man looked up from his drink, assuring himself that Thomas was still there.

And who might this be?

He'd never been one to bask in the spotlight—he preferred to be left alone—his mind worked better that way. *He* was the one who analyzed and dissected others; he detested the idea that someone else was doing it to him. Suddenly, a tall glass of water was slid in front of him, breaking his concentration. Its transparent surface reflected the dim light of the bar into his eyes.

"No ice?"

The waitress stopped mid-step as she was walking away.

"Ice machine's out of ice."

Thomas stared down at his glass. He wanted to do something but didn't know if it made sense. But he couldn't stand it any longer.

Glancing over at Pete, who had already gulped another tall one down, he poured his water into his empty glass.

"Hey, Tommy, what's the idea? They've got people for that."

Pete belted out another round of idiotic laughter. He seamlessly shifted directly into one of his embarrassing stories about Thomas. Thomas got up and began to approach the man who seemed so interested in him. His eyes locked on him and noticed a pitcher of water on his table. It only had a few melted ice cubes left floating in it. A small but important detail suggesting how long the man had been there. Thomas needed to know more. Who was he and what was he doing? He watched as the man shifted in his chair as if getting ready to flee. But once the man realized Thomas was coming straight at him, he relaxed back into his seat.

"Mind if I pour myself some of your ice water? Ice machine's broke, so says the waitress."

The man's eyes receded slightly, but he quickly put on a warm, welcoming smile.

"Be my guest. Last I checked water's free here."

Thomas forced an amiable smile of his own. He carefully lifted up the pitcher and poured himself a glass of water.

"Don't think I've seen you before; you from around here?"

The man lifted up his own glass and took a sip. As he did, he stared distantly off into the bar.

"Nope, just passing through on business . . ."

Thomas gave him a rapid once-over. The man was in a fitted suit, had a professionally maintained haircut, and a definite persona. He, much like Thomas, appeared to be out of place. There had to be more than to him than meets the eye. Forgoing any form of eloquence, Thomas went for the throat.

"So . . . I noticed you've been watching me. Actually, you've been watching me for quite some time now. Is there something I could help you with?"

The man squirmed in his chair for a moment but replied cordially.

"You must be mistaken. If I gave you the wrong impression, I apologize."

Thomas felt an instant gut check. The man was lying; he had to be. He could recollect the whole evening perfectly. There was far more

One Down

than happenstance at play here.

"Cut the crap—you've been gawking at me like a hawk—so, there's either something you want, or we've got a problem."

The man's face changed from friendly to slightly hostile. He furrowed his brow in defiance.

"Look, buddy, it's a free country. I can sit at any bar I want to."

It was clear that Thomas' interjection into the man's life wasn't a welcome one. The man took a glimpse at his watch and snarled.

"Damn it! I'm late. Thanks a lot buddy. Because of you I'm going to miss my bus."

Thomas shrugged. He felt no responsibility for the man's inadequacy to keep track of time. Suddenly, the sharp sensation of cold hit his wrist. He had over-poured his cup. A few icy drops of water trickled down to the floor.

"You really know how to carry a conversation, friend," said the man getting out of his chair.

Thomas watched as he headed for the door. The entire time, the man fidgeted with his watch as if he was confused by it. Unable to contain his curiosity, Thomas followed him. He wove around odorous bodies, swaying around clumsily to the dated music that was blasting through the cheap speakers. He didn't want the man to know he was being followed, but Thomas also needed to stay close; he didn't want to lose him. As the man burst out through the doors that led outside, Thomas was close behind. Once outside, he saw something shocking. The man was standing at the edge of the sidewalk staring right at him.

"You following me? Look, buddy, I think you—"

The man's words were suddenly cut off by the incredible force of an out of control bus. The bus swept the man along with it as it barreled into the back of a parked car. The deafening crash echoed through the streets as astonished onlookers screamed for help. Shrapnel from the impact shredded the air, sending Thomas to the ground. Within the blink of an eye, Thomas had seen life pass into a burning pile of metal. As sirens sounded off in the distance, he felt himself drift. The delicate balance had been broken; death was knocking at his door.

7

BRINK

Still not comprehending everything that had happened, Thomas had wandered aimlessly for what seemed like hours. How had it happened? Was it an accident or was there something more—something he'd failed to see? For a man who could usually recollect everything, he was coming up blank. Perhaps the man had just been in the wrong place at the wrong time. Stewing on him immediately took him back to the organization. He couldn't stall any longer. He had already wasted enough time.

Finding his way back to the door that led into the enigmatic building, he knocked. It seemed preposterous to him that such an unexceptional door led to such exceptional things. His images of what a secret organization should look like had been replaced by the mundane reality. It was still just a workplace. But if what they had told him was true, it held some real power; power that he now had a great interest in.

There has to be a way.

Suddenly the door opened and before him stood the figure of authority he now knew as Roslin. Roslin's face looked tired and upset. Thomas could plainly see that he had had little to no sleep. Things were far worse than he had supposed.

"Come inside. We've got a lot to talk about."

Thomas did as he was told. He was starting to understand the routine. Assimilation into the system was the only way to keep things fluid. Walking into the building, Roslin was quick to direct him back to the same room he'd left Thomas in before. He escorted them through the doors to the inside.

"Take a seat. Agent Mathers will join us in just a moment, along with someone else who's going to get things started."

"But I still haven't said anything. For all you know I could be taking a walk."

Roslin slammed his fist into the table. The forceful impact made it rattle.

"Take a seat."

Thomas didn't know what to say. He'd never seen this side of Roslin before. All of his sarcastic jests would have to be placed on hold. It was obvious that things had escalated. Reluctantly, he did as he was told. Right as he felt the cold chair press into him, the doors to the hall rushed open.

"Mr. Ghune—I'd like to introduce you to someone."

Thomas looked up to see Banks staring back at him earnestly. And he wasn't alone. To his side was a very odd looking man. Thomas stood up to greet him. As he did, the man's odd appearance came into full view. He was a portly man, wearing deep, thick glasses with wide brims, topped by waxy, brown hair. He was wearing a quirky shirt that paid homage to an old rock band. He appeared clumsy and off-balance as he stood there.

"This is Julius Orson, one of the lead scientists here."

Julius approached Thomas, rapidly jutting a hand out to greet him. Thomas watched as the soft hand grasped his and shook it weakly.

"You can call me Jo. It's a lot easier that way. Everyone I know here does, which isn't that many. We've all got our nicknames around this place. I'm assuming you've met Banks or *Man in Black* as we call him behind his back. You'd swear he never smiles. A real storm cloud that one."

Thomas started to respond when his mind latched onto Jo's matted hair. Layers of what appeared to be greasy clumps of straw jutted this way and that. Mesmerizing—so many patterns on such an odd head—it was almost magical.

"Is he okay? He's staring at me."

Roslin swirled a hand through the air.

"Mr. Ghune, are you there?"

Thomas shook his head. His brain had been spinning in circles over the frivolous details of Jo's overtly nerdy appearance.

"I'm fine. I was just thinking."

"Can we *please* do some thinking at the *table?*" asked Roslin, sounding annoyed.

Thomas obliged Roslin and headed back to his chair, leaving Jo behind, still staring blankly. Thomas' weird introduction had put him off, but he too reluctantly followed suite. Once at the table, he sat down cautiously. Banks sat beside him, keeping his eyes locked on Thomas at all times.

"Right, let's get started. I'm sure Agent Mathers has clued you in on some of this, but Mr. Orson is the real wizard here. As I'd rather not waste any more time, let's just get all the questions you have out of the way now."

Thomas shifted in his chair, examining Roslin nervously. He didn't know why, but something about the man made him feel uncomfortable. Or maybe it was the fact that Banks was staring at him like a piece of steak he was ready to gnaw on.

"Right now, I only want to know *how* and *why*. You all claim to do something absolutely ridiculous, and yet I still find myself sitting here. And by *how* I don't mean the nitty gritty. I just want to understand what exactly I'm getting into. After *that*, let's find the why."

Jo's eyes lit up with pure jubilation. His on switch had been pressed. Roslin looked at him and nodded.

"It's really something, isn't it? Taking the very fabric of time and rolling it out like a red carpet. The immense number of complex singularities, energy patterns, and possibilities is truly mind-boggling."

"Jo, get to the point," said Banks, interrupting him.

Jo cringed. He looked upset by everyone's enthusiasm.

"Fine . . . we created a form of time travel, only it's probably not what you're thinking."

"I'm not even believing it at this point, let alone thinking about it."

Jo's smile returned. Roslin's incredulous challenge had been accepted.

"Picture the world as you know it now, only flattened out and stretched. On this flat floor are all of the energy patterns created by gravity, electrons, and a literal smorgasbord of other things. But in the end, it's all energy. This energy creates patterns that exist in instances throughout time; your first birthday party, your first kiss, your first time with a woman . . ."

Jo blushed at the mention of the word *woman*. His vivid imagination was getting the better of him.

"These instances are tied to you. You're forever bound to them. From conception until the end, you have a unique pattern; a pattern that can be traced and accessed. We've merely figured out how to access that moment in which your instance existed. There we create a temporary distortion allowing you to go back in time!"

Thomas rolled his eyes.

"Are you kidding me? That's insane."

"Insane, yes, it's absolutely, deliciously insane. That's what makes it awesome!"

Jo closed his eyes for just a moment, relishing his show of intellectual superiority.

"But we have limits. Picture that same flat floor. To access an instance taking place when you existed in the past, we bend it, like a donut. A scrumptious, sugar coated donut!"

"Jo!" scolded Roslin, getting annoyed.

"Nobody likes metaphors? Anyways, it takes an astronomical amount of energy to do so. This makes the time in which you can be there short. It also makes the window narrow. And on top of that, everything would be relative. Your current self would exist in a temporary time lapse where things would be happening around you at an almost snail-like pace. It's like being on super speed; the rush of a lifetime!"

Thomas' mind had already formulated a plethora of questions. But he quickly organized them into a hierarchy of what he cared about most.

"So you're telling me that I could hop back in time, but only long enough to take a power nap? And then what am I supposed to do? Come back and just say everything looks great?"

Jo clapped his hands. Thomas' inability to understand it was thrilling him.

"Normally, yes; we do it all the time. Ever been alone and felt like someone was watching? Ever thought you saw a glimpse of something that wasn't there? Ever feel like something changed without you knowing it? We're the ghosts in the shadows, the watchdogs of time."

"But it's those watchdogs that are being murdered, including one last night!" exclaimed Banks with high emotion.

"Wait, wait a second. You were following me, weren't you? At the bar, that man, he was one of your guys!" yelled Thomas furiously.

"We told you we'd be watching, Mr. Ghune. There was no way we were going to let you just walk away after being here. This isn't that simple," continued Roslin.

"That man's dead! I watched him get ripped apart by an out of control bus! Don't lecture me on what's simple!" screamed Thomas passionately.

"And don't you think I know that? Don't you think I haven't regretted that decision? I'm not going to apologize for doing my job and making the hard decisions. But you have to understand that our line of work comes with risk. Risks that can sometime require the ultimate sacrifice!" bellowed Roslin.

"That man was a friend of mine—a good agent—he didn't deserve to go out like that," added Banks soberly.

Thomas closed his eyes and took a deep breath. His emotions were getting the better of him and he needed to take it down a notch. If he was going to beat this he needed to stay immune to it all.

"Ok, I'm sorry. It's just disturbing is all, and to be honest, horrifying that someone can do that with such a slight yet calculated sleight of hand. So how can you stop someone who's hopping back in time? You said it's all relative for the traveler, but what does that really mean if we collide?"

Roslin looked at Jo who resumed his gleeful babble.

"I thought you'd never ask. Your instance and theirs would coexist. But your windows would have to be the same. As all things are relative, his window could pass in the blink of an eye, leaving you none the wiser should he arrive at a different point in time. There's no way of knowing when he jumped back; all we can do is trace the event, the ripple. We would be placing you within that variable time frame that we can support. If you're lucky, or judging by current events unlucky, enough to meet this person head-on, you both would adhere to the same physics or laws. This also means either one of you could die. I'd imagine that to be a last resort."

Thomas cringed at the mention of death in Jo's sentence. He felt as if the room's walls were somehow closing in around him. There would be no turning back.

"So why are they dying now? Why didn't whoever this is just go back and push their tricycle out into the street and call it good?"

Jo shook his head.

"One thing you need to understand here are the instances themselves. Your past is, for lack of a better explanation, in the past. It's happened. Its energy pattern has been made. To change something like that would be utterly impossible. But our future, the here and the now, well that's wide open. If you could foresee a pattern and calculate a response by changing tiny details of the past, you could alter the future, or as in our case, murder. It's the most elaborate game of chess you'll ever play, using all of the pieces to finally get what you want; where past movements eventually force a result in the present."

Jo's eyes watered with emotion. The mental exercise and intricacy of the problem was captivating him deeply.

"This is insane. So, if I'm understanding all this sci-fi hoopla, potentially, I'd be traveling back to a time that puts me on a crash course with some psychopath, where I'd then have but minutes to figure out what this looney has changed and link it to the present? That's like me pushing a pebble down the mountain and then trying to tell you if an avalanche is going to happen. This isn't some game; this is the puzzle of a lifetime."

Jo began to respond but was cut off by Roslin.

"One that you're going to have to solve, Mr. Ghune—that's why you're here—we wouldn't have pulled you into this world had we not ran out of other options. The truth is we aren't winning. The truth is there's too much evil out there that needs to be fixed and we don't have the resources to do it."

"Resources? You mean talent—some freak like me—why don't you guys just call it what it is? You only need me to save you. I'm nothing but a means to an end. Then what? I miraculously save the day and get an honorary recommendation? You're just going to let me walk away from all this?"

Roslin put a hand up to his head. The incessant questioning from Thomas was whittling him away.

"This isn't about us or you. This is about what's right. I'm not at liberty to say more, or care what you decide to do with yourself. It's up to you to decide what you think is right."

Thomas shook his head. There were so many things he didn't like. So many parts of the story that still seemed wide open. But he hadn't stopped to ask the very simple question; what *did* he think was right? What was right to a man who had lost everything? Did he even know the difference between right and wrong anymore? Or was he floating somewhere above it all in the selfish pursuit of purpose and vindication. There was only one true way to find out.

"Let's say I'm in. Where do we go from here?"

Banks moved forward on the table.

"You'd be partnering up with me. With the recent murder of Agent Stathis, that leaves only two of us. If you were to join, that'd put that number to three. We've lost three agents thus far. Our odds aren't looking good. But the longer we wait, the more whoever this is will accomplish. Everybody is at risk here."

Banks pulled a watch-like gadget from his pocket that mirrored the one he was wearing and placed it on the table.

"It's yours. You need to be trained, but from then on you'll temporarily be a part of this team. It comes with all the responsibilities of wielding something like this. We don't give gifts like this lightly."

Thomas looked down at the incredible device. It sat silently, beckoning him to pick it up. A part of him wanted to without question, but his pride held him back. How did they know what was and wasn't possible? How could anyone possibly understand the complexities of time? The amount of arrogance in the room was repugnant. But he didn't really have any other choice. Slowly, his hand worked its way out of his pocket and grabbed the watch. He twisted it around his wrist and latched it tightly.

"Good, good, let's not waste any more time than we already have. We're way behind so we've got to do some serious catching up. Agent Mathers can show you the ropes. Use Mr. Orson for anything else. If you need me I'll be around," Roslin said as he rose to his feet.

"And where are you going? Have some other, more pressing, issues to deal with?"

Roslin responded over his back as he continued without pause.

Brink

"You have no idea."

"I think it's time you really learn just how complicated things can get. We'll teach you how to use what we call "the brink" to take glimpses back. I'll show you the ropes of something you never would have imagined possible. But I cannot stress enough the importance of never losing your device or damaging it. The implications could be disastrous."

"Brink, glimpse, and disaster—who could possibly say no to all that?" remarked Thomas sarcastically.

Jo let out a sudden burst of laughter that he quickly contained. It appeared he was enjoying Thomas' dark, morbid humor. Banks gave him a very upset look that shushed Thomas on the spot.

"Mr. Ghune, you need to start taking this seriously. If you don't, you will lose—I promise you that."

Thomas felt the sharp comment stab at his pride. Immediately, his defense mechanisms heightened in preparation for retort. But he was quick to calm himself down. He couldn't let his ego demolish the few flimsy bridges he'd built so far.

"Alright . . . I'll try. You just have to understand how ridiculous this all seems upfront. I'm still having difficulty processing."

Banks put on a microscopic smile that faded quickly.

"You sound a lot like I did all those years back. Don't worry; it gets better. Soon it'll become almost second nature."

The group huddled together. The explanations that came were astounding. The brink was nothing short of spectacular. All of the years of research and secret funding had created a true epitome of human creativity. But this brought another question; just what else was there? If the brink program existed, how many others did as well? These questions needed a place and time to be answered, but it wasn't now. As the hours dragged on, the only thing that mattered to Thomas was the only thing he couldn't change—the past.

8

TEWSDAY

Thomas looked down at the array of graphs, readings, and other data hovering around his wrist. It was amazing. Never in his wildest dreams could he have imagined such a thing being possible. It seemed to defy all forms of logic. For a moment, he felt like a young boy again. His imagination was being jogged around a track containing all possibilities. He had rehearsed the steps many times now, with Banks's aid. He was now competent enough to attempt an actual glimpse, as they called it. But he still wasn't sure. Somehow, he felt like they hadn't told him everything. Would his deal with the devil go sour?

"Are you ready or should we rehearse?" questioned Banks, standing a few footsteps away.

Thomas smirked.

"You really don't get just how good I am at this, do you?"

The comment looked to have mildly insulted Banks.

"Right . . . as you keep reminding me. Just try and remember one fact, alright? It's one thing to play your little game of hocus-pocus and then take a bow *here*. When we step back, it's a whole new world. Forget everything you know about physics right now. I promise you that nothing you've done up to this point will have prepared you for this."

Thomas' eyes rolled around in one full circle. It was clear that he felt Banks's depiction of the soon-to-be was a bit exaggerated. Thomas had been on many cases and seen many things; so what if it was at another place in time. He could tackle anything.

"As for encounters, I've never had one, but in the event you do, be ready. There's no way back once you're dead. Your line ends."

"So do we even know what to look for, and in what general area?"

"The brink will put you as close to the epicenter of the ripple as possible. From there you are on your own. With any luck you'll be close enough to stop whoever this is. So far, we haven't. We're either too early or too late to catch them before they jump back to the present."

Thomas looked up at the white ceiling. His mind was wandering about, trying to formulate a plan.

"Are you coming?"

Banks shook his head.

"It doesn't work that way. Our windows would have to align in order for us to exist relative to each other. If not, I'd pass you or you'd pass me in a flash. Remember—it's all relative. But you can use the brink. It can help lead you towards the epicenter of the ripple. But it's not precise enough to track exactly *what* created the ripple. That will be up to you to find."

Thomas rested his eyes for just a moment. He could feel his nerves humming in anticipation. This would be the moment that he would put all of their so-called technology to the test.

"I'm ready to do this."

"Alright, then fire it up," said Banks.

Thomas hovered his hand over his wrist. Instantly, an array of projections streamed out, prompting him for input. Quickly he began recanting his training. He set the date and time given to him by Banks's intel.

"How do you get this thing to target again? Is it acquire, target; or target, acquire?"

Banks looked displeased.

"For someone that remembers so much, you'd think you could remember the order."

"Always had a bit of a problem with order; it's the details I never forget."

Thomas input a few more parameters before gazing over at Banks. Banks sat patiently watching as a teacher would a student; arms crossed, eyes focused on Thomas.

"I think I'm ready," said Thomas.

An ever so tiny smile returned to Banks's face but was quickly erased. "Good, let's go then. Oh, and one more thing I almost forgot. When you do jump, it's going to feel like a million icy daggers are stabbing into your heart. It's a horrible feeling, but you get used to it with time."

"Wait, *what*? Are you *joking* right now?"

Banks grinned. It was obvious he was going to enjoy this. Without hesitation, he thrust his hand over to Thomas' wrist and hit a small button. The world instantly began to slow down. The images of reality shifted around Thomas like dripping paint. He watched as Banks's silhouette rapidly disappeared into nothing. Then, without warning, came a piercing ray of light. The light swirled around his body, blotting everything else out of view with its blinding luminescence.

What's happening?!

Soon the light had completely enveloped him. It pulsated around him like a beating heart. But the awe inspiring beauty was shattered by his deafening scream that echoed into nothingness. The description that Banks had given was accurate to the letter. The shocking amount of pain ripped him into another sense of reality. His eyes jutted wide open, while his veins began to surge with rushing waves of pulsing blood. Then, at the very precipice of being able to take no more, he collapsed down to the ground. Instantly, the blinding light was gone and all that was left behind was a world unlike anything he had ever experienced.

The scene around him was slightly familiar; a cramped over-priced apartment building in the big city. What had him completely stupefied was the weird tempo of the objects and people that were frozen in time. The few things that appeared to be moving at all moved at such a stagnant pace that they appeared almost motionless. A woman sat crouching next to him addressing her child's bad behavior. A man was stuck in limbo trying to catch his beagle who had run off, leash in tow. Another man was gulping down a soda, letting it hover just inches above his mouth. Thomas lingered for a moment. The sugary stream sparkled as the slowly moving liquid slid down the man's throat like toothpaste. It was surreal.

Intrigued by his new surroundings, he touched the pouring, bubbly stream caught midair. In complete wonder, he watched as the liquid pressed back against him, fighting to keep its place in time. He licked his finger. There was the slight hint of flavor left behind. Glancing down at the dog on the run, he could see its drooling mouth exhibiting the same behavior. It was beyond belief. His curiosity began to overflow, pouring itself out into a delightful parade down the hall, touching, grabbing, and prodding as he went. It felt godlike to do so. He was so caught up in his mindless amusement that he almost had forgotten why he'd come in the first place.

Tommy, get it together. This isn't play time.

He stopped and did his best to contain his out-of-control mind, which was screeching in delight. The power, the ability, was incredible. But he had a job to do. He had seen the very real, palpable pain that Banks had. He was beginning to understand the dire consequences of altering the past. There wasn't any time for his selfish indulgences. Looking down at his watch, he saw the epicenter of activity on display, and he had arrived close to it. Realizing this, he began working his way rapidly through the building. He took a couple of turns, doing his best to dodge all of the objects and people on the way. He then went up a flight of stairs; the signal was getting closer.

This is unbelievable . . . absolutely unbelievable.

At the top of the stairs was yet another hallway filled with dazzling images. It was like a 3D painting that he could interact with first hand. He was now very close to the source of the signal. Looking around, he could see it all perfectly. He let his mind open up its insatiable appetite and feast. A literal ocean of details came funneling into him in just seconds. His eyes were truly the only limiting factor. But he had to be fast. That's when he saw a door that was slightly ajar. Not knowing what else to do, he entertained the idea of entering it. As he scooted past a slender woman dressed in her workout clothes and talking on the phone, he met her eyes dead on. He felt a wave of panic ensue. It was beyond strange to be so close to someone, literally staring them in the face, and have them not see you. Perhaps a part of her would see him, but it would be forgotten in a brief flash.

I hope wherever you end up you don't remember any of this.

The truth was, to her he would be nothing but a ghost passing in time, a ghost on a mission. And it was the mission that troubled him. It was completely chaotic. There seemed to be no logical cornerstone holding the house of cards together. But this detail was overshadowed by the paramount importance of stopping whoever it was that was setting up the murders. He was going to beat this.

Heading towards the cracked open door, he peeked inside. The center of activity appeared to be here. But from what he could see, it looked completely normal. Just another city apartment slammed between shoddy, thin walls. But the devil would be in the details. Grasping the door, he attempted to move it and slide inside. The door remained immobile. Its energy fought the rapid change trying desperately to keep its place. Frustrated, he dug his fingers a bit deeper to get a better hold. He arched his back and pulled. The door moved slightly, sending out a small wave of distortion through the air. The crack was now just wide enough to fit his body through. Sucking in, he threw himself inside of it as the door burst back into place. The force threw him to the floor.

This is insane.

The impact with the floor took his breath away. He could feel the jolts of pain race through him, reminding him that he was anything but god-like. He was very much human. He would have to be careful. Rising up slowly, he adjusted his hat and suit. Banks had yet again been correct in his description. He had never experienced anything like this. Even in his own unusually creative imagination, something like this seemed farfetched. He now clearly understood Banks and Jo's explanations about change. If that was the amount of energy it took to only temporally displace a door, what would it take to permanently alter something? But he was sure of one thing. The pain he felt was the same regardless. The last thing he wanted to do was to become a victim in some brief moment of happenstance.

Okay, what now? What do you do now?

He immediately began scanning the room. All of its many interesting details screamed at him, begging for attention. There was a kitchen sink full of dirty dishes. That day's newspaper was sprawled out on the table next to a half empty glass of orange juice. And then there was a strange arrangement of magnetic letters on the fridge, spelling out the day of the week. Thousands of images, all containing something that he wanted to examine. But he had to prioritize. He needed to use every bit of his experience and ability to stack and attack them in order. He glanced down at his watch. He was directly on the epicenter. In his head, he was also tracking the time he'd been glimpsed. It had been just a few minutes—but a lot can happen in a few minutes. When would the change occur? What would it be? His heart raced under the bleak understanding that the killer was possibly sharing his space. Maybe he was being watched. Looking at the date on the paper he gasped. It was three months ago.

Calm down, the odds of him being here are slim. Just do your job.

He took a deep breath, and continued going through each part of the room, as quickly as he physically could. Something caught his eye. In the studio apartment was a small bed. Its covers were partly draped to one side. But it was what was in the bed that intrigued him; a beautiful woman. She lay dozing away, comfortably tucked under her warm covers. Thomas' mind erupted. With the eruption came all of the painful memories of his time spent with Jena. He missed her tender touch, the warmth of her body. Here was what he could no longer have. This kind of life was someone else's; it didn't belong to him. And it was something he would never have. His heart ripped itself apart in jealousy and pain. It wasn't fair. Standing just inches from the bed, he felt a tear stream down his cheek. Was he really so human? Would he ever be free?

I'll find a way.

Suddenly, a brief blast of light pulsed through the room and then disappeared. His watch hummed as readings streamed across its face, divulging its details.

"What was that?"

Turning back towards the rest of the room, his eyes pranced wildly about. But he was feeling sluggish. His emotional fog was overcasting his ability. He needed to focus; he needed to forget.

Damn it, Tommy, just let it go. Why can't you let it go?

But he knew the answer. He didn't want to. Pacing back through the room, he began heading towards the door, discouraged. But a spark from his mind suddenly ignited a burning curiosity to look more closely at the fridge. Even with all of his moping around, his eyes had caught sight of it and made a note. He stared at the quirky, magnetic letters arranged on the front. Something had changed. The letters had been altered. It was subtle—so subtle that anyone else probably would have missed it. Where the letters had once properly spelled out the word *Tuesday*, it now incorrectly spelled *Tewsday*. It seemed so alarmingly insignificant. Why would anything that trivial matter?

Why, why would you change that?

He stepped up to the letters on the fridge. He tried to rearrange them but found that he couldn't get them to budge.

What is going on?

He closed his eyes and dwelled for a moment in time. He was streaming over the possibilities that the slight change could create. Perhaps it was a distraction to modify someone's schedule, if ever so slightly. The real question now became, what schedule was being modified? Looking around the room he desperately searched for any clues. Stacks of magazines, unopened envelopes and some empty boxes, but nothing seemed especially out of the ordinary. But maybe that was what he needed to look for, the ordinary. Realizing his time was probably short he darted around the room looking for anything he could find. He wanted to know this person, whoever it was. Soon his efforts were rewarded with a small, crisp business card.

David Schilling - Plumber

Now his mind was a sky of bursting fireworks. What could it possibly mean? How could this clue, buried in the past, help him save a life in the future? This was an unbelievable puzzle that he had been thrown into alone. One thing was for sure; he needed to track down David Schilling. This man was somehow connected; connected to a nefarious plot to murder yet another agent. Instinctively, he reached down to pick up the flimsy card. It stuck to the table like glue. He had to remember what he was up against. He would have to leave all of the laws of physics he knew behind. Taking a deep breath, he turned back towards the bed. He looked at the woman still stuck in time. Her luscious lips were slightly open. No doubt, her significant other had left her there, carefully sneaking off to work after a night of passion. He couldn't resist. Sitting on the edge of the bed he breathed in the essence that was still frozen in the air. The tiny molecules that displaced themselves tantalized his nostrils. The alluring scent of her perfume was mixed with a peculiar musk of cologne. It was intoxicating.

"One day, I'll have her back."

Tewsday

He began to stand up when a bright light began to form directly in front of him. The light swirled uncontrollably until it encapsulated him entirely. The same blast of pain from before came along with the mind numbing lapse in thought. A scream of agony rang through the nothing before it came to an abrupt stop. The trip of a lifetime had just come to an agonizing end.

9

GLIMPS

"Thomas . . . Thomas . . . can you hear me?"

The world of light suddenly gave way to darkness. Everything hummed with a vibrant energy as things sped back up. The tornado of light and energy dissipated, leaving the normal world behind, and with it an extremely disoriented Thomas.

"What happened? Where am I?"

Thomas flung his arms wildly about while he staggered around, desperately trying to keep himself up. He felt beyond dizzy. It was as if his brain had been put through the spin-cycle a few thousand times. He found it incredibly difficult to even stand, let alone think clearly.

"Calm down, you're back now."

Thomas looked over to trace the source of the voice to see Banks's worried expression. Banks watched attentively as Thomas continued to struggle to regain his composure.

"Why do I feel so sick? I feel like I'm going to throw up."

Banks put on a slender smile before shoving a bucket Thomas' way.

"Everyone's first couple runs usually end this way. It doesn't hurt to just get it all out. We get that a lot around here."

Thomas hunched over the bucket and let it rip. The sensations he was experiencing were both incredible and terrifying at the same time. He felt as if he had just experienced an out-of-body moment.

"Your mind is just reconnecting to the present. It's like slamming two worlds together for just a flash. It takes some getting used to."

Thomas continued to wobble around, but his mind was finally

beginning to return to its normal, freakish self. As it did the flood gates opened, spewing out all of the details he had witnessed in the past.

"I saw the change back there; or at least one of them. But it's so insignificant I can't possibly imagine how it would affect now."

Banks walked slowly around Thomas, inspecting his every move. He looked very concerned.

"Well, what was it you found?"

Thomas looked down at the floor. The information streams were blinding him at the moment.

"Just some letters on the fridge—they were rearranged—it was just the day *Tuesday*, around three months ago. I have no idea what it means."

Banks looked slightly disturbed by the result but nodded.

"Okay, well, there has to be more."

"I have a name—David Schilling. He's a plumber."

"Anything else?"

Thomas cringed as his mind accelerated, relaying back to his brain the entirety of the room. Every detail it had found of interest was there. The only thing he had truly omitted was his distraction.

"Thomas, anything else?"

Thomas noticed the lack of professionalism that Banks was expressing. He had dropped the titles for the moment. Now he was treating him as more of an equal.

"That's it; that's really all I've got."

"So, your time in the past only brought back two discerning pieces of information. You'll excuse me if I'm slightly underwhelmed."

"I was distracted. There was a woman in a bed who reminded me of someone, that's all. It was nothing."

Banks approached Thomas and put a hand on his shoulder.

"Thomas, it's obviously not nothing if it's effecting your work. We're trying to save lives here! We can't let our personal lives screw this up. We have to stay focused. We have to stay strong."

Thomas flung Banks's hand off his shoulder.

"And just what would you know about that? You have no idea what it's like to have someone ripped right out of your hands; taken away! I was robbed on what was supposed to be the best day of my life!"

Thomas watched closely as Banks instinctively rambled off a date and time almost completely silently. But it meant nothing to him, did it? Quickly, Banks retorted in anger.

"I know a hell a lot more than you think! You'd be surprised what secrets we all have. Let's just say I understand your sentiments. But just because I do, doesn't make it right!"

Thomas started to lash out with a verbal retaliation but paused. Had Banks just expressed some truth? Was one of the unbreakable, inhuman agents actually expressing emotion? Now his curiosity was tying itself around him, binding him to the question. What had Banks lost? Letting out a long sigh, he let his fiery embers of frustration dampen. He suddenly remembered another acute detail that had bothered him greatly.

"When I was back there, I tried to fix the letters on the fridge but couldn't. Why? I was able to slightly displace the door, and yet, no matter how hard I tried, was incapable of moving the letters."

Banks shook his head and looked away. The complexities that he knew as common place kept rearing their ugly heads.

"It's because it had already been altered. To alter it again would require even more energy. Once something finds its place and then is forcefully moved, it only adds to the energy keeping it in place. Time doesn't like change. Whoever did this knew what they were doing. That's why we have to get it right the first time."

Thomas blinked then responded.

"I also believe I saw a flash of light. It came and went before I could see its source. It appeared that the change happened right after."

Banks nodded his head.

"Well, then you were in the right place. The flash of light was the alteration adjusting itself into your instance. For a brief moment in time you were standing in the same room as the killer."

Thomas let that sink in for a minute.

"That means he saw me! I would have been sitting wide out in the open!"

Banks shook his head.

"Look, I don't understand how everything works, but I'm sure he didn't see you. Your instance and his are dwelling in their own relative window. To you what seemed like minutes, in reality was at best a second or two to everyone else at that time. You'd be nothing more than a flash of light. If you two line up, *then* we've got a problem. We've never documented an occurrence of two instances in the same glimpse. And to be honest, we've never tried to."

Thomas felt sick. Despite Banks's reassurances, he still felt violated. He recalled the blank expression on the woman in the hall. How could he shake off the feeling that he was being watched?

"Fine, let's say he didn't see me. If this guy is as good as you say he is, how long before he comes for me?"

Banks let his head collapse onto his chest. His emotional state appeared ragged at best.

"Odds are he already is. That's what makes this so incredibly difficult. He's always a step ahead. Each time we get close, or think we are, we lose somebody. In essence, either one of us could be next."

Thomas recalled the minor changes he had noticed since his involvement. Barb's office, the hat store; had there been more? Had these changes been intentional or just coincidence? His fate was now hanging from wires of looming questions. If he was going to win, he'd have to outpace and outmaneuver the killer.

"Then we don't have time to dig deeper. We need to find this David Schilling. Whatever was altered started with him. This only happened three months ago. Who knows what this has compounded into?"

Banks's eyes seemed to tell the story. He was showing some deep remorse about failing thus far.

"I'll call our intel and get him traced. In the meantime, we'll need some transportation."

Thomas kept repeating the man's name and job title over and over in his mind. What was the link? How could a deviant mind use this man to create mayhem? There was a reason and he was going to find it.

"Call the other agents. Find out where they are right now! Tell them not to move a muscle until we can provide further details."

Banks gave Thomas an odd look. He was taken aback by the brash tone in Thomas' voice.

"I'll see what I can do."

Thomas looked around the large, white room.

"And what am I supposed to do?"

"Well, you said you're good. So figure it out. There must be more to this than you realized."

Thomas didn't like the idea of being locked up in some secret room in a building that didn't exist. He felt like a caged tiger, pacing like mad. His mind needed a target. He wanted more information and he wanted it now. For him things were moving far too slow. If he had to wait every time for the others to finally catch up, he'd lose. Sooner or later he would have to make his move. But for now, he would play nice. The dictates mandated it so.

"Just hurry; if I'm right, somebody may already be dead."

As he said the words his heart skipped a beat. That somebody could be him.

10

CAT PEOPLE

The ride towards the mystery man's apartment seemed to take
a lifetime. Thomas felt as if he was being held back by all things
tangible. Feeling frustrated, he gazed out of the blacked out windows
of the car he was stuck in. He saw the faces of all the people bustling
about their normal city lives. At times he envied them. They were so
oblivious to anything around them, so apathetic in their interactions
with each other. The many details that each carried were utterly
wasted on faked cordial greetings exchanged on mundane schedules.
It seemed almost alien to imagine himself in such a life. Even now,
as he was being dragged even deeper into the madness, he was finally
starting to feel like himself again.

"Back there . . . I'm sorry if I came off a little rough. I'm just sick of
losing people . . . friends."

Thomas looked over at Banks who had remained quiet for most of
the ride thus far. He was also gazing out of the car window, letting his
eyes run over the world passing them by.

"I understand—it's fine—I know I can be difficult at times."

Banks looked at Thomas out of the corner of his eye.

"You think you can really catch whoever this is? It feels to me like
chasing two tails at once."

Thomas slunk back into his seat. Inside his head, his form of reason
was traversing through the never-ending parade of fact and detail.
Each passing moment a new piece of data would present itself, only
to be slaughtered by some loose end or gaping hole in logic.

"Catch isn't my job. I'm here to pick up all the bread crumbs. I'll let you guys do the catching."

Banks shook his head slightly. Thomas' overbearing attitude was getting old.

"We can do our job just fine. It's yours I'm worried about."

The car came to an abrupt stop, interrupting a would-be rebuke from Thomas. The car quickly emptied as each suited enigma moved rapidly out.

"You sure this is the right place? Seems like David Schilling could be a pretty common name."

Thomas rapidly recited every David he had ever met that was of interest.

"I'm sure," Vaun assured him. "Our intel is the best. As long as the details you provided me accurate, we'll find him."

Thomas rubbed the back of his neck. The seats in the car were horribly uncomfortable. For it being a car belonging to a secret organization with a seemingly blank check, it was a failed oversight. Stepping out of the car, a strange feeling swept over him and skewed his thoughts for a minute. The building they were standing outside of was foreign to him, and yet it wasn't. Something was distinctly familiar about it.

As the pair walked into the main entrance, they were met by a literal cavalcade of human life. People coming and going, all caught up in some sort of seemingly important activity. No one seemed to notice the duo's existence in the slightest. A small dog came into view.

"I know that dog," said Thomas aloud.

A portly beagle pranced by tugging its slender leash behind him. The owner of the dog suddenly came chasing after it.

"Trixie! Get back here!"

Thomas didn't know why but he smiled. It was like he was revisiting a warm piece of his own past.

"Dog?" questioned Banks.

"Forget it; it's meaningless."

Thomas watched as the owner of the dog finally caught the tail end of the leash and reined in the loose canine. He was so caught up in the moment that he neglected to move out of the way of a woman heading towards the door. His shoulder plowed into her sending her reeling back. A slew of profanity instantly erupted.

"Hey! Watch it, buddy!"

Thomas glanced over to see a slender woman dressed neatly in workout clothes. He caught her eyes and gasped. It was the same woman from the hallway. He couldn't shake the image of their intimate encounter in the hall. Unable to break his stare, the situation only worsened.

"Hey, creep, what's your problem?"

Thomas was unable to find the right words to say. He only remembered her as a still statue frozen in time. The vibrant woman that stood before him now was unbelievable. Taking one last look at him, the woman shook her head and wandered off. As she passed she let him have a few more choice pieces of her mind dipped in a heavy vat of obscenities.

"What's your problem? You keep stalling and making a scene."

Thomas shrugged.

"Just adjusting to reality, I guess. I'm a little behind the times."

Banks rolled his eyes at Thomas' witty pun. But he was not amused. To him the situation was dire. Every moment they wasted would be one they would never get back. But to Thomas it was just more dots. Millions of dots, all moving about, somehow connected to other dots. It was an infinite game of relationships. Never before in his life had he seen such a clear standard of cause and effect.

"He's upstairs. Let's be quick and avoid any more attention, alright?"

Thomas nodded his head. He already knew where to go. Everything was falling into place. It was as if his own glimpse into the past had now become a part of him. Nostalgia crept into his heart like somehow the place actually meant something to him.

What is happening to me?

Taking one of the nearby elevators, the two stood quietly for a moment. The elevator chimed as it passed each floor. Quaint, retro elevator music played producing ambient background music. While standing there motionless, Thomas looked over at an elderly woman holding a ball of fluff. The ill-mannered feline growled at him, watching his every movement. Feeling slightly put out, he smiled at the owner to help remedy the situation. She glanced at his hat and suit and sneered. He looked away and sighed.

"Cat people . . ."

A ding and a whoosh announced that they had arrived at their floor. Looking behind, he watched as the old lady repeatedly pressed the *close door* button. Did he really look that threatening?

"Should be a couple doors down this hallway."

"I know where it is. I actually took the stairs last time."

Glancing down the end of the hall, he saw a little sign sitting in place as a warning. It appeared the stairs were under construction. This brought on another extremely odd feeling. To him, the change was rapid and dramatic. It felt like just a few moments ago he'd raced up them.

This is out of control.

"Thomas, stay focused. You're really dragging me down here."

Thomas puckered his lips and blinked. This was far more difficult than he had imagined. He was struggling to target just what tail to chase at the moment. Banks was right. Purging all of the convoluted mess from his mind as best he could, he sped up to catch Banks. Once he reached him, he saw the door. It was the very same door he had seen before. Only this time it was tightly closed. This begged a question he had not asked; why had it been ajar before? Perhaps a lackadaisical morning with a few things forgotten had left it that way. At this point it seemed irrelevant.

"It's locked," said Banks, turning the knob.

"Maybe you should try knocking first?" suggested Thomas.

Banks shot him an annoyed look but obliged. He gingerly knocked on the door and awaited an answer.

"Just where exactly are you from anyways? Nobody's going to answer with that girl-scout-cookie knock."

Thomas pushed Banks aside and rapped on the door. He waited for a few passing seconds before pressing his eye against the keyhole.

"Looks like nobody's home. You got another plan?"

Banks let out a long sigh. Carefully, he pressed himself between Thomas and the door. He was prying a small piece of wire into the tiny keyhole. He maneuvered it about with expert precision.

"Where I'm from there's no such thing as a closed door. Or did you never learn?"

With a quiet pop and moan the door jutted open. Thomas blushed slightly. His ego had dug the hole he was getting deeper in. Feeling slightly suspicious, he examined his surroundings quickly. No one appeared to notice the false owner's entry into the room. The apathy of the city was astounding. So many eyes were readily available yet no witnesses could be found.

"Never been big on closed doors; most are closed for a reason."

Cautiously, the two of them moved forward. Once inside it was as clear as day to Thomas where he was. Everything was still so fresh in his mind. The only real detail that was by-and-large gone was the woman. He didn't know why, but a part of him wished she had still been here. There were some loose strings attached to her that he would have liked to tie up in order to calm his probing mind.

"This is it, but now what do you propose?"

Thomas lingered on Banks's question for a moment. Just what was he going to do here, now, in the present?

"Now we play the game of connect the dots. Only we have to do it faster than ever before."

"By all means," said Banks, taking a seat on a couch sitting in the center of the room.

"What a bum."

Thomas began perusing the room at lightning speed. He was doing a major overhaul on his cross-checking. Every item that had changed was noted. Everything that had remained in place was tossed to the side. He knew he needed more. He quickly tore through stacks of envelopes, piles of papers, and any drawers he could find. He had to find the more intricate details to fill in the holes.

"We need to understand his schedule. Where he goes and when; from there someone can work on the *why*. All I care about is his role in his monotonous day-to-day existence. He's some sort of plumber; what does a plumber do, *plumb*? There's got to be more to this."

Without hesitation, Thomas ran to the fridge. He saw the jumble of magnetic characters with only one word clearly defined—*Monday*. This was obviously a habitual practice. Looking down at his watch he realized it was now early morning. More than likely the man was already at work, waiting for the clock to chime five to go home. So why would it matter that three months ago the word *Tuesday* had been changed to *Tewsday*?

Thomas muttered the word over and over again. It wasn't the word he needed to focus on but the order of the letters.

"Get up and start looking for books this guy reads. Maybe he leaves notes or something like that."

Banks look appalled by the request, but did as he was told. He rummaged through books, papers, and anything else he could find. Meanwhile, Thomas continued to ponder the word. There were so many relationships regarding the word Tuesday, that at some point he had been exposed to. But he needed the right one.

"I think I've got something here. Some books about astronomy, signs, and interpretations. This guy was really into this stuff."

Thomas practically flew across the room. He looked down at the books and began scanning them frantically.

"Turn to anything that describes Mars."

Banks flipped through the pages until he found a few worn pages describing the red planet. The pages were filled with meticulously scribed notes, all containing cryptic correlations of one type or another.

"What is all this?"

Thomas snatched the book out of Banks's hands and let what he had been cultivating inside burst free.

"*Tuesday*—the name has origins. One is *Tiwedaeg*, or *Tewesday* in ancient English, thank you history class. It has a connection to some god's name, which I can't recall."

"What do you mean you can't recall? How can you remember all that other nonsense but forget that part?"

"It was college . . . there were a lot of distractions in that class, alright!"

Thomas remembered the tantalizing image of a brunette girl leaning back to stretch. This had taken precedence over the delicate details he was missing.

"But I do remember it's related to Mars. Do you know Latin?"

"Why would anyone know Latin?"

Thomas felt frustrated with the limited resources he had to work with.

"Forget it; let's just focus on what we've got. A man thoroughly involved in astrology signs or semiotics, a man who's obviously got some interest in big red up there. Suddenly, in his daily routine his fridge reads *Tewsday* instead of *Tuesday*. What would he do then?"

The scene was coming together. The left ajar door, the half glass of orange juice, the lover left waiting. Scrutinizing the fridge for something he hoped had been left behind, he saw it—a tiny business card. On it was a peculiar set of cards with a giant eye hovering over them.

"It was there the whole time! Why couldn't I see it?"

Thomas suddenly picked up his phone and began searching.

"What are you doing?"

"If I'm right, this minor alteration has probably spiraled out of control. I need some validations here. When's the last time you've been to a psychic?"

A moment of reprieve came as a local listing which matched the business card came up just a few blocks away.

"Let's go, we don't have any time to waste."

Baffled beyond belief, Banks quickly followed behind. He was blown away by the sudden transitions from one train of thought to another. Just trying to keep up with Thomas was proving to be mind-boggling. But like a hound on a trail, Thomas was in hot pursuit. With a fresh new target in sight, there'd be no stopping him now.

"Where exactly are we going? Could you please stop being so vague?"

Thomas paused for just a moment. He let the words stumble out of his mouth carelessly.

"To try and stop a murder."

11

PIPE PLUMBER

A clock slowly ticked away another second in time. A cramped room smelling of burnt incense was dimly lit and silent. Both Thomas and Banks had no idea what to expect. Neither of them seemed too familiar with the setting, let alone the purpose for being here. Thomas had tried to explain the situation that was unraveling in his head to Banks, who quickly fell into a sloshing pit of confusion. It all seemed so clear to Thomas; why was it so hard for Banks to understand? Feeling annoyed with their sluggish progress, he slammed his fist down on the tiny bell sitting on the entry table one more time.

This is a joke. Could anything else possibly go wrong?

"Maybe nobody's home; it's pretty early."

Thomas shook his head. She had to be here. He needed some answers and he needed them now. Looking back out of the door through which they'd entered, he saw the morning's light showering down. He had lost all track of time in the present. He hadn't slept. Mental and physical fatigue was crying out to him, begging for some rest. But he couldn't rest. He couldn't let himself slip—not again—not like before.

"What the hell is it? Can't you read the sign? We're closed! Just how did you get in here anyway?"

A wiry looking woman stepped out adorned in eccentric cloth. Her head was draped with what looked like a festive tablecloth. She reeked of multiple layers of old smoke and perfume. The smell was nauseating.

"We'd like to ask you a few questions."

Pipe Plumber

Instinctively, Thomas reached for his pocket to pull out his credentials; only there was nothing there, nothing but an empty pocket void of any real authority. Luckily, Banks was on tap to produce his own. He pulled out just one of his many identities from his pocket.

"The Feds? What you want with me? I ain't done nothing wrong."

The woman produced a cigarette like magic out of thin air. She lit it casually and began puffing away.

"This isn't about you. We're here looking for some information," said Banks as he tucked his credentials carefully back into place.

"I don't have anything and I don't know anybody. I'm a tarot card reader—I just read cards—I don't go diving into anybody's life here."

The woman took another long drag of her cigarette and released a small, noxious cloud of smoke in Thomas' direction. She was eyeing him curiously. She seemed to be deeply interested in him.

"We're here about one of your clients; one David Schilling."

The woman shrugged.

"Doesn't ring any bells. You'll have to do better than that, honey."

As the puff of smoke passed over Thomas he felt sick to his stomach. He definitely felt completely out of place here. But his patience had run its course.

"Look—we're trying to find a guy who has some high interest in signs. He would have come in here rambling about astrology, Mars, or something along those lines. I'm sure you don't get that type every day."

The woman's eyes narrowed. She tightened her lips around the end of her slender stick of poison and inhaled.

"Oh, yeah . . . I remember someone. A few months back some weirdo came barging in, telling me he just received a sign from god or something crazy. I seem to remember him being rather good looking."

Thomas exhaled. Finally, there was what appeared to be a potential break.

"That's the guy. Can you remember what he said, when he came?"

The woman put out her cigarette on the counter before flinging it off somewhere into the room carelessly.

"Look, honey . . . I can barely remember my own name most days, let alone conversations with some nut job three months ago. I just read the cards and let their imagination do the rest."

Thomas took in a deep, slow, breath of air. The woman was truly testing his patience. Banks interjected.

"Well, you're a business, of sorts. You've got to keep *some* kind of records of your clients and appointments."

The woman looked displeased.

"I keep some books, sure. Doesn't everybody? But I don't take kindly to peeping Toms."

Banks gave the woman a very stern look, reminding her of who he was.

"Fine, have it your way. I'll go dig out the old pencil scratches. But don't think you'll find much information there—just times and names."

It's the time we care about, lady.

The woman dug her cat-like, acrylic nails into an old Rolodex. She took a couple of long drags off a new cigarette that had, again, magically appeared in her hand. The smoke slithered out of her mouth like a vanishing snake.

"Here, here's what I've got. That's strange . . ."

"*What?*" demanded Thomas.

"Seems like your little pal was here bright and early once, but only once; I thought I remembered him. We had a few words . . . he didn't like what the cards were saying. Burst out of here in a temper tantrum."

Thomas turned to Banks and shook his head.

"We're behind. Whatever needed to happen has. We need to move now."

Banks looked from Thomas to the woman. He appeared momentarily flustered.

"And so where do we go now?"

Thomas closed his eyes. He was allowing the electric freeway of his mind to open up. There was one question above all others he needed answered.

"We need to find him. I need to know just exactly what David Schilling the plumber does."

Banks's flustered look came to an abrupt end. They stepped back through the door, leaving the crabby woman behind.

"Bunch of freaks!" she screamed after them.

Thomas glanced at Banks who was already dialing his phone.

"Can you pin this guy? We won't have much time. Whoever is doing this has always been a step ahead. I feel like we're close now."

Pipe Plumber

"I'm on it."

Thomas turned away from Banks. He examined the world before him for a moment. Colorful, animated humanity was skittering about the streets. The city had come back to life, switching from night to day. Its nocturnal dwellers receded back into their homes.

Where are you? Are you watching right now?

He knew that whoever the killer was needed to study his victims. He needed to know every intimate, intricate detail he could in order to orchestrate the perfect set-up. Despite the killer's obvious aptitude towards deviant perfection, he had flaws like anyone. It was possible that he would need to try more than once. A memory from the recent past came into full view—the bus—the bus that had so nearly thrown its force right through his body. He had dodged it by mere inches. Were the darts already being thrown at the target?

"Got him. He's downtown working at the stadium."

"Perfect. Let's go."

Banks looked down at his watch fervently.

"What is it with you and that watch? Let's go!"

Banks grimaced at Thomas' remark. He hurriedly put his arm down. "When you're in the business of time, it's good to keep track of it!"

Thomas rolled his eyes. They jumped into their parked car and drove away. Inside the car there was a quiet hum of energy. Both men appeared to be stewing away on their internal suspicions. Were they as close as they thought? Who was the target this time? He didn't know why, but he felt like he was making a connection with Banks. Their recent time together had forged an unspoken bond. It truly felt as if it was them against the world. Maybe there was a future for the bickering partnership.

Thomas watched as the massive silhouette of the football stadium could be seen through the murky clouds of smog. There was something primal about the place; an arena for modern day gladiators to bash each other into oblivion. He had no real interest in sports—it was just the idea that grabbed him. In truth, he didn't know what to expect in such a barbaric place. Maybe one day he'd give in to his inclinations and see what all the fuss was about.

Weaving through a few more lanes of traffic, Banks pulled the car to the front entrance of the stadium. He looked out of his window.

"What's all this about?"

"What?"

Thomas glanced over to see a man being escorted from the stadium in handcuffs. In a sheer moment of panic, he burst from the car and yelled.

"Hey! What's going on here?"

The policemen hauling away the squirming man looked over at him and scowled.

"Pipe down, buddy. This is none of your business."

Instead, Thomas escalated things by approaching them aggressively. He couldn't miss his chance to find the man of interest.

"Who is that man? What's his name?"

The police officers pivoted and reached for their side arms. It was clear they weren't about to budge on the issue.

"That's none of your business, sir. Now step away!"

Thomas looked at the man in handcuffs. His eyes darted wildly about. It was clear that he was beside himself.

"I just want a name!" screamed Thomas, taking another step.

"Sir, I'm warning you!" one of the officers yelled as he unhooked the strap to his gun.

"Hold up!" roared Banks, finally catching up.

He flung open the badge he was carrying in his hands.

"We're with the Feds. Just looking for a man who goes by David Schilling."

The officers slowly removed their hands from their guns. One looked over the badge carefully before responding.

"Well, you're in luck. You've found him. Got a call about some erratic behavior and vandalism this morning. Guys been spouting off for hours. We're taking him downtown to clear him up a bit."

Thomas swooped in on Schilling quickly. He was finally getting to see the man he had been dissecting. His eyes looked tired; his posture, decrepit. He looked wildly unkempt. Large brown puppy dog eyes looked up at Thomas intently. A bristly beard covered most of the finer points of his face. He looked to be out of his mind.

"These bastards don't understand. This is the place! It's here! I didn't understand for so long, but now I do. You've got to believe me!"

Thomas shook his head in an attempt to clear out the sticky

cobwebs and crossing paths of logic in his head.

"What are you talking about?"

David fought with one of the officers who kept trying to move him along.

"The signs . . . the signs are everywhere—it's changing us all—this is where it will happen!"

One of the officers pressed Schilling's head towards the ground. He howled in anger, doing his best to fight back.

"Alright, buddy, you've had enough prophesying for one day."

"Wait—I need to talk to him; I need to know more."

The officer nearest to Thomas put on a smug smirk.

"Sorry, buddy. I've got a schedule to keep and I'm already behind. You want any more answers, you can come downtown."

Thomas began to move towards him but was stopped by a stern hand from Banks.

"Let it go. It's not worth it. We'll just follow them down."

Waves of frothing adrenaline surged into Thomas. He couldn't stand it.

"We can't just let him walk away!" Thomas growled as David was being shoved into an awaiting police car.

The two of them watched as the car sped away. Thomas' heart sank. He was so close, so very close. As the car roared away, his mind latched onto its details. There was something peculiar about it . . . . He realized it was the exhaust pipe just as its poisonous output disappeared around a corner.

Gas . . . what about gas?

His thoughts were suddenly interrupted by a deafening round of gunfire. Both men threw themselves behind the car. In a flash, Banks pulled out a gun from his suit.

"What's going on?" screamed Thomas.

They looked up ahead and saw a terrifying scene unfolding. A man with a small pistol had burst from an alleyway.

"Death to the pigs!" was the man's lunatic decree.

He blasted a few rounds directly into the back-seat area of a cop car. When his pistol was emptied he quickly ran off. The police officers were stunned but reacted rapidly. Bursting from their car, they fired off a few rounds before following the shooter in hot pursuit. Thomas erupted from his safe spot and sprinted towards the stopped car.

"Get back! Don't run out into the open!"

Thomas disregarded Banks's plea and pressed forward. He had seen the officers leave the car abandoned. To him, there was only one conclusion. But it was a conclusion that horrified him in its bitter reality.

"David!" screamed Thomas as he approached one of the cop car's back doors.

He pulled on the handle but his hand slipped out under the abrupt force. It was locked. He could see that a few rounds of bullets had blasted their way through the car window. Inside, David's limp body was bent over to one side. Streams of blood ran from his chest. He was clearly dead. Thomas furiously kicked the side of the car before collapsing against it. He put his head into his hands.

What's happening? Why can't I stop this?

"Thomas, what are you doing?" demanded Banks as he rushed to his side.

"That guy could still be out there! Darting out like that could make you a target!"

Thomas heard Banks but didn't care. David Schilling was gone and with him all the answers Thomas needed. The timing had been immaculate; the set-up superb. Everyone had been in the right place at exactly the right time. Were they just victims of circumstance, or was there something more? Had the killer caught their scent?

"Forget it. We've failed. He's gone, along with everything he knew."

Banks slammed the back end of his pistol into the car after seeing the dead body. It was obvious that it disturbed him to deal with this twisted form of reality.

"So, what? We just wait until another agent dies? We just give up?"

Thomas squeezed his eyes shut. The swirl of human emotion inside him was taking precedence over his sharp logic. He needed to separate the two; he needed to survive.

"The stadium—he kept saying it was there—we need to find out what he was talking about."

Banks kept his eyes on the dark alleys around them. He looked anxious, as if he was expecting another wave of fiery lead to blast out from their depths.

"Fine—but no more running off. You've got to start being a team player."

"Team? Since when did you think we were a team? I'm not here to be on a team."

Banks's chest heaved in and out as he did his best to contain his anger. Thomas' attitude was melting over him like a suffocating wax.

"Look—let's just focus on solving this—this isn't about you and me at this point."

Banks spun around wildly facing the other direction. Through gritted teeth he responded.

"Let's hurry up. Unless you've got something better to do."

Thomas got up off the ground. The image of the dead body in the car was now permanently affixed forever in his mind. He'd never forget it. Looking down at his own watch, he saw the time glaring back at him. They were losing the battle; with each passing second they were that much further behind.

Sprinting to the stadium, Banks flashed his credentials at a man near the door who let them in. Once inside, they found themselves lost in its labyrinth.

"Now what? This place is massive."

Thomas had an answer this time; one he'd been working on for what seemed like an eternity to him.

"He's a plumber—probably stopped by to do some maintenance— that means he left a log somewhere. These places usually keep track of who fixed what and when. We just need to find it."

Looking back at the door they had just burst through, he targeted the man who had let them in. "Where do you guys keep records for maintenance issues?"

The man looked taken back. He seemed to be fumbling around for the right words to say.

"Please hurry. We're running short on time here."

The man blinked then nodded.

"We've got a list of who comes and goes in the main office. But what's that matter now? Didn't you see that guy get blasted? This whole place is going down the toilet!"

"Just take me there, alright?"

With a huff and a puff the man ushered the two of them along. Banks began prodding at Thomas for some answers. The truth was, he didn't have any; at least not yet. He needed to solidify some ideas that were floating aimlessly around in his ocean of logic. He needed more info.

The man led them up a few flights of stairs before he jostled out a massive set of keys.

"Guy came in this morning on some maintenance call. Seemed normal enough until, well, you saw. I swear this city's got some sort of disease or something. Should have listened to my mother when she told me to get out young. Now look at me, just a bag of bones."

Thomas watched as the man tried one key then another. His anxiety was palpable. With each failure, he had to resist the urge to snatch the keys from the man's hands and do it himself. It was all happening so slow.

"There she is . . . always the last one you try. You guys aren't going to tear this place apart are you?"

"Don't worry about that. We'll be in and out no problem," said Banks.

The man stepped into the room and brought out a clipboard. His long eyebrows twitched around as he read through the list.

"There he is—one David Schilling, the plumber—must have been the on call for the burst pipe we had."

"Where? Where was the burst pipe?"

The man gave Thomas a look of exhaustion, as if begging him to let it go. But he wouldn't. Letting out an apathetic sigh, he looked back down at the clipboard.

"Downstairs. One of the snack bars. Looks like it was the hotdog stand *Astro Buns*. Fixed a faulty gas valve and pipe. Things are so oily, it's no wonder to me. Speaking of oil, been trying to do one of those cleanse diets to clear me out, you know what I mean? Wouldn't believe what that stuff does to you."

Without warning, Thomas darted out of the room.

How did I not see this? It was all right there in front of me!

"I thought we agreed to no more running away?" Banks grunted, doing his best to follow.

Thomas charged down the stairs, passing a few weary-eyed janitors on the way. Once in the main commons, he unleashed his pragmatic mind. A solid row of commercial, food, gluttony ran through the stadium only broken apart by a few cliché signs.

Pipe Plumber

His eyes searched as his feet hammered against the ground. Suddenly—he found what he was looking for—*Astro Buns*. Jumping over the counter, he slid into a ketchup dispenser which fell onto the ground, spewing its contents. He was looking for something specific; a trigger. Something that would have set off the time bomb that had been festering inside of David Schilling and eventually led to his murder. The place was completely trashed, but there it was. It would have most likely been overlooked by anyone else. It was so subtle, and yet so deliciously suggestive. The special of the day was none other than the *Astro Mars Dog*.

The playful cartoon figure of a dog in a spacesuit, holding out a ketchup-dosed hotdog, came into view. Tomatoes, red peppers, and paprika—the perfect combination of reds to symbolize the red planet—but it was the ads that had pushed the boiling mental state of David over the edge.

"It's coming for you!"

"It's almost here!"

"Mars' best hotdog!"

"Time is running out!"

Thomas immediately felt his inside shift around. A squeamish feeling percolated up him like a toxic poison. The subtle yet direct nature of the signs around him divulged a truth that he had not foreseen.

"What is it? What did you find?" asked a breathless Banks.

Thomas could feel the hopelessness of it press in on him with a chilling embrace.

"This is what broke him. It's absolutely magnificent. I didn't see it coming."

"What are you talking about?"

Thomas shook his head. He was searching within himself for something to grab hold of to pull himself out of the dark pit he was in. Then, like magic, there it was, sitting right in front of him—a grill.

"He works on grills and gas pipes. He's not the kind of plumber I assumed he was. He's been playing our ignorance. I've never been here, I've never cared about any of this, until now. This is unbelievable."

Banks began to speak but was cut off by Thomas' panicked voice.

"Find the remaining agents. We need to get to them *now!* If I'm right one, of them is going to die *soon*."

Banks immediately dialed his phone, sending out the dire message. Thomas drew himself closer to one of the animated signs.

"Time is running out," he mumbled.

But with David now murdered, whose time was it?

12

BOBBIES

The phone calls brought on an upsurge of commotion. Finding each agent was now Thomas' number one priority. He needed to get to them before the altered course of time ripped them apart. As their car screeched around another corner, he could hear Banks screaming into his phone's receiver.

"Where are they? We need to know *now*! I don't care about protocol! You need to tell me—they are in immediate danger!"

It appeared that even in a secret organization, all of the proper strings had been properly attached by gluey, procedural bureaucracy. With a few more insistent demands, Banks finally appeared to be making some headway. Slamming his phone shut, he looked over at Thomas and sighed.

"You'd think I'm the killer the way they treat me. It's ridiculous how much red tape they put up."

"So did you get anything? I'm not enjoying our downtime here."

Banks took a deep breath in.

"They're out for breakfast."

Thomas cringed at the mention of their whereabouts.

"*Breakfast*? I thought those guys were on lockdown?"

"They are, but they still have to eat, don't they? Last I checked we all do."

A gurgling slurp and slop in Thomas' stomach reminded him that was also running on empty. But his mind took precedence. It was unrelenting.

"We need to get to them. Can you call them?"

Banks nodded his head as he pressed his phone up against it.

"Already on it; I got their numbers, finally."

"You guys always so disconnected?"

"You have no idea."

Thomas slipped into the car as Banks rambled on the phone. His attitude was one of both concern and annoyance at the process. A process that, by design, was supposed to keep agents safe, and was now the one thing barreling them towards disaster. As the car screeched down the streets of the city, he took a moment to reflect. David Schilling the plumber had been spooked by the minor alteration of the words on a fridge. He had tried to make some sense of it by running to a cigarette-addicted tarot card reader, but she had given him no relief. Tiny pebbles rolling down a mountain—tiny pebbles that had created a massive landslide that had just climaxed. This was art; perverse, disturbed art. The challenge was amplified by the urgent nature of it. Had he bitten off more than he could chew, let alone swallow?

"This should be the place. They're fine, or so they've told me. They're together and technically out in the open, but I know these guys. They wouldn't just wander into something blind," Banks said, looking towards an old diner on a street corner.

Thomas silently agreed with the statement. Sitting in a diner, the odds of anything drastic happening seemed slim. But there had been a shooter; a shooter who was still at large. But it couldn't stay that way, things needed to start to come together. This diner had to have something in it that could help him start putting the madness together; some sort of evidence or clues.

"We'll figure that out once we're inside. It looks like the place just opened anyway."

The store was just awakening from its nighttime slumber. A retro neon sign buzzed, assuring that the doors were open. Through aged windows, Thomas and Banks could see two agents discussing something over an empty tabletop. They quickly walked inside. A wonderful mixture of pan-seared bacon, griddled waffles, and hash browns met them. This came as a clear-cut reminder of human necessities. Banks was the first to put a card on the table.

"Hungry? I can't imagine you've really had much time to eat. I know I haven't. Might as well grab a bite."

Thomas shuddered at the mention of slowing his progress. He didn't like it.

"No time for that."

"You're no good to anyone starved. I suggest you speak with these guys, clear your head, and refuel."

Banks took the lead, moving cautiously towards the two seated men. Thomas followed reluctantly—he was piecing apart the building—so many floating points that needed to be addressed. His head ached. His body was raising the stakes in his game of overcoming it. Looking at Banks, he watched as he greeted the two men and sat down.

"This is Mr. Ghune. He is currently working with me on our project."

The two men turned and examined Thomas, who stood at an awkward distance from the table. Banks gave him a stern look of annoyance. The strange behavior was embarrassing him. One of the agents sitting closest to the outside put out his hand to greet Thomas.

"I'm Agent Matthews and this is my partner, Agent Reynolds."

Thomas moved in close enough to shake Agent Matthews' hand. He let it lay as lifeless as a dead fish in Agent Matthew's grip. An unsettled look crossed over Agent Matthews' face.

"You there, Mr. Ghune? You're not looking so good."

Thomas put on the best façade he could. The smile he conjured looked as fake as ever.

"Yes, sorry, just a lot on my mind."

"So I've been told," chuckled Agent Matthews.

Forgetting his place, Thomas released a torrent of, until *now*, internalized questions on the unsuspecting agents.

"Anything out of the norm happen today? Any interruptions to your schedule or habits? Anything at all? Notice anything out of place, perhaps, or a sudden change you weren't expecting?"

Agent Reynolds put down a sugar packet he was reading and looked at Thomas and then back at Agent Matthews. It appeared that *Thomas* was the unforeseen, out-of-place oddity of the day.

"I mean . . ."

"No, I get what you're going for there. And the answer is no. We've eaten at Bobbies so many times I can't count them. And nothing is out of the ordinary," said Agent Reynolds.

"Well, actually, it did open slightly later than normal—the cook showed up late because he was recovering from a cold or something," added Agent Matthews.

Thomas noted the statements and nodded for them to continue.

A cold—opening late—where is this going? But as for this table, looks pretty safe to me. Only issue is our food we ordered ten or fifteen minutes ago. I'm starved."

Banks smiled and took a seat across from Agent Matthews. He motioned for Thomas to do so but was denied outright.

"I want to go poke around a bit. Maybe talk to some of the people around here."

Agent Reynolds picked up another sugar packet and weaved it through his fingers.

"Have it your way. You'll want to order the bacon here, it's amazing. Just relax, buddy; we're on our toes here."

Thomas smiled and turned. Looking around, he saw sparse morning traffic passing by outside and an early morning skeleton crew inside. A waitress painted in cheap makeup and who looked stuck between her fifties and sixties skulked around the room. At the counter a corpulent cook walked back and forth, eyeing orders before disappearing to the back to fill them. Thomas tried to catch his attention by waving his hand in the air.

Come on, bubba; pay attention.

Frustrated, he walked up to the counter and rang the order bell. The moment he did, a large man who gave him a very bothered look came out from the back.

"Yes, can I help you?"

Thomas immediately sprang into action.

"Do you work often?"

The man nodded. He looked over Thomas' shoulder and shrugged.

"I'm a regular . . . what of it?"

"Notice anything out of place recently, perhaps today?"

The man sniffled, congestion making it difficult for him to breathe through his nose.

"It's a diner; how out of place could anything be? Now, if you don't mind I've got some orders to fill, and I'm not feeling too chatty."

Bobbies

"It's important, alright? Any pipe problems or plumbing issues?"
The man frowned.

"Do I *look* like a plumber? You're asking the wrong guy. I'm just another Monday guy. I show up for work and go home. I don't look into that crap."

Thomas now frowned as well. This was going nowhere. He watched as the man sucked in a long, labored drag of air through his stuffed nose. The thought that the same man was cooking the food made him instantly nauseated.

"Why don't you go home and take care of that. It's disgusting," grunted Thomas as he walked away.

"Who are *you*, my doctor? Shmuck."

As Thomas headed back towards the table, he could see that Agent Reynolds was missing. Panicking, he ran the rest of the way.

"Where is he?"

Agent Matthews and Banks looked up from their conversation.

"He's in the bathroom. People gotta use it sometimes, you know?" answered Agent Matthews.

"Where's the bathroom?" demanded Thomas.

Agent Matthews pointed towards a hall leading away from the kitchen.

"What is it? What's going on?" probed Banks.

"Nothing—well possibly—oh, I don't know . . . I just need to make sure," responded Thomas.

He looked ill. The dots in his head were forging connections with the streaming reality he was in. It was weighing him down. But which possibility would it be? What was this leading up to?

"Hey, why don't you calm down, Thomas? These guys come here all the time. They've been on watch and under protection. This is as safe of a place as any."

Thomas ignored Banks's placating remarks and he headed towards the bathroom.

"Where are you going?" called Banks.

"I need to take care of something."

Thomas wiggled his way around tables and chairs as he rushed towards the bathroom. As he did, he scanned the room with his mental radar, letting his surroundings sink in. But there was nothing—nothing that stuck out—nothing that called to him. It was an empty, white canvass with no discerning color. Then, something caught one of his other senses—an odor—a faint yet apparent odor. It was incredibly difficult to focus on as it competed with the more flavorful smells that had been caked onto the diner's walls. But it was still there. What was it? Taking a few more steps towards the bathroom, a sensation from somewhere in his past came tingling into his mind. A sensation with a direct tie to David Schilling that was tied inseparably to something that was just about to happen. What had taken months to put together, took mere seconds to all fall apart. The blast blew out the bathroom door, sending a wave of flame with it. On the other side of the wall there was a booming eruption that shot pieces of the kitchen through the air with incredible force. The moment seemed to pass by slowly, frame-by-frame. Dancing flames etched their way through the air at Thomas' body. The invisible force gripped him in its arms, throwing him back into the diner as if he were a small child. His screams were muffled by the chaos playing out around him. Suddenly, everything went dark. Had death's icy fingers finally squeezed what little life he had left out of him? Had he finally found his place as another martyr; as part of some psychopath's quest? Only time would tell.

13

BIG BLUE

Thomas woke up screaming. Sharp bolts of stinging pain raced around his body like a swarm of frenzied ants. He had lost himself; lost himself completely to the immense force that had so nearly taken his life. A beautiful game of chess masterfully planned and executed by the unforeseen killer. How many intricate details had it taken? The sick cook, the timing, the location, and the execution. In a sick way he admired whoever was doing this. They, much like him, seemed to be plagued by their gift, their obsession. Their efforts to purge themselves clean of it had led to this.

"Hello?"

Thomas let out another scream and opened his eyes. A slender beam of light fell around his head, giving him an angelic aura. He looked over his body and saw some deep cuts and gashes that had been carefully bandaged. He could still feel the heat from the room. One faulty pipe, negligently forgotten, as one lunatic David Schilling went on a quest, forgoing his agreed upon schedule. A pipe that one spectacular weekend had broken free within the wall, spewing out a recipe for disaster. The smell had been there; just enough to be detected. But the cook had been sick—his thoughts, somewhere else. It wasn't his job to care; after all, they had maintenance people for that. All it took was a spark to ignite the time-created bomb, blowing up one unsuspecting agent sitting in the bathroom sky high. A literal trail of interconnected subtleties and clues that the killer had left behind that had finally lead up to an explosive end.

You're good, really good.

"Thomas, are you okay?"

Thomas looked over and saw Banks standing by what looked to be a hospital bed.

"Yeah, I'm fine . . . just really shaken up."

"You had me worried back there. Whole place went to hell; never seen anything like it."

Thomas looked past Banks and scanned the room. He thought he must be in a hospital; all visual cues pointed in that direction.

"The Agent . . . Agent Reynolds . . . is he—"

Banks closed his eyes and shook his head.

"Pulled the damn carpet right out from under us. He didn't stand a chance. But at least it was quick."

Thomas felt a sharp pain in his heart. He had lost again. Although Agent Reynolds had meant virtually nothing to him, the reality that he was gone reminded him of the game at hand. He couldn't let it continue like this.

"I need to get out of here. I don't have time for this."

Banks stuck his hand out in protest.

"You need to rest—you're half-way to death—you can't keep running on empty like this."

Thomas cringed. He didn't care. Instinctively, he reached up for his hat.

"My hat! Where's my hat?"

The sudden change in tone shook Banks out of his slightly melancholy state. He responded by walking over to a rack behind the door.

"It's here, relax."

Thomas snatched it away from Banks and grimaced. Its once vibrant red was now mixed with a dark charcoal singed around its edge.

"It was all there again. But I couldn't connect it fast enough. Whoever is doing this is playing off my ignorance. I have no memory of these places or things."

Banks took a deep breath.

"Look, Thomas—that may be true, but it won't matter if we all die. We still don't even have a lead on this guy. The organization I work for is growing restless. We need results. This just proves that no one's safe; not even us."

"Then get me out of here. I can heal later. We need to glimpse again, follow the ripples, and destroy their creator. I'm done playing nice."

Banks looked surprisingly put off by Thomas' sudden courage but acknowledged the task. Looking swiftly down at his watch, he nodded.

"Get dressed; I'll take care of the rest. I made sure they didn't touch anything they weren't supposed to."

Banks walked out the door, slamming it behind him.

In a tornado of movement, Thomas gathered his effects, dressed himself, and began heading towards the door. As he did, he was suddenly troubled by the absence of something. His anal attention to detail wouldn't let him move forward without an answer. He slowly scanned himself and realized his watch was gone. Pushing on the hospital door, his wounds hollered in pain. It would take some time before he'd feel whole again. But being blasted unconscious had provided him with some much needed rest, even if it was by force.

Keep it together, Tommy. You've got work to do.

Banks was standing just outside of the hospital door. He gave Thomas a once-over and then smiled broadly.

"That hat . . . it really is something."

Thomas frowned.

"Just stick to the plan, alright?"

Banks's smile faded to a frown. He suddenly shifted his emotional standpoint.

"Roslin wants us back at base. He's not happy with any of this."

"And why should I care? The guy is a complete tool!"

Banks's frown dug even deeper into his scruffy face.

"I think it's something personal. It's not like him to do this."

"Personal, with Roslin? Is that even possible?"

Without saying a word, Banks turned to leave the hospital, Thomas following. Like the master leading the student, Banks's experience was still directing Thomas' gift. Neither could free themselves of each other's limitations. They would have to rely on each other at every turn.

Returning to the facility, Thomas saw immediately that something had changed. Things had been tainted. The once impervious fortress now looked like a revolving door of possibilities. Every agent, every item, and every detail posed a viable threat. But as with any malicious plot, it had a direction. It was that direction that Thomas intended to divulge. He needed to understand the overall picture in order to get a step ahead—but to do so might mean sacrifices—sacrifices that could very well include his life.

"Gentlemen, it's good to see you both alive."

The hard-nosed tone of voice could belong to no one but Roslin. He met the duo head-on in the hallway they were walking through. His face looked contorted and worn. The especially long hours of his unforgiving schedule were starting to take their toll on him. Who knew what skeletons a man of such power and secrecy had in his closet?

"I need to glimpse. But I can't do it without Jo," stated Thomas, disregarding all formality.

"Mr. Ghune, I hate to remind you of the reality here. We just lost another agent. An agent we had under protection that was still blown to pieces in a diner. Now, follow me."

Thomas had so much more to say. He had been so close; so close to narrowing the wide gap between himself and the killer. Despite the lingering scent of charred flesh and blood, he had been there; right at the precipice of stopping it from ever happening.

Roslin moved with purpose. He looked largely upset at the seemingly endless stream of problems he suffered valiantly. There was obviously a burning fire in him that just could not and would not be extinguished. Going through the layers of protocol, they finally walked into the white room. Thomas erupted.

"Look, I appreciate all of the games but—"

"No! *You* look!" interrupted Roslin. "I've got another dead agent, I've got a killer on the loose altering reality, and you're not doing your job! We brought you here to do one thing and you're not doing it!"

His brash tone spurred Thomas into a defensive posture.

"I'm doing the best I can. If you think you can do better, then by all means, please, go ahead. At least I was close!"

"*Close? Close?* Who *cares* if you were *close?* Agent Reynolds is still dead! An agent who was under our protection was killed! It's plain and simple. The astronomical resources we put into this project need justification, and so far there is none. We need results!"

Thomas noticed the slight change in resonance in Roslin's voice.

Big Blue

Something was different about this; something was personal. Although he couldn't even begin to understand the persona that made Roslin Tanner, Roslin Tanner, he understood loss. He had experienced it intimately. The same rage dwelt within him as well. This led him to a bold yet conclusive statement.

"Something happened; not to any of us, but to you; didn't it? This isn't just about the case anymore, someone got to you."

Roslin looked poised to blast Thomas across the face with a tightly clenched fist. But the carefully constructed words from Thomas had found their mark. Within Roslin's drumming heart there was a harmonization of truth; a truth he had been too proud to admit, until now. He suddenly couldn't seem to muster the energy to speak. It was his silence that finally planted the seed of truth in Thomas' mind; Roslin had been hurt.

"Look, I get it, alright? You're the big, bad director in some secret organization. Really, I get it . . . must have felt nice being untouchable until now. But if you're going to rip me then you better start telling me the truth! Whoever this is has a direction. And if there's a history, I better know about it."

Roslin paced away from Thomas, allowing his shoulders to slump down for just a moment. It appeared he had an internal battle waging that just wouldn't subside. Becoming human would mean losing his immortality. But in order to succeed he'd have to, less he lose everything.

"You see a lot of things when you're in a job like mine . . . a lot of things. Some are beyond belief; others . . . others just get locked away in some dark place. But the one thing you always hold as pure is family. Family, in one shape or another, is all you've really got at the end of it all. But I left that behind ages ago. Protection, progress, results—those were the reasons—I was ready to handle the consequences, until now."

Thomas glanced at Banks who was eyeing Roslin intently, watching his every move and reaction. It appeared that he had never seen Roslin like this. Thomas looked back at Roslin, who was facing the two of them directly now.

"I received a message this morning. A message that only held meaning for one person and one person alone."

Roslin pulled out an old baseball glove. The worn, aged leather stood as a testament to its place in history. Years of playing catch had shaped it to a conforming fit.

"My brother is missing. He disappeared this morning. Whoever is doing this has just raised the stakes. Now it's personal."

Thomas analyzed the glove, then Roslin. The two were now tied together. Their history was unknown but the sentimental attachment was clear. It was lonely at the top for a man like Roslin, but even he had a heart. It was a heart encaged in secrecy, lies, and deceit, but it still felt the harrowing pain of losing a loved one.

"When did you last have contact?" probed Thomas.

"Haven't—not for years—that's part of being me."

Thomas nodded his head. He had already known the answer.

"Sir, had I known I wouldn't have just barged in here with Mr. Ghune."

Roslin put up a hand to stop Banks's apologetic tone.

"Don't, just don't. That's what whoever did this would want us to do—break down. We've got more important things to think about at the moment."

Roslin's finely tempered self had returned. All that remained was his chiseled, emotionless face. He quickly put the glove away and pointed towards an open white door.

"Jo's waiting."

Thomas took a step but paused. He had forgotten to mention something. His queue of priorities had omitted it until now.

"I'm missing my watch, or whatever you call it."

Banks sprang up to his side. He slithered Thomas' watch out from one of his pockets.

"Took it off you for safe keeping—you can never be too careful with something like this—I forgot to tell you."

Thomas gave Banks a rather incredulous look of uncertainty. But all-in-all it made sense. If a nurse or someone else were to stumble on such a marvelous piece of technology, who knew what might happen. Even Thomas still had an inferiority complex when it came to its utilization. He took the watch from Banks who immediately looked back at Roslin. Roslin looked indifferent.

"Let's get going. I don't want to fall even further behind."

"I expect the best from those I deem as such. Let's not have this conversation again," Roslin said as he left the room hurriedly.

"Does that guy ever stick around? Where's he always going? What's his job here, anyway?"

Banks disregarded Thomas's curiosity driven questions.

"Jo, what can you tell me?"

Thomas looked up to see a befuddled Jo scrambling around his futuristic playset. An amazing array of technology was at his fingertips.

"We think we've got something—a systematic alteration that's resonating—the probability of an accurate access point looks good."

Jo fumbled his fingers around each other in anticipation.

"In English?" demanded Thomas.

Jo's expression said it all; it was painful for him to have to drag himself down in order to give what he considered to be a child-like explanation to them.

"I've got a good point to glimpse to. Somebody's screwing around in the past. Meaning, you need to get back, figure it out, and avoid another blast. The blast from the past . . ."

Jo's eyes twinkled. His dark wit had struck again, but no one seemed to follow. His notion of the comical was far too twisted for anyone even *slightly* normal   even Thomas.

"Just give me a frame so we can glimpse," said Banks, frowning.

Looking slightly deflated, Jo did as he was told. Turning around, he spouted out the numbers. Banks's eyes widened.

"What, what is it?" asked Thomas.

"It's nothing. I'm sure it's nothing. Let's just get in there and finish the job."

Thomas struggled to fight the urge to dig deeper. He resisted the temptation, at least for the time being.

"Can you at least give me a location, reference, *something*? I don't want to keep rolling the dice."

Jo let out a quiet snicker that was promptly chased away by Thomas' scowling face.

"I'm sorry . . . it's just . . . ironic; you asking all these questions. I was told you know everything; that you had an insatiable hunger for knowledge."

Jo placed his hands up by his neck and practically purred.

"Please?"

Jo rolled his eyes and shrugged.

"Where's the fun in that? *Fine* . . . have it *your* way."

Hammering away at some keys, he leaned in and adjusted his thick glasses. He grinned as the unbalanced glasses fell to the side again.

"Somewhere in the ocean . . . the *ocean*? That's awesome! I've never seen it—come to think of it, there are a *lot* of things I've never seen—I really need to get out more."

Thomas' brain stalled for a moment. Had he heard Jo correctly? The *ocean*? Was he *serious*?

"Time to get moving. The longer we wait, the more that what happened amplifies."

Rehearsing the steps, Thomas synced the data to his watch. The seamless interaction between it and him was now almost intuitive. He could feel the tension begin to swell up inside him. The vivid memory of his first trip ushered in waves of extreme sensations that frightened him.

"Thomas?"

"I'm ready . . . sorry."

Reaching down to activate the device, he was stopped in his tracks by a frantic cry from Jo.

"No! No! Not in here! What are you, *crazy*? Don't stand so close!"

Thomas rattled his head around trying to grasp the situation.

"What? What's wrong?"

"You don't light a fire next to the fireworks, do you? Seriously! That would create uber-levels of problems. You should never glimpse when someone is that close, especially someone with one of the watches!"

"Why?"

Jo's mouth shot wide open and hung for a moment, as if the answer was blatantly obvious.

"Imagine if you damaged it or accidentally set it off; I mean, seriously bad juju there."

Jo tenderly began shoving Thomas into the large white room.

"What if it gets damaged in the past? What if it breaks while I glimpse?"

The timid ushering ceased. Jo stood straight up and let his eyes wander. He looked woefully lost in his own intellect. But suddenly, the moment was interrupted by a gleeful shout, accompanied by a pointed finger.

"I don't know! I have no idea what would happen if two identical energy patterns were trapped in the same time and space. Wow, you're really giving me a headache with this!"

Thomas perused the prospects that ran into the walls of his own conclusions. He, too, was largely ignorant to just how fragile time could be, even in all of its seemingly infinite power. But would he be willing to test those bounds? Would he be willing to push the limits?

"That's funny . . ."

Banks looked over at Thomas as he emerged from the technology filled room into the open white space.

"What?"

Thomas winked at Jo sarcastically.

"I thought Jo was the guy that was supposed to know everything."

Jo grimaced. His pride had been dealt a well-placed blow. He quickly retreated back to his technologic cave, a slew of profanities slipping from his mouth.

"That guy is an absolute freak," muttered Thomas.

Banks disregarded Thomas' childish conversation. Instead, he opted to move forward.

"Please get this one right. I don't want to state the obvious, but our lives *do* depend on it."

The response the old Thomas would have given somehow never came. He had changed. His confidence was being dragged along a rocky road, one excruciating bump after another. Reaching down to activate his watch, he looked on as Banks distanced himself. Banks's expression told more of the story. They were at risk of losing everything in this high stakes game of chess. They couldn't fail.

14

EYE OF THE TIGER

As before, light and chaos swept Thomas out from his current place in time and pushed him into another. He collapsed onto a rickety floor that creaked beneath his weight. A thick musk of salty, humid air infiltrated his nostrils. His body was covered in tiny beads of sweat. The environment was foreign to him. Never before had he felt like he was drowning in air. He became aware of the repugnant smell of mold, mildew, and fish all around him. It appeared that the location had been justifiably described; he was somewhere in the ocean.

"Okay, what now?" he mumbled.

To his great delight, he realized he was sitting safely inside what appeared to be some sort of cargo ship. The massive boat was being held in place at the mercy of time. Everything was almost at a standstill. Clouds of puffy steam sneaking their way through the cracks were suspended in midair. The rocking motion of the ship was on pause. All of the items scattered about the cavernous hull were beyond imagination. A world set aside momentarily, ready to be examined. But he faced the same problem as before—which ones were clues? He needed to find the important details; details that would lead to clues that would lead to conclusions. Without them, this was a complete waste of time. But where should he start? This place was as foreign to him as the moon. But to the killer it held a purpose—to send a tiny snowball streaming down the hill on route towards the decimation of someone's future.

Not wanting to waste another second of his precious time, he looked down at his watch. He had landed a bit further away from the epi center of the disturbance than last time. He needed to get moving. Taking a few long strides, he paused upon seeing a shabbily dressed man cradling a large vat of alcohol against his chest. The man jangled an exorbitantly large set of keys looped around his wrist. No matter how many times Thomas tried to convince himself he couldn't be seen, the idea still tickled him with possibility. Passing the strange man, he realized he was walking between massive storage containers and crates. Crates filled with unidentified goods, all carefully packed away in the dark.

A cargo ship? Why would he come to a cargo ship?

His mind was so energetically engaged in the question that he didn't notice the large, free-hanging knotted rope just a few steps ahead. It smacked hard against the side of his head. He was knocked to the ground and his head rang like a cymbal. It took him a moment to realize what had happened. Standing back up, he was struck in awe for a moment at the image before him. The rope sat mid-swing, reacting to the forces caught in its relative domain. The configuration seemed supernatural. And yet when his head bashed into it, it had remained just the same. Unable to fight the urge, he grasped the rope in his hands. It felt as solid as a rock; almost completely unmovable. Straining himself, he heaved on the rope, pulling himself off the ground. It was astonishing. The angles—the shapes—it was like a funhouse beyond imagination.

This is ridiculous.

The lost toys of time were a distraction; a distraction meant to derail his fuming locomotive. He needed to focus, but there was a part of him that wished to dive further into the physics that dictated this time-warped world. Suddenly, he caught a whiff of something odd. The tiny particles suspended in the air flowed into his nose, shepherding in a stray memory from recent times.

I know this smell.

It was much like the cologne he had smelled on the bed of the woman. It was a common scent, nothing too eccentric or traceable about it. He had known many men to splash a layer of it on routinely. It was unfortunately mixed with the gagging combo of alcohol and murky water. So many sensate memories caught up in the clutches of time.

Moving forward, he stared down at his watch—he was getting closer. Meandering his way through the hull was becoming difficult. It was a literal maze. No path seemed to lead in any desired direction. It was a scramble of effort just to stay on course. This was accompanied by the ridiculous nature of methodical interactions. Objects stuck out in unnatural states of time and energy cluttering almost every step of his way. Even a spilling over barrel of peanuts proved to be an exhausting task. But it was remarkable. As his weight pressed down on the suspended peanuts, he could see them shift slightly under the force. But their relative immobility kept him afloat. It was the closest thing to walking on air he had ever experienced.

I can't believe this is happening.

Passing over the last few barriers, he glanced back down at his watch. He was directly on top of whatever had been altered. Now it was a waiting game. Focusing on his insatiable mental appetite, he feasted. All the details of the ship came rushing in. It was proving to be quite a task to keep them organized. The ship was filled to the brim with important details. Crates, metal boxes, tightly bound parts, cages, and other items strewn about stampeded through his mind. But none of them were any obvious threat; at least not yet. For the time being, everything appeared tame enough. He had become so caught up in his inspection of the area that he neglected to watch where he was backpedaling.

A large cage, mostly covered by a thick blanket, slowed his progress. When he turned, he was met by the dark eyes of a wild tiger. The deep melody of orange hues mixed with yellow gazed back at him ferociously.

"Woah, whoa!" he screamed, falling down and away from the cage.

From where he landed, he could see the beast's head that accompanied its nightmarish stare. It was locked away inside of a cramped, rugged-looking cage. Its eyes had seared like fire into his soul. He had never been so close to such a magnificent, yet mortifying creature. Standing up slowly he met its gaze dead on. He felt himself tremble. Such little protection lay between him and an almost assured death. But in his relative space, he would go unnoticed as only a passing moment of déjà vu. He was a ghost.

Don't want to see what you're like outside of that cage.

Eye of the Tiger

But it was the cage that suddenly interested him the most. This lead him to another point in memory—the man; a drunken man skulking around in the midst of the giant hull. A routine, a job, a purpose; was there something there? Looking back at the cage, he scrutinized its ever detail. Aged steel and rusty locks made for appalling living conditions. He racked his brain for answers—using his present to unlock the dire possibilities of the past. Now he was running into a problem—he was looking for potential game changers—things subtle enough to be changed, yet vital enough to be the predecessor of catastrophe. In the bowels of a humongous cargo hold, everything seemed to carry some weight on the topic.

Where are you?

Things had not yet been churned into motion; he would have to wait. He recalled the anomaly that flashed like lightning during his last glimpse. It had all seemed to pass so quickly. Relative time lapses were incredibly complicated to understand. But to him it felt like passing another car going the other direction on the freeway. You both were in the same moment and space, even if only for a second. There was something else that was gnawing in his mind; a strange, eerie feeling. Unable to shake it, he began searching around. Occasionally, he would stop and attempt to peer through the gaps in the carelessly thrown together crates. But the darkness therein seemed to be shrouding any prying eye. That was until he found a rather odd shaped crate marked with only a few indiscernible letters.

What kind of ship is this?

A trickling beam of light had found its mark, almost perfectly putting the contents of the crate in full view—guns—a whole mess of them. They were tightly packed inside the box. The image took his breathe away. Something was beginning to take shape in his mind that was sickening him. He was on a ship teeming to the brim with illegal contraband. Ships like this had only been figments of his imagination up to this point, but now he was standing dead center of one. If the high number of ways to utilize any one of these items had been overwhelming before, it seemed utterly daunting now. Reaching his hand out, he ran it over the rough surface of the crate.

So this is where it starts.

His mind was looking for the final piece of the jigsaw puzzle he was caught in. He felt like he was onto something. Suddenly, he thought he caught something twitch out of the corner of his eye. But that was impossible. Although relatively new to the process, he knew that all things were behaving in relation to him. That meant there should be no movement. Yet he was sure he had seen something, so he replayed the moment over and over again in his mind like a skipping record. *Something* had moved.

Curiosity swelled inside of him until it burst. He had to investigate. Turning around, he saw the large rows and columns of containers, crates, and other objects. Quickly, he honed in on the point at which he swore he had seen movement. He dwelled there for a minute. If something had moved perhaps it would move again. But there was nothing. Everything stared back at him, frozen in time, and bearing false witness to the conclusion that his mind was merely playing tricks on him.

What is happening?

He wasn't going to stop. His progress hastened. Zeroing in closer and closer to the point in question, his breathing became erratic. He was nervous. There was suddenly a slight trace of fear in the room. Had the framed picture on the wall come to life? That's when he saw him; a man standing motionless, facing into a dark shadow in one of the ship's countless crevices. His clothes were a layered conglomerate of different shades of black. His face was shrouded in darkness. But that wasn't what was pulling Thomas in; it was how out of place he appeared. Much like himself, something about the man didn't seem to belong. Unable to resist, he approached him. Soon he was standing just inches from his back. Not knowing why, he extended his hand to touch him. His shaky arm crept closer and closer, inch-by-inch. At the precipice of contact, a whirlwind of chaos erupted. The once statue-like man swung around and dealt Thomas a vicious blow across the face. The force sent Thomas sprawling to the floor.

Wriggling around on the floor to try to gain his bearings, he watched as the shadow-like man sprinted away. The improbable had just happened—he and the killer were now firmly planted in the same glimpse. His worst nightmare had come true.

"Stop!"

Thomas' scream went completely unanswered. The man was

gaining distance from him with every passing second. Fighting the immense pain, he pushed himself off the ground. He did his best to control his faltering legs and bolted after the man. His heart leapt in his chest. Was the man armed? Would he be running right into a trap? The only thing that was crystal clear was the man's ability. He was brilliant. But he was losing him. The man weaved his way in and out of objects with expert agility. He had obviously done this many times before. It was no wonder that Banks and the other agents had such a healthy fear of him. Thomas thought about screaming out another plea to stop, but quickly realized it was pointless. Whoever it was wasn't going to do so. In the dark shadows of the ship, he found himself alone and defeated.

Damn it!

The killer had left him behind. Bending over, he let his weight fall on his hands and knees. He sucked in the thick, ocean air in greedy gulps. His high levels of adrenaline were leaving him breathless. Somewhere in the hull was a killer whose ability severely trumped his own. If he was caught off guard again, who was to say he wouldn't be the next victim on the list? Suddenly, a flash of light streamed through the world around him. Something had changed.

Digging deeper into his already exhausted fuel supply, he began moving again. He needed to find the source. He needed to find the ripple. He and the vile murderer dwelling in the same glimpse could mean disaster. But he had to risk it. If he didn't, there would be another potential murder in the future. His desires would have to be put to the side for now.

Where are you?

His pace had dampened to a slow walk. He skulked his way along the large crates, ducking in and out of the shadows. In a desperate attempt to boost his chances of surviving, he was trying to adapt. He had never been in such an unbelievable situation. Not even in his wildest dreams had he ever deemed anything like this a possibility. There had to be a way to beat the killer's deviant plan. There had to be a way to end the madness. Coming around another corner, he saw where the chase had led him. He had gone in a massive loop, back to the crates of guns and the caged tiger. Looking down at his watch, he saw the prompt displaying the calculated epicenter. It was strange that to him it had just happened, but in the future so much time had passed. He shook his head.

Stay focused.

He felt the strange sensation that he was being watched from somewhere out in the shadows. He spun wildly around looking for the source. But there were too many places to hide, too many dark corners.

"Who are you?"

His scream echoed through the room, but there was no response. In the unnatural quiet, he could hear the deafening drumming of his heart. He knew the man was still there, watching. Was he preparing to make his move? Had he been just as shocked to find that he was not alone? Suddenly, he felt the presence of the man somewhere behind him. The man's eyes were burning a hole through the back of his head like two fiery pokers. Turning slowly, he looked into a dark space between two massive steel containers. Once there the sharp pain from the blow swayed his hand up into a trickling line of blood coming out from his mouth. Would he tempt his fate again?

"I know you're there. You've got to stop this. You have no idea what consequences you are creating. You are destroying lives!"

For a moment he thought he saw something shift in the dark. Then, without warning, a small card slid into view. It had a strange symbol inked on it—a symbol he had seen before—three triangles locked together. He bent to reach for it when suddenly the world around him began to shred itself apart with brilliant rays of light. His time was up. Taking one last desperate look into the dark he saw a black glove suddenly burst free. It pointed directly at him. Both he and the man were swept out into time and space leaving a million unanswered questions behind. In utter awe, he watched as the card was ripped into a billion fragments. This answered his lingering question—*What happens to things left behind?*—with a horrible solution. But it didn't matter now; the poison had been planted. Who was going to die next?

15

ROGUE BEGINNINGS

Thomas collapsed onto the serene blanket of cold white. He was heaving for air. A million tiny needles felt as if they had been pulled out of him in a mere heartbeat. The feeling was overwhelming. Still gasping for air, he did his best to pull himself back together.

"Like I said, you'll get used to it."

Looking up, he saw Banks hovering just above him, extending out a hand. He slapped it away, feeling his damaged pride.

"I'm fine. Just give me a second."

Grunting in pain, he rose to his feet. The blow he had been dealt persisted. Placing one of his fingers up to his mouth, he felt the warm stream of blood dripping from it. He was quickly reminded of the card. Along with the memory of the card, came the correlation he had made almost instantaneously.

"Where's Roslin? I've got some questions."

"Hold up, alright? Just let me know exactly what you're talking about. Roslin doesn't really show up on request, if you know what I mean," said Banks.

"The killer showed me something—a card. It was a card with some sort of symbol on it. I've seen it before. I've seen it on Roslin."

Thomas caught Jo's head out of the corner of his eye. He was hovering around curiously as if caught in a stupor of thought.

"Can I help you?"

Jo put on an impish smiled.

"So he gave you something? A literally physical, tangible object that had been transposed into that singular, relative time and space?"

Thomas' eyes glazed over. He suddenly felt annoyed and tired at the same time.

"Do you even know English? And he didn't give it to me, directly. He just put it where I could see it."

Jo frowned. The finding appeared to be disappointing. Thomas, however, was just beginning to burn.

"I watched it get ripped apart into a million pieces. I guess that answered one of our questions about what happens to things left behind."

Jo's frown turned upside down. He squirmed in excitement.

"I knew it! The momentary energy being sustained was destroyed in the very moment the connection was severed. It's mind numbingly awesome!"

So many profanities popped into Thomas' mind that trying to keep quiet merely plugged a ready to burst dam. But Jo's excessively eccentric personality was starting to grow on him. He truly had found his place in the circus. He took a deep breath.

"Fine, fine! But why would he do that? Why give me something? This whole thing has blown wide open!"

Banks looked perplexed. He was silently debating the new information.

"It's a trap. He could have just been trying to manipulate you *then* to affect you *now*. You've seen it before, unless we've forget David Schilling."

At the mention of the name, Thomas shuddered. It was true. A pebble had been dropped into the pool of time and its ripples changed reality in the worse way possible before coming to an abrupt end. He couldn't be sucked into the same game. And yet a part of him needed to know. He needed to delve deeper into the mystery. The attention to detail displayed by the killer was immaculate; almost as good as his own. He wouldn't have released such a whimsical detail for nothing. There was a deep purpose here. There was a deep, dark purpose.

"I understand. But this is different. He saw me. He knows who I am. Surely, now, he knows what I'm doing. And if that's true, he's already onto me. He could have killed me."

Banks suddenly looked shocked at the possibility. He peeked over at

Jo, who looked just as surprised. Thomas took on a much quieter tone.
"He was right there. Literally just a few steps in front of me. But he
tricked me. He hit me and ran. Then he did what he had gone back to
do. He had wanted me to survive. He wanted me to see it, but why?"

Everyone sat silently. It appeared that none of their imaginations
were creatively inclined to answer such a complicated synopsis. But
Thomas' mind had moved on, like always. It was now journeying
through all of the possibilities and compounding them into the script
that had been played out. Every detail he had seen and experienced
played a part. He felt he had an answer.

"Where do you take a tiger?"

The abrupt and odd question glued both Jo and Banks to their
spots. Their mouths hung wide open in combined confusion.

"Thomas, I have no idea what you're talking about."

This comment had been the last straw for Thomas' patience.
He needed to do something to speed things up. He needed to do
something extreme.

"I need to get to the docks, *now*! I've got a ship to find. But I want
to go this one alone; I've got some things I need to do, and I need to
do them fast."

Banks shook his head.

"Absolutely not! You're not going rogue; not now. We've got too
much at stake for you to play your own game."

"It's either that or we both end up dead. You're of no use to me
out there. You haven't seen what I've seen or understood what I
understand. You're only getting in the way!"

"I understand and have seen more than you know! Don't be so
arrogant! You'd risk more lives just to go out on some selfish quest?
Are you really that prideful?"

"Believe me! I don't like it! But whoever this is would expect us to
be together, wouldn't they? If we keep playing by the same stupid
rules than we're playing his game!"

Banks let out a burst of anger before he turned away. He saw
two beady eyes peeking out from the corner of the tech hub room,
belonging to a retreated Jo. He felt the sour taste of logic beginning to
win out against his sworn allegiance to order.

"No promises. I'll do what I feel needs to be done. But if you think this will help save lives . . ."

"It will."

Banks looked confounded by something he wanted to say but couldn't. The moment passed. Without saying another word, he walked out of the room, leaving Thomas behind. Once alone, Thomas suddenly felt the cold touch of reality trickling down his back. He was going solo. In almost the entirety of his career he had always had a partner. Even if not by choice. But now he had pushed the only human connection he felt he had away. In his mind, there was only one person he needed to see, but the thought of forcing himself to do so made him want to vomit. Could he possibly endure what was to come?

16

EXOTIC DETAILS

The precinct looked to be bustling like always. His memories of the comings and goings of the place brought on a warm blanket of nostalgia. It had been his home away from home at one point in his deranged life. Now it was inaccessible. Long gone were the days of simple cases. One John Doe left in a garbage can—a white collar suicide turned homicide—seemingly pointless details to others that had locked many evils away. But now was pointless. Success meant nothing compared to the current tragedy unfolding. Walking up the stairs towards the entrance he saw all the familiar faces; at least to him they were. The normal people around him only gawked at him to speculate on his unusual hat. It, as always, was drawing in some unwanted attention. But as soon as he opened the front doors, a booming voice erupted that caught him off guard.

"As I live and breathe! Tommy Gun, here in my office? The hens have come home to roost!"

Two thousand, four hundred, and thirty eight times; that's how many times, his brain calculated, he had heard that phrase.

Doing his best to blend into the scene, he put on a falsified smile.

"Pete, it's Pete," Thomas responded, slurring the words slightly.

Pete came at him like a sweaty wall of uniform mass. The abrupt noise alerted all of the surrounding men and woman to Thomas' prodigal return. Each eyed him curiously as if expecting an answer of some kind.

"You sure know how to ruffle the feathers. But one's got to ask, what

129

brings you here? Last we spoke of this place it was on your burn-it-to-the ground list. But don't let my greasy wheels speed ahead."

Pete looked winded despite the short distance he had come. But like always, he was pouring the social charm on loftily. It was acutely strange to Thomas how Pete had ever come to the position he was in. But politics eluded him; there was no logic to it.

"Just stopping by. It's been awhile."

Out of the corner of Thomas' eye he saw Vaun. He was wearing a rather disturbed look before trading it for one more suited to a meet-and-greet. He nodded, placed some papers down, and headed over.

"Good old family reunion we've got going today. Remiss that I didn't prepare for the occasion," said Pete, pulling out a white cloth to rub the sweat from his forehead.

"It's fine. Like I said, just stopping by."

"Tommy Gun, give me one reason why you'd come back to embarrass yourself? Thought you'd *never* come back."

Thomas cringed at Vaun's tart remark. The blatant jabs had returned. Time hadn't faded their toxic relationship. He preferred Vaun drunk.

"It's good to see you, too, Vaun. I was telling Pete that I was just stopping by."

Immediately, Vaun's face contorted to one of pure disbelief. It was obvious that he didn't believe a word of it. The vibe was mutual. Pete also looked like he was swallowing glue.

"Let's head to my office. I've got a minute. We can catch up there," said Pete, slapping Thomas' back.

Thomas' smile faded as he caught Vaun's eyes. Although silent, there was a sense of anger lingering about him. His eyes were glaring and focused.

"Age before beauty," said Thomas playfully.

Vaun put on a sliver of a grin. Slowly he nodded his head.

"Sure, Tommy; sure."

Walking through the office, a wave of eyes swept over Thomas. It was the same wave that carried on it the hatred of each member of the office who knew him. His special treatment and long leash had always fed festering jealousies. How many of them would like to see him fall quietly off a cliff?

"I'll tell you what, Tommy . . . it's been hard around here lately. This city just won't sleep. Which reminds me, you were but a waltz away from watching that fed get plowed like a corn field. You holding up?"

Thomas looked up at Pete, who was holding the door to his office open for him. He saw Pete's pudgy face mold into a serious look of concern. It appeared that Pete's almost parental instincts for his officers hadn't been dampened by Thomas' absence.

"I do alright. Never was one much for sleeping."

Pete shook his head before closing the door behind them.

"Look, Tommy, I love you like a son . . . I do. But you and I both know you're not here to just say hi. You look like a train wreck. Vaun's filled me in on everything he knows. Tommy, it just sounds downright paranoid—you stalking around the city, hanging out with the Feds—just what on earth is going on here?"

Thomas looked at Pete, and then over at Vaun who was sitting silently. The baying dogs wanted reprieve.

"It's *nothing*. You been following me, Vaun? You *can't* be serious?"

Vaun frowned.

"I haven't been following; just watching. I hear things, Tommy. The city's full of little birds. What with you just up and leaving us here, what was I supposed to think? I was looking after you."

Now Thomas frowned.

"Looking after me? Vaun, that's the last thing you'd ever do. You'd rather light me on fire and burn me at the stake."

"Boys, keep the tantrum down. And Tommy, Vaun's got a point. This is a precinct, not a coffee shop. Now, I suggest that you put down the mask so we can get this ball rolling. Everybody knows you're into something, Tommy, so what is it?"

Tommy looked down at the floor. A logical dilemma was facing off against his moral self. The truth was beyond belief. Even he still struggled to believe it. But to lie would mean turning his back on those he used to call family. He knew what he had to do, but just didn't know how to do it. A mind like his own wouldn't allow him the comfort of an easy passage through the web of lies he was spinning.

"I've been searching for Jena's killer. I want to find him and make him pay. It's possible, but I've made some deals with the devil to do it."

Both men looked repulsed by the answer. Vaun, even more so, looked incredulous. His time with Thomas had made him question almost everything; even Thomas.

"Tommy, he's gone. She's gone. That guy was a junkie. Trash like that always ends up in the gutter. We all did our best and you did your best. You've got to come to grips; what was done was done."

"Don't say that! There's always another way. You can't expect me to just let it be. There's no justice in that!"

Vaun started to speak but was promptly cut off by Pete.

"That's exactly what you need to do. It ain't about justice anymore. What you're talking about is revenge. Nobody's gonna win that game, Tommy. There's no justice in revenge."

"To hell with justice! It's justice that got me into this in the first place! Always trying to do what's right just gets you burned."

"But that's what we do; we do what's right. That's what we took an oath and swore to protect," continued Pete.

"I'm not under that oath—not anymore. I walked away from all that."

"You never walk away," said Vaun soberly.

Thomas closed his eyes. His emotions were getting the better of him. What was happening to him? Were the layers on the surface slowly being eroded away to a rotten core? Was he not the gallant hero he so desperately dreamed of being all those years ago? Perhaps reality was far greyer than he realized.

"I need help. I've gotten into something I don't understand, but I know I can't do it alone."

Pete looked out of the door to his office. He caught a few eavesdroppers who quickly scurried away.

"Tommy, you know I can't do that. You're not thinking straight. Why don't you just walk away and we'll forget this conversation ever happened," whispered Pete, trying to calm the tempo.

"Pete, I'm not asking you on a professional level. I'm asking you as a friend. I need this."

"You know that's wrong, Pete. We can't dish out favors to old personnel. If anyone outside this room ever caught a sniff of this we'd be through," pleaded Vaun.

"He's right, Tommy. Whatever it is you're going to ask for, I just can't give. I'm afraid it'll have to be no."

Thomas felt sick. But he couldn't falter; he needed them too much.

"Just give me *one* last favor. I'll never ask anything of you ever again."

"Tommy, it's not that simple."

"Please, Pete . . . for me and Jen."

Pete looked at Vaun, who turned away.

"Tommy, you're putting me in a bad place here. I don't much appreciate it."

Thomas kept his silence. He was affirming his stance by doing so.

"Just do it, Pete. If you don't, you and I both know that he'll just keep asking," said Vaun.

Pete chomped his mouth as he slowly closed the blinds on his office window.

"You realize those people out there want your head; right, Tommy? It's things like this that keep the pitchforks coming—but I know you—you wouldn't press this if it wasn't important."

"I need some information. What can you tell me about the docks? I need to know everything. All the cases you've had in the past months. Things going on, rumors, even a hiccup if you've heard it. I know we keep that stuff compiled and locked up."

"Locked up for a reason. Not just anyone can go poking around there," said Vaun.

"Don't you think I know that? I just need to go through what you've got. Filter some things out and see what's connected or not. After, I'll put it all back like nothing happened, I promise."

Pete looked largely displeased with the request.

"That's it? You came here with all that hype and build up just to proofread some of our case files? Tommy, you had my last working artery ready to pop!"

"I'm sorry. I just don't—"

"Understand human beings? Yeah we know," interrupted Vaun.

"The docks, Tommy; things haven't been so squeaky clean that way. You sure you want to go digging around that place alone? A lot of rats hiding in those cracks, Tommy."

"I'm sure, Pete. This is bigger than me."

Pete looked at Vaun who shrugged.

"There's been the usual illegal trade coming in and out of there. Nothing unusual, but recently things have picked up. Word on the street is there's some high ticket event coming up with only the top tier scum getting the invites. Probably just another shark den swimming with prostitutes. The DA is pretty good at snuffing those out."

"Vaun's playing it lightly. Those suits pack heat. But we're so bottlenecked by paperwork that we'll probably only get around to it by the time the dust settles. We'll clean up a few bodies, roll the yellow tape, and take pictures," added Pete.

"But anything strange? Out of the norm for such a place?"

Pete let out a bellowing chuckle.

"You gotta wax those ears, Tommy! There's nothing normal about that place. You'll be walking to your grave if you catch the wrong eye."

"Sorry, sometimes I can't hear what I'm saying," replied Thomas.

"Never have, never will. One reason we mixed like oil and tequila."

Thomas glanced at Vaun who gave him a tiny smirk.

"I'll watch my back down there. I've been in worse."

Vaun shook his head.

"That damn pride."

"Tommy, don't want to be the one to put the lid on a boiling pot, but Vaun's right. You'd be writing your obituary."

"Just let me see the files. I need the history on this place and I'm losing valuable time."

"Have it your way. But if you wind up another body in the river, I'll never forgive myself," sighed Pete heavily.

Cautiously, he peeked through the blinds then swung open the door.

"Wait here. If the docks don't kill you, these people will."

"It's unbelievable, it really is. You always get special treatment. I'll just never understand why," Vaun huffed.

"Vaun, let's just forget our past. I know I've done some stupid things. I can be a real prick," Thomas answered in response.

"Now you're speaking some sense for once."

"Can't we just put it aside?" Thomas asked. "I'm not doing this for me. I never was."

Vaun looked repulsed by the statement.

"Tommy, it's *always* been about *you*. Your little gift has always kept you in the spotlight. You never cared what the rest of us normal people had to do. A bull in a china shop, that's what you are. You just leave the rest of us behind to clean up your messes."

Exotic Details

Thomas began to answer but was cut off by Pete staggering into the room holding a large box of file folders. He squirmed his foot around in order to shut the door.

"This is all we've got that you might find of any interest. But to be honest, there's nothing here that hasn't already happened a thousand times since. That place is a broken record, Tommy."

Pete sprawled the folders out onto the table. Immediately, Tommy pounced on the files, looking for trigger words, contrabands, arms, drugs, illegal trade, and murder. Then he focused on the things he had seen himself. The one thing that stuck out more than anything else was the tiger. What place did a caged tiger have sitting alongside crates of illegal weapons?

"What about exotic goods? Any surge in those?"

Pete looked like he'd just swallowed a sour grape.

"Just what type of exotic are you talking about?"

Thomas looked up at Vaun who eyed him carefully.

"A big cat."

Pete put a hand up to his sweaty face.

"A bit of overkill just to find your neighbor's pussy cat, don't you think?"

Still locking his eyes on Vaun, Thomas replied.

"This one could take your head off."

17

BEARS AND TIGERS

The murky waters of the ill kept shipyard sloshed about, churning up a healthy froth of white from its depths. Old wooden structures, weathered and worn by time, dotted the edge where water met land. It was late in the evening. The last rays of sunlight were rapidly thinning into nothingness. The eerie chill from the water was whisked through the air like a silent ghost. Many dark places hiding many dark secrets loomed about. Amidst it all stood Thomas.

He puffed in and out a few breathes of the chilled air. His nerves hummed like overcharged electric lines. He had been to many loathsome places, but the docks always topped his list of most hated. Proximity towards the water created a myriad of dark possibilities that could easily drown-out thought. All one had to do was give a push, and a world of details would be lost to the sea. How many secrets lay at its bottom? How many questions unanswered?

What the hell am I doing?

Thomas looked around, suddenly feeling the urge to turn around and dash home. But he stood his ground. There wasn't time to indulge his selfish, human nature. To succeed he had to pause his concerns and replace them with reasons. But the docks proved to be a formidable opponent to his courage. He knew just as well as any what despicable things lurked in the shadows. It was a watering hole for evil.

You can do this, Tommy.

He looked around until he was content that he hadn't been

followed. His demands had been explicit. He needed to walk this part alone. The killer had seen Thomas, which meant he was more than likely already studying him too. If this was the case, he needed to cease being who he was, and quickly. Pulling up the collar of his coat, he inhaled the crisp air. Cautiously, he proceeded into the unseen places in the dark.

At first he was largely disappointed. Apart from a few homeless wanderers, the area was dead. Nothing but empty beer cans, cigarette butts, and garbage dotted the scene. Perhaps all the hype truly had been overstated. That was, until he found himself walking towards a peculiar looking building. It was just another tossed-together example of the make-shift architecture popular here. It reeked of stale fish and rot. But on its only door was a handmade sign with three triangles tightly locked together; three triangles that he had seen many times before in his thoughts. Now more than ever, he wished he would have seen Roslin. There was something he needed to know; something deviant in nature he suspected was being played out masterfully.

Walking up to the door, he ran his fingers over the frail piece of paper that had been intentionally placed there. With little effort it fell into his hand.

Three triangles . . . three triangles . . . what does it mean? Come on, Tommy. What is this?

As hard as he tried, no answer appeared. The odd symbol meant nothing to him. Its cryptic meaning was a mystery. But one thing was now becoming certain; the killer had a purpose. It was finding this purpose that now consumed his thoughts. Balling the paper up, he tossed it roughly to the ground. Reaching down, he tugged on the door handle. It didn't budge. Frustrated, he tried again. It was locked. But why would the killer lead him to a locked door? What was his plan for Thomas?

Letting loose a few lines of exasperated profanity, he threw himself into the door. It creaked slightly against the force. He repeated the process again. This time he put everything he had into his shoulder and heaved forward. With a sudden crack and a pop, the door flew open, sending him flying inside. He slid onto the ground and rolled into a few barrels that held miscellaneous tools. The impact sent some of them whirling through the air, making a ferocious racket when they landed.

There goes the element of surprise.

Putting his hat carefully back on his head, he dusted himself off and got up. His body was beginning to feel more and more like a crash test dummy. How much more could he possibly take? He felt down his thigh towards his gun. At least he had remembered his weapon. Without it he had felt naked and vulnerable. He felt it helped him slightly level the playing field.

What's that?

Suddenly a flickering stream of light dancing its way up a mysterious flight of stairs appeared before him. This oddity seemed to be sourced from somewhere down below. This was obviously very out of place. Looking around the room, he realized that there was only one choice left to him. He would have to go down and meet whatever was waiting for him head on. For better or worse, he wanted it to end. He was ready to do whatever was necessary, even if the thought of it petrified him.

He had to move forward. Time wasn't going to safely abide at his side for long. If someone was being targeted, the current of motion in time had already begun ripping them apart, one tiny detail at a time. Going down the flight of stairs, the light began to grow until it completely enveloped him. Along with it came the rowdy voices of a large group of men. He now realized that he was moving into a potential pit of vipers. Releasing his gun from the side of his hip, he gripped it tightly in his hands.

I can't believe I'm doing this.

Step after step, he cautiously worked his way down. The intensity of the clamor below grew and grew. It was now deafening. Drunken slander, contempt, and joyous overtures filled the passage to capacity in equal measure. Realizing he was just a few steps away from leaving his concealed position in the stairway, he paused. Now more than ever he regretted coming alone. But he had done so for a reason. If he was being targeted, he was going down alone. There was no sense in dragging someone else into the claws of death.

Feeling his finger slide over the smooth edge of the trigger, he peeked around the corner. What he found left him utterly amazed. A massive room opened before him, crudely lit by a jungle of connected lights. Men stood shoulder to shoulder in the thick smog of cigarette smoke. Their faces were shrouded in shadow. Cackling demons dressed in their fancy suits.

What is going on?

Looking around it soon became clear that the epi center of activity was the middle of the room. From where he was he could make out a large recess with high, towering walls filled with men cheering loudly. Tables filled with guns, knives, and all other manner of contraband lined the walls. Scantily clad women moved seductively through the crowd serving drinks. A true den of vice.

Taking one last deep breath, he carefully hid the gun in his coat, concealing its threat. The last thing he needed was to draw any unwanted attention. If he was discovered, a bullet square between the eyes would be the last human interaction he would ever have. He moved forward, feeling the immense heat from the packed-in bodies in the room rubbing up against him. The fowl air made him choke and cough. This drew the attention of a few onlookers who looked him over suspiciously. Each looked as if they had been inside a cage for most their delinquent life. They dismissed Thomas quickly. Amongst such a diverse group of underbelly scum, he was just another odd face.

Pressing his way through the crowd, he could sense the tension in the room. It was almost palpable. The alluring scent of debauchery passed by him, its wearer brushing against his side. He glanced over to catch her eyes.

"Looking for a good time, honey? I'd run a special for you."

The raspy voice came from a slender, part Asian-looking woman. She winked at Thomas as she continued on her way, sensually presenting her goods. Her scent lingered behind, making Thomas' normally sharp wit dull slightly. It appeared that no matter one's intellect, women always held the carnal keys.

Turning back around, he rammed face-first into the broad chest of a very large man. A large fist quickly snatched Thomas by the collar of his coat.

"You have a problem with walking?"

Looking up at the mountain of flesh, Thomas shook his head.

"Sorry, I've had one too many tonight. Left my good leg at home."

The man released him and burst into gleeful laughter. He moved on past Thomas pursuing the slender woman who had propositioned Thomas with her bold touch. Relaxing his body, he felt his hand shift beneath his coat. He had been clenching his gun tightly in anticipation. His heart sank. He needed to be more careful. A gun fight in a place like this would not end well. Moving forward, he came across a beehive of underworld activity.

Tables were filled to capacity with illegal arms and imported explosives. Stolen government goods, top-secret documents, and other damning items were on open display as if it were a flea market. This was all hidden quietly in the dark, far from the view of those with a legal interest. In his entire career he had never seen anything like it. All of the details in the room were zooming through his mind, connecting dots to faces. It was a literal treasure trove of potential for resolving unsolved cases. But he wasn't here for that. He was here to stop a madman from altering time; something more dangerous than any of the weaponry embellishing these tables.

"You placing a bet?"

Thomas was caught off guard. His mind came to a screeching halt, when a moment ago it had been whizzing around a race track. A wiry man with clouded eyes gazed blankly at him. He held one of his hands out before Thomas like a beggar, his eyes remaining intently focused on him.

"I'm sorry?"

The man blinked slowly. From behind his yellow stained teeth came a gurgling reply.

"The fight—are you betting or not?"

Thomas took a glimpse around the large pit surrounded by the drunken gathering of deviant men. It was clear as to what he was referencing.

"No, no, not tonight. Got money to spend elsewhere."

The man looked confused. He looked Thomas over carefully, only stopping on his hat.

"How much for the hat? Haven't seen one like it in an age. I like it."

Thomas pointed up towards the burnt, red feather stuck in his cap.

"Sorry, can't part with this one."

The man scowled and moved on, heading toward the darkest shadows in the room.

Bears and Tigers

The fight, it's got to be there.

Moving even further into the mob of vile men, Thomas began questioning his resolve. He had obviously been led here by the killer—a killer who had cleverly crafted the murder of numerous professional agents—agents trained in how to stop men just like him. There was no chance that this was accidental. No chance that he didn't already know that Thomas was there. He would be watching from somewhere in the darkness. He must be there, his sinister plan unfolding, one passing moment after another. In a deranged way, Thomas looked forward to finally capturing him. He felt there was much he could learn from such a brilliant, yet destructive, mind.

Pressing through the remaining outer edges of a packed circle around a large pit was like maneuvering through a fleshy maze. His progress was suddenly halted by a mind numbing roar. It rang through the room with blood-thirsty ferocity. It didn't take long for imagination to anchor into reality. He had found his missing tiger. Now he had to see it. He needed to validate his intuition. Finally making some headway, he could see the wicked marvel in front of him.

You can't be serious . . .

A massive pit, dug into the very foundation of the room, opened below him. A tiger was pacing back and forth, panting heavily. The same tiger he had met face-to-face in his glimpse into the past. But instead of the horrific but still statue, it was now an animated mass of deadly prowess. Another blood curdling growl came from the horribly abused animal. It was obvious what type of set up this was. The thought of it sickened him. What kind of people found joy in such primitive behavior?

Scoping out the edge of the pit, his eyes came to an abrupt stop on one area of interest. In their own private booths sat a select few men, all dressed in their finest garb. Each was surrounded by a few of their constituents who looked into the thrashing crowd, tempting someone to try. Some of the city's most repugnant leadership was in attendance, and Thomas was a mere stone's throw away from them. He suddenly quietly hoped that he had been followed; that Vaun or Banks would come storming in, armed to the teeth with a swarm of backup. They could accomplish more in five minutes here than they would ever accomplish in years out on the streets. The killer was here.

He had to be. But where was he? He hated the idea of being watched by someone he knew nothing about. He hated playing the puppet.

"Last bets are being called! Get them in!"

A rumbling voice blasted through the air from a large man holding tickets. Thomas eyed the audience carefully as a few remaining men returned to the man, adding to his supply. Thomas looked over his way. He looked at the man's grisly features. Then he noticed something else—standing just behind the ticketholder was the outline of something that struck him as oddly familiar. He had seen that body before. It was a shot in the dark, but perhaps he was on to something. Forgetting his place, he tried desperately to wiggle his way towards the other side of the pit. As he made his way, he did his best to focus on the dark silhouette. It was still. It appeared the man was also watching, waiting. Perhaps his inclination had been correct. But he needed a face. He needed a face on which to pin all of the atrocities that had been committed.

"What's your problem?" questioned a snake-eyed man, practically hissing as Thomas squeezed by.

"Mind your business!" hollered Thomas, looking back.

He was growing weary and impatient. If he was going to catch the killer, he'd need to kick things up a notch. With a few more strides he was within striking distance of the man. But to his utter dismay, the man was gone. Somewhere along the way he had slipped out of view. Now finding him seemed completely out of the question. He had undoubtedly blended back into the humming cesspool in the room.

This can't be happening!

Frustrated beyond belief he let out a growl. The growl was suddenly amplified by the growl of the tiger still pacing in the pit. Everything for a moment began to mix together. All of the profanity and banter slid into his mind like poison. His thoughts were clouded. With no clear direction, he was suddenly feeling himself slip into a brief moment of madness. Just why had he come here? His thoughts shattered into a million horrifying pieces as the body of a man caught up in a fight was thrown into him.

He felt himself weightlessly cutting through the air. The impact of the force had sent him flying towards the bottom of the awaiting pit. He let out a shriek of terror when he realized what had happened.

Bears and Tigers

With a massive thud, he landed in the pit, letting out a groan of terrible pain. The chaotic room above him looked on curiously. With a bit of a racket, his hidden gun burst free from his coat, clattering across the floor. But the calamity and racket was further amplified by the soul-piercing growl of a tiger that was already on its way to pouncing. A surge of adrenaline blasted its way into Thomas' veins, propelling him back to his feet.

His first instinct was to retrieve his weapon, but the tiger was almost directly on top of it. Out of sheer panic, he leapt to one side and backed into the wall. From somewhere in their midst came a voice of accusation.

"He's a cop! I know I've seen that face before!"

Suddenly his odds of survival had been weighted with an even more unpredictable element. If things had been bad before, they were now plummeting quickly to hell. The tiger let out another mind-numbing roar as it approached Thomas, testing the boundaries. The hushed room erupted into elated cries of joy. What else could they possibly ask for than a suspected snitch falling dead weight into a pit with a tiger? The set up was nightmarishly perfect.

"Looks like the game's got another contender!" said the leathery looking man holding the tickets.

He looked over at the powers-that-be sitting comfortably in their chairs. One of them gave him a silent nod. Things had been approved to move forward, so Thomas' life was in jeopardy. Rolling to one side, he watched as the tiger's movements became more and more bravado. Its bloodlust was overcoming its fear of its captors. It eyed Thomas as it would prey stuck lower on the food chain. It lunged. The chase was on—a chase that Thomas stood zero chance of surviving—the adept predator would rip him limb from limb.

Panting like mad to keep himself moving, he dodged the tiger's lunge, letting it crash into the side of the pit's wall. He sprinted away doing everything he could to put distance between him and the beast. The mob went wild. They had been awoken by the potential blood frenzy. But there was only one thing on Thomas' mind—his gun—if he could at least get to his gun he stood a minute chance of survival. He was now on the opposite end of the pit. The tiger was repositioning for another life-ending pounce. It followed his every movement as a cat would a mouse. Its long, flesh-puncturing fangs dripped saliva, driven by its insatiable urge to feed. Taking in a long drag of air, it tensed its body and leapt. For Thomas, it all passed in slow motion. The outreached claws of the tiger slashed through the air on their path towards his exposed throat. Soon the powerful jaws of death would clamp around his trachea and squeeze what little life was left out of him.

Do something, Tommy! Do something now!

Not knowing what else to do, he whipped off his coat and threw it at the face of the leaping tiger. It landed well and temporarily blinded the animal. It promptly slashed the coat to pieces. But it had bought Thomas just enough time to get to the other side of the pit. He snatched up his gun and pointed it at the tiger. His finger quivered in anticipation, he aimed to make the kill. Just as he did, a loud roar of cheering arose, as a large panel was opened.

The panel was embedded in the wall of the pit. It opened to reveal yet another horror that burst free from the shadows, thrashing at the air as it moved; Thomas found himself facing a massive bear. It rolled into the pit in a direct beeline towards him. Without hesitation, he blasted a few rounds into its thick hide. But it kept coming. Its fury was unchecked. Its only desire was to end his life. Feeling the hairs on his neck prick up, he threw himself out of its path. As he did, the bear met the tiger head-on. The two behemoths clawed at each other ferociously, spittle flying, pushing each other into a corner. Large electric prods lowered from above pushed them back towards each other and the vulnerable Thomas. Large crimson drops of blood ran from the bear, leaving a trail as it paced around the middle of the pit.

"Stop! This is insane!"

But the blood thirsty crowd roared for more. They were relishing every moment of the drama before them. No one was going to put an end to the madness. Looking towards the two animals that were being forced back on him, he felt his heart sink. He had finally come to his end. The path towards it had been laced with the obvious. Any minute now, two dynamic forces of nature would be on top of him. His pistol, holding just a few more measly rounds, would be his only defense.

I didn't think it would end like this. Is this really why you lead me here?

Feeling his back press forcefully into the pit's wall, his eyes watered.

Bears and Tigers

The two enraged animals were now within mere footsteps. Their thrashing bodies were sweeping in like a tornado of tooth and claw. But there was something else. At the rim of the pit. Upon its safe embrace sat a man; a man with the same outline and shape of the one he had pursued so foolishly. His face was shrouded in a dark mask staring down at him. It was the killer. The very same man from the glimpse that had left his bloody print on him.

"You did this!" screamed Thomas, looking up at him.

The man put out his hand and pointed directly at Thomas. He then disappeared mysteriously back into the throbbing crowd.

So it's true. He wanted me to come here to die. Why were you so stupid, Tommy?

At the sheer precipice of no return when the frenzied beasts were upon him, there came a crash of thunder. From somewhere above him, a wave of energy blasted through the room. Suddenly, a giant rafter broke loose, and plummeted down into the pit. It struck the center with a dreadful thud. It was soon joined by another rafter that fell just outside the pit, squashing a few of the spectators where they stood. The world around him erupted in chaos. The building appeared to be falling apart. Now, practically chewing on his own heart, Thomas searched for an escape. Miraculously, the first fallen rafter had provided the miracle he so desperately needed. Its long stretch of plank gave him an exit at the top of the pit. There was a way for him to get out, but there was still a more prevalent issue—the bear and tiger. Forgoing his quick escape, he looked ahead, expecting the worst. To his great relief, the two apex predators had forgotten all about him. In the acute moment of chaos, both seemed to have opted for a rapid escape.

He watched in terror as the two enraged animals sprinted up the rafter past him into the panicked crowd. A few gun shots were heard as the tiger pounced on top of a fleeing man, easily ripping him to pieces. The man's screams were suddenly dampened by another thunderous wave of energy. This sent a piece of the building plummeting directly down towards Thomas' head. Just in the nick of time, he rolled out of its trajectory, letting it smash itself to pieces on the pit's floor.

Time to go, Tommy. Time to go now!

Doing his best to only focus on the exposed beam, he ran for his life. The world around him was literally falling apart. Pieces of falling debris were pouring from the air. The screams of fear and panic were ear-splitting. His feet struck the beam hard, throwing his body into a contorted effort to balance itself. He carefully scaled toward his salvation at the top of the pit. Once there, he immediately leapt forward, leaving it all behind. With a massive crash, another beam from above ripped its way through his exit, smashing down into the pit. He had made it out without a moment to spare. Not willing to test his fate any further, he pushed himself to his limits. Propelling himself through the buzzing hive of bodies, he slammed his way through. The stairs leading towards the only known exit were just a few leaps away. But progress was painfully slow. The tension was eating him alive.

"Get off of me!"

He screamed at a man who had looted one of the tables now collapsed on the floor. The man flung himself into Thomas' path, holding a long, serrated knife. It looked as if his intention was to rob Thomas, but suddenly a bullet blasted its way through his chest. The man fell limp to the floor, lifeless. Thomas' eyes bulged open like two giant bubbles, ready to burst. Punishment in the underworld was dealt with promptly, apparently.

I've got to get out of here.

Another powerful blast from somewhere in the room tossed him forward. He fell to his knees, feeling the impact rumble through his body. With what little energy he had left he rose to his feet and fought valiantly to get back to the stairs. His efforts were rewarded when with a few more labored steps he reached them. Rushing up the stairs as quickly as he could, he burst into the tiny room, and threw himself through the open door. He collapsed onto the ground, groaning in pain. With another deafening roar from somewhere beneath him, the small building folded in on itself. Somewhere in the distance the echo of sirens wailed in the darkness. But his body had reached its limits. His mind was in a paralyzed stupor. Was he going to make it out of this alive?

18

SYMBOL PRICE

Streams of cool air passed by Thomas' face. His mind felt fuzzy and dislodged. He wasn't sure where he was or what he was doing. But one thing was for certain; he was moving. Doing his best to open his eyes, he could see the hazy outline of the man driving. He appeared to be intently focused on the road ahead.

"You up, Tommy? You alright?"

Thomas heard the man's words and immediately recognized who they belonged to. It was Vaun. At first this came as a great relief. Vaun had come to the rescue. But that thought was quickly spoiled by the obvious—how had Vaun found him? Racking his brain for answers, he couldn't remember just how he had arrived at being in the car. He needed some answers.

"How did you find me? Where am I?"

Vaun glanced over for only a heartbeat. He appeared nervous and flustered.

"It doesn't matter. That place was falling to pieces back there, Tommy. I had to snatch you up before the law did. Just what the hell were you doing back there?"

Thomas struggled to gain his bearings. Slowly his sight returned to him, painting him a clear picture. Suddenly a brilliant dawn burst through the foggy mist in his brain. Instantly, he remembered everything—the utter chaos that had nearly taken his life—the same chaos that had taken the lives of so many others. Just how many had died in the explosions? Was this justice demanding its needs be met?

"Vaun, it matters! I told you not to follow me. You could have very well been in that building, buried a hundred feet under. Just stop the lies for once and tell me the truth!"

Vaun took a sudden turn into an alleyway and brought the car to a screeching stop. The smell of burnt rubber only heightened the burning anger he held inside.

"Because I don't trust you! Nobody does, Tommy! You go all rogue on us, just up and leave, and now this? It's crazy, that's what it is. I'm not going to let you run around starting fires! I'm just not!"

"And what about you? Should I trust you? All these years you've been riding me into the ground? You're always trying to take a piece of me every time we're together. And for what? Just to see me fail?"

"I just saved your life! The least you could do is thank me. I could have left you behind so those blue buzzards could slap one indictment on you after another. But I didn't! Stop believing that there's something there that isn't!"

Thomas felt the anger inside him swell. He let the words drop into his boiling vat of resentments. Vaun's jealousy had driven a wedge directly between them, built of doubt and paranoia.

"Thanks, thanks for picking me up. I apologize that I reamed you so soon. I've just been through a lot lately."

Vaun's demeanor shifted from one of anger to a more relaxed, receptive one.

"Why can't you just tell me what's really going on? You go pull Pete's chain to come down to the docks? The docks, Tommy—*really*? Look, I'm no spring chicken. Just what have you dug yourself into?"

Vaun looked over at Thomas' exposed watch. His eyes dwelled there. Thomas tucked it out of view.

"I don't know what to say. To be honest, you wouldn't believe me even if I told you."

"Try me. I was paired up with you, remember? There's a lot of things that I'm willing to stretch on these days."

Thomas felt the urge to say something but refrained. To do so meant condemning his relationships with Roslin, Banks, and whatever organization had granted him his overwhelming responsibility. But he felt betrayed as well. The killer had shown him one of his cards. A card etched with a cryptic message that had kept his mind revisiting it. It was obvious that he wanted Thomas to know something. But what was it? Was the supposed untouchable organization contaminated? With Roslin's own brother being reached, just how far did the treachery go?

"I'm changing things; things that when set in motion have the potential to create devastation, much like you saw back there. I've struck a deal with the Feds and have been working with them ever since. Really, that's all it is."

"Then why all the secrecy? Why now? You treat the rest of us like strangers. People you've worked with for years are suddenly ostracized by you and your secretive quest. You can't just keep pushing people away, Tommy. Heaven knows you're already running thin."

Thomas looked out the window into the dark alley. A part of him wanted to abandon it all and just go back to mourning his loss. Everything had become so horribly complicated. Nothing was what it seemed. Every corner now harbored the dark shadow of death; one disease-filled tide, sweeping its way through time, destroying the future.

"It's because I can't. I can't bring someone else into this. Whoever this is, is winning. People are dying wrongfully. This isn't about me anymore. I left me back with Jen."

"Tommy, what are you talking about?"

Thomas closed his eyes. For once he didn't know what to do. Everything was so woefully out of place. But he knew he was right. Vaun wasn't ready for the world he was in. The last thing he wanted was innocent blood on his hands merely to satiate his human need to not feel alone. The puzzle was becoming a literal hell. Without words, he reached for the door handle to exit the car. This immediately set Vaun off like a fire alarm.

"Tommy, think about what you're doing here. You can't just go back and change this."

Thomas felt his heart sting. Despite their rocky relationship, Vaun had stood with him many times before. But now he had to leave him behind. He had already left behind almost every other aspect of his past self; now he was shedding what little was left. He was being bored down to the very core of who he was and he didn't like what he saw.

"I know."

Thomas slammed the door behind him. He could feel Vaun's

emotions practically oozing out, submerging him in their reflective abyss, trying to pull him back in. But it was too late. With the screech and burn of rubber, Vaun was behind him.

"I'm sorry, Vaun . . . I really am."

Thomas knew that he needed to get back and glimpse again. He needed to push himself to the very fringe of time and stop this madness. He needed to see this through.

"So, it's not just me, then? Man, you've got a real way with people."

The voice came from somewhere in the shadows. It only took a moment for the source of the voice to walk into the open. It was Roslin—the very man who had plagued his thoughts since the beginning of this insanity.

"I thought we agreed to no following—you've got a way of hiding things—things people should know about," said Thomas, eyeing the small pendant he was wearing.

Roslin nodded.

"I'd recite to you the gravity of me telling you any of this and the implications therein, but something tells me you just don't care."

"At least you're finally getting something right."

"I've known about your little gift for some time. We've had our eyes on you for some time. It's what we do. But I guess your question is, who are we?"

"Spare me the backstory. Why would he show me that symbol? Why would it matter?"

Roslin turned and began walking away. Cautiously, Thomas followed.

"The symbol is a reflection of what our organization does. It goes back ages, has survived the rise and fall of many governments. It has been weathered, tested, and proven. But everything comes with a price."

"What are you talking about?"

Roslin stopped for a moment.

"The world can't know what we do; it isn't ready. We stand between humanity and utter chaos. This often requires sacrifice."

"Like your brother?"

Roslin turned, his posture turning aggressive.

"*No—not* like my brother. He had nothing to do with this. I made my own choices. He's done nothing wrong."

"It's those choices that are haunting us all now. You can't possibly *believe* that you're untouchable. Everybody has their boiling point; even *you.*"

Roslin looked down at the ground. He appeared to be in deep thought.

"I've worked tirelessly to remove everything I was in order to become something more. All that matters now are the results. I won't condemn the many just for my own selfish desires."

"You're a monster! How can you just stand by and do nothing? This isn't about some secret organization. This man wants to destroy you and everything you stand for! It's no longer about results. If you don't start telling me the truth, he'll win!"

"Don't you think I know that? It's not that easy! When much is given, much is required, plain and simple. I've earned my stake—have you?"

"I couldn't care less about what stake I have. I'm trying to save people's lives! Innocent people who are being destroyed. I just watched a building collapse on top of a crowd of people. They may not have been innocent, but many didn't deserve to die like that. Whoever this is will do whatever it takes to win."

Roslin put a hand up as if to refute the remarks but let it fall back limply to his side.

"So what do you propose? We've already lost most of our team. We almost lost you."

"Let me do things my way. You've had me in handcuffs ever since I came onto this program. Take them off. Let me do what I'm good at."

"I know what you're trying to ask me but the answer is no. We are struggling too much as it is to track one disruptor, let alone two. To have both of you playing a game of cat and mouse could be disastrous. I just can't risk it."

Thomas took a few steps towards Roslin. He did his best to look him straight in the eyes.

"If you don't, we've already lost."

The comment struck Roslin who sat quietly for a time. He was considering the idea poised against his twisted sense of duty. But Thomas had played his card with purpose. He knew that Roslin wanted results. It seemed that was all that mattered. Had he pressed the right button?

"Jo isn't going to like it. You've already got him rambling off line after line of adjunct possibilities. He won't like the idea."

"Believe me, neither do I. If I felt like I had another option, I'd take it."

Roslin turned and began walking away.

"Where are you going?"

"You know."

Thomas sat quietly in the dark. Was he alone? Was he truly ever? His sense of loneliness was quickly being replaced with one of paranoia. He wasn't safe. He was never going to be safe again.

"I know, but I just don't like it."

He took a moment to reflect. There was something wildly out of place inside of him. His heart seemed to jostle around in his chest with every breath. What was real anymore? Who or what could he trust? He had enticed anger at almost every turn. Now the killer was undoubtedly studying him down to every last detail. And yet he was still alive. What twisted game was being played? There was only one person he wanted to see now. In a prayer from his heart, he just hoped she was still alive.

19

CLIFF NOTES

It wasn't like Thomas to behave like such a stalker. He mostly had kept to himself in the past. But his acute sense of detail had recollected the directions clearly. Walking up the long, stony steps towards a gated door, he dwelled on what might happen next. Should he even be here? By coming had he damned the last real connection to the real world he so desperately wanted? This brought on some serious questions that had been growing in his mind. Why did he keep coming back?

Raising his hand up to knock on the door, he was shocked to see it swiftly open. Standing before him was Barb. She was draped in a nightgown, her sultry body tucked in tightly beneath it. She looked straight at him. Her eyes told the story.

"Thomas, what are you doing here? It's the middle of the night and half the force is running around with their heads cut off. Thomas, there was an explosion down at the docks. I tried to call you but you never picked up! What's going on with you?"

Thomas hadn't realized it until now, but he had been ignoring his phone completely. It had been more of annoyance than anything to him. Pulling it out of his pocket, he looked to see a long list of missed calls; Barb, Vaun, Pete, and even a few unmarked numbers. All of which he had let go unnoticed.

"I'm sorry about missing your call and how late it is. Can I come in anyway?"

Barb frowned but opened the door. Thomas realized he had never been inside her house before. It was a beautiful blend of modern architecture dabbed with a hint of a subtle taste for the classic. Her perfume masked the air, chasing away all other scents.

"Thomas, you've got me worried. You stop by all enigmatic and problematic and promptly leave. Then you disappear, there's an explosion, and I try to call, only to get no answer. Thomas, what is going on? Normally I try to keep things professional, but you have to see my angle here."

Thomas felt himself sink. He felt like an emotional train wreck. Pieces of him seemed to keep burning away.

"Let's sit down. I feel sick."

Barb led him to her front room. He was met with the same comfort and warmth of her office. He also noticed a picture that had once lived in his memory somewhere else.

"Your fat dog. I've missed that photo."

Barb sat a steaming cup of tea in front of him. The herbal essence lingered in his nostrils tantalizing his senses.

"Not everything has some deep meaning. I just wanted to bring it home for once, change things up."

Thomas put the warm cup to his lips where he allowed the cozy steam to warm his face. It helped clear his mind. There was something he had always overlooked—human nature. To someone like him it was an illogical point of weakness. But it was true. Human's changed all the time for little to no reason. Perhaps the bulldozer of change that many people secretly hoped for was driven by nothing more than boredom. Change for change's sake. It was the overriding factor in the equation that proved that even the killer couldn't succeed every time. There had to be more there to understand.

"Change . . . it's something I struggle to deal with. It seems that it comes so fast, with no logical path or conclusion, and then leaves. A real party crasher."

"Of course change is hard for you, Thomas. Look at you—you memorize dictionaries and miniscule details that boggle my mind. But those details don't just suddenly change on you, or cease to exist entirely. It's like you saying *abyso* . . . oh, whatever it was, now just doesn't exist! Your brilliant mind struggles to understand why."

"It's page twenty six—*abyssopelagic*—of, like, or pertaining to the depths of the ocean. I'm impressed you remembered that."

Barb shook her head as she sipped on her own cup of tea.

"I didn't remember all the details, just the part that mattered; the *meaning* of the conversation; the *purpose*."

Thomas froze. A part of him was suddenly dancing around inside, screaming like a small child.

"*What* did you say?"

Barb tucked a corner of her robe back around her body as she shifted in her seat.

"Normal people don't remember every little detail, Thomas. We just do our best to remember the overall idea; the cliff notes, if you will."

Thomas grinned. He had been so blind. His ability had driven him into a corner. He had spent so much time going over every aspect with a fine toothed comb, that he'd forgotten the bigger picture. Whoever the killer was, he was gifted. *Gifted* but also *human*; a fact that he was uncovering more and more with each passing day. His sinister prey still had a drop of humanity. Now he would need to rely on a part of himself he'd never cared for—his understanding of other people. The weakest weapon in his arsenal was his struggle to understand the motives of people; the motives of evil. To him it just didn't matter. One dot connected to the next and would ultimately draw a picture. Maybe it was time for him to change.

"Barb, you're a genius! I can't believe how stupid I've been."

Thomas sunk his head into his hands. He'd been played. The killer was merely showing him the pieces, one catastrophe at a time.

"Thomas, what are you talking about? Quit speaking in riddles. Just tell me the truth for once."

The fight to keep his lionhearted promise to an organization he didn't really trust was waning. Barb meant something to him that traversed those boundaries.

"I'm aiding a secret organization whose origins are still largely under question. They recruited me at the bridge where I was trying to kill myself. Since then, I have literally been jumping back in time to try and stop a madman who crafts his murders into the most elaborate chess game I've ever seen. And it should be noted, that I'm losing. He's always a step ahead and now I don't really trust anyone. Except you, of course. I feel like I'm losing my mind. Nothing is making sense anymore."

Barb let her cup of tea drop from her hand. Her mouth gaped open, her brows furrowed. She was shocked by the utter insanity that he had just described so cavalierly.

"Thomas . . ."

Barb's words trailed off as he put his own cup down and took a seat next to her. He gently took her dwindling, trembling hands into his own.

"It's all true, Barb. You know I don't lie. I suck at it. Trust me; I still don't believe half of what I've been through myself. And yet it's still there every time I open my eyes."

Barb's mouth slowly closed has she listened thoughtfully before speaking. "Okay, whoa. That's a lot to take in. I'm not even sure what to say right now. Secret organization, time travel, and murder? Thomas, that's some muddy stuff there. You honestly expect me to believe any of it?"

"No, not at all. But honestly I don't know what else to say. All I know is people are dying out there. And I'm almost positive that I'm on the to-do list now as well. That means you could be at risk too."

Barb shifted in her seat, putting a little distance between her and Thomas. She slowly brought the cup of tea to her lips and took a sip before responding.

"I don't know what's crazier. Everything you just said or the fact that a part of me wants to believe it. But it's impossible."

Thomas brought his watch into full view. He held his hand flat over its top. Instantly, a world of scientific imagination beamed out from it. Barb had never seen nor dreamt of anything like it. Her eyes were wide with disbelief. It was incredible.

"This is what they call a *brink*. But forget the name. It allows me to temporarily glimpse back in time. I'd tell you how it works, but honestly, I have no idea. All I know is I can access anywhere in time that I've existed. From there, I have a small window to figure things out and then, *boom*! I get blasted back here."

"Thomas, that's ridiculous. If someone could do that they could change the course of history."

Thomas shook his head.

"It's more complicated than that. I'll spare you the torture, but there are limits. Only the smallest things can be changed, but they

create the tidal waves we see today. Just like a snowball running down
a hill can turn into an avalanche . . . or whatever. It's hard to explain.
But that's why they dragged me into this—the details—there are
so many details and possibilities that they needed a freak like me to
chase after them."

"Why would someone do that? Why would someone risk altering
time? Assuming any of your crazy claims are true, many people would
be at risk. It's sadistic!"

"That's exactly what I'm up against. At first it was much more
refined, targeted; now it's becoming a loose cannon. I'm pressuring
whoever this is and they're reacting. I think you should get out of
town, Barb. I don't want you anywhere near this."

"And what? Go *hide*? I don't hide, you know that. If this is as
serious as you say it is, it wouldn't matter anyway. If any of what
you just said is real, Thomas, you need to stop it. This can't go on
for *any* reason."

Barb put down her cup and slid closer to Thomas. She put a hand
on his knee. Her small gesture sent a dizzying wave through Thomas.

"Are you going to be alright? Why not let someone else take this
burden? You don't have to do this."

Before he could respond, Thomas felt his phone buzz in his pocket.
Remembering the previous round of missed phone calls, he looked
at it. There was just one message in the form of a text; unmarked,
unregistered, and untraceable.

It's time.

He put the phone back in his pocket. The killer was unrelenting.
Not even giving him a moment's rest. What passionate hatred could
drive such a person?

"There is nobody else."

Thomas smiled at Barb. For a moment he swore he saw the ghostly
image of Jena smiling back at him. His heart ached. Had it really
been so long now? Were the wounds dug in so deep? His eyes began
to sting from the remorse of his lost commitment.

"Thomas?"

Barb gave him an endearing look he had never seen before. Their
relationship had always been mingled with professionalism. But by
allowing him to enter her home, a barrier had collapsed.

"I've got to go, Barb. But please do what I said. You're all I have left."

Thomas left Barb's home feeling like he had just left a part of himself behind. He wanted to return to simpler days. He wanted to stretch out and continue with some witty banter. Because it was true. She was all he had left. His warped notion of family deemed it so. Perhaps in an alternate reality there could have been something more between them, but not in this one. Not with this calamity.

20

ABSOLUTE AUTHORITY

Morning came and the crowded city came bustling back to life. The once muted streets clattered with activity, each person moving with purpose towards their next destination. Each blissfully unaware of how each and every one of their choices would echo on into the future. Thomas was among them. He was nearing the mysterious building he was beginning to call home. He knew what was inside; a literal universe of thought provoking options. But for now it was just a means to an end. He needed to finish the job and put an end to this prevailing misery.

He approached the plain, unmarked side door and waited. He was going to knock but knew better. They knew he was here. Looking down the alleyway, he saw a homeless man staring blankly back at him, scuffling around in a pile of garbage. Was he homeless? Was he real?

"I thought you'd never come back."

Thomas looked up to see Banks filling the doorway. He had a smirk on his face that was quickly replaced by one of concern.

"I get that a lot lately. I wouldn't be here if I didn't have to be," said Thomas pointing towards his phone.

Banks nodded and went back inside.

"A lot's happened since you decided to go roaming about the city. Don't think we don't know what happened. There are at least a hundred bodies still being dug up. You *knew* to be there; I'm not sure how, but you did. I'm not at liberty to say this openly, but screw it. You've really pissed some people off. Including me! We're supposed to be a partnership. Now, I get your suspiciousness, but look what happens. Is it really worth it?"

Thomas shrugged.

"You tell me? Has anything improved here?"

Banks stopped for a moment, allowing a few suited men to walk by. This gave him a moment to collect his thoughts.

"Roslin's on the warpath. He's being stretched thin, too much on his plate. And with his brother's absence, he's been aside himself. He claims it's of no concern to the agency. But I beg to differ. He's tearing this place down."

"So what's he doing? I can't imagine such a soulless machine could ever come completely apart."

"You'll see. Let's just say nobody's future here is secure. We picked a bad time for this to happen. Too much else is going on."

"Like what?"

Banks pursed his lips before he spoke.

"Even I can't answer that."

The two entered the large white room. They were met by Jo, who looked unapologetically disgusted by Thomas' presence.

"You look horrible. Like you've been sucked into a neogenic recombinator or something. Seriously, get some sleep."

Thomas scowled at Jo who immediately cowered behind Banks. But Banks wouldn't provide the emotional bulwark he so desired.

"We've got work to do. Thomas has been through hell."

Jo's eyes darted across the room. Both Thomas and Banks followed them, tracing a path directly to Roslin, who stood to the side like a fuming volcano. In his hands he gripped a newspaper tightly. He jutted forward and slammed it onto the table.

"What the hell is this? We agreed you could go solo to help *stop* this, not make it *worse*! We've had our men working around the clock to scrub the scene and erase any evidence linking you to us. Men we don't have the luxury of giving up to janitorial work! You better have a good reason as to why I shouldn't have my men escort you out of here right now and throw you behind bars!"

Thomas snorted in anger.

"I was solving this case! Did you think that when I started putting the pressure on, things wouldn't escalate? We're dealing with a psychopath, a brilliant, dedicated psychopath. He doesn't care who gets hurt. He only cares about winning! Sure sounds a lot like you, doesn't it?"

Banks started to interject but stopped. There was a sparkle in his eyes. Perhaps Thomas speaking up to Roslin had harmonized with something in him. The overreaching arm of Roslin seemed to touch everyone's life who was involved with him.

"You've got a serious attitude problem! I made a mistake bringing you here. You've done nothing but create more problems! I should have never—"

"Never *what*? *Tried*? You knew this was going to happen one way or another. And whether you'd like to admit it or not, you're letting this hit home. Your brother is merely another part of the equation."

"Don't you *dare* bring him up! He's got *nothing* to do with this. That's personal!"

"It has everything to do with this! This whole case is personal! Look, I get how you feel—I've lost someone—I'm sure we all have. But this isn't about that. You're brother still has a chance; he's still out there. And so are *they*—everyone that *has* suffered or *will* suffer if men like this aren't stopped. You want to know what stake I have in this? It's one I'm willing to put my life on."

Roslin threw a chair across the room and then ripped the newspaper in two. Jo darted towards his room. Roslin put two hands on the table and braced himself. He was panting like a dog, trying to contain his emotions.

"I was brought back for a reason. I don't have time to keep explaining myself. Either you can deal with the consequences or you can't. Either we do what it takes or we don't. But just realize that the more we don't trust each other and do what's necessary, the more he'll take advantage of it. He doesn't share our moral compass."

Roslin looked up at Thomas. His eyes burned like two fiery coals, but Thomas could see he was beginning to understand his point of view. People were being sacrificed now at an alarming rate. And things were only going to get worse. There was no turning back. Doing his best to regain his steadfast composure, Roslin got up and quietly left the room. He muttered only six words, but with absolute authority..

"Just do your job or else."

The exit door slammed, leaving the remaining men alone.

"Let's get things moving. I'm tired of wasting time."

Banks's eyes were still fixated on the door. He had a fierce look on his face. Had Thomas crossed the line?

"Did you hear me?"

Banks shook his head as if to clear it.

"Talk to Jo. He'll get you dialed up."

Thomas approached Jo, who was still cowering inside his futuristic room, his safe place. When Thomas entered, Jo cringed as if expecting pain.

"Relax, it's over. Big daddy has left the building," Thomas assured him calmly.

Jo squirmed around awkwardly, trying to adjust his lab coat, which was draped over a dark black shirt, embroidered with a classic rock band's logo. The image made Thomas curious. What sort of hobbies could someone who kept himself locked away in a secret facility possibly have?

"Okay, okay, about all that . . . I . . . I was going to get this going."

Jo wiped the sweat from his face that had accumulated during the tense encounter. He began tap dancing his fingers across a keyboard, pulling up an array of information and data.

"We had an event. This one has really upset the flow here."

Jo pointed towards a monitor, where there was a crisp image of waves of transcendent energy radiating from one acute point out into a much larger field.

"That looks intense. But I thought you said nothing significant could change so rapidly?"

Jo looked completely befuddled.

"It can't. But this point has upset other portions that are behaving like some sort of superimposed harmonic! The wave pattern is being amplified by natural occurrences that were already going to happen!"

"English?"

Jo sighed. How many times would he be forced to teach remedial time travel classes?

"The killer changed something that is piggybacking off of things that were going to happen anyway, therefore, amplifying the possibilities. It's brilliant!"

"Just get me back there. We're already behind."

A betrayed look came across Jo, who glanced out at Banks sitting patiently in the white room.

"He's not happy with you."

"I know, just give me the coordinates."

Jo did as he was told. His thick brimmed glasses perched precariously on his nose as he programmed the coordinates into Thomas' watch.

"And don't forget—"

"I know, I know . . . Remember? I don't forget anything," interrupted Thomas, exiting the room.

"This time when you get back, we work together. No more running around solo. We either beat this as a team or lose. Is that clear?" Banks asked tersely.

"What are you, my boss? You're talking like you own me here, which you *don't*."

Banks looked away. Thomas was proving to be too much to handle at the moment.

"Just do it. It's not your choice anymore."

Thomas ignored Banks. His mind had already revved up. As he stepped out into the middle of the room, he pressed down on the prompt to glimpse. As he did, the skewed images of Banks and Jo were slashed to bits by the powerful beams of energy. The world as he knew it slipped out of view. But would the world he knew still be there should he fail? Would the world succumb to darkness?

21

PLANES TRAINS AND AUTOMOBILES

Radiant beams of sun pelted down like a warm shower from the sky. A pleasant ambience was wrapped around the world like a warm blanket. Thomas squinted his eyes, raising one hand just above his brow to inspect his new surroundings. Blue sky, green lawns, and a plethora of suburban, cookie-cutter homes. He had never been in a place like this before. It reminded him of the old TV sitcoms with the quintessential neighborhoods he had often wished to burn down to a more acceptable state of ruin.

Where am I?

Moving forward, he felt his shoes press into the soft blades of freshly cut grass. Inexplicably, he found himself standing as if on a bed of nails on top of the time frozen blades. Despite his various glimpses into time, he still felt like a child exploring the world for the first time. Walking through the grass, he glanced at his watch. The epicenter was somewhere nearby. He swallowed a pool-ball sized lump in his throat. What if the killer was here? What if he was watching?

Keep it together . . . just keep it together, Tommy.

Taking a quick three-sixty of the area, he felt confident that he was alone, or at least confident enough to keep moving. Looking up ahead he saw more seemingly identical homes. They, much like the rest, lacked any real distinction or vivid detail.

Who lives in these places?

Down the street, he could see people out enjoying the pleasant weather, all frozen in time. A group of young kids were dashing away from a man spraying them with a garden hose. A dog leapt in midair reaching for a Frisbee that was just out of reach. Cars sat like broken down pieces of hardware in the bustling street. Conversations, smiles, smells, and all the other spectacular images had Thomas lost in wonder. He was so caught up that when his legs pressed into a forceful wave of pressured water, he barely had time to yelp.

He tumbled over, plowing head on into a tiny garden gnome that pressed back against him before ultimately falling down. At the same time, a flash of light shot through the air, leaving him still trying to regain his composure.

Dammit! Well, I hope that doesn't ruin anything!

Thomas glanced at the fallen gnome who had valiantly given up its previous place in time given the right amount of force. He had bitten a fleshy chunk of the inside of his cheek. It felt like a thousand snakes were squirming around inside of him. But how could one silly lawn ornament change anything?

Looking back at what had sent him flailing, there was a revolving sprinkler spewing out glistening streams of water. It had been a stream that he had run into. It had provided just enough resistance to knock him cleanly off his feet. Reaching down, he felt the remnants of moisture that had stuck to his pant leg.

This is ridiculous!

Shaking it off, he pressed on. He needed to be quick. The vile intent of the killer was maturing into something far more destructive than before. It was one thing to target an individual, meticulously calculating the method of their murder. But now he appeared to be being playing impulsively and wild. The detonations at the docks had claimed many lives. Taking out the lowest common denominators was just a trivial practice. Whoever the murderer was, he wanted results. Everything else was just collateral damage.

Weaving his way towards the front door of the home, he took another look at his watch. He still appeared to be going in the right direction. But something else was present, another dot. At first he panicked, not immediately understanding what it meant. But soon the details he needed to see marched out of his mental barracks. It was clear. He had changed something. The incredible piece of technology had registered it and was reporting correctly. Which means if he could see it, so could Jo. This was a recipe for trouble. Undoubtedly, he would be skewered alive when he got back. But it did bring up a couple of interesting ideas . . .

Not now, just shut up and focus on this! Please!

At the door, he rehearsed the back-breaking routine he'd need to get it open. At first it held its ground, refusing to succumb to his violent yanking. But with a few more firm pulls, he was able to wedge himself through it, allowing it to vibrate back into place. Waves of energy passed over him like a transparent flock of butterflies. It was miraculous. The inside of the house was the perfect picture of an ideal American home; spotless countertops, cheap, trendy furniture, and a warm plate of cookies, sitting front and center in the middle of the room. Seated around the snacks was a group of young adults, smiling ear-to-ear. Their pearly-white teeth shined like the keys of a new piano. All were dressed in the latest fashion, each one working hard to keep up their facades. It made Thomas sick. Looking them over quickly, he found them to be utterly useless. The sea of details around him was turning out to be nothing more than a kiddie pool.

He took a few more steps towards the kitchen. Once there, he took in every detail in the blink of an eye. Standard living equipment for the standard billboard family. Thomas could see nothing of note. But there *had* to be something. The killer was brilliant—defiantly so. He wouldn't waste his efforts on a whimsical trip to the past just for fun; especially not to visit a quaint, middle-class neighborhood like this. There *must* be something hidden here.

Continuing through the kitchen, the enticing scent of freshly baked cookies filled his head. The left-over cookies were still on a cooling rack on the counter. Thomas thought them lucky to need not suffer the mindless banter undoubtedly occurring at the living room coffee table. They looked delicious. His stomach started to groan. He was hungry. His insatiable curiosity had been trumping his physical needs. Even a freak like him needed to eat once in a while. Pausing at the rack of cookies, he let his stomach take the helm. He bent over them, letting even more of their tantalizing scent tickle his nostrils.

Well, I've already ruined the universe with a gnome, why not?

Snatching a cookie, he opened his mouth, preparing to sink his teeth into his top contender to be devoured. Unfortunately, his choppers were stopped by the resilient forces of time. But he had tasted the tiny bits that had broken free and they tasted like heaven. As he lingered over the sweet tease, he noticed something interesting. On the fridge was a calendar that had something written across the top:

Planes, Trains, and Automobiles

It appeared to be in pristine condition; a true vintage classic of a great flick.

I really liked that big guy.

He looked more closely at the calendar to inspect the dates. He knew now that dates could be critical in an investigation of the past. Aside from the year and month, there were blank boxes displaying the days, but nothing was written in them. It was completely devoid of detail. This area was worthless. He had taken nothing in that his mind marked as critical. But the plain needed to be assessed as much as the odd. Maybe the vintage calendar held some importance to its owner. A hobby or career connection? He was stymied.

Moving from the first level to the stairs leading to the second floor, he was bombarded by family photos. Each hung in an aesthetically pleasing location, with the family in matching outfits and appropriately themed backgrounds for the occasion. It was really becoming too much to bear. At this point, he felt that the entire family was either guilty of being the most perfect family ever conceived in a laboratory, or being closet, homicidal maniacs with a secret basement filled with bodies. Either way, he knew he didn't belong here.

Where are you, murderer of mine?

Sneaking a peek at his watch midway up the stairs, he saw that a few minutes had already elapsed. But aside from his alteration, nothing had happened. The center of activity was close. It could be upstairs, downstairs, or in the basement. All Thomas knew was that something needed to happen to make his glimpse worthwhile. Should the overlap fall at the end of his glimpse, this might ultimately be a pointless waste of time.

Time . . . always with the time. I hate time.

Getting to the top of the genealogical display on the stairs, he took a deep breath. Even briefly passing by the pictures had left his mind buzzing.

Mikel Parry

Mrs. Whoever, what is it with you and those damn turtle necks?

The upstairs was as scrupulously decorated and put together as the basement. Additional pictures dotted the walls alongside generic quotes about home, family, and other saccharine subjects. There were only a few rooms off the hall, with a wide open door at the end. It was that one that caught his interest. The room's placement suggested it might be used as a home office, or at least a hobby nook. The potential for juicy details was much higher in there. Never mind the extra perk, that he wouldn't have to wrestle with a belligerent door that didn't know when to quit, just to get in. If he ever saw this place again, he'd kick the front door down.

With a few quick strides, he made his way through the hall. Brief glimpses through cracked open doors divulged additional details. Two girls and one boy, or at least that's what the room's décor suggested. In one room a young boy was sprawled out on his bed, playing with some sort of gaming system that accurately resembled a grey brick. Thomas' mind pranced around, gleefully absorbing the information all around him. It felt at times as if he and his mind were actually two different, distinct life forms. Maybe in the future he could get a lobotomy. The Egyptians pulled the brain out through the nose. *Excerebration . . .* that was what it was called. But that wasn't done until after the person was already dead.

Get a grip!

Shaking his head violently to calm his overactive mind, he stepped into the room. His hypothesis just became fact. The room was an office; the type of office that someone who was afforded the luxury of working from home might have. Here was the real meat of the find. Maps of highways, railroad tracks, subway systems, and a plethora of other related items were scattered all about. It was an astounding amount of data to take in, but Thomas' brain was working in overdrive to try and make it happen.

"What is all this?"

Foraging through piles of maps and notes, he was looking for the delectable, potential trove of new info he could use to begin connecting the dots; dots that would have repercussions for years to come. He found himself impressed by what he saw—impressed by the genius like intellect of the mysterious man who was orchestrating this. The set-ups were impeccable—the execution—nearly perfect. His idealistic acclamation quickly faded to the horrible reality. Was he really going to be able to beat this monster?

He felt his thumb slide over the rigid edge of an exposed piece of paper. It nipped into his flesh, leaving a narrow slit behind. A few tiny drops of blood squeezed out before he stuck the finger into his mouth. *Still sharp.*

As he sucked on his finger, feeling the sting of his minor injury, he saw something that made his heart jump. Directly across from the desk, fastened tightly to the wall, was an enormous map of a city. The city needed no introduction. He knew it like the back of his hand; it was *his* city. Every street and tunnel was accounted for. Each purposefully labeled, showing an overall picture. So many lines going this way and that, all connecting one point A to another point B, or C, and so forth. It was a true marvel of organization and design. Like a massive spider web splattered on the wall, it loomed over everything else in the room. Encroaching on the giant tapestry of paper, he saw a few other interesting clues. Small pins with yellow string stretched over various areas of the map, perhaps pointing out the changes to future renditions of the city that he knew in the present tense. There were so many lines crisscrossing each other all over the map. It was a super-sized serving of mind clutter. Even with his unusual ability, it was exhausting. He glanced at his watch. Still nothing.

Where are you? Why here, why now?

Feeling frustrated by the deluge of what seemed to be unhelpful details, he exited the room. He decided to check for a basement when he found himself curiously drawn to the room of the small boy. The door was just ajar enough to see in, but with a few forceful jerks, it was open. He looked curiously around the room; cartoon character posters, superhero figurines, and a tiny basketball hoop dangling out from the closet. It truly was an amazing room for any child to aspire to have. He glanced at the boy, who looked far-off and indifferent. To Thomas, it was the look of pure ecstasy—to have his mind dwelling on something as pointless as a video game for hours on end—to be able to finally close his eyes and blank out. The thought alone was intoxicating enough to induce in him an emotional high.

He took a step towards the boy and clumsily plowed his foot into something on the floor. He spewed out a slew of profanity as he picked it up. Fighting rising anger, he looked down to see a large train set. It was laid out on the floor carefully. The miniatures created an almost satirical design compared to what the real world looks like. Little crops of corn suddenly transitioning to a quaint little town, with only the most necessary of buildings allowed. Happy, smiling faces on disproportional bodies stuck forever in some artist's rendition of how life should be. Then there was the train; its tiny details carefully placed with a dot of adhesive on plastic. It was stuck half way inside a slender little cave that led into a forest green mountain of plastic.

I wish I would've had one of those . . .

Feeling a bit of nostalgia, he closed his eyes. Perhaps in another life he could just spent his time playing with trains. His eyes jutted wide open as suddenly a flash of blinding light lit up the world he was standing in. He knew all too well what had just happened. He wasted no time. Scanning the room frantically, he tried to find anything that had been moved, changed, or altered. But he was coming up dry. The child's room was barren of anything of interest. Out of frustration, he gritted his teeth forcefully.

"Come on! Where is it! What have you done this time?" he growled under his breath.

Looking at his watch, he could see all of the vibrant activity animating its outputs. It looked like an electrical storm. And yet, in his own relative space in time, nothing appeared out of place. Perhaps he wasn't as talented as he had thought. Unwilling to give in, he pressed even harder. He closed his eyes and pressed a finger into each temple. He took the photograph of everything he had seen and began dismantling it down to each pixel. But still the room held nothing. That's when it hit him. He was in the wrong room! The tight space between the walls had convoluted the location. It wasn't accurate enough. But the daunting task of dismantling the room next to him was near impossible. He hadn't seen all the maps, read all the notes. Even for him it would be an impossible task. Lowering his arms, he let out a furious cry of anger.

"I can't let this happen! Not again! I'm running out of time!"

As he allowed his eyes to slowly open, he let them rest on the train set ahead of him. He felt the world muffle itself to a whisper.

He imagined the small boy playing with it. It reminded him of the half-filled balloons, streaming down sidewalks, being tugged along by the display of youth and energy he held in his memory of children from somewhere long ago. The train sticking part way into the tunnel, stuck in its place in time.

Planes, Trains, and Automobiles . . .

Without another moment's hesitation, he burst from the room, squeezing himself through the door, before sprinting into the office. Once there, he let it flow.

"Trains, automobiles, and maps . . . What does this guy *do*? It doesn't matter! All that matters is what was *done*! Come on, Tommy! Don't be so stupid!"

He bolted through the room like a streak of lightning trying to find ground. He needed to find something that had been changed. Had it had been here all along? Altering a substance like cookies had been draining. Whatever had been done, must have been minor, yet important enough to start off a catastrophe. He gazed up at the massive map on the wall.

There's so much there. Too much. I can't do this!

But deep down inside he knew he had too. The ripple in time had to be here, and in his mind it had to be the map. He closed his eyes and pushed his brain to its upper limits. It began to resonate within his skull like a humming generator. Every single detail it could possibly pull out from the cerebral synapses that were popping like fire crackers it brought forward. There was a picture of the room—the room from just moments ago in his relative space—the clutter of papers, the mess of maps, and the large city on display. It was the city he focused on. There had to be a logical reason for the map to be changed, but what was it? It had been so many years before; what possible effect could it be?

You can do this, Tommy! Come on!

A sharp river of pain crept out from his head and into his body. The pieces of string streaming across the board were being traced at breakneck speeds by his mind. Each ran to a location marked as correct by his memory. Time and time again he repeated the process feeling like the world around him was on the verge of collapse, sucking him back into its time warp.

Faster, Tommy. You don't have time for this.

The pain in his head and body was now excruciating. He pressed his mind faster and faster. His hands were clenched tightly. The slender cut bled in a trickling stream under the immense pressure. One string here, another there, another, another, a line connected, a location identified. Suddenly, he felt an immense wave of energy begin to swallow up the room whole. Time had finally run out.

No, no, not like this! Not this time!

Fragments of a past reality broke free, swirling around him like a tornado. But he continued to focus, continued to push himself past his limits. Another string, another location, a sprawl of possibilities. He felt himself begin to drift into the tremendous force of time ripping him away. The board was falling apart now; all that remained was the image in his mind. In the final moments, at the very last second, his eyes shot open and took one calculated glimpse at one very specific location. With a scream of anguish, the spiraling light and energy enveloped him. His trip to Pleasantville had come to a hellish end.

22

MANNEQUIN TORSOS

"You've got to get up!"

Thomas felt the world swirling about him in a hazy, incessant fog. He struggled to reclaim himself from the profound depths he had pushed himself into. It was so fragmented. It had all happened so fast. He felt the normal nausea that accompanied his jaunts through time. But it was being overshadowed by the uncontrollable pain that buzzed in his head. He felt completely exhausted.

"Get up, Thomas! Jo, go get help!"

The words reached Thomas's ringing ears. They seeped like molasses into his train of thought. Where was he? *When* was he?

"No, I'm alright, I can get up," he said, struggling to grapple with his shaking body.

He saw Banks standing over him with a very concerned look on his face. He remained there, examining Thomas thoroughly.

"Get him a glass of water!"

Thomas' eyes rolled to one side where he saw the perfectly white floor glaring back at him. He was beginning to loathe its presence, as it was a cruel reminder of where he was. He gazed up, watching Banks snatch a tiny, plastic cup from Jo's shaky hands. He held it out to Thomas carefully. It took some grunting for Thomas to heave himself up into a seated position on the floor. He grabbed the cup out of Banks's hands and began sipping on it gingerly.

"It's such a small cup. You think you guys could afford some bigger ones."

Banks's eyes glossed with a mixture of relief and frustration.

"What *happened* to you? You glimpsed, and then came crashing back like a bat out of hell. Jo practically fainted on the spot."

Jo's face peeked into view. He was biting his lip nervously. His glasses shifted towards the end of the runway that was his nose. They dangled loosely.

"I swear I'm never standing in this room with you guys again. Every time I do—"

"Relax, Jo. Nobody got hurt. No need to press the issue."

Jo looked upset. It was obvious he was tired of being told what to do and how to do it. He *was* the genius, after all.

"I'm not pressing anything. All I know is this guy brought in the storm of the century on the brink! I also saw two, that's dos rifts! Meaning, he changed something! That is a big fat no-no!"

Banks was poised to reprimand Jo, but then looked curiously back at Thomas, who stood up slowly.

"What's he talking about? You changed something? We went over this before. You aren't supposed to change anything."

Thomas waved a hand in the air as he crumpled up the empty glass and tossed it behind him nonchalantly.

"It was an accident. Besides, it was stupid. It doesn't matter."

"Doesn't *matter*? Doesn't *matter*? You can't go creating rifts in the very fabric of time, realigning the future in the most butterfly-effect kind of way! The unforeseen consequences could be disastrous! An assassinated leader, an event that shouldn't of happened, happens! You're a reckless freak!"

Both men looked at Jo, who was gasping for breath once his rambling ceased.

"Could you just shut up? It obviously didn't work that well, because you're still here!" said Thomas.

Banks put on a tiny sliver of a smile that he quickly shook away, doing his best to remain professional. Instead, he gave Thomas a very stern look.

"What was it? We need to know."

Thomas rolled his eyes. He looked down at his hand, which still carried the slender cut.

"A damn lawn gnome. One of those dainty, stupid lawn ornaments that people seem to like. I tripped on it and it fell over. It also pretty much broke my ankle, thank you very much."

Jo began to speak but was shushed by a finger.

"Okay, let's hope you're right. You'd be the only one that would know anyways, seeing that I and Jo were stuck back here. Let's forget that and cut to the chase. What did you find?"

Thomas blinked his eyes slowly. The pain was just beginning to diminish. His brain felt like a sloppy pile of dough.

"I know where to start. He changed a reference point."

"A reference point?" asked Banks, looking decidedly underwhelmed.

"A line on a map—a location—whatever you want to call it. The guy had the layout of this entire city. Some sort of planner or construction guy probably, I don't know. All I know is one of the lines changed. I saw it. But I'm not entirely sure what it means."

"Could you repeat that? It kind of sounded like you were a little off!"

Thomas ignored Banks who had shed his professionalism for the time being.

"I mean, I know where it is, but . . ." Thomas stared at Jo, who immediately leapt out of his sight.

Planes, Trains, and Automobiles . . .

"Planes, trains, and automobiles—that's got to be it."

Banks shook his head.

"What are you talking about?"

"Can you get me a map of the city?"

Banks snapped his fingers at Jo, who quickly fetched a slender tablet device. His fingers danced over the screen before he shoved it into Thomas' hands.

"There, what do you have?"

Thomas' eyes rattled back and forth as he swooped in and out on the massive city sprawl. Then, in pure elation, he spotted the exact location he had burned in his memory. Without warning, he headed for the door.

"Where are you going? We agreed no more solo trips!"

Thomas paused. He was so caught up in the chase, he'd forgotten the obvious—the target—the events cascading into the present from the past, with a dreadful purpose.

"Where are the other agents?"

Banks cringed at the mention of the word *agents.*

"You mean us and the one other? That's what we're down to."

Thomas felt sick to his stomach. They were dropping like flies. After his last experience in the pit of blood, he no longer felt the security net of protection he once had.

"Where is he? The last one besides us?"

"I don't know. I'd have to make some calls."

"Do it, *now!* We need to get there! He's in a lot of danger."

Banks pulled out his phone and began dialing.

"Is that psycho coming here?" questioned Jo, looking frantic.

Thomas shrugged.

"He doesn't have to. He, or whoever it is, can get into anywhere. For all we know, he's already here."

Jo looked as pale as a ghost. As was routine, he retreated back to his blinking room of lights and shut the door.

What a closet freak.

"He's at a safe house located on the east side of town. He's being watched as we speak."

Thomas swallowed a burning pool of acid that had pooled in his throat from the anxiety. He tried to think calmly and clearly. How would he do it? How could he do it?

"Let's get to him."

"And then what? We've got to have a plan or something. I haven't forgotten what happened last time we went all wild-west."

"It doesn't matter. The longer we wait the worse it becomes. I suggest we forgo the pointless arguing and just get moving."

Banks looked exhausted but agreed. He was slightly reluctant. It didn't take long for them to exit the building. They'd left in a blur of motion, leaving a few dumbfounded agents behind. Something else was troubling Thomas. Where was Roslin? For having Thomas on such a tight leash, the man was surprisingly off the radar. It wasn't like him to just disappear, leaving his precious program in the hands of those he deemed less worthy. Who knew what the man was hiding?

"You're sure he's there?" probed Thomas, looking at Banks, who was weaving the car through the busy, street.

"Positive. He's been there since the last incident."

Mannequin Torsos

Thomas' guts shifted to one side as Banks screeched around a street corner. A few muffled cries of anger rattled through the windows from some onlookers.

"Why is he doing this? Why destroy an organization created to protect? We've only been doing our jobs!" declared Banks, letting his foot press down even harder on the gas pedal.

Thomas gulped as the sudden forward motion forced him to sharply suck in a mouthful of air.

"It's not about us. He's after all of it. I don't understand his motives or why he's doing it, and frankly, I don't care. All I know is these murders are painting a picture we just aren't seeing. Roslin's brother being gone, numerous casualties, explosions, fire, wrecks; the killer's been rattled. It's only going to get worse."

Banks looked disturbed by the comment. His fingers clenched the wheel of the car tightly. He glanced down at the needle measuring his RPM's and saw it deep in the red. His frustration and anger was almost palpable. Suddenly, the car began to decelerate. It caught Thomas off guard, as he had been securely fixed in thought.

"What the hell is this? You've got to be kidding me!" stammered Banks slamming his hands into the steering wheel.

Ahead of the car was a scene of absolute chaos. A fire truck blocked the road, with a large crowd amassing at its perimeter. All stared at what appeared to be an overturned semi-truck. A few flickering fires could be seen around its edges dancing playfully. The truck's contents had spewed out onto the street like litter. Shattered glass and debris joined the array of random objects, further complicating the deciphering of the collage of clutter.

"This is unreal! What are we supposed to do now?"

"How far away are we?"

Banks pulled out his phone and fumbled around.

"Less than a quarter of a mile—just a short jog from here—in that building." Thomas swung the car door open and sprinted down the sidewalk. He couldn't be stopped now. A man's life could very well be at stake. *His* life might be at stake. Nothing was sure anymore. Anyone could be on the verge of an untimely demise. The only thing to do was to keep moving. It was always harder to hit a moving target; even harder if the target behaved erratically. If he couldn't outwit the murderous chess game wizard, he would out stupid him. Continue behaving stupidly, doing reckless things to press his own advantage? The mere idea of it was madness. From behind him, he heard Banks slam the door in anger.

"I thought we agreed no more running off."

Thomas ignored his plea. He kept moving. Once he arrived at the outskirts of the accident scene, he was stopped by a wall of bustling bodies. He leapt up into the air to get a better view. He needed to get closer. Pushing people aside, he began forcing his way through. A few people felt his urgency was insulting and lashed out at him verbally as he pressed his way through.

Just shut up and let me do my job, people!

At the front of the crowds he could finally see it all perfectly. All around the overturned semi were mannequin torsos strewn about. A few had been ignited on fire, some were already smoldering into ash. The truck itself had been vacated when the emergency response team had snatched the barely living driver from the clutches of disaster. Gasps of terror could be heard throughout the swaying crowd. Had he been too late? He looked across the street, past the barrier of legal enforcement, and saw an antique store. He recoiled at what he saw—a garden gnome—one that eerily resembled the piece of lawn decor he had hammered with his body. For a moment he felt a shrill sensation of fear tingle through him. But his logical brain stomped it into oblivion.

That's impossible. You're being a complete idiot. They made millions of those things.

Looking past the disaster area, he eyed the building that Banks had pointed to. It, like all of the organization's buildings, was completely innocuous; just another old, run-down, ragged piece of construction. But, as always, it was what was on the inside that counted. He looked back again at the crash scene. Was it truly coincidental? Or was it a part of the pot he kept stirring, trying to find the right action to bring the real threat out of hiding. He didn't have the luxury of time.

"What do you think you're doing? You can't just jet off like that, leaving me stuck in traffic!"

Thomas turned to look at Banks, who was practically jumping out of his shoes in anger.

"Look, I don't have time to apologize. We have to move. This thing works fast. We waste any time, any time at all, we lose. Simple."

"So what the hell did you want me to do? Leave a car in the middle of the street that shouldn't exist? Does that sound like a good idea?"

Thomas couldn't believe what he was hearing. There they had a man's life at stake and Banks was rambling on about the car.

"You take care of the car! I'll meet you inside!"

"You don't tell me what to do!"

Thomas clenched one of his fists tightly. At times, he wanted to smack Banks across the face, wiping his undeserving sense of authority away.

"Fine, but let's get going!"

"This is on you if anything goes wrong. This isn't how we do things!"

"Isn't it always on me?"

Both men stewed in a silent rage. Their game of pride had reached a stalemate. Neither was going to back down. But they needed to keep it together, at least for now. Thomas led the way, plowing through more onlookers as they circumvented the accident towards their destination. All the faces they passed were logged away along, with as many details as Thomas' mind could capture. Everyone, at this point, was guilty until proven innocent. *Everyone.* Was any of it connected?

"It's right there around the corner, in the alley."

The pair passed a donut shop and a decrepit looking laundromat before coming to a screeching halt in front of an unremarkable door leading into a tall, skinny building.

"What is it with you people and alleyway doors? Can't you get something better?"

Banks shot Thomas an extreme look of annoyance.

"You got a better way to hide things in the middle of everything, that's financially sound? I'd love to hear it."

Banks glanced at the door and produced a badge that glinted with reflected light. He held it up in the air. With a loud crank and a snap, the door slowly opened. A few men with guns watched them closely. One of the men ran a scanner over each of their faces before stepping aside. Thomas and Banks stepped inside, just as the thick metal door slammed shut behind them. Large bars slid across it, making it a literal wall of metal.

This is more like it.

Thomas looked at Banks, who pointed.

"Up this way. He should be in one of those rooms. We'll find out which one."

They approached a desk where more suited men were standing. Banks flashed his credentials again before spelling out his demands.

"I called ahead. Where is he?"

A woman behind the desk looked both of them over carefully. Her eyes closed into slivers of suspicion as she checked them out before answering.

"He's on the second floor."

Banks nodded then immediately moved away from the desk. Thomas followed closely, doing his best to dodge the incredulous looks he was getting. Continuing up the stairs, they arrived at yet another level of secrecy.

What is it with these people?

But in truth, each one of the agents, staff, bystanders, and even Roslin himself, at this point, were possible suspects. They had been gutted open from the inside out. No one was innocent anymore.

"He's just up around the corner."

Thomas lifted his eyes rapidly to see even more black suited men standing guard outside another impervious door. One of the men stepped out to stop them. Banks looked flustered by all the dramatic distrust he felt he was receiving. This was *his* organization; or so he once thought. Things were definitely changing.

"Seriously, how many times do we have to flash a badge around here?" said Banks, showing his credentials again.

The man reluctantly stepped to the side to let Banks and Thomas enter through the door. It closed behind them with a cavernous whoosh of air. Inside, was a large room filled with every living accommodation imaginable; a windowless prison in the most opulent sense. In the center of the room sat the agent. His eyes looked glazed, almost as if he was looking right through them.

"Agent DeMarques?"

The man looked up slowly. He looked worn and ragged; his complexion pale; his demeanor, one of defeat.

"What do you want, Banks?"

Mannequin Torsos

The clear tone of his voice reflected his obvious state of hopeless. "You know why we're here. Things are getting worse. Outside it's anarchy. And they've got you set up in the suite? How long were you going to hide in here?"

Agent DeMarques got off the couch he had been slouching on, his postures firmly aggressive.

"Just can it, Banks! I've watched my last two partners on this program die! No funeral, no records, just gone. So I'm done playing the part of bait. He'd get me just like he's going to get you! We're losing this!"

Thomas glanced at Banks, who wore a look of understanding. *But who's he, who is this killer really?*

"Fine, let's drop it. What can you tell me?"

DeMarques shook his head. He began pacing around the room.

"Nothing, I've got nothing. We've been tracking, glimpsing, just like you. But the occurrences have increased, the disruptions, greater. It's a joke. We don't have the man power for this; we never did. And still no one has found the leak. But we're all that's left, aren't we? I mean, damn, this is it. If it's not me or you, then who?"

Banks's eyes were filled with sympathy. The remarks were impacting him greatly.

"I don't know either. This whole thing is just one big cluster. We've never been this disorganized. Roslin is on a rampage back at home. The whole program is in jeopardy."

"Forget the program! We're all in jeopardy. Don't you get who you sound like right now? You're a clone of him; *Roslin*. Screw him and this program! We're supposed to be watchers, protectors, not street warriors running for our lives!"

Thomas watched as at the mere mention of Roslin's name, Banks's demeanor shifted to one of resolute anger.

"Look—I don't see eye-to-eye with Roslin either. But we have rules and systems for a reason. They keep us all in check. Without them, it's pure anarchy."

"But anarchy is the name of the game now, isn't it?" interjected Thomas.

Both Banks and DeMarques paused their ongoing argument to stare at the strange oddity that was Thomas. Feeling his head begin to swelter from the pressure beneath his hat, he removed it for a moment, letting it dangle from just two fingers.

"Well, isn't it? Look at us? We're being herded like cattle to the slaughter. Each time we do what's expected. We follow the rules, the stupid processes, and for what? To end up crammed in some safe house like a dog stuck in his kennel. The anarchy is calculated. It creates the logical end result that we don't see, and then we die. In each case, we die. That's all that matters to him; one game piece at a time until the board is clear."

"Forgive me if I'm not impressed, but tell me something we *don't* know," responded DeMarques, crossing his arms defiantly.

"I know that instead of having one agent in one place, we now have three. That seems as good a time as any to whack us."

Banks and DeMarques caught each other's eyes. They appeared to be looking to each other for some unspoken affirmation that what Thomas suggested was pure lunacy. They were safe here.

"Look, buddy—I know you're Roslin's new toy—for *now*. But this place is one of our secure safe houses. Nobody's getting in here," continued DeMarques.

Just then, a deafening thunder rumbled from somewhere outside. It seemed to reach beneath the building, vibrating its very foundation.

"What was that?" yelled Banks.

Without thought, Thomas burst free from the room. In the hallway, a few men were struggling to get back up to their feet, the shock wave having knocked them to the ground. Then he heard the horrific screams. Outside, the amassed crowd was falling into madness. In a few gigantic bounds fueled by adrenaline, Thomas found a window and looked outside. The street below had cracked from the immense pressure that had swelled from somewhere underground. People were scattering like roaches under a spotlight, each trying desperately to distance themselves. The crack extended past the fallen semi to directly under the building itself.

Thomas ran as fast as his legs could carry him down the stairs, leaving Banks and DeMarques behind. He reached the bottom floor, shoving his way past the armed, black-suited sentries heading towards the door. Sternly, they put a halt to his progress. A strong arm blocked him from the exit.

Mannequin Torsos

"Nobody goes in or out until we know what happened!" barked the man blocking his path.

Thomas wanted to rip his head off. But it wasn't over. In the street they heard the blaring horn of another out of control semi. It came blazing down one of the side streets, heading directly towards the safe house. People jumped out of its way as fast as they could, leaving a floor of bodies in its wake. The driver jumped free from the car moments before it collided with the building.

Thomas barely had time to react. It came so fast it seemed surreal. The incredible force blasted its way through one of the nearby walls, propelling him through the air like a rag doll. He watched helplessly as one of the agents was torn to shreds by the catapulted debris. Tiny pieces of shrapnel raked his exposed flesh, leaving little crimson pools blossoming on his flesh. Then, with a mind-numbing thud, he hit the ground. His ears were ringing like church bells. Everything seemed to be passing by frame by excruciating frame. The pain-filled screams, the waves of fire, and the scattered debris was a horror movie. The once impenetrable safe house sat ravaged and wide open.

He tried to put his legs underneath him. Was he paralyzed, injured, dying? He needed to know, so he needed to move. It felt like he was made of rubber. Each time he tried to upright and balance himself, he would collapse back to the ground out of breath. He saw a stream of blood and sweat mix together and drip on the floor. Taking in one last, gasping, gulp of air, he let out a tortuous bellow of agony. He could feel his wounds begging him to give up, lie down, and wait to die. But he knew better.

"Thomas! Thomas! Are you alright?"

He turned to see Banks running toward him at top speed. His eyes looked wild and scared. Once at Thomas' side, he helped him to brace himself up.

"I'm fine, just seriously rattled."

A small explosion erupted next to them, where the semi had come to a rest on its side. The sounds of sirens echoing in the distance were closing in fast.

"We need to get out of here. Where's DeMarques?"

Banks gestured with his head.

"He's upstairs. I've got to make some calls, this is bad!"

Thomas cringed in pain. His body felt like the wreck that had nearly engulfed him. The semis, the explosion, the correlations between events, the lines connecting the dots; this had just been a distraction; a distraction that had successfully left one Agent DeMarques alone in the middle of absolute destruction. Scampering up the stairs, still feeling woozy and disjointed, he arrived at the room's door. A few of the armed men remained.

"Where is he? Where is Agent DeMarques?"

Both men abruptly looked behind them before one responded.

"He's inside. Nobody's come in or out. We'll be evacuating soon."

Thomas shoved the man aside and entered the room. Aside from a few jostled items, it appeared to be stable. But there was only one problem—no Agent DeMarques.

"Where is he? He's gone!"

The men outside the door burst into the room, guns drawn. They looked completely befuddled. How could something be missing from a safe room?

This isn't happening.

Grabbing his head, Thomas let his frustration out. This was pure madness. This finely crafted attack had ripped the world he knew apart. Where could DeMarques be? He had to be close. He'd *just* been here. Leaving the other agents, he ransacked the room for clues. That's when he saw it—the bathroom—the only room that firmly dictated the need for privacy. He punched through the door, crunching shattered glass beneath his feet. Looking inside, a sudden sense of terror surged through him. A gaping hole had been blasted open just beneath where the bathtub had been. Broken water lines spewed water into the air like a kid's water park gone mad.

This can't be happening . . .

The hole was adequate to fit a man through; or perhaps, to force one through. He looked behind, not wanting to be followed. He was tired of being stalled by slower mentalities. But at the same time, a gruesome death could be awaiting him in the dark. Still no sign of Banks. Undoubtedly, he was busy calling in the clean-up crew. Roslin wasn't going to be happy, wherever he was. Guilt prickled at Thomas' mind like a tiny cactus. But he still couldn't peg it on anyone. He needed more. Taking one last look behind him, he plunged down the hole, gripping the slippery pipes with all his might.

Streams of water rushed down his face, blurring his vision. He was in a wall space; a wall space that had been carefully sought out to gain access to a multitude of safe rooms. Like the filthy rat that he was, the murderer had gained access using the chaos as his malfeasant distraction. He had timed it perfectly. How long had he been waiting in the walls for his beautifully crafted work to eviscerate the world within them? Had he been listening to everything they said?

I'm going to kill you.

A darkness swept into Thomas' heart that grew in intensity as he struggled on. He hated this man. He hated what he was doing and how he was doing it. But more than anything, he hated that he was losing. *He* was supposed to be the *freak*. *He* was supposed to *win*. The repugnant smell of sewage suddenly hit his nostrils as he went deeper. Just where the pipes led? He had no idea. The air was thick now. It was getting so dark that even his own hands disappeared in front of him. His progress was painstakingly slow, but with a squishy splash he suddenly hit the bottom.

His arms were screaming under the exhaustion, his body threatening to soon follow. The intensity would not cease. He could feel his own mortality beginning to fade, taking over his consciousness, unsure of how much more it could take. Then he heard it; a muffled cry from someone hidden in the darkness. Blinking his eyes rapidly, he tried to adjust them to the low light. It wasn't much, but he was able to see a tiny speck of light. Like a firefly, it moved about rapidly, swooping this way and that. Had Thomas finally found him?

"Stop! You have no idea what you're doing!"

Thomas's scream echoed off the cement walls. The light ahead paused for just a moment before quickening. The muffled cries of someone being dragged further intensified. Forgetting his own pain, Thomas sloshed through the water. Sewage tunnels, drainage tunnels, and an array of other shafts poked through the walls. He was pushing his way through the dark underbelly of the city. Thomas pulled his phone from his pocket. He began waving it around in the air like a torch. The miniscule amount of light helped guide him through the foul world he was traversing.

He was panting like a dog. His sides ached from the exertion. But he was closing in on whoever it was that had orchestrated this nightmare. The pain was becoming more and more unbearable. He needed to catch the madman before he succumbed.

"What do you want? What are you gaining?"

The bobbing light was growing larger. It appeared to be a tiny flashlight, being held by a black glove. Thomas strained his eyes to try and see who he was following. But the dark shadows skewed the image beyond recognition. What *was* clear is that they were pulling a body through the tunnel. It sloshed in the filthy water as they moved.

"Why don't you at least have the courage to face me? You're a coward, hiding in the shadows!"

The light stopped. It was not far now. Pushing past his own limits, Thomas got within a stone's throw of the mad lunatic he had been pursuing for so long. He finally saw him. The same lifeless, dark mask he had seen in the pit. His eyes receded into its depths. This was the monster who would forever darken his thoughts. At the man's feet sat the incapacitated DeMarques. He appeared to have been medicated, legs battered. His eyes were rolled back in his head. His chest gradually rose then collapsed; he was still alive.

"Leave him. He doesn't need to die! You can stop this!"

The man put away the flashlight and pulled out a slender, silver revolver. He pressed it carefully into DeMarques' temple. The groggy, faded look in DeMarques' eyes still registered a tinge of horror.

"Don't do it. He's done *nothing* to you. I won't let you do this!"

Thomas reached inside his coat and pulled out his gun. He hoisted it into view, carefully aiming it directly between the eyes of evil incarnate.

"I'll kill you if I have to!"

Silence. Whoever the man was, he was holding steadfast to his unwillingness to be heard. A moment passed. All that could be heard was their breathing. The tension in the room was suffocating. Thomas' finger twitched over the trigger of his gun. Sweat was pouring into his eyes with a painful sting. Neither man moved. What was going to happen? Did he truly have it in him to take a life?

Please, just put the gun down!

Thomas took one brave step forward. The man's arm tensed, plunging the revolver even deeper into the exposed temple of

Mannequin Torsos

DeMarques. Thomas stopped mid step. He wasn't willing to risk it. But if he didn't, he'd lose what he so desperately wanted; to catch that lunatic. If he didn't, the hell would continue and more people would die. What was one agent's life when stacked against the potential future loss of life? Was his one life worth that much?

"Last warning! Put the gun down or I shoot!"

The darkness of the tunnel was creeping into Thomas' soul. Death's icy clutches were reaching for him, ready to show him the way. His finger pressed slightly in on the trigger. The hammer of his gun jerked back slightly. At the edge of insanity, just as his finger was ready to pull, a horrendous crash of thunder roared through the tunnel. An out-of-control subway train surged through a thick slab of concrete wall spewing shards of debris. It jettisoned out into the tunnel, screeching wildly beneath the unimaginable force. Sparks spewed from the sides of the locomotive as it continued crashing down another tunnel towards its demise, cutting a perfect path between Thomas and the dark evil he was pursuing. The shock wave threw Thomas to the ground. He felt his body seize up. Pain washed over him, threatening to steal his consciousness. Trying desperately to get back up, he watched as the tail end of the train passed, thundering forward down the old track. The man was gone. Left behind was the lifeless body Agent DeMarques. His sluggish look had been replaced by a wide-eyed, last glimpse of life mask, compliments of a bullet to the head.

Tears filled Thomas' eyes. He threw his head back and let out a deafening scream of anguish. As his head dropped back down in exhaustion, his eyes caught a tiny, flimsy, piece of evidence uneventfully left by its owner. A card, just as before—three triangles linked in the center—the symbolic creed of a secretive world locked away beneath deception and lies. The world around him began to fade into darkness. His fate was left to the depths of an abandoned tunnel, brimming with nothingness. He had failed.

23

BURN BRIDGES

The gurney shook wildly as it was being pushed frantically down a hospital hallway. A small team of nurses crowded around, all trying to work on the body and run at the same time. The wheels of the gurney squeaked with their effort.

"He's got some bleeding but nothing major," said one of the nurses.

"Buddy, can you wake up for me?" said another, waving a hand back and forth.

Once reaching a room, they carefully hoisted the body off the gurney into a hospital bed. They immediately sped off, leaving the body with a nurse who had remained behind. The remaining nurse carefully jotted down the health information that had been gathered, and then left.

Thomas' eyes felt like two large bags of sand. His body ached, his mind was scattered, and his whereabouts unknown. He gulped down two soggy mouthfuls of air in an attempt to clear his head. Each time he tried to open his eyes, the blurred image of the masked killer would leap at him from the darkness. His heart raced madly. It all seemed so unreal. Everything was just one big nightmare. Letting out a rough grunt of pain, he awoke suddenly. His eyes opened and he instantly began taking in the world around him. He was obviously in a hospital, but as to which hospital where, he had no idea. The smell of medications, cleaners, and the crisp linen sheets made him feel nauseated. He needed to get out. Without thinking, he tried to sit up. He felt each and every cut and bruise buzz with horrible pain. Now in a seated position, he could see the entire room, and he wasn't alone. Standing near the door were two men and a woman, standing close together. They were staring at him with deep concern.

"As I live and breathe, I thought that boy was a goner."

"Thomas, are you okay?"

The voices required no introduction. The first belonged to Pete, who was dabbing at his sweaty, bulbous face with a handkerchief

Another voice was a very much needed and pleasant surprise— Barb. She was standing a few steps from Pete, arms crossed. Her face said it all; she was beside herself with worry. And then there was Vaun; his face looked relieved but with a slight edge of anger. Perhaps he had been dragged along. In Thomas' mind, he fought hard to try and convey his thoughts. There were so many things spinning wildly about in his head, it seemed impossible to calm it down. As he tried to speak, a glob of saliva dribbled from his mouth where it had pooled while he had been unconscious.

"I'm alright. I mean, I'm a complete wreck, but alright."

"Still babbles like a baby," laughed Vaun, walking up to the hospital bed.

"Thomas, where have you been? Vaun says he spotted you being dragged out of that horrible disaster like a corpse!"

Thomas glanced at Vaun, whose eyes remained locked on to Thomas.

"Vaun, you guys *know* each other?"

"We've made our introductions. We've had a few hours playing babysitter together here," said Vaun, winking at Barb.

The way Vaun looked at Barb made Thomas suddenly defensive.

"Just the wrong place, wrong time, I guess. Just lucky to be alive."

"Tommy, I'd be doing you a disservice if I didn't just tell it to you like it is. You stink son, you stink *bad*. And I'm not talking about the sewage water you apparently were neck deep in. You don't think I've got a nose for BS? Tommy, I practically wrote the book. Why don't you just start telling the truth, and maybe we could help you," said Pete.

"He's got a point. Let's face it, we're all you've got," added Vaun, looking at Pete for back-up.

Barb immediately cleared her throat to make her presence known.

"He's right, Thomas. When I saw what happened on the news,

I just somehow knew you'd be involved again. That's *two* major disasters that you were just *coincidentally* involved in. Thomas, you can't expect me to believe these things aren't related. A lot of people have died!"

Barb turned away to hide the flush reddening her cheeks.

"Would you all stop crowding me? I've barely woken up and I'm already being interrogated. I don't need to answer to anyone as to where I've been or what I've been doing!"

"Tommy, you're going down a dangerous road. You ain't gonna like where it takes you," said Pete.

Thomas could feel his anger surging up and down. Why was he so angry? What was happening to him? Overwhelmed, he felt like he needed to get some air.

"Look, I've just been through a lot lately. I'm working out some serious personal issues and just need some space. I promise . . . I'll be fine.

"I told you he'd do this, didn't I? You just keep doing this, Tommy. We're supposed to be a team, but all you are is some shooting star, blasting your way through the universe before disappearing again, like nothing ever happened. What a joke," blasted Vaun, pointing a finger at Thomas.

"Vaun, I'm done explaining things to you! I don't owe you anything!"

Vaun clenched his fists and took a step toward the bed. He was easily stopped short by Pete.

"That's enough boys. This ain't some fight club therapy, alright? We're not in our right heads."

Pete turned around slowly and gave Thomas a sympathetic look.

"Tommy, we've just been through hell and high water running around town, cleaning up messes. It's by an angel's sweet grace that we only have to deal with what falls on our table.. We came down here to check on one of our own. But to be frank, Tommy, you ain't seeing it that way. You're treating us like we're the enemy here," said Pete.

Maybe you are . . .

Thomas felt defeated. He let out a long, drawn out sigh before attempting to gather his high-strung emotions.

"Alright, alright, Pete . . . I get it.

"Could I get some time with him, alone?" Barb asked suddenly.

Pete looked at Vaun, who threw his hands up in the air while walking out the door.

"I'm done with this. Just keep lying, Thomas. What a joke."

As Vaun left the room, Pete said one last thing before following him.

"You best get that head screwed on right, Tommy. You're burning some serious bridges here."

Thomas felt a part of him yearn to just let it all out. Let all of his secrets and lies shower down on Pete like acid rain. But he couldn't; he wouldn't. He couldn't risk it. He'd already said too much to Barb, who he feared was high risk now. He couldn't drag anyone else into his filthy mess. As the door to the room shut, his view was filled with nothing but Barb's lovely, but concerned, face.

"Thomas, what is happening to you? I've thought long and hard about what you told me last time. But it doesn't make any sense. Thomas . . . you sound like a raving lunatic. I've known you a long time, and I know you can be . . . eccentric. But lately . . ."

Thomas threw his legs to one side of the bed. He realized he was still wearing his scuffed up suit. His shoes lay at the side of the bed, one neatly next to the other.

"I'm a freak, Barb; plain and simple. I wasn't lying. All of it's true and it's getting worse—the explosion at the docks—the semis at the building. I was there trying to stop it. But then, it just happens again. Over and over, and I lose every single time. No matter how fast I move, he's faster."

"Who's he?"

Thomas slid his shoes on and tried to stand up. A few of his bones sang out a melody of juicy cracks under the pressure.

"The killer. And I don't know who he is. I have a truck load of details—clues—and no idea what they mean."

Thomas peeked down at his watch. He was greatly relieved that it was still there. The last time it hadn't been.

"I'm just completely losing it. This city, the world, it's on fire. I swear, every day it's getting worse. And then to see you like this . . . I can't keep doing this," said Barb, looking away.

Thomas searched for the words to say. His logical self had no place here. This was in the realm of emotion. For him it was like being thrown into water without knowing how to swim; he was doing his best just to stay afloat.

"Maybe it is getting worse. I don't know, and I don't care. Maybe you and I are both losing it. To be honest, I don't know what to believe anymore. But I know you, Barb. If you can put up with my pointless rants for hours on end, you can do this."

"What exactly do you mean?" questioned Barb.

"Maybe I need your help. I'm good at what I do, really good. But I lack the common skill set that most people have."

"And what's that?"

"Understanding people—understanding their motives, reasons, and purpose—until now, I've never cared. But you made me think about it the last time we spoke. Maybe it's not just the details, but the overall purpose that's *tied* to those details, that keeps eluding me. Each time I fail, I come right back to where I started; literally, this time. But sooner or later my luck is going to run out or the game is going to end."

Barb nodded her head slowly. She was debating the absolute absurdity of everything Thomas had told her. But she cared for him. In what shape and form, she still wasn't sure. But he was near and dear to her, nonetheless. But by entertaining his story, she was forsaking her own affirmation to never become one of her patients. Was she really that crazy?

"I'll help you, Thomas, but I refuse to get involved with any of this time travel hocus-pocus you keep blabbing about."

Thomas started to laugh but cut it short, feeling his injuries begin to scream with pain. Barb saw him cringe and frowned.

"Thomas, you need to rest up. You look terrible."

Thomas shook his head.

"Can't rest, Barb. Too much going on right now. I saw him—the killer—twice. He wears some sort of dark mask. Never seen one like it. Always hiding in the shadows."

Barb narrowed her eyes as she thought out loud.

"What else?"

"He keeps showing me cards with a symbol on them. A symbol I've seen before; in the organization that dragged me into all this. He's targeting the men in the organization. It's like he's one of them, and yet he wants them dead. The only problem is that there's no one left. Then at the docks he killed people that had nothing to do with any of this. It's like one moment he's focused and tuned in, and the next he's shotgunning everything in his path."

"Maybe he's confused. Many people behave irrationally when they have mixed emotions. Maybe a part of him embraces whatever he sees as his reason for doing all this. But there's another part, albeit a teeny tiny part, that doesn't. Guilt can create rage, which in turn repeats the guilt process; a vicious cycle. Would explain why things keep escalating."

Thomas walked through Barb's carefully crafted response. Her wit was as sharp as ever. He started to respond but she cut him off.

"The real question is what drove him to this? There has to be something you've missed."

Thomas felt his mind flash through all the details stored there. But there were still too many loose ends. At the precise moment he tried to respond, the door to the room opened. Outside stood a few men in dark suits; they stood aside as both Roslin and Banks walked between them. Roslin pointed at Barb.

"She goes. *Now.*"

Barb began to protest but was interrupted by Thomas.

"He's right, Barb. I'll see you as soon as I get the chance."

From Thomas' tone alone, Barb knew he meant it. Their discussion would have to wait. Before she left, she leaned over and kissed his forehead, and then stared him in the eyes.

"You know where to find me."

She reluctantly left, scowling at the men who crowded the doorway. As soon as she was gone, Roslin shut the door, leaving him alone with Banks and Thomas.

"What the hell is going on? I've got another catastrophe on my hands, the cops are crawling down my neck, and I'm dealing with massive clean ups. We've lost another agent *and* some bystanders. All *that* just for you to end up back in the hospital? Let me repeat; what the hell is going on?"

Roslin's self-discipline had wilted away to reveal the thundering mountain he was now. He wanted answers. He wanted results. But to Thomas, his behavior was exaggerated. It appeared that Roslin's firm grasp on things was quickly coming undone.

"I was trying to stop it! I almost had him. He was as close as he's ever been."

Thomas recalled everything; the underground explosion, the semi crashes, and the out-of-control subway train. It was beyond belief. The tempo was beating faster and faster.

"But you didn't! Damn it, you didn't! *Again*! We've spent an astronomical amount of our resources and time here. We have too many things on our plate to be focusing on this. You need to solve this or—"

"Or *what*? You shut the program down? We've already been down this road. I'm close—so close now—and the killer knows it. He's squirming, trying to get out. He's getting sloppy. We've got to ride this to the end, or get out now. I'm sorry he's got your brother; I'm sorry that innocent people keep dying. But I'm doing everything I can here. I'll either beat this maniac or die trying."

Roslin took a deep breath. The normally huge gap between his professional life and personal life had grown very narrow. He was letting his very human side continue to ooze out. He was breaking down.

"Jo's got an event triggered. But this time it's different," Banks said, breaking up the argument for the moment.

Thomas felt sick. Was there no mercy? How much longer could this possibly go on? Did the world he knew have to burn to the ground before this would end? Roslin nodded slowly. He looked down at his watch and then at Banks. With an accompanying flash of black suits, he was gone.

Banks approached Thomas cautiously.

"You alright? I can't believe you survived that."

Thomas looked around the room. Instinctively, he was looking for his hat. It somehow brought him comfort. He looked at Banks; the quirky fedora was clenched tightly in his right hand. Banks saw Thomas' eyes fixate on it and offered it to him warmly.

"Oh, your hat. Thought you might want it."

Thomas snatched it out of Banks's hands.

"He was *right* there."

Banks listened closely and then paused to examine what Thomas had said.

"Look, you can only move forward. Roslin's falling apart, there's no doubt about it. His cage has been rattled. We're all that's left and he knows it. And like it or not, you're a part of this. If the project burns to the ground, you'll go down with it."

"Why does he keep showing me the same card? He's done it twice now. What is he telling me?"

Banks looked perplexed by Thomas' aimless comment.

"What are you talking about?"

Thomas looked at the hat he was holding. It looked battle worn now. And yet, it still maintained its overall shape.

"Secrets—this organization is full of them, isn't it?"

"Everybody's got their secrets. This is no different."

"There's a lot more here than *normal* secret organization stuff going on. Who would want to see this all come crumbling down? Who would want to see Roslin six feet under?"

Banks shrugged.

"Besides *everybody*? We piss a lot of people off around here. Granted, we're ghosts, but even then, bound to step on some toes somewhere."

"What about internally? A leak, some loose end, a disgruntled past employee?"

"If you haven't noticed, the selection process around here is extremely stringent. If you as so much as hiccup a bit of doubt, they're not opposed to canning you. Most of us are here because we have no connection to the real world. Why do you think they wanted a freak like you? You're the perfect candidate . . . aside from your knack for destroying things."

Thomas let the words sink in slowly. Banks was right. Having a mole was possible but improbable. Especially a mole who had such intimate knowledge of the program. But that's how things were now; perhaps the past was different and held something darker. Maybe he'd been focusing on the wrong time and place. He decided he needed to start playing with time on *his* terms.

"We should get going. Jo's probably already wet himself in anticipation. Guy seems to struggle with containing his emotions."

Banks put on a sliver of a smile.

"Yeah, but he's a good guy. Just all brains and no logic. Ya gotta feel for him though, locked up in there like Roslin's little lab rat."

Thomas put his battered hat back on top of his head. He was going to keep fighting. His body ached, his mind felt torn, but he wasn't going to give in. Even if it killed him.

24

SINGULARITY

The drive over was silent. Neither Banks nor Thomas spoke a word. Whatever was going on in their heads was being carefully protected. Thomas was swimming through the darkness that filled his mind. It was chaos. The images of the people who had been lost so far whirled around and around through his mind like a carousel. Even Banks still made a part of him feel a little suspicious. The organization, Roslin, Banks—none of them could whitewash the filth away—so many questions, so many doubts.

Arriving at the organization's main building, both men rehearsed the routine as best they could. It was clear that things had changed. There was an unspoken animosity between them. Looking at Banks as they entered, Thomas could see he was as resolute as ever in his belief in the organization's principles. A true zealot of their workforce. Thomas' time with him had proven that. Something inside Thomas was beginning to shift; his ideas about allegiance and duty were changing. Perhaps his time in Roslin's circus was coming to a grand end.

"Let's just remember why we're doing this, alright? I know it's gone out of control. But it's all got to end somewhere, sometime," decreed Banks.

Thomas looked at Banks, who had finally broken the silence. They were only a few steps from the door leading into the white room. They both paused.

"I don't need to remember anything. There's no purpose or reason with this guy. And if the killer doesn't need a reason, than neither do

Singularity

I. I'm going to stop this. I'm going to kill this guy," added Thomas.
Pressing on, Banks opened the door. Thomas pushed past him
impatiently. Banks mumbled at his back.

"Everybody's got their reasons."

Once inside, Thomas couldn't miss Jo, who was walking in tight
circles in the center of the room, holding a large tablet. He was
scanning over streams of data that appeared to be confounding him.
Jo's usual fearful self had diminished to one of pure frustration.

"This is improbable—illogical—just plain redonkulous! These
numbers—these readings—*what's* going *on?*"

Thomas caught the tail end of his muffled banter. Without asking,
he already knew something was wrong.

"What is it?"

Jo looked up at Thomas, who was standing just an arm's length
away. His face contorted into a look of disgust for a nanosecond
before returning back to one of complete confusion. Taking a
courageous step forward, Jo shoved the tablet towards Thomas.

"Look at this pattern . . . and notice I said *pattern*, not *patterns*.
Does that strike you as strange at all? Where's the fireworks, where's
the light show? Know what I mean?"

Thomas wanted to plug Jo's mouth with a cork. He almost never
understood what he was babbling about. Did anyone? The man was
completely crazy.

"Does it *look* like I know what you mean?"

Jo looked displeased. He pursed his lips together and let out an
exaggerated sigh. As he did, Banks joined the fray. His eyes locked
onto the tablet but then came back up rapidly.

"That looks odd. Don't recall seeing any like that."

Jo swung his arms open as if offering a massive bear hug.

"That's what I was trying to tell Mr. *Weird* Hat, here. There are no
waves coming off this node! It's a specific singularity. One that's pretty
faint, but undeniably present. This is warp zone wild!"

Both Banks and Thomas looked like they had just sucked on a
piece of sour candy.

"Okay, so let's go see what it is then. Seems simple enough to me,"
said Thomas.

Jo's mouth dropped open. The ignorance in the room was insulting to him. But like a dog being scolded, he hung his head and walked off to his technological masterpiece of a room.

"Coordinates, Jo?" said Banks.

"Yeah, yeah, you can come get them. Just know that I think this is crazy. I have no idea what you'll find."

"Do we ever know what we'll find? Seems pretty normal to me," mumbled Thomas.

As Thomas entered the room, he saw the coordinates on display on one of the many panels in the room. He snapped out his wrist and hovered his hand over it. Though he'd seen it work its magic many times before, the watch, with its almost magical interface, always mesmerized him. What an unbelievable amount of science and effort for something so very small. As he plugged in the coordinates, he felt sick to his stomach. What was he getting himself into? . Every time he glimpsed, the world he came back to was on fire. But he had no choice. People's lives were being destroyed at an ever increasing rate.

What are you up to now, you sick freak?

In his heart, a burning hatred had been festering, fueled by the ongoing events. A dark piece of his soul had grown two-fold in size and presence. How could he continue fighting against something so heinous without losing himself to it? Was he strong enough?

"You be careful. If Jo's right, there's something different about this one. I saw it too"

Thomas glanced at Banks, who had distanced himself. He looked upset. Thomas wanted to say something, but found he was lacking for words. The glimpse had taken precedence. The valve into his genius had been opened, and with it came a flood of memories and details. As the image of the room began to swirl madly out of control, he closed his eyes. Time was of the essence, and it was running out.

An abrupt wave of pain swept through his body. This was expected. Thomas recoiled. It was still very painful. A few moments passed and the world that had been thrashed apart began putting itself back together. Tiny pieces of the puzzle assembled themselves behind a blinding light before crashing to a stop. Thomas felt the icy shards of air cut into every inch of his lungs. His eyes shot wide open with the shock of the change in climate. He felt himself dipping slightly into the ground he was standing on. Taken by surprise, he fell to the ground. A few crunchy layers of icy snow pushed back at him like a cement floor. The impact rang through his body.

Where am I?

Putting his hands down to stabilize himself, he felt the cold permeating deeper into his body. Pulling himself back up, he inspected the area around him. The view was breathtaking. Snowcapped mountains extended along the horizon. A slightly clouded sky backed by a brilliant, crisp blue added to the epic scenery. He had never seen anything like it. Since all of his days had been spent dwelling in the bright lights of the city, he had never experienced the grandeur of the heavens above.

This is amazing.

Still struggling to gain his bearings, he focused on the ground around him. Snow and rock. The jagged edges of time-shaped stone jutted from its white, powdery cover. It was a world unlike any other. Disregarding his body, which was now beginning to shake from the chill, he glanced down at his watch. He saw the shining dot representing where the next event was supposed to happen. It, like all the others, was relatively close. But there seemed to be a slight problem; he was on the side of a mountain.

Oh, you've got to be kidding me!

Following the directions of the prompt, it became apparent that the only way was up. Up the side of what appeared to be nothing short of an assured death. He closed his eyes and let his head bob around. He was beyond exhausted, but had committed to something utterly insane anyway. Taking one last long look at his watch, he practically gagged when his heart jumped into his throat. He was going to do this.

Or die trying . . . that's what I said. Why did I have to be so heroic? Thomas, you're an idiot!

Doing his best to stay away from the edge of the mountain, which fell thousands of feet down into a white abyss, he examined the rock wall ahead. Small crags, crevices, and weather-chiseled edges dotted its landscape, producing a seemingly innumerable number of paths to take.

This is so stupid, Tommy. What the hell are you doing?

Letting his mind wrap itself around the problem at hand, it instantly began to toss the most logical paths to take back at him.

Looking up, he realized there was a slender shelf above him. But the shelf was far out of reach, unless he climbed.

It must be there. Where else could it be?

Digging his fingers into the first logical crevice, the cold stone clamped down on his flesh. He felt faint. A tinge of fear had fallen into his toxic mixture of courage.

Just keep looking up. Don't look down.

After adjusting his hat with his free hand, he dug his fingers into a predetermined location. His feet soon followed, and then the whole process was repeated. With each gut wrenching pull of his own weight, he could feel his body scream at him to stop. But it was his heart that pressed him forward. His thoughts had turned to those still alive; those who still had a chance. Perhaps it was possible that he could still save them; that he could stop this in time.

His right hand grabbed at a tiny ledge. As his fingers tried to clamp down on its surface, it slid out from under them. His body was flung out into space, on course to go tumbling down into doom. With a surge of adrenaline, his other hand dug deeper into the crag it was gripping. The sharp granite sliced open his skin leaking a trail of blood. He let out a shriek of terror as he saw the world swivel. Throwing all of his remaining energy into one swift movement, he spun back around, digging his feet back into the rock face while fighting to find a spot for his loose hand to grasp on the wall of rock.

Stupid variables! Ice!

He found a solid piece of rock to grasp, and once he felt secure enough, he began gasping for air. Breathing was difficult in any time-locked environment; it proved to be an even greater burden at this altitude. But miraculously, he recovered. The blood from his sliced hand was pouring onto the rock like a miniature waterfall. It was a stark reminder that he was on the verge of extinction.

Just keep going, Tommy!

Fighting the pain and fatigue, he pushed himself up the rock face. The bitter cold numbed his touch. His hands felt like to useless nubs. But he could see it now; the crest of the edge. With a few more torturous heaves, he threw himself on top of it. He rolled and collapsed onto his back. Shivers vibrated through his body like pulses of electric current. The nightmarish climb was still streaming through his thoughts. But he had made it—exactly to *where*, however, he did not know. Rolling to one side, he saw something that practically stopped his heart—a corpse. And it appeared to be the corpse of a woman.

She was frozen in time, literally. Her face was one of pure exhaustion that had finally been able to rest. Although Thomas was no doctor, it was apparent that some of the woman's bones had been shattered. Across from her resting place was a small cave bored into the side of the gigantic mountain. The remains of a parachute, various gear, and other specialized equipment was strewn about.

You landed here?

Thomas looked into the woman's face. Her eyes were frozen shut. She looked so peaceful. The dire cold had probably taken her in her sleep.

You were stranded.

He continued his inspection of the area, looking for clues. He looked at his watch. He was standing on the epicenter of the change. But the peculiar nature of it struck him as odd; a change that hadn't created a rift? Maybe Jo had been seeing things. This couldn't all be mere coincidence. That's when it caught his eye. The woman was wearing a large coat that was slightly opened at the top. There, beneath the layers of clothing, was the edge of something familiar; a pendant. Forgetting his place, Thomas tried to bring the pendant out just a few inches more so he could see it better, but the force of time fought his efforts, keeping everything in its place. He already knew without looking what was etched on its surface—three triangles, connected in the center. A symbol he was so tired of seeing that it practically made him explode with rage at the mere thought of it.

Again and again and again . . .

Looking over the body, he found nothing else that hinted at anything vile in nature. Now it was just a waiting game; waiting for the burst of light to sweep across his present world and set things in motion. Thomas waited. The seconds that passed in this relative time and space ticked by painstakingly slow. His heart beat faster with each passing moment. What was going to happen? He searched his mind for answers. He looked for lines connected to dots in both the past he knew, and the present he lived in. But there was nothing. At least nothing that screamed loud enough to be heard above all of the other competing details. But there was something . . . He felt the hairs stand up on the back of his neck—he felt the presence of something—a presence he had felt before. Turning around, he looked into the cave. Because of the icing of winter it was almost completely shrouded from view. The woman must have taken shelter in there until finally succumbing to the elements outside in one last desperate act of survival.

I know you're there!

Squinting his eyes, he strained to see into the opening, but it was too dark. The contrast was too strong. Forgetting his fear, he left the frozen body and entered the dark embrace of the cave. Once inside, he saw the world turn to darkness as his eyes struggled to adjust. Apart from a few tiny trickles of light, there was nothing but a black blanket extending endlessly.

"I'm done chasing you! I'm not afraid anymore! You will get caught, and when I catch you . . ."

He heard a crack coming from somewhere behind him. It was the sound of a misplaced footstep breaking through a microscopic layer of ice. In the darkness, a miniscule burst of light shone through to the floor ahead. Feeling intrigued, Thomas honed in on the location. As he stepped forward, he was careful to keep his balance. Ice was slippery; ice, frozen in time, was *ridiculous*. Further inside the cave, he saw something unexpected. In the dim light, he swore he saw a name etched into the wall:

JOHNNY

Who is that

He took a few steps forward on shaky legs. Winter's frigid fingers were pressing into him like jagged knives. Something needed to happen soon; he wouldn't last much longer. He put his face as close as possible to the carved letters.

How long have you been here? Lost, forgotten, or worse?

Suddenly, from out of the darkness, an arm wrapped itself around his exposed throat. It choked the air out of him, leaving him breathless and silent. As the arm had passed over him, he had seen a watch, accompanied by a dark glove. His fate was all but sealed now. His foolish endeavor—his quest, his story—would ultimately be plagiarized by a murdering psychopath skipping through time. With his last bit of strength, he tried to fight back. Then the world around him began to spin.

It's too early. That much time hasn't passed, has it?

The man's grip on him increased in fervor, keeping Thomas tight against his body. Fragments of reality encompassed them entirely. The bolts of pain that accompanied the miraculous leap came. The ice capped mountains faded into nothingness and were quickly replaced by a faceless floor of white. He felt as if he was falling. At last, the man released him.

Thomas hit the floor with a loud thud. He let out a howl of pain and rolled to one side. He saw a sea of white that he knew well. But how could this be? Confused, Thomas painfully pushed himself onto his feet. His hand dripped blood, which splashed on the floor. His head felt like it weighed a thousand pounds. His body was beyond exhausted.

"Where are you?"

Thomas' scream came out sounding like a maniac on a rampage. He was tired of the cat and mouse game. Either he was going to kill or be killed. This had to end.

Holding his chest, desperately trying to gather his emotions, he examined the room. It was a room just like the room in the organization's building where he had glimpsed several times; a room he had come to loathe. But he suddenly realized that it *wasn't* the room he was used to. He noticed subtle variances, but they were obscured by the bizarreness of the scene that was frozen in place in front of him. He couldn't believe his eyes. Was it even possible?

Solidified in place and time was a small group of men. Each was professionally adorned in the organization's standard black suit. But there were two men who stood out from the rest—two men that he had come to know by some twisted stroke of fate—Roslin and Banks. Looking at the group of men, it was obvious to Thomas that there had been a highly heated argument going on, with each man accusing the other of something. Whatever was at stake had inspired a passionate level of emotion in the room.

What was it? What happened?

He slowly approached Roslin. As always, the man stood like the unbreakable statue that he was. He was a force of nature, plowing his way through the realm of reality to get results. His eyes were narrowed. It was clear that his mind was mulling over the subject matter deeply. And then there was Banks. He appeared to be going straight for Roslin, stopped only by the few men who were desperately trying to hold him back. His eyes were watering, filled with both anger and something more elusive. Thomas was horrible at recognizing human emotions, let alone understanding them. Yet something about Banks's composure made his heart sink; was he in pain?

What did they do to you?

There was an audible sound of movement from somewhere in the room. It had come from somewhere behind the frozen figure of Roslin. Thomas' mood suddenly changed from one of deep inspection to rancid anger.

"What do you want from me? Why are you doing this?"

His emotional plea rang through the time and space he was locked in. His eyes darted back and forth looking for who he knew had to be the killer. Much like cancer, he was looking for the malignant tumor that had started this ongoing nightmare. His heart pounded against his chest in anticipation; he *was* going to *kill* him. The burning anger he felt was unquenchable. The only thing left was satiating his need for revenge.

"Show yourself!"

Examining the white room he was in, he saw that there were various rooms that branched from it. Each was cloaked in a heavy blanket of darkness; each one a potential place from which prying eyes could watch.

"Why did you kill them? Why did you kill all of them?"

In a fit of rage, Thomas swung a fist through the air in an attempt to release some of his pent up tension. He spat a stream of saliva onto the ground. He was losing control. His eidetic memory was encircling him like a python, squeezing him with too much disjointed information. But the overlying concept was about his failure. Lives had been lost and there had been nothing he could do to stop it. More blood would be spilled if things didn't change. Looking at Roslin, he felt a dark hatred form. Who was he *really*? What was he capable of? Lies, secrets, and more lies.

Singularity

His eyes began to sting as tiny droplets of sweat slithered their way into their corners. He wanted to scream, lash out—but then he saw something. As always, it came at his emotional precipice. Three triangles joined at the center, printed on a flimsy card. It lay at the opening of one of the rooms; its menacing presence undeniably ushering in a wave of sheer terror.

No more! I'm so tired of this!

Forgetting his unfavorable position or that a homicidal maniac was hiding in the shadows, he stampeded forward. His eyes locked on the tiny card. He allowed himself a moment to ponder over it, its meaning still unclear, and its origin infuriatingly unknown. He picked it up with surprisingly little effort. He felt around its crisp edges, letting his mind wander. For a moment he felt disjointed, separated from the very reality that he was trying desperately to salvage. There was but one real question front and center; why was he still alive?

Why haven't you killed me?

Looking into the darkness of the room beyond, he pondered something sinister. Was the man showing him something for a reason? Was this man truly evil incarnate or something more human? There was a true purpose here, one that had been carefully constructed throughout time. Going over the faces in the room apart from Roslin and Banks, he could see them one-by-one. Two of the men he knew, or at least he had seen them in their last moments of life. The others remained a mystery. Could one of them be connected? In another time and place, what was now few, was once many. With so much death, the agency's numbers had dwindled drastically of late.

Is this what you want? To see me fall apart?

Thomas shook his head. He was letting himself drift off into a stupor of thought. He had to bring himself back; there was too much at stake. He heard movement once more. Letting his clasp on the card loosen, it floated back-and-forth on its path to the ground. He took a step forward. At the edge of the light, his eyes strained to see inside. As he instinctively reached for a light switch, a black glove shot out from the darkness and grasped him by the throat. The swift and unexpected force took him by surprise. Gargling on his own saliva, he fought to breath. He was staring directly at the dark mask. Its eye sockets appeared empty and soulless.

"I'm going to kill you," Thomas hissed, barely able to choke out the words.

The man's grip on Thomas' throat relaxed. He was surprisingly strong. For the first time he spoke. His words came out through a convolution of shattered tones, masking his identity.

"I'm already dead."

The man flung Thomas forward, his back plowing into the sharp edge of one of the tables in the room. He collapsed to the floor, gasping for air. He felt his eyes fill with blood from a lack of circulation. But his will was pressing him on. He wasn't going to give in.

"What is it you want to show me? Why play these games?"

The man stood motionless, his lifeless mask examining the room carefully. The aura of evil was pronounced by his looming presence.

"Answer me!"

The man's head turned slowly towards Thomas, who struggled to get to his knees. The killer gazed on in silence. It was as if he was trying to understand Thomas. What he was, why he was, how he was, who he was . . . deep questions that seemed to elude him. Thomas was about to demand an answer, when he was again cut off by the inhuman voice.

"Truth has many forms. I am one of them."

Thomas paused. The statement was profound to him for some reason. The word *truth* struck a nerve that hummed in his soul. As he was finally getting control of his breathing, he watched the dark mask looking back at the quarreling group of agents. It was as if he was asking Thomas to see; to understand; but he couldn't. He couldn't possibly understand this man's perverse mode of thinking.

"What do you want from me?"

The man let his gaze rest on the frozen group of agents. Another drawn-out silence pressed Thomas' to his limits.

"Freedom or slavery . . . you choose the path you walk."

Thomas spat out a salty pool of saliva onto the ground. He adjusted his hat carefully, feeling a power reignite from somewhere inside. His thoughts turned towards his last moments with the only true love he ever had—Jen. His heart began to throb in his chest. He needed to dig deeper.

Singularity

"I know what this is. I know what you're trying to say. And I say *no*. I'll never help you."

The man turned his head slowly towards Thomas. Again the soulless eyes began picking him apart. In the silence, Thomas felt his hands start to tingle with anticipation. What was going to happen? Without warning, he bellowed out his denial once more.

"Did you hear me? I'll *never* help you! You're a sick freak!"

This time the response came quickly. The man's posture tensed. He was preparing himself for what he was about to do.

"Time brought you here and only time will set you free. I regret what I have to do."

Just as the man reached for his pocket, Thomas pounced. He had to use every fiber left of his being. He threw himself at the man's legs, ripping them out from underneath him. The man fell, losing grip of his silver revolver. It clanged against the ground as the crack of bones hitting floor broke the world into chaos.

The man fought to get out of Thomas' grip, as Thomas fought like mad to gain the upper hand. He tried to snatch his own pistol from his coat. The man spotted his attempt and thwarted it, back-handing Thomas and sending him sprawling backwards. The force broke Thomas' concentration, just as his fingers had barely pried his gun loose from its holster. It spun across the white floor, sliding through a narrow path comprised of the legs and feet of the group of agents. Thomas' eyes bulged wide in horror.

Without hesitation, both men fought their way towards the revolver. It was close enough that their misplaced feet kicked it around the floor, sending it careening in all directions. Thomas ducked as the man threw an expertly placed punch, missing him by just inches. Thomas responded by throwing a gut punch of his own, digging his fist deep into the man's body. He felt one of his ribs shift to one side. The man was quick to respond to the pain, ramming his knee into Thomas' face. He scurried away while Thomas caught his breath, snatched up the revolver and pointed it.

Thomas saw him out of the corner of his eye and made a desperate move to stop the inevitable. His hand shot up, pushing his aim to one side. A fiery round erupted from the chamber. The bullet ricocheted off of one of the walls before bouncing off another. The powerful force of time propelled it back at every angle. After dealing his adversary an elbow to the face, Thomas slid his finger onto the gun's trigger and pulled back on it. The chamber emptied, sending another four bullets blasting through the room. Both men paused for a moment, realizing what had just happened. The once tame, unassuming room had become a death trap. In awe they watched as a bullet blasted one of the agents directly in the back, shredding a tiny part of his suit. Instantly, there was a flash of light, marking the reality of the change.

"What the hell did you do?" screamed Thomas.

The man responded by hammering Thomas with another fist to his side. As he did, the dark eyes of the mask locked on the remaining pistol. He turned on his heel and sprinted towards it. Thomas followed suit. He desperately fought through his horrific pain to beat the killer to it. The murderer arrived first, only to be sent reeling backwards by the force of a stiff, accusing arm, stuck in time, belonging to one of the men standing in the group. Thomas tried to weave between the impervious walls of flesh, as the pistol had come to rest in the center of the stilled agents. A literal jungle gym of bodies lay between him and the only upper hand. Another flash of light flashed through the room; a second bullet had altered something. Thomas rolled out of the way as one of the bullets ricocheted just inches away from him.

This is unreal!

He glanced back at the pistol and saw a hand trying to weave its way through the forest of legs. Not wasting another moment, Thomas sprang to his feet and quickly assessed the situation. The man's fingertips were just about to reach the pistol. He had to do something. Without thinking, he climbed onto one of the men standing closest to him. Using arms, shoulders, and anything else he could, he climbed up and over the human obstacles and dropped onto the killer, his full weight slamming into him. The man let out a painful wheeze. Quickly, the killer retracted his arm and rolled away. Both men stood up slowly. Blood trickled down Thomas' lips. The blood from his hand was smeared all over the mask and clothes of the killer. Both men heaved for a minute, gasping for breath. The clanging of bullets echoed now from the depths of the room. The flashes of light came one after another as if on a timer. Thomas prayed that they hadn't unleashed hell.

"What do you think you'll accomplish? Kill me; kill *everyone*! Watch the world collapse, and for what?"

The masked man stood firm. He watched as Thomas picked up his hat from the ground and placed it back on top of his head. An evil, bitter cold rushed into the room. It wasn't over. The man came at Thomas again, this time with a renewed vigor.

"Justice!" the murderer shouted coldly.

Thomas dodged the first few attacks but fell victim to a well-placed fist across his jaw. He felt it unhinge and then snap back into place. The acute pain awakened his desperation to survive. He couldn't lay down and die—not like this. Trying to defend himself, he threw a punch of his own. The man ducked, sending Thomas' clenched fist into the back of one of the agent's heads. It smashed like jelly hitting a cement wall. Thomas roared in pain and collapsed to his knees feeling torn and broken. The clang of bullets was closer again; the flashes of light intensifying. When he looked up to find the masked man, he instead saw the hollowed out end of his own gun pointing at him. The killer had won. Soon he would be blasted into oblivion.

"Do it! I'm tired of the games! Either you go or I do!"

He watched as the man paused, his finger twitching. Just as he pulled the trigger, an out of control bullet caught his shoulder. The force knocked his shot off course. The killer let out a yelp of pain as a pool of blood spread on his suit. As he raised the gun again and took aim, the world around them began to shred apart. Shards of light ripped at their current reality like a tornado. The man aimed and fired. Thomas closed his eyes. His mind went blank and he fell limply to the ground. The maelstrom of time had finally come to an end.

25

STATUES OF TIME

"Thomas! Thomas!"

Screams from an indiscernible source echoed off the fuzzy walls distorting reality completely. Thomas felt his heart beat once, twice, and then again. He was alive. His mind felt shattered, his body torn to pieces. The incessant battle had finally taken its toll. He desperately tried to open his eyes. He could hear but also feel the buzzing pleas for his life vibrating through his body. But still he remained paralyzed by fatigue.

"Grab me a cup of water!"

Thomas pried his eyes open, straining to lift his eyelids. He saw the silhouettes of a few men standing around him. One person stood closest. This was a feminine form he knew well. Pixel by pixel, the outline of a woman materialized into someone he loved—Jen. Her hazy image was looking down on him and smiling.

You're alive! But you can't be.

Thomas' eyes began to water. Mixed with the incredible pain was something more; the indelible imprint that she had left on his life forever; his greatest gift taken at the moment of fruition. The disdain for the abject suffering he was experiencing was too much to bear. He closed his eyes.

I'm sorry . . . I'm so sorry, Jen.

When he opened his eyes gain, her swaying image faded away like smoke rising in the air. It was quickly replaced by a more masculine frame that was coming at him quick. A splash of ice cold water pelted against his face, suddenly rocking him back to reality. He coughed up a mouthful of water and saliva that sloshed onto the pristine white floor. His insides churned. He felt like hell.

"Thomas, are you alright?"

The voice was now recognizable as Banks's. He stood empty cup in hand, towering over Thomas, vigilantly awaiting his return. But he wasn't alone. Jo and Roslin had joined the fray, all looking down on him earnestly. Upon seeing Roslin a surge of energy burst through his body, propelling him off the ground. He slammed his body into Roslin's wide frame and let loose a coiled up fist of anger. It struck Roslin across the eye. Roslin respond by grappling Thomas into submission, as both Jo and Banks helped to calm Thomas' out-of-control anger.

"Liar! What the hell did you do to them? What's going on here?"

Roslin's body tensed. It looked as if he was preparing an assault of his own. But he stood his ground, firm and resolute.

"Don't you *ever* come at me like that again! I'll make sure *that* never happens again!"

Thomas continued trying to fight while in Banks's firm grasp, accompanied by the almost absent touch of Jo. He was struggling to keep it together. He watched as Roslin covered his eye for a moment, still feeling the bolts of anger surging through his body.

"What are you talking about?" screamed Banks at Thomas, still pulling him away from Roslin.

Thomas looked down at his chest. He remembered just how close he had come to death. He had been sucked out of the past at just the right time. His luck wouldn't endure, this he was sure of.

"I saw her, I saw you, back in time! I saw you all fighting! I saw—"

Thomas turned and looked at Banks whose grasp on Thomas eased.

"I saw both of you there—stuck like statues, fighting and screaming—and then there was the woman . . ."

Thomas put his face in his hands. He felt like screaming.

"What do you mean, a *woman*?" probed Banks.

Thomas looked up sternly at Roslin.

"You left her, didn't you? You left her to die."

"What are you talking about? Left who?"

Thomas' mind rattled around in his skull like a rock in a can.

"Who are you talking about?" added Banks.

"I don't know. I don't know who she is."

Nothing was making sense. Even Jo had a grimace etched into his face. The sudden violence had put everyone on edge.

"That's it. I'm pulling the plug on this. We've already lost too much just to have you come back answerless. I've got too much on my plate to keep entertaining this."

Thomas thought to respond but refrained. In his mind, he was taking each of the men apart, even Jo. He didn't trust any of them anymore. All could be guilty, all could be dirty. He knew what he had to do but just didn't know how he was going to do it. He would be saying goodbye to the organization that had brought him in. He would be saying goodbye to almost all of the only deranged family he had left. His path would be walked alone.

Roslin started to speak but was promptly cut off by a loud buzz emitting from his pocket. He reluctantly answered his phone. He said nothing. His eyes said everything. They sunk deep into his skull, brows furrowed deeply. He responded with a meek, single word.

"Understood."

Once he put the phone back into his pocket, he stared blankly out into the white room. His composure had shifted from anger to profound sorrow.

"We'll deal with this later."

He turned suddenly in an attempt to make a hasty exit.

"Where are you going?" yelled Thomas.

"Why does it matter to you?"

Roslin left the men alone in the room. Now Banks's pocket buzzed. He put his phone to his ear.

"This can't be real," he sputtered through tightened lips.

Although Banks hadn't divulged what had happened, the facts were all present. Thomas's brilliant mind had already begun fitting them together. And someone else was dead.

"Come with me, *now!*" demanded Banks, as he headed for the door.

Thomas did as he was told. He needed an exit. As he left he glanced at Jo and nodded. Jo did nothing back. His thick glasses seemed to be temporarily fogged up by the onslaught of emotion he was experiencing.

This is goodbye.

Leaving the building, both men climbed into Banks's car. He sped off like a bullet, screeching his tires against the pavement.

"This isn't good. This is bad," he mumbled angrily.

Thomas remained quiet. As the car approached the center of the city, he could see the commotion. A crowd had gathered, people standing around in shock, eyes fixed on one location. Cameras were flashing like fireworks trying to capture the harrowing event. In the midst of it all, dangling from a rope, was a man; his neck broken, his last breath taken. Across his chest hung a sign, and on it, written in bold letters, was a message to the world:

JUSTICE AND TRUTH

Thomas felt faint. He pressed a hand against the dash in front of him. The image of the deceased man swaying carelessly in the air horrified him. What was happening? Banks stopped the car and got out, leaving Thomas behind. He burst into the crowd, pushing people out of his way as he went. More sirens could be heard approaching in the distance. Things had fallen apart. This atrocious spectacle just threw things into the limelight.

Getting out of the car cautiously, he let what was happening sink in. Another death, another unknown reason, sealed in death. But this man was no agent. He was slightly aged and wore similar features to another man he knew—Roslin. Even though the thought of it disgusted him to the core it, was apparently true; Roslin's brother was no longer among the living. His tortured soul was finally released, but in the most heinous of ways. Now was the time to sever his last tie to the organization. His trust would have to lie elsewhere. The sticky web of lies and deceit, the unspoken plans; he could only trust himself now.

Turning away from the madness, he walked towards an empty alleyway. He was within a few footsteps from disappearing into it when a powerful hand gripped him by the shoulder. He traced the hand to its source—*Roslin*. The man looked completely beside himself. His eyes were filled with remorse and anger. He squeezed Thomas' shoulder violently.

"Hell's been unleashed and you're leaving so soon?"

Thomas tried to step away but couldn't. Roslin's grip was too firm. Taking a deep breath, he responded reverently.

"Let me go, Roslin. Let me go *now*."

Roslin's arm trembled. His professionally character was in shambles. The truth had sunken in. His brother was gone. Despite his efforts to remove himself by departing from mainstream society and its cares, he had been whittled to the core. No one was above the pain of the loss of a murdered family member . . . no one.

"If I let you go, you can never come back."

Thomas pushed his sleeve over his watch. He calmly adjusted his fedora to center it just perfectly on his head. Once he was satisfied, he looked Roslin sternly in the eyes.

"I don't plan to."

Catching him off guard, Thomas broke free from Roslin's clutch and sprinted down the alley. From behind, he heard Roslin give a brief chase, and then the pounding of footsteps came to an end.

"Thomas! Thomas!"

Roslin's screams seemed almost inhuman. The tortured words of this broken man echoed off the bricks and mortar. But Thomas pressed on. He left him behind. He left them all behind. His body trembled from the fatigue and injuries he had sustained. He wouldn't make it far. He needed a place to go. Jutting the watch on his wrist into full view, he waved his hand over the top. He had seen Banks do it, watched carefully, and memorized the steps. He was sure that manipulating their technology would result in the rest of his life behind bars. But he didn't care. After just a little effort, the watch warned him about what he was about to do. He quickly disabled its tracking device. He was going rogue. From here on out, his goal would be to leave no trace. No breadcrumbs for the organization to follow once they launched their internal witch hunt for him. He reached into his pocket and pulled out his phone. He hurled it against the wall and watched it break into a dozen pieces. He was cut off. Instinctively, he reached into his suit to pull out his gun. It was gone. But he knew that. It had been left behind with the killer. A relic now in the past, manifested again in the future and into its new master's hands. Why had he reached for it? The thought troubled him yet intrigued him at the same time. Despite his brilliant memory, he was still just human.

I need to get out of here.

Leaving his shattered phone behind, he darted down the alley. He prayed that she would still be there; he prayed that she was still alive.

Standing outside of Barb's apartment door, he felt himself shiver. But it wasn't because of the cold; something else was gripping his heart in its icy clutches. The firm understanding of evil he thought he once had, had evolved into the monster he now knew. He didn't know what to believe anymore or who to believe in. She was his last chance, his last hope.

As the door to her apartment opened, she shot a hand out and quickly pulled him inside. She glanced outside, assuring herself that no one was watching. She quickly shut the door and began examining him.

"Thomas, you look like death!"

He rambled a few lines of gibberish before collapsing against the wall. "Barb, I don't feel so good."

She ran to his side and tried her best to hoist him up. She grunted under the weight of Thomas' body as she helped him into a room with a partially made bed. She removed his coat and hat and let him lie down.

"Thomas, your face, your hand! What happened?"

Thomas rolled onto his side. He felt himself drift slightly. He was diligently trying to fight the urge to succumb to his exhaustion and pass out.

"He won again, Barb. Someone else had to die."

Closing his eyes slowly, he heard Barb's voice echo through his train of thought. The last thing he thought he heard her say was that she couldn't lose him. But it seemed like she was just about to.

26

MOUSE AND CAT

Thomas awoke to a tender touch, something he hadn't felt in what seemed like ages. Slender fingers worked their way methodically back and forth across his forehead. He smelled an alluring perfume that lingered in his nostrils. It was pleasant and refreshing. Opening his eyes, he saw the decorative ceiling of Barb's room. Everything was blissfully peaceful. Everything was quiet. But soon his mind was busy revving itself up. All the things that had happened came back to him, taking his breath away. Feeling a sudden sense of panic, he bolted upright, frightening Barb who had been tending to his wounds.

"Thomas, don't do that to me!"

His mind rapidly came to the present. He looked at Barb, who was holding a damp rag and bowl. She had been taking care of him the entire time.

"How long was I out?"

Barb smiled gingerly before dabbing at his face again.

"A few hours—you pretty much ruined my bed sheets—thanks."

Thomas smiled. He had missed Barb's thorny wit. He felt much better than before, despite his ongoing fatigue.

"I'm not safe staying here . . . they're probably looking for me."

Barb's smile continued.

"Then let them. As far as I'm concerned, you don't exist. And I'm an excellent liar, unlike you. I am a psychiatrist, after all."

"He wanted me to help him, Barb . . . the killer. When I refused, he tried to kill me."

Thomas could still feel the powerful fingers clutching his throat.

"Don't blame him. Having someone like you on his side would definitely sway the teeter-totter."

Barb paused for a moment and Thomas gazed up at her. She had a strange look about her; one he had seen a few times before; she looked as if she cared for him. Thomas put his guard up, realizing that he had lingered a touch too long on her eyes.

"Doubt that. All I'm good at his burning down bridges and pissing people off."

Barb plopped the soaked rag into the bowl and shook her head.

"You've pissed me off and I'm still here. Besides, I think I've lost my mind."

"What do you mean?"

"All of the things you've told me about—a murdering time traveler, the disasters, the secret organization, and Freud knows what else, may he rest in peace. Thomas, I'm actually starting to believe them. The other day I was doing some laundry and couldn't find one of my black socks. I always keep things organized and know for a fact that it had to have been by my bed. But something had changed; isn't that how it works?"

Thomas smiled. He glanced over at Barb's feline companion who was chewing on a pile of black threads.

"Barb, your attention to detail astounds me."

She crossed her arms and let out a puff of frustration.

"You're not taking me seriously? You think I can't understand something like this? I'm seriously losing it here."

Thomas took her hand.

"Barb, trust me, it's real. And that's what worries me the most. That's what I was trying to say; you're not safe around me. This guy's a seriously bad egg who will stop at nothing to finish what he's started. And now that I've thoroughly upset him, I'm as good as dead."

Barb absentmindedly pulled a pen from her pocket and began gnawing on its end nervously.

"Maybe not."

"Maybe not? Haven't you been paying attention? And in case you've forgotten, I'm the one who keeps ending up in a hospital or your apartment, not him. This guy's too good."

"Would you just shut up and let me think?" Barb said, rolling her eyes.

Thomas puckered his lips and pouted. There was something about Barb's feisty side that intrigued him. A few moments went by as Barb paced in a tiny circle in her room before collapsing into an arm chair in the corner. She sighed a few times before finally speaking.

"Screw it, just screw it. This is such a bad idea, but the hell with it."

Barb sat up and crossed her legs. Her professional demeanor had returned. She looked at Thomas like she used to; a patient she was examining.

"Maybe you're right. He's just too good. But even the too-goods have weak points. I mean, from what you've told me, this person has some serious issues with this organization, and all of humanity, in some deranged way. Perhaps it takes understanding him a bit more."

"But you know I can't do that. I barely register as a normal human being, let alone one who understands people. Just give me the facts."

"Then, like I said, screw it. Make him chase you. You've been getting beat to hell and he's been leading you around by the nose. Maybe it's time *you* start doing the leading."

Thomas took a deep breath. The thought had crossed his mind many times before. But the rules were clear; one does not go gallivanting into the past for any reason other than to protect it. And he knew his way was anything but the right way to do things. He could potentially open Pandora's Box.

"So just sit back and watch the world burn down? I'm not following you here, Barb."

"No, not burn *down*, per say, just hit with a little controlled bonfire. Find a pressure point and start pushing. We all have them. I've known you for a long time now and we both know you're good at being especially aggravating. With your ridiculous attention to detail, there's got to be something you could scrounge up. Isn't there?"

Thomas pondered over the entirety of what had happened. So many hazy dots and connections streamed through his mind. But one picture was clear—*Roslin*. Either he was involved or he was being victimized, tortured. Roslin was as good a starting point as any, and there was also the woman.

"There was a woman. He took me to her. Tricked me into taking the bait. But when I got there she was long gone, frozen to death on the mountain. She had scribbled something on the wall—a name—one I haven't been able to connect to any of this. She's obviously someone near-and-dear to this psycho. The only question left is who is she?"

Barb uncrossed her legs and slouched forward onto her elbows.

"Bingo. The deranged psychopath used to be a sweet little lover boy. Or maybe she was family, or a near friend? No way of really knowing. Did you see him with her?"

Thomas shook his head.

"He took me away before anything else could happen. He just wanted me to see it."

"Then what?"

"I saw a bunch of men fighting. They looked to be on opposing sides of an argument. Two of them, Roslin and Banks, are guys I've been working with. Both of them looked very upset. But I've been around them many times now, and have never seen them behave like that. Banks's pretty much Roslin's little stooge, and Roslin's just a complete jerk. But their eyes were so angry."

"That's a start. Maybe that's the hole worth going down."

"I was told I could never come back. Like I said, I'm really good at burning bridges."

"Thomas, if any brilliantly gifted, unemployed, practically homeless man can figure out a way, you can. I've got faith in you."

"I think you were right, Barb. Pretty much like always."

"You've got my attention. Please indulge me."

"You were right about finding a purpose. I think Jen would have wanted me to keep doing this. It's just a messed up situation, is all. Something that feels so right, and yet, it's so wrong."

"That's not surprising. It's always difficult to discern between the two. It's a fine line to walk."

"The two?"

Barb pursed her lips, putting on an impish smile.

"Good and evil. It's in all of us. We all like to believe we've got a halo floating above our heads, but the truth is, we don't. I've often questioned how capable a person really is of doing things completely out of character when dropped into the right circumstances. A disaster, a tragic loss, a change of heart; these things intrigue me.

"You always had a way with words, Barb. Full disclosure—I'm not even sure I know which side I'm on. Am I supposed to care that a bunch of underworld thugs got buried in rubble? Am I supposed to care that some secret organization's agents were plucked out of existence? In truth, I really *don't* care, and yet I do. It's confusing."

Barb stifled a chuckle. She let her eyes fall on Thomas and linger. She found him to be delightfully complex.

"This is why I missed you. No matter how hard I try, I almost never understand you. You're like my own personal crazy koosh ball. I just want to keep squeezing until something finally happens."

Thomas rolled his eyes and sneered.

"Barb, are you sure that you're not already skirting that fine line we just talked about? Maybe your halo is starting to droop a bit."

"My halo? Oh, that old thing? It's been in the closet for years; haven't even dusted it off."

Thomas smiled. For a moment he had forgotten where he was and what he had just been through. He thought there might be something special forming between the two of them. But he quickly dismissed the notion. His heart was still an ice box to which there was no key. The idea of it, however, still remained, tantalizing his imagination.

"You naughty girl. You know that things are going to get ugly if I do this. I can't imagine what's going to happen next."

Barb's demeanor adjusted itself into one of a more serious nature. She was thinking through what she had suggested—it was both sweet and sour—a chance to end the madness, but at the expense of even more catastrophe. What other choice did they have? Thomas swung his legs over the side of the bed and let the fresh air sift into his lungs. Could he really do this? Alone?

"I need to get going. There are some things I need to do."

Thomas stood up slowly. His movement was akin to a rusty, mechanical robot. But he was still alive. He had meant it when he'd said he would die trying. If this was his only purpose left in life then he would defend it as such. He covered his eyes for just a moment, suddenly feeling a chill of darkness sweep through his mind. The dark mask of the killer plagued him like some incessant disease. It was always there, watching. He wanted desperately to rip it off, put a face to the crimes, the injustices. He wanted a target at which to expend his deeply buried hatred. Looking up, he saw his hat on the edge of the dresser. It reminded him of so many things now.

"My uncanny desperado. It's a wonder how a man like you stays single."

Thomas put on a cheesy smirk that quickly faded away.

"I still think you should leave town, get out of here. I mean it, Barb. It's just not safe anymore."

Barb put her own façade of seriousness on.

"That's not going to happen, Tommy. It'll take more than a time traveling killer psychopath to make me leave my apartment. It's taken me this long just to get my own parking spot."

She looked like she couldn't really believe she was actually saying that. But she had left all logic behind when she had decided to share this nightmare with Thomas.

"I'll be coming back. Not to sound cheesy, but you're all I've got now."

Barb's face softened. Her eyes were talking again. But with a few blinks, the moment had passed.

"You know where to find me. I'm a creature of only two worlds at this point; the office or home."

Thomas looked back down at the bed to see fresh linens had been stretched over it.

"Yes, you owe me some new sheets. A girl like me likes to be pampered, so you'll understand when you get the bill. Not to mention the clean-up," Barb said, drawing a circle around her own face.

Thomas smiled as he headed towards the door. Once there, he paused. He briefly wondered if what he was about to do was right or not. It was all so convoluted, it didn't matter. Turning the doorknob, he opened the door and began stepping out.

"I didn't think women like you ever slept. We'll talk about the bill later."

Thomas shut the door, cutting off Barb's retort.

I got the last word. Barb will love that.

Looking at his wrist, he let out a sigh of relief to see the dimmed lights of his watch staring back. Although he knew that the organization couldn't track him directly, they'd undoubtedly be able to see his glimpse to the past. Or would they? The intricacies of the brink technology were like a magic show to him. Smoke and mirrors with the real guts of it hidden beneath absurd complexity. It would take someone like Jo a million years to dumb it down enough for him to understand it fully. But all he cared about were the results. The technology was a means to an end. That's when it hit him; he was acting just like Roslin; hiding in the shadows, keeping secrets, going behind everyone's back. Was he becoming the very monster he so loathed?

What's happening to you, Tommy?

He stepped away from Barb's apartment building and worked himself into a wide alleyway. He hadn't spent much time on this side of town. It was well outside his territory from his days on the job. But it still felt like home. He saw a man covered in rubbish sitting next to a large trash can. When he noticed Thomas, he looked offended and straightened up. As Thomas began fumbling with his watch to plug in some coordinates, he heard the man grumbling.

"Not another one of you freaks! Why can't you people just leave me alone? First the gangly one, now you . . ."

Thomas disregarded the comment, his thoughts elsewhere. He looked at the display on his watch which was prompting him to enter some coordinates. He had watched Jo read them off and had learned how to put them in. But for some reason, this time, he paused.

I shouldn't do this, should I?

He knew it was wrong, and yet it felt very right in this moment. To senselessly indulge in the idea of it was intoxicating. Perhaps his time with Barb had accidentally left the door to the cage of his locked-up emotions slightly ajar. It felt uncontrollable. A need he had to satiate. A selfish desire he wanted to indulge.

Damnit it, Tommy, just let it go. Why are you doing this?

With trembling fingers, he punched in the date and time. He knew it like the back of his hand, down to the very second. It had been seared into the very tissue of his brain. It was a place in time that would never be forgotten by him. He took a deep breath. Was he merely damning himself to a tortuous circle? Why was he doing this? In a tornado of fragmented light, it no longer mattered. His heart ached with an insufferable pain. His worst nightmare had returned.

27

REBEL

Slamming into the floor, a literal wave blasted his every sense. The smells, the sights, the feel; it was all there, just as he remembered it. Every acute detail accounted for—everything in its place—nothing had changed. Pulling himself up off the ground, he looked around the room quickly, his mind ablaze, his heart racing.

It was him, the old him, at an angle he could have never imagined. He was literally staring at himself, what seemed like ages ago. And there she was. Her eyes filled with light, her elated smile enticing him into a sense of glee he had long forgotten. His heart skipped a beat. Looking at the Thomas that was frozen in time, he could see the ring, the exotic ensemble of flowers, and his stupid hat. He had worked so hard to be normal at that point. To sweep Jen off her feet and never let her go. She had said yes, the most affirming answer he had ever received from anyone. It was pure, delightful, and good. Tears filled his eyes. The flood gates had been opened. Allowing himself to drift into the currents of his roaring emotions, he bit his lip and cried. It was both horrible and beautiful to be able to see her again. Why had the fates been so cruel?

He paced around the room before taking his place next to himself, kneeling and smiling ear-to-ear. Only he wasn't smiling; everything had changed. He was tainted, torn, and broken. The contrast was remarkable. The simple times in his life were long gone. The suffocating nostalgia of his broken past was too much to bear. His heart grieved his loss. Standing up slowly, he stumbled to Jen's side.

He brushed his fingers against her delicate skin. Its suppleness was denied by the powers of time, locking it in place like cement. And yet it was still there, the perfect memory. Unable to resist, he kissed her gently. Her face remained unchanged. She would never know he had been there. She'd never know that on the same day his heart had nearly exploded with joy, it had also nearly collapsed with sorrow. Such a warped twist of fate; such a painful moment.

Screw it. Screw all of it.

Looking back down at his watch, another date and time came to the forefront of his mind. This date and time brought in a harrowing reality that he wasn't sure he could face. But he had to. He had to try. He didn't care what they had told him about the rules of time, the rules of brink. This was beyond that. He had never done it before, but had witnessed it firsthand. He was going to glimpse to another moment in time, just minutes from the one he was dwelling in now.

I've got to try.

Plugging the data into the watch, he pressed into the tornado of light. He watched with tears in his eyes as the love of his life was rapidly shredded apart. Within the blink of an eye, he was back again. The glimpse was largely anti-climactic. He was in the same room. But so much had changed. His heart plummeted into the bowels of despair he harbored within. Could he relive this moment?

Not this time. I'll stop it, I swear.

Looking around, it was as it had always been; the greatest tragedy of his life. There stood the man, gun pointed, bullet fired. Just ahead of him was the frozen image of himself, begging the soon-to-be killer to stop. Behind them, Jena cowered. Her eyes were filled with terror. Their perfect moment, ravaged.

I'm here, baby.

And there it was—the embodiment of what had become the end of his fairy tale—the bullet. It was suspended in air on route to its final destination, Jena's chest, his frozen-in-time self mere inches outside of its path. He approached the bullet and frowned. How could something so small wrench apart a life, leaving unhealable gashes behind? It was beyond him. Had his body been just a step to the right, he would have been the one struck, rather than Jena. The thought of this pained him. He felt like a coward. Why hadn't he done more? What hadn't he stopped it?

Unwilling to fight the urge, he reached out and grasped the small bullet between two fingers. Its place in time nailed it firmly to its course. Suddenly, the fire that had been boiling in his veins erupted in a scream filled with anguish. His fingers pressed tightly around the bullet, he pulled on it with every fiber of his being. Yanking and contorting his body, he tried again and again to veer the bullet off course, even if ever so slightly. With each effort, his soul shriveled up just a bit more. It wouldn't budge. Despite his most valiant efforts, the change was too drastic. Jena's timeline had ended. For a moment, he thought about trying to change a few minor things in her past. Perhaps he could play the killer's game of chess and somehow salvage the situation. But somehow he knew, deep down inside, that the justice of time had to be met when it came to death. There was no greater sacrifice or loss than one's life, whether given or taken. The unchangeable event would not be robbed of the soul it had claimed that day. The past could not be changed.

Thomas collapsed to his knees, defeated. He had expended every ounce of energy he had in his vain effort. Tears streamed down his face. He hated it; all of it. He wished he had never opened this door. Why couldn't he change the past? Why did she have to die? He put his head in his hands and let loose. He knew that his time would soon be up. Jo would trace the event and warn the team. Their foolish oversight ultimately made him a vigilante on the run; a vigilante running from a secret organization that he now felt was teeming with evil.

I'll find a way, I swear it.

Unwilling to get back to his feet, he looked at the man carrying the gun. He knew the face well now. It had lived on in his nightmares. The strung out junkie who had no name, no real purpose. Someone looking to score his next fix by stealing an expensive ring. The ring had meant nothing to him. But to Thomas, it had meant everything. Walking up to the man, he looked him straight in the eyes. Panic, anger, and confusion were the emotions that dwelled there. A man who obviously wasn't completely sure he had just done what he had just done. Behind that was the emptiness of failure. The sick, sour taste of defeat.

When the lights flashed and the room began to unravel, he felt himself lose something—*hope*. Was it all really worth it? Did it even matter without her? An acute ripple of pain ran through him as he was rapidly ripped away, back to his present world. He collapsed with a thud against the concrete ground in the alley. A wave of energy swept up some of the discarded garbage and then dumped it in all directions. He felt sick. Unable to fight the urge, he ran directly to the nearest garbage can and puked. Even though the sensation that glimpsing brought him was more manageable now, mixed with his intimate visit to one of the most painful moments in his life proved too much for him. As he finished heaving his insides out, he wiped away the remnants from his mouth and stood up. He saw the homeless man he'd run in to before gazing back at him blankly.

"You aliens stay away from me. I ain't caused no trouble."

Thomas shook his head. The world was still fuzzy. An evil smile crept over his face. He was imagining the sheer panic he must be causing in Roslin's organization. He could practically hear Jo's educated banter streaming like a broken record. For some strange reason that was even beyond his understanding, he actually missed it. Perhaps his time with them had somehow sprouted roots in him, like a fungus. He threw the sentiment away. There was more he needed to get done. But now he was up against what seemed to be insurmountable odds. How could he dig up the past of a secret organization that had so painstakingly kept everything swept under the rug? What would he find?

The memory of the feel of Jena's skin still lingered in his mind. He needed to remain focused. He couldn't dilute himself any further. He was going to find the one answer that still stewed his cerebral juices; who was the woman on the mountain? What could she possibly have to do with everything? Perhaps it was time he took Barb's advice.

Screw it.

If he couldn't change the past, he could at least use it to his advantage. He'd be a ghost passing like a chill. No one would ever know he was there. The only problem was, *where* was *there?* How could he use his gift and technological windfall to his advantage? He'd have to remember it all, every moment he spent in the mysterious building. Every discussion he had ever had with anyone connected to the secret organization. Words could translate into clues. Little breadcrumbs ready to be followed.

It wasn't clear, but opaque. The path to vindication was filled with obstacles. But it was all he had now. Perhaps he needed to retrace his steps. But there was something else; things had changed. What was once presented as an impossible anomaly had now occurred several times. He had shared his relative time and space in a glimpse with the killer, not by happenstance, but by design. If the murderous wit of a madman could figure it out, so could Jo and the organization. With each glimpse he'd be baiting them to try to catch him. And if that wasn't bad enough, the killer could just as easily be lurking in the shadows. It was a web of malicious design. His actions would strum its fibers, alerting one monster or another. It was a game of tag with everything at stake.

Let's do this. Come on, Tommy, let's do it.

Thomas repeated his silent mantra over and over. He needed the courage to face whatever was going to happen. One date and time came slamming into the forefront of his mind. It felt like he had just left it. Pressing even further into the alley, he went over in his mind's eye what he had already seen. The homeless man cowered as Thomas passed. He looked as if he was seeing a ghost. But aside from his mumblings and grumblings, he stood his ground. Thomas ignored him completely. He was intensely working his way through things. Passing a T-junction in the alleyway, he finally reached the pivotal end of his walking path. He stopped. He'd have to be quick. The glimpses would have to be expertly executed, one seamlessly transitioning into the other. If he was right, his time would have to be brief. The agents or even the killer could be waiting to pounce.

You can do this.

His heart thumped up and down as if prepping for a cardiac arrest. The tension was humming in his ears. Hovering his hand over his watch, he rehearsed the protocol. The watch prompted for the coordinates; he gave them. For a moment he was breathless. This would be the adventure of a lifetime. He would be a true renegade of time and space. As the maelstrom of light surrounded him, he knew that his time had come. Thomas Ghune was dead. Tommy Gun was who he needed to be now. A law breaking rebel who wasn't going to stop until it was over. He clenched his teeth as the world disappeared. Waves of intense energy ushered in a true sense of his mortality. If he failed this time, he was as good as dead.

28

DECASTRO

The frost bitten ground gnawed into Thomas' exposed hands. He could feel the ice cold weather slither through his veins, making him shiver uncontrollably. He'd been here before, and yet, it still felt like a foreign world. Snowcapped mountains, blue skies, a seemingly endless sprawl of celestial skyline. If he had been a more spiritual man, perhaps the scene would inspire in him some mode of reverence. In his own attempt at supplication, he was just thankful to still be alive to see it. Looking up at the side of the cliff, he gasped. It almost seemed nonsensical to test his fate again, but he had to. Digging his hands back into the frozen rock face, he began writhing his way up the path he had taken before in what seemed like a past life. His mind recalled every detail, every crag, every crevice, and even the iced rock that had so nearly taken his life. Everything was going as planned until he felt the hairs on the back of his neck stand tall. He wasn't alone. Looking back down, he saw them. Two agents, dressed to kill, as always. Both were climbing after him. They must have glimpsed close, too close to his location. He needed to move quickly.

With a shot of adrenaline that muted everything else, he propelled himself up and over the ledge. The agents were closing in fast. It was clear that their intent was to capture him. But if given the right reason, an extreme decision might have to be made. Once at the top of the ledge, Thomas immediately dove into the scene like never before. The woman was there, frozen solid. The mess of items from the crash was still strewn about like discarded laundry. Then there was the cave; he had to have missed something. Sprinting inside, he could hear the agents struggling up the last leg of the climb. He opened his mind—the name on the wall, the leftovers from a vicious wreck, a crumpled up parachute tucked neatly into the corner like a bed.

Her bed.

Running to the place she had slept, he looked it over in full detail. The imprint of a body was still there, pointing to the woman's time spent alive here. The woman was an agent; there was no doubt about it. He had seen the symbol. But that wasn't enough. She was connected, but to who and what? Hunching over, he let his thoughts linger.

Who are you?

Off to the side of the make-shift bed laid a tiny notebook. Its brittle pages looked like thin sheaths of ice ready to break apart. He carefully inspected it. The repetitive use of it had creased it to a natural open. Digging his fingers into the top of the notebook, he threw his back into an arc. He let out an enervated scream. The notebook fought to keep its place, but with a few more herculean-like pulls, it gave way just an inch. A flash of light burst throughout the world. He gasped. In truth, he hadn't expected it to actually happen. But he had to seize the opportunity. He looked at the pages that had opened; the last entry, the last testament. A few scribbled lines clumsily put together. She must have known her time was short. It looked to be a goodbye. The same name that was on the wall appeared, tenderly addressed. Barb had been right; there was something far deeper here. Just then, he heard the groans of the two agents as they rushed into the cave.

Here we go.

Thomas' eyes darted back and forth through the notebook. That's when he saw it. Like all wishing to leave their mark in the last moments of life, she had done just that. A signature. Although barely legible, it provided a clear enough image to read.

Taylor DeCastro

His mind only needed but to see it. Now he had some ammunition. He looked up as the agents rushed into the cave to stop him. He couldn't waste a second. Throwing his wrist into the open, he quickly

plotted in the coordinate of his next glimpse. He had seen it for a
fraction of a second on the killer's wrist. But it had been enough.
The watch hummed as the agents leapt at him. With the usual flash,
the whirlwind came, sweeping him out of the ice cave on top of the
world into a place he knew very well. The white floor came blindingly
fast at him. His body struck hard, bringing pain to his entire being.
He yelped loudly. He slid onto his side and gasped for air.

Get up! Get up now!

Pushing himself to his feet, he saw it all again. Roslin, Banks, and the
agents, stuck in time. Each one was standing in the exact same position
as before, their hellacious argument seemingly extending on forever.
But it would end, and the results would continue on as a mystery.
Thomas ran up to Roslin and looked him over. He had already done so
once before, but this time he was seeing him through different eyes; a
lost woman, a fever-pitched argument, and a trail of blood.

What is it? What are you hiding?

He inspected each agent before him, one-by-one. All seemed to
be fervently involved in the discussion. But none of their faces had
appeared at any point in his own timeline, except for Banks. The
persona of Banks was that of a steadfast, devoted agent, willing to
do what it takes. But Thomas had also seen another side of Banks;
one that had begun to question the agency, and even Roslin, if ever
so slightly. Perhaps there was more to Banks and Roslin than met
the eye. Years of working together could taint anyone's relationships.
There were always things kept hidden.

But the woman . . . what about the woman?

The room seemed barren without her. So what if the agents
were in an argument with one of their higher ups. Roslin was the
sheer definition of arrogance. His take-all, win-all attitude had
assuredly been one of the reasons he'd escalated up the ranks of the
organization. With an attitude like that, he wasn't short of enemies.
But were any of these men capable of such heinous acts? The question
loomed large within Thomas. As he continued his search for truth,
there was a forceful pounding on the door. Almost jumping out of
his skin, he turned to see what he so desperately had been hoping
he wouldn't; the same two agents who had followed him up the
mountain were now throwing themselves into the door, leading into

the room. The only deterrence was the forces of time refusing to
secede their position. But he knew it was possible, he had done it
himself, after all. They would be upon him in mere moments.

Focus, Tommy . . . focus or die.

Working his way past the crowd, he headed for the room from
which the killer had been watching him. The murderer, now absent,
had waited patiently for him to see. To see the world through his eyes.
To give him the truth. But the truth about what?

What is this to you?

The door to the room was almost wedged open wide enough for
a body to push its way through. Ripples of energy moved through
the air like transparent waves in an ocean. He could hear the agents'
heavy breathing. Thomas stepped into the dark room. He was met by
a treasure trove of filing cabinets, each filled to capacity with folders
containing a library of information. Information carefully locked
away, never to be seen by those unworthy of the privilege. One of the
cabinets was ajar; jar enough to have been recklessly shut. Perhaps
the argument had ensued at this point. His eyes scanned the tops of
the folders that were out in the open. Names, carefully organized,
mysterious in nature. His mind organized the data and came to
a conclusion; a folder was missing. Recalling the signature, the
connection was made. How hadn't he seen it before? The killer had
practically given it to him.

Why didn't I see this?

Stepping back into the room, Thomas could see that the agents had
finally worked their way inside. One pulled his gun out and pointed
it directly at Thomas' chest.

"This is where it ends, Mr. Ghune."

The cordial title was very Roslin-esque. No doubt, these were
some of his new henchmen. It was likely that even Banks was being
contained at this point. Roslin was out of control. But there was
one more thing he had to see, one more detail. Looking desperately
around the room, he found it. The folder was on the table near
the agents. It lay open, divulging the intimate details of one Taylor
Decastro's life. Who knew how much was there? The papers were
slightly scattered. Thomas looked at Roslin. How had he not seen it
before? His infuriated stance, much like a magic trick, had led his

eyes away from it. Clutched tightly in the hand at his side was a piece of paper. Taking a deep breath, he looked up at the agent who was closing in on him.

"Don't make me do this."

Thomas took a deep breath and leapt forward with everything he had. His mind shot straightaway into pure panic mode. He hadn't planned on this happening. Waving his hand over his watch, he quickly plotted in one of the dates that flashed into his mind. It didn't make any sense, but it didn't matter. As the world was spinning wildly out of control in shards of light, he saw it. He'd taken a gamble that had paid off. The folder was missing its most recent entry; a paper with a photo, a name, and a description with three bold red letters. Luck graced his eyes as he saw the one line that hammered the open question.

T. DECASTRO - KIA

Electric pulses of energy blasted him into another moment in time and space. He felt himself roll over a desk covered with paper. The momentum he had gained in his leap drove him hard into the ground. His hands instinctively shot out in front of him to help absorb the impact. Gasping for air, he sprung up and began running. He had to outlast them. The chase couldn't go on forever. Sooner or later the agents would capture him and his fate would be sealed; just another face that mysteriously disappeared to a nameless fate. He grimaced at the mere thought of it. Looking around, he paused, if just for a heartbeat.

It's good to be back home.

Police men and women were stuck frozen in time in the middle of their daily hustle and bustle. Stacks of papers, fresh brewed coffees, and a plethora of police force nostalgia filled this world to its brim. A warm blanket of belonging came over him. Why he had chosen this date was a mystery. Although, then again, everything he was doing was becoming more and more random. He wasn't himself anymore. There was Vaun. He sat innocuously at his desk, rummaging through some papers. His face was much younger, much brighter. It hadn't been aged by Thomas' incessant demand for more details. It had been Thomas' first day on the force. His introduction would be imminent.

Looking over his shoulder, he saw Pete and the old, but physically younger him. His eyes gleamed with the prospect of becoming the unsung hero of the police force. A weapon for justice. Had he known then what he knew now, he would have probably turned tail and ran. The moment resonated with him. It was miraculous. So many things had happened since then. So many things had gone so terribly wrong.

Suddenly Thomas heard the loud thudding of heavy footsteps coming from somewhere lower in the building. The agents had arrived. Something told him that the situation had escalated. He had directly disobeyed their command. His life may well be considered a necessary loss for the good of the whole. He wasn't going to stick around to see. Turning to run, he saw the agents burst through a pair of doors at the exit. His heart sank as they both reached for their guns. Looking around the scene in front him, his mind plotted a million different options with a million different results. It was a race against time to stay alive. He needed to endure until the brink took him back to his place in the present. Glancing over, he saw one of the routes his mind had exhaustively put together. It was illogical, unheard of, and complete insane. The open room was surrounded by a stair railing that skirted the second level. Above him was a hole he could get through if he could maneuver it right.

I'm going to die.

The men shouted their demands just as Thomas took off full stride. He pressed his fedora down on his head as he ran in a furious sprint. A shot rang out and ricocheted just a few inches from one of Thomas' feet. Thomas leapt up onto a desk. From there, he climbed onto a man's outreached arm as he passed some papers to his desk mate. He carefully placed his foot on the stack of papers which bought him a few more inches. His body swayed slightly as he tried to keep his balance. Another shot rang out in the room. It flew just over his head before bouncing off of a cup of coffee being sipped on by one of the policemen. He plowed his foot directly into a man's face from where he launched himself towards the wall. A large American flag stood motionless in time. Its smooth fabric rippled slightly by the small breeze created by the vents in the building. He reached his hands out as wide as possible and hit his target dead on. In a moment of reprieve, his hands grasped the flag pole tightly, hoisting him higher.

It was surreal. His weight outside the brink would have easily toppled it over. But here the rules of physics were temporarily suspended. It was a playground for the imagination.

The two agents watched in awe as Thomas quickly climbed up the flag, hoisting himself over the railing. But they just as quickly returned to the chase. They had but one job to do; eliminate the threat. Thomas' short cut to the second floor had bought him some time. But the stairs weren't far, and he was running out of options. Looking across the gap in the floor, he saw an open door leading to the roof. But it was on the opposite end. He looked for the closest connection. His heart sank. It passed by the stairs. The same stairs the two agents were scrambling up at a blistering pace.

Can't I ever catch a break?

The agents appeared at the top of the stairs and took aim. Thomas grabbed at the only path available—the lights. They were hung by scrawny, decorative pieces of wires that were suspended from the ceiling. In any normal realm, his attempt would be utterly insane. But here it was his only option. Running straight at the railing, he flung himself over it and flew through the air, arms outstretched, hands desperately grabbing for the flimsy piece of wire. The agents fired a few rounds at him, the bullets streaming by before glancing off a half-opened door. His heart was ripping itself out of his chest. Incredibly, he found his mark and clutched at the wire. It slid through his hands, leaving a small laceration behind as his feet finally came to rest on the pathetically small island that was the light fixture. The world seemed to be rocking back and forth. He tried desperately to keep his balance by steadying himself with the wire. The intense game was pushing his core to its limits. But he had to keep moving. Another wave of well-aimed bullets flew by. The agents had only one goal in mind—kill Thomas Ghune.

Come on! Keep going! You can do this!

Swinging from the time-regulated light fixture, his eyes ballooned out of their sockets as he watched the world below him fall in and out of focus. If he missed, he'd end up a broken pile of bones. The second light fixture came at him more quickly than anticipated. He missed the wire completely. Screaming in terror, he flung one of his hands behind him in a desperate attempt to save himself. His luck rang true as his flailing hand was able to grab the wire just above a glass bulb. His momentum rag-dolled him backwards like a whip. He could feel his joints violently popping. But it wasn't over. His hand was beginning to slip. His weight was forcefully sliding his hand down the wire onto the smooth top of the fixture.

"No, no, no!"

In horror, he watched as his hand slid free. In one last-ditch effort to save his own life, he let go and stretched both hands towards the light bulb. It went against every logical fiber in his body. His mind poisoned him with doubt. But miraculously his hands locked around the bulb just as the force of his velocity stopped him midair. He sighed out a nauseous moan. That sensation was quickly replaced by searing pain. Like grasping a fiery coal in his hands, the light bulb was scorching his flesh. He let out a grunt of agony as he fought the powerful urge to let go. Another round of bullets streamed past his wriggling body, suspended in the air. For a moment he felt like he was going to succumb to the pain and let go. But he dug deep, deeper than ever before, and began pulling himself up.

Come on, Tommy! You can't die now, not here!

One of the agents had reached the railing. The other had preemptively gone down the stairs. They were going to trap him. But they had underestimated his resolve. Fighting against the scorching pain, he pulled himself up to the wire and then onto his feet. Sweat was pouring down his face. He looked back to see the agent pointing a gun directly at him.

"Mr. Ghune, it's over! Don't make me do this!"

Thomas' eyes glinted with emotion and energy. He was panting like a marathon runner. His body screamed in distress.

"It's never over!"

He launched himself at the next light fixture. As he did, the man holding the gun fired off another round. His gun clicked; he would need to reload. The man gave a prompting look to the other agent who was now directly below Thomas. The agent sprinted back up the stairs. He was going to cut Thomas off on the other side. Thomas felt his insides shift as he whirled around the third light fixture's wire like a pole dancer. He came to an abrupt stop upon reaching the top. He was swaying back and forth from the momentum of his jump. He was so close to the other side now, it was just within reach. Peeking over his shoulder at the man near the railing, he saw him begin to reload.

Where do they find these guys?

The heavy steps of the agent dashing up the stairs echoed through the room. Thomas had to make a move. Bracing himself for his soon-to-be ungraceful landing, he closed his eyes. Could he really jump that far? With the sound of a clip clicking into a holster and the echoes of bullets ringing through the building, he vaulted from the light fixture, feeling it give, even if ever so slightly. Amidst a flash of light, another fiery round passed by him, tearing through his suit. His fingers caught the railing and slid. He floundered wildly trying to stop his inevitable plummet. With an excruciating stretch, his fingers found the top of the railing and dug themselves into it. With a magnificent burst of adrenaline, he pulled himself up and over it.

He rolled onto the floor. Looking towards the stairs, he could see the black, polished shoes of the encroaching agent. It was enough incentive to push him on. Springing up from the floor, he flung himself through the door onto some stairs. As he did, a ricocheting bullet whizzed by, sending the agent sprawling to the floor. Thomas pressed his hat onto his head. It was time to run again. Scanning the stairs ahead, he began to feel like death at the hands of the agents might be a better option. He was beyond fatigued. The lumbering pace of the nearest agent resumed. Thomas' time was again running short.

Where is the storm? This is an eternity!

Scaling the stairs two at a time, he looked back to see the agent pointing his gun and firing. The shot missed him and bounced directly back into the massive room. Faint flashes of light were being emitted from the impacts each bullet had on time itself. Directly in front of him was the door to the roof. It was tightly shut. He swallowed a throbbing lump in his throat. He felt ill. His luck had finally run out. He could hear the agent closing the space between them. Soon he'd be joined by the other agent. There was nowhere for him to go.

Damnit, not like this!

Unwilling to give up even now, he grabbed the door handles and pulled. The agent behind him was nearing but had also run out of bullets. He paused only to pull a clip out to reload. Thomas continued thrashing about like a fish out of water. He was fighting for his life. The door had to move. Beads of sweat dripped into his eyes making them sting horribly. If this was going to be the end, h would go down fighting. With another gut wrenching pull, the door moved slightly. Now familiar with the physics of relative time, he jammed his foot into the gap. He grunted with pain as the door pressed into his foot, trying to push its way back to its original position. But it worked. His valiant effort had produced the sliver of opportunity that he needed. Just as the agent secured another clip and aimed, Thomas slid through the gap, letting the door slam shut behind him. Ripples of energy swept through the air. He had bought himself some time, but it was still of the essence. The agents would breach the door soon enough. Where was he going to go now?

Now what, Tommy? Now what?

The roof was an open canvas with no saving grace apparent. He was on the verge of extinction. Frozen in time—birds, garbage, and the still world populated the outside. Feeling overcome with frustration, he furiously kicked a nearby pigeon. The impact vibrated through his body like he'd kicked a rock. But the worst was far from over. Hearing the sound of voices, he looked back and saw the two agents heaving on the door. With both of their energy properly applied, it was opening quickly. In a moment of sheer panic, he ran. This time he had no direction and absolutely no plan. He was stuck on a roof. The only quick route back down would be his last one. What now?

"This is not good, not good at all!"

He ran to the edge of the building. He skidded to a complete stop as his shoes dug into the abrasive cement. His heart skipped a beat. The world down below seemed much further than he had expected. His eyes were wide open. A noxious mixture of adrenaline and exhaustion were competing with each other in his body. He heard a wave of sound as the door to the roof slammed shut. Someone had made it through. Glancing behind him, he saw one of the agents, gun in hand, approaching him slowly. The other one struggled, his body pressed between the frame and the door. The agent approached Thomas cautiously.

"Last chance, Mr. Ghune. I promise I won't keep missing."

Thomas looked at the agent and then at the edge of the building.

His train wreck of a mind was oddly curious about what would happen if he jumped. What would happen to his body? What would happen to the present he was trying to get back to? Would he end up as nothing more than a pile of flesh and bones squashed on the sidewalk below?

"I'm warning you, Mr. Ghune. You either come with me or I end this here."

Again, Thomas looked at the agent then back over the edge.

Where is brink? It's never gone this long!

It all came down to an extreme surge of adrenaline. This moment in time and space was breaking down, frame-by-frame. The agent's finger tensed. A life ending piece of lead was about to exit the gun's chamber. Thomas' life was hanging in the balance. He had only one choice. As he jumped off the building, a part of him let itself die. It was the part of him that still feared death, our final destination, the be-all, end-all, of life events. He knew it was inevitable now. He closed his eyes as he heard the bullet whiz by him. He let his arms flail in the air. The cruel grace of time was now sweeping him away. His future now trapped forlornly in the past. It was ironic, really, that his final resting place would be where he had first started his journey into justice.

I'm sorry.

The ground was rushing at Thomas at a heart-stopping pace. A sudden cloud of pulsing energy and light appeared. Like an omnipresent angel finally coming to the rescue, it swept him away. His time really had finally come to an end.

A blast scattered loose debris into a perfect circle. Thomas' body collapsed to the ground with incredible force. There was a sickening thud as his body's mass conformed to the pavement. He let out a shrill, shriek of pain and terror. The world around was fuzzy. Rolling to one side, he saw a polished set of black shoes moving towards him. It appeared his last-ditch escape effort had only dropped him into the waiting arms of the organization. As his consciousness weaned, he closed his eyes. It appeared that time had finally taken his soul.

29

BANKS OFFER

The early morning air was thick with a salty fog. The sun crept up over the ridge, slowly turning the world to color. The light hit the fringes of Thomas' eyes. He awoke abruptly with a scream. The speeding carousel was violently spinning inside his head. His unique brain was replaying the latest events like a recorded video. It only gave pause to the final moments, the black shoes. Shoes he had seen many times before; shoes that belonged to the agents of the organization. He attempted to open his eyes, regretting it immediately. How long had he been out? Where was he? His body felt trampled. But surprisingly, he felt softness beneath him. Probing with one of his hands, he found he was lying on a carefully stacked bed of plastic bubble wrap.

What's going on?

He squirmed a bit, trying to resurrect his paralyzed limbs. He felt sharp nails of pain in his back. The fall . . . he remembered the fall. At what point the brink had taken him back to the present, he didn't know. But he was alive. That in and of itself was a miracle. He pried his eyes open again, ignoring the intense burn. But where were the agents? Where was the white room he'd grown accustomed to seeing? Where were the handcuffs? He wriggled around like a worm, trying to get his bearings. The boisterous sound of bubble wrap popping filled the air.

"I'd relax for a minute if I were you."

Thomas froze. His face contorted into confusion. But it was

confusion based not on the source of the voice, but why it was even there in the first place.

"Banks, what are you doing?"

Banks hovered near Thomas, holding a bottle of water and a packaged sandwich. He eyeballed Thomas closely, intently looking him over. He made himself busy adjusting a few commands on Thomas' watch. The sequence was recorded in Thomas' mind.

"Hiding . . . just like you. I see you turned off the tracking function on your brink. Always another surprise with you. I doubt we'll have any visitors here."

Thomas pushed himself up to a seated position.

"You know that's not what I'm asking."

Banks looked Thomas in the eyes before responding.

"Roslin's brother's dead. Of course, you knew that. The man's lost his mind. Accusation, interrogations, the whole damn system is collapsing in and on itself. I've never seen anything like it. And then you conveniently go missing. Last seen with yours truly. And to think after all these years . . ."

"Roslin let me go. He saw me go rogue."

Banks sneered at the comment.

"Roslin would never—"

"He did."

"Why?"

"How should I know? You're his little stooge; why don't you tell me?"

Banks looked insulted by the comment.

"This little stooge just saved you. I dragged you halfway across this city making sure not to be seen, and still saved time to help tend your injuries and pick you up a sandwich. Is this how you always say thanks?"

Thomas relaxed his assault on Banks. It was true. Banks could have easily turned him in if he had so desired. But he hadn't. Now, by association, he was on the organization naughty list; a list that no one *ever* wanted to be on.

"Look . . . I'm sorry. It's just been crazy. This whole project has been blown to hell and back. I've been on the run, beaten, bashed, and I don't even remember what else. So let's just ditch the cordial tone and be straight with each other."

Banks Offer

Banks shoved the sandwich and bottle of water into Thomas' hands. He turned around, inspecting the room they were in.

"We're it. That much is clear. Everyone else is dead. The agents tailing you, or rather *us*, were brought in. No doubt Roslin has escalated the issue. We've got no motive, no suspect, nothing. Now the very people I've worked to protect want to see me hung from a noose. How did Roslin let it come to this?"

"You're wrong."

"How so?"

"There is a motive. One that's as cliché and typical as that stupid suit you wear."

Banks paused, letting Thomas fill the silence.

"Love. This killer, this whatever, was in love. Or at least I think he was." Banks shook his head.

"That's impossible. Agents are cut off from the world unless given proper approval. The connection would be obvious. In case you haven't noticed, we run a tight ship."

"Look, I know what I saw. Whoever this guy is led me there. I went back. I'd missed something. But now I've got it all up here." Thomas motioned to his head. "It isn't going anywhere. Next, I've just got to find her."

"You're proposing we go find some lady while Roslin's got all his hounds on our trail? Do you ever listen to yourself?"

Thomas nodded.

"Always; that's the problem. What other options do I, do *we* have? Love it or hate it, we're stuck in this mess together."

"Well, you're right about that . . . I hate it. Since you were brought in, everything's been complete chaos. We've lost agents, *good* agents, and others who were just trying to do the right thing."

"There is no *right* thing anymore. We're in survival mode now. You adapt or die. It won't be long before either Roslin or that psychopath finds us. He's already tried to kill me; what's stopping him from killing you?"

Banks looked disturbed by the comment. He appeared to be waging an internal conflict.

"How can I trust you? You've been less than honest with me since day one."

241

"That's cute how you use that word. I was just going to ask you the same thing. How did you find me?"

Banks shuffled his feet, looking slightly guilty.

"You didn't honestly think I'd just let you walk. You're good at what you do, and I'm damn good at what I do. You'll have to try a bit harder next time."

"So you followed me?"

"Not exactly. But once I found your trail, I put my nose down."

The two let a little time pass before speaking again. Each one was juggling their ideas about trust and allegiance. Once Thomas felt content that they were on the same page, or at least in the same book, he walked towards the door.

"Why do you do that?"

Thomas heard Banks's question but ignored it. Instead, he pursued his more pressing ambitions.

"How do you find someone that doesn't exist? That's what you guys are, right? Ghosts?"

"We try to be. But despite what Roslin might tell you, we're still human. At least some of us are. There's always something left behind."

Banks suddenly looked sickened by his own comment.

"Then that's a place to start. I'm going after this."

Banks shook his head.

"We need to lay low, find somewhere to catch our breath. Things are just too hot right now."

"I don't have time for that. Who knows what is going to happen next?"

Banks took a deep breath.

"Look, I've been with this organization for a long time . . . too long. And I promise you, if you go gallivanting around asking for trouble, you'll find it. They don't take going AWOL lightly."

Thomas was furious. It was a no-win situation. Sit around and wait for it to all come crashing down, or run straight into the lion's den.

"I'm not saying we don't do anything. But we need to recuperate. You already look like crap."

Thomas could feel his weakened body still humming with pain. He looked down the alley, filled with millions of details. So many random objects all worthlessly connected to nothing . . . what a waste.

"Fine, what do you propose?"

Banks Offer

Banks put his hand near his mouth. He was slightly emotional about what he was going to say. His nerves were getting the better of him.

"I know a place. I used to duck Roslin and the organization there, back in the day. It's been abandoned for years. No one would have any reason to look there. I can tap some power, and maybe even get us some water to clean up with."

The idea of hiding in an abandoned building was not inspiring. But Banks's logic was sound enough to agree with; perhaps a day at most, to let Roslin's hounds increase their search radius to away from them. Then he could enact his plan.

"Fine. But a day at most. And even that is generous."

Banks reluctantly nodded his head.

"Why did you want to dodge Roslin and the organization?" probed Thomas.

A brief silence hung in the air. Banks rolled his eyes.

"Wouldn't you, working with those guys for that long?"

Thomas watched Banks carefully. A part of him felt an urge to investigate further. But in truth, he just didn't care enough. Banks was just a means to an end. He knew deep down inside that both of their futures were ruined. Sooner or later they'd be brought in. Sooner or later they'd vanish into a drawer full of paperwork, never to be reviewed.

"Let's go."

Banks was pleased by Thomas' acceptance of his plan. The two had formed an inelegant partnership, but a partnership nonetheless. They had to rely on each other now. Neither of them had anywhere else to turn.

Walking quietly in the shadows of backstreets and alleys, Thomas pondered. He could see all the nodes of information in his mind pulsating like distinct lifeforms, constantly evolving. He would trace a path to one then to another before finding a roadblock. The process infuriated him. It was as if each of his attempts were just a comical jest. The killer's chess pieces were all scrupulously placed with an intent and purpose that was beyond him. This belied his deeply embedded feeling that he was getting close. He knew he had to be. He'd seen so much at this point. He had some ideas. There was someone he still needed to talk to, someone who helped stoke his logic furnace—Barb. Despite his inherent brilliance, she always found some angle that his inhuman self just couldn't see. But for now it would had to wait. He couldn't risk it.

"It's not too much further. Just keep your head down."

Thomas listened to Banks's words while his mind continued to latch onto ideas, images, and details. It was exhausting. He had never been pressed this hard. So far it had been the ride of a lifetime, but he was ready to get off.

"Here it is; there's a back window I can slip through. I'll come up to the front and let you in. Just make sure nobody's watching. And I mean *nobody*. These guys can look like anybody."

Banks walked around to the back of the building. Its old, boarded up windows and peeling paint were testaments to its long held place in time. It had likely been condemned by now, waiting for a new purpose that had never come. Places like these were havens for the homeless and occasional drug addict. But Banks was right on one accord; nobody would ever think to look for them here. As he watched Banks shrink into the distance, he mumbled under his breath.

"It's not *them* I'm worried about."

Feeling suddenly strained from all of the tension in his body, he sighed out a gust of stale air. He began to survey the area. It was the run-down side of town for sure. Common to large cities, there was nothing particularly special about it; just another unexceptional collection of rundown buildings and clutter. That's when it dawned on him—but it couldn't be—it was absurd.

No way . . . it couldn't be, could it?

Suddenly his brain was creating a collage; the credit card machine, Barb's relocated photo, and every other altered or out of place detail in between. Was his paranoia getting the better of him? Banks had assured him that no one would know they were there.

Keep it together, Tommy.

But the feeling wouldn't leave him. It needled him like a pestering child, pleading their case, nonstop. Was this a set up? How many intricate threads had been woven into the tapestry of madness that was his new reality? How many times had he fallen into a trap so carefully fabricated? He perused his doubts, ran through his logical walls. Roslin and Banks were all that was left of the so-called originals now; Roslin, Banks . . . and him.

Scrutinizing the immediate area around him, he saw a large, dusty sign. It had been placed in an obscure corner of the lot. Its dirty face rendered it unreadable. Unable to fight the urge, he brushed his fingers over the surface to reveal its message:

DEMOLITION SCHEDULED

Now his heart was racing. He realized the obvious. The building's life was coming to an end. With shaky fingers, he removed the remaining dust and saw that the date had been changed. The new date was today, but there was no one around. He recognized the calling card of a malicious genius. All hell was about to break loose.

"Banks!"

Screaming as loud as his vocal chords would allow, he ran. This time he wasn't running for his life but Banks's. Banks, who had disappeared into his old hiding spot to open the front door, something he'd done many times before. A pattern, a habit, a point of predictability; how could Thomas have been so foolish?

He flew around the corner of the building. He didn't know *how* it was going to happen, he just knew it was. The game was in play and another pawn was about to be sacrificed.

"Banks!"

His scream was mixed with hopelessness. Where had he gone?

"Banks! Where *are* you?"

Tears of frustration filled his eyes. Banks was nowhere to be found. He grumbled profanely under his breath. He was about to lose again. He continued to find himself on the receiving end of catastrophe. He plowed over a pile of debris, feeling himself lose control. A feeling of desperation welled up in him like an unwelcome guest. He couldn't shake it off. He jumped from the garbage pile and tripped on some aged wooden boards. He lost his balance, sending him plunging to the ground. He landed hard on his knees in the filth surrounding him. He let his head hang.

Banks, where are you?

With his eyes closed, he breathed deeply in an attempt to collect himself. It was all he could do not to just give up. Then he picked

up a scent. He had smelled it before; Banks's cologne. It was a trail
of hope. Hopping back to his feet, he did his best to track the scent
to its source, but it was near to impossible. Every breeze would wisp
it away, making its remnants that much harder to find. Letting out
a guttural scream of frustration, he continued yelling for Banks,
hoping he would respond. As his voice went hoarse from his effort, he
spotted a window.

It had been pried open. Banks had to have come this way. Thomas
swallowed the acidic lake that had formed in his mouth. Was he really
going to try this? He had no choice. He had to try and save Banks's
life. Banks had saved his; it was the only decent thing to do.

Here we go.

As he took a step towards the window, there was a sudden
rumble. The rumble quickly turned into a deafening clap of
thunder, accompanied by a shock wave that rattled the ground. The
detonations were going off.

"No!"

His scream was muffled by another detonation. The building began
to shake itself apart. Shrapnel was raining down on him in a vicious
storm. Throwing his hands over his head, he crouched down. After
another soul-shattering explosion, the building began to collapse. His
nerves were exploding in hysteria. The mayhem was coming down
with incredible force, like death casting its shadow from above. He
had no choice but to flee. Despite his depleted state, he put everything
he had into the rhythmic pumping of his legs. He could feel hunks of
debris scathing the exposed portions of his clothing and flesh. His heart
jostled around inside its bony cage like a bouncy ball. If he couldn't
clear the blast zone, he'd be crushed then buried in rubble.

"I'm not going to die here!"

He let out a guttural scream fueled by his desire to survive. The
fates couldn't let him die here; not like this. His work wasn't done, his
purpose unfinished. He felt like the very bowels of hell had consumed
him, and yet he remained. His legs felt like two burning match sticks,
their usual strength vanishing away into thin air. Feeling the last
ounce of strength he had leave him, he made a last-ditch attempt at
salvation with a behemoth leap. The materializing shadow continued
to grow and grow, consuming his body entirely. With outstretched

arms and his heart pounding in his throat, he collapsed to the ground and rolled. The monstrous racket enveloped him along with a thick cloud of dust. Then, everything got eerily quiet. Only an occasional crack or pop broke the silence as the remaining parts of the building finally accepted their fate.

Turning to his back, he gasped for air. The dust stung his eyes. The thunderous blast was still ringing in his ears. Banks . . . Banks was dead. Pounding the ground like a mad man, he let loose his rage; the pointless losses, the bitter taste of defeat, the hatred. His eyes watered, caught between an emotional outburst of both sadness and anger.

"No, no, no, no!"

His mind was bogged down by a thick layer of pestilent filth. His brain was spinning out of control; so many sensations, feelings, and pains.

"Stop, stop it!"

He pressed his hands against his head. Rolling over, he plowed his face into the ground. The tears of disappointment and rage dripped to the ground, forming little muddy marshes in the dust.

Why didn't he hear me? Why didn't I see this coming?

He couldn't tell what was real anymore. Somewhere in the distance, he heard the banshee-like call of sirens. Soon the site would be buzzing with activity. If he was found, who knew what would happen? Maybe it would just be better that way. Maybe the more he tried, the more things would continue to get worse. But now there was no one. The safety blanket that was Banks was gone. Now more than ever his heart burned with an evil desire. He wanted to kill the demon; the demon who had orchestrated his hell from the dark.

"I'm going to kill you, I swear it."

Pulling himself to his feet, he picked up his hat. It looked battered and worn. It now seemed like a lifetime ago that it had come into his life. Such a stupid thing, his hat was. But there was a lot of history in that hat now; people's faces and memories of the past, mixed with the terrifying present. Sniffing the air, he put it back on. He was going to beat him. And he was willing to die to do it.

30

MR. AND MRS. SMITH

Banks's loss had hit home harder than Thomas had expected. For someone he had largely held at a distance, he had to admit that Banks had grown on him. But he was gone. Crushed beneath tons of uncaring rock. There was no way he could have survived. His body might eventually be found, launching an insidious cover-up. He hated the organization now; all of them. How could they ostracize their own the way they did? How could Roslin be so blind as to launch an internal witch hunt for those who had risked their lives for a better tomorrow? A part of him wanted to believe that Roslin was behind it; the master puppeteer using those around him to advance his position ever further; a power whoremonger. But it didn't make sense, did it? It was for this reason he had to see her; he had to see Barb.

It had taken hours to skulk his way through the backstreets and shadows. Occasionally, he'd pass a vagrant begging for a momentary reprieve; a dollar here, a nickel there, unperturbed by the world burning down around them. But it didn't matter. Sooner or later, the evil he now knew so well would show up on everyone's doorstep. It had to be stopped. He wondered what to say and how to say it. He felt so dark now, so cold. His emotional state was a dire one. Perhaps he was finally losing himself. Rapping on Barb's door, he let himself slouch. He felt utterly deflated.

The door opened slowly. He saw two eyes peer out cautiously. When she saw it was Thomas, she ushered him without hesitation.

"Thomas! Thomas, you're covered in dust! You've got blood all over you!"

Thomas nodded his head. Her presence was a welcome one. It was like a breath of spring had come to his wintered heart. He put on a weak smile.

"I'm fine; really, Barb. I just had a little tussle with gravity."

"You're such a horrible liar. Here, let me—"

Barb tenderly began brushing him off.

"What happened? What's going on?"

Thomas felt his heart sink as he responded.

"They're dead. All of them. Every agent on the program is gone. Banks was the last, and I practically walked him to the hearse. I was so stupid, so damn stupid! I was so distracted by my emotions I didn't see it coming, like always."

Barb stood tall in response.

"You're not stupid, Thomas. You're one of the smartest people I know. You can't blame yourself for everything. That's what this psycho wants you to do. He's breaking you down."

Thomas slapped a few objects off the table near where he stood. They crashed onto the floor loudly. He put his head into his hands and did his best to muffle a scream of anger.

"They're dead! Every one of them! Banks, the other agents, the men at the dock . . ."

Barb sensed the progression and put a hand on his shoulder, looking at him gently.

"Jena . . ."

Thomas rocked back and forth, unable to contain his overwhelming feelings.

"I know, Tommy, I know. And there's nothing you can do about that. They're gone, Tommy. You've got to let it go."

"But I can't! I can't, Barb! I'm . . . I'm scared."

Saying the words, he felt his emotional dam burst open. He collapsed into one of Barb's over-sized chairs. The truth had final set itself free. *He was afraid.* Not just of losing, but of being alone. Almost everyone he had ever had ties with was either dead or estranged. His life had become an empty existence. He didn't want to be alone anymore.

Barb slowly walked up to his side and grasped one of his hands firmly in her own. She looked him sincerely in the eyes. The glint of caring had grown twofold. She was close to him now, a critical brick in his building of life.

"You're scared. You're scared that no matter what you do, you'll end up alone. That those you care about most will be the first to go. Tommy, I understand. But there's something *you've* got to understand now."

Thomas winced as if in pain. His eyes pressed tightly shut.

"What?"

"That even though they're gone, they've never left you. Each and every one of them is a part of you. In some way, shape, or form they helped mold you into the man you are today. Each of them left an indelible imprint on your life. Their stories are a part of your own. That's the real power, Tommy; recognizing that. Recognizing that you're never truly alone."

"Why couldn't I save them? Why couldn't I make things right?"

Barb kneeled down beside him. She placed Thomas's other hand into hers.

"Because sometimes our losses can help us appreciate what we have. Losing someone can sometimes help us save ourselves."

Thomas looked into Barb's eyes. He could feel the warm flame of friendship that had grown between them. But now there was something else; a tiny spark that seemed to be igniting in a shutdown part of his heart. He dwelled on the feeling a moment before dismissing it. This wasn't the time or place. Her words had touched him. As always, she had a way of making his mind slow down, forcing him to pay attention.

"Okay, okay . . ."

Thomas got out of the chair and wiped his face off with his sleeve. He turned slowly back around.

"I don't know what to do now. I, I've got all of this," said Thomas, pointing at his head, "but nowhere to go. I'm just running in circles."

Barb conjured a pen and began gnawing on its end. She took over his vacated spot in the chair. Her position implied that he should continue.

"All the agents are dead, only leaving this Roslin guy. But then there are the people at the dock, the other people harmed. I'm not seeing a connection."

"Maybe there isn't a logical connection. That's the point. Maybe this guy is running blind."

"Running blind?"

Barb stretched her arms out while gazing at the ceiling.

"Well, let's start with the unknowns. Who is the woman?"

Thomas recited the name the instant her inquisitive sentence ended.

"Taylor DeCastro an agent like the others."

"So, I'm assuming she's probably off record, as they say. This guy wants you to see her, and then tries to shorten your lifespan by a few decades. But he initially wanted you to *see*. That's the point here."

Thomas shook his head. The point seemed dull.

"I don't get it. Why go through the trouble?"

"That's exactly my point! This guy, for some reason, slipped up. He let his emotions trump his logic, not that you'd know what that's like. He didn't *have* to show you; he *wanted* to. His emotional bark wanted to be heard. He wanted you to feel something."

Thomas let his mind drift for a moment until her image came to him.

"Jena?"

"Jena."

"But that would mean that whoever this is has had eyes on me —"

"For who knows how long, maybe using his little wrist rocket like yours. He did his homework. He obviously felt like you and he shared some connection."

"But there's the problem. Everybody's dead. There's just me and that jerk Roslin. I don't have time to go dig up the other men in that room. I'm almost positive they're already dead anyway."

"Forget them for a moment. Let's figure out *her*."

Barb got up and sat back down at her computer. She opened up a few browsers and began typing. Thomas took her place on the couch. He continued mending his wounds as best he could. Barb let out a long sigh.

"Nothing . . . not surprising. At least nothing that looks remotely interesting. There's got to be something else."

"They're ghosts. They've probably deleted most, if not all, of her history. But there's still the name on the wall. I've got an idea."

Thomas got out of his chair and nudged her over to look at the screen.

"Hey, I'm enjoying myself here! Not every day I get to look up dead, secret organization agents involved in some deranged love story."

"You are a genius. Barb!"

Barb looked confused. Thomas tapped the keyboard wildly.

"That's got to be it. The name on the cave wall . . . maybe it was a nickname or something. And the love thing, maybe there's something to that."

"What do you mean?"

"Right before this last agent died, he told me that romance within the organization is generally frowned upon. If you saw these people, that would come as no surprise. So what if that happened? What if an agent fell in love with another agent but they hid it from everyone?"

"They eloped! How dreamy."

Barb clapped her hands together.

"Stick with me, Princess; this dream turned out to be a nightmare."

"Fine . . . typical male ego. I'll indulge the idea that the fairy tale didn't work out. Always looking at the negative in things Tommy. So what's your plan?"

"If I was going to elope and I was handcuffed to the organization, where would I do it? I mean, where would you find the time to do something like that?"

Barb puckered her lips.

"Oh, Tommy, you just lack imagination. You don't need time, just the right setting. Dark night, sneaking out to some secret spot, saying the vows before shaking the bed posts, bodies tense, fingers wandering . . ."

"Barb, please, stick to the details. We're not writing a romance novel here."

Barb frowned.

"What I was getting at is that there's probably a record somewhere.

"Barb, you always outdo yourself."

"I'm an amazing specimen, this I know."

Thomas' fingers were blazing across the keys. Barb shoved him away playfully.

"Hey! I'm investigating here!"

Barb rolled her eyes.

"You lack creativity. This requires a woman's touch."

She quickly pulled up a list of all the hotels she'd swooned over with her friends. She asked Thomas for more information.

"Where's this little organization's hub, the beehive, if you will?"

Thomas pointed.

"Odds are these guys are on call almost all the time, like you. So keeping to schedules is a must. So they'd need somewhere quick and easy. Bingo!"

Barb turned the monitor for Thomas to see.

"Cupid's Eros! That phrase doesn't even make sense."

"It's a play on words, Thomas. It's cheesy, quaint, and accessible. It's well within the search parameters. And trust me—I'm a lady—we *love* this hopelessly romantic crap."

Barb pulled up the number for Cupid's Eros. She dialed, and then snapped her fingers.

"What was that name again, the one on the wall!"

Thomas looked baffled but responded.

"Johnny, but it's just one name. The registry would have two, wouldn't it? Assuming they were that stupid."

"Trust me, they were."

A voice picked up on the other line. Barb politely asked about the hotel registry. She lied, stating that she and her husband had visited there for a celebratory night, and had forgotten the date. She covered the mouthpiece of the phone with her hand.

"What's the last name? This lady's going along with it, but wants our last name."

"*Our?*"

Thomas gave Barb a wink. She responded with a sarcastic sneer. Thomas' brain quickly scanned over every name he had ever known. From there, he broke it down to the most likely of candidates. But it was stupid, sloppy, and completely arrogant. Would someone sworn to a life of secrecy be so cliché?

"Smith . . . try Smith . . . I don't know."

Barb smiled.

"See? You're finally starting to get it."

Barb looked around her desk until she found a pen and paper. She jotted down a few details as she listened.

"Ask for the time. The time they checked in."

Barb looked slightly confused, but obliged.

"And when did they, *we* check in that day?"

Barb's was magnificent. Her acting, spot on. She put down her phone with a smug look.

"Guess what I found?"

She gave the piece of paper to Thomas who looked it over. The date, times, and names stared back at him.

June Smith

Johnny Smith

"But why be so stupid? I mean, assuming this is even right. Someone could easily track this down with the right information."

Barb sighed.

"And here I thought I had you at abysozologic . . ."

"*Abyssopelagic*; of, like, or pertaining to . . ."

"Whatever. Point is, nobody found anything because they didn't have a reason to look, until now. This was an act of defiance, but a part of them wanted the world to know. They wanted to prove that their love superseded all the stupid rules. A true Romeo and Juliet. My heart's practically throbbing out of my chest right now."

"Well, that's all great until Juliet dies. Now Romeo is burning down the whole city."

"A vengeful heart looking for relief. I imagine he's a very conflicted fellow."

Suddenly something lit up in Thomas' mind. A little light bulb surged with current, illuminating paths in his mind he hadn't explored before. Was it possible? Could it really be so sinister? Thomas dabbed at an open wound on his face before he responded.

"I think I have an idea of what to do. I just hope I'm right, and that you're right."

Barb smiled. She swayed across the room before collapsing into her favorite arm chair.

"Thomas, I'm always right. You know that."

Thomas' eyes suddenly widened, his heart skipping a beat. He was having déjà vu. Barb walking across the room, sitting in her armchair . . .It was all so . . . *predictable*. The hairs on the back of his neck stood straight up. A tingling sensation permeated his body.

"Barb! We've got to go *now*!"

Mr. and Mrs. Smith

Thomas leapt from his chair with an inhuman strength. He threw himself at Barb, tackling her from her chair and onto the ground.

"Thomas! *What* are you *doing?*"

Barb's scream was instantly muted by a deafening crash. Barb's apartment wall collapsed in on her chair, crushing it flat beneath the enormous weight. From outside, someone screamed. A massive crane was whipping back and forth, out of control, its operator holding on for dear life. It passed through the apartment again, ripping another segment away like it was made out of cardboard.

"Watch out!" screamed the operator.

Thomas pulled Barb off the ground.

"Go, *now*! This whole place is going to collapse!"

Barb nodded silently. She looked terrified, but mechanically did as she was told. Thomas pulled her to her feet and they ran for the door. The crane ripped through the floor behind them, large chunks of the apartment collapsing into the rest of the building. The screech from the immense power of the crane shredding both steel and rock were gouging out their ears. The trail of destruction nipped at their heels as they ran. With each passing moment, it was closer to swallowing them whole. But just as it appeared that the end was upon them, they saw the front door.

"Keep moving. Don't stop for anything or anyone!"

Screams could be heard echoing from every direction. The chaos had awoken everyone to a new state of fear. Nothing was safe anymore. Sprinting down the stairs and out the door, they watched in horror as a massive chunk of the building fell free. It thundered down, landing on top of a few parked cars that were squashed like toys. Fires erupted randomly, as an array of broken pipes haphazardly spewed water over the scene. Sirens sounded off in the distance. The madness was just beginning.

"Thomas! Watch out!"

Barb suddenly shoved Thomas hard as motorcycle veered off course nearly crashing into him. The cyclist panicked and overcorrected, sending himself flying like a rag doll across the ground as his motorcycle smacked into a thick wall of brick. It burst apart into a hundred pieces. Thomas couldn't believe his eyes. The world around him was crumbling around him. The scene was horrifying.

"Keep moving, Barb! Just keep moving!"

Thomas grabbed her and began hurling her forward. All the while his mind scanned every angle, every detail, and every possibility. Hell had been unleashed. The devil was coming for him at all costs. Everything was just collateral damage at this point, even human life. An explosion erupted down the street that sent another crowd of people scrambling for their lives.

"He's not sure where I'll go, so he's just going to blow up the whole damn block!"

Both he and Barb were sprinting as fast as they could. Thomas felt like he was having a very bad dream. As they rushed down the sidewalk trying desperately to flee the worst of it, they heard out of place. The sound was being reinforced by powerful waves that pulsated in the air and the whooshing of metallic blades cutting through matter at a blinding speed. Looking up, they saw a helicopter. Its pilot had abandoned his post, thus vanquishing all hopes of controlling the destruction his aircraft was inflicting. And it was coming right at them.

"We've *got* to get off the streets, *now!*"

Thomas grabbed Barb by the shoulder as the helicopter cut its way through the overhead power lines. Sparks rained down from the sky like fireworks. The helicopter struck the ground creating an ear-splitting screech of metal against asphalt. Its battered blades spun madly, ripping everything in its path to pieces. Its velocity was incredible, and it was now within striking distance of Thomas and Barb. Just as their escape appeared to be futile, an alley presented itself like a path to paradise. They expended every last bit of energy they had to dive out of harm's way. The think blades narrowly missed their flailing legs. The immense force of the blades whipping through the air propelled them further down the narrow passage. They were both screaming at the top of their lungs.

They fell hard against the ground, knocking the wind out of them. The helicopter continued spinning wildly out of control.

"Where can we go?"

Thomas didn't know what to say. All he cared about was assuring Barb's safety. He could feel his own life force beginning to fade. He couldn't last like this much longer. All of the damage to his body was overcoming him.

Mr. and Mrs. Smith

"Barb, we need to split up. You can't stay with me. Is there somewhere you can go?"

Barb's eyes were rimmed with tears threatening to spill. She was trembling in fear. Thomas remembered seeing this same emotion a lifetime ago in Jena, and it broke his heart. Some of the parameters around his purpose were changing. The fiery flues of his hatred were being soothed by love for Barb, and those he'd left behind. She had been right; they were all still with him. Their faces empowered him to go on. He put out his hand to hold Barb's, which was shaking uncontrollably. He drew her close and hugged her. He didn't know why, and he didn't want to know—he needed it. He let the moment linger before letting go of her hand and repeating himself.

"Is there anywhere you can go, Barb? Somewhere no one could find you; not even me. I can't know."

Barb was crying frightened tears. But she kept her composure.

"I think so, yes."

"Then go there, now, until this ends. Don't come out until it does."

Thomas looked into Barb's eyes and did his best to show her his deeply felt emotions; he genuinely cared for her. Suddenly, another explosion went off somewhere behind them, sending a wave of debris into the alley. Thomas threw his arms up to shield his eyes.

"Thomas . . ."

Barb's voice sounded faint. Suddenly she collapsed to her knees.

"Barb!"

A piece of rebar was sticking out from her side. It had punctured her clean through. A crimson river of blood gushed out of the wound with each heartbeat. Her complexion went white. She was fading fast.

"No, Barb! No! Don't do this to me! Not now! We've made it this far!"

Barb smiled weakly; a smile that even Thomas knew was fake. As her eyes rolled back in her head, she muttered her last words.

"I'll be fine. I've got you, don't I?"

Her body went limp, her last breath drawn. In complete anguish, Thomas collapsed on top of her. He let his heart relinquish all of its pain in a soul-shattering wail; a ravaged heart's last plea for redemption gone unanswered. He was now utterly and truly alone. As the city shook around him, he could feel himself beginning to slip into darkness. Death's shadows were closing in on him too.

31

A GOD'S JUSTICE

Staggering through the unkempt streets, Thomas could feel his heart breaking apart in a furious frenzy. Love's sweet reprieve had again been stolen from him. Now his soul burned only with hate. He was going to finish this once and for all. There was only one man he wanted to see; one man who plagued his mind like a festering infection; *Roslin*. He was someone who held all the keys and who had conveniently been absent at some of the most critical moments; a mysterious man with a manor-sized closet of secrets. It would take everything he had not to kill him on the spot.

I'll make them pay, Barb. All of them.

He was careful, more careful than he had ever been before, not to be spotted. To not follow his normal routes. His mission now was to not be himself. But in all honesty, he wasn't himself. Not anymore, how could he be? The evil that he professed to want to destroy was now dwelling inside of him. A vile seed most sinister, growing bigger with each of his heartbeats.

An explosion erupted somewhere in the distance. Undoubtedly, more innocent lives had just been lost—another dart thrown at the board that missed its mark. Their lives were taken by mistake. A human mistake. He saw it now more clearly than before. The killer was *human*. Even more human than he'd expected. Evidenced by the mindless violence he was inflicting. A few dots connected in his mind. Dots strung together not by logic, but emotion; a human experience that had eluded him for much of his life.

A God's Justice

The bleeding heart of a psychopath.
Arriving at what would be his final turn, he approached the corner cautiously. He was at ground zero, where it all began. Where he had been introduced to the program and the organization. Where he had glimpsed for the first time. Where the snowball from hell had begun rolling downhill. Glancing around the corner, he saw the world he once knew in flames. The street was ablaze; mobs full of mindless violence dotted the landscape, looting stores, vandalizing property. Agents were strewn about dealing with issues as they haphazardly presented themselves. The back alley door to the ominous building was being loosely guarded. With the right physical persuasion, he could get in. Instinctively, he reached for his gun and badge. They were gone. But he had known that. So why did he still react the way he did?

A creature of habit. Habits . . . humans have habits. Even I have habits.
Taking a deep breath, he prepared himself for the feat of strength his battered body would have to endure. No one could know it was him. No one could know who he was coming for. Retracing the steps of the building in his mind, he calculated the quickest route back to the white room. But just what he'd find there remained a mystery.

Let's go, Tommy. Let's do this!
Bursting out into the open, he tap danced around a mob of looters tussling with the local authorities. Screams of panic could be heard all around. The city was literally falling to pieces. A few agents had pinned a man to the ground who was screaming out the reckoning of god. He did his best to skirt past them without making eye contact. He moved like a ghost passing in the night. Within a few steps of the organization's entrance he came to an abrupt halt. Two men were there, each armed to the teeth. They deflected any would-be-assailant by their mere presence alone. Thomas's heart sank. How could he possibly get by them? Although distracted, one foolish move might ultimately be his last. But he had to try.

Waiting for just the right moment, he joined a passing mob who had dared press their number advantage on the agents. The agents drew their guns and began issuing ultimatums. The chants for violence from the crowd grew in intensity. But then he found the miniscule window of opportunity that he had been looking for.

With the distraction of the unruly crowd taking front and center, the agent's stronghold on the entrance had slipped. Taking an almost half-dive at the gap, he lunged forward. His momentum propelled him past the squabbling guards and through the open door.

He could see the white hallway in front of him. Inside, more chaos was unraveling things like a spinning top. He was stopped abruptly. So abruptly in fact, it had knocked the wind clean out of him. As he tried to catch his breath, one of the agents grasped his shoulder firmly and pointed a gun right between his eyes.

"Where do you think you're going? This area is off limits! We will use appropriate force if necessary!" the agent bellowed.

Thomas' normally brilliant mind had somehow gone offline. He could think of nothing to say in response. His heart was practically pounding its way out of his ears. Just as the agent looked poised to apply the *appropriate force* he had mentioned, a shot rang out from somewhere in the crowd of bodies. Everyone dropped to the ground, petrified with fear. The perpetrator was the would-be prophet who had somehow managed to wriggle himself free and get a hold of one of the now-slain agent's guns. He continued his lunacy by blasting another bullet towards the agents at the door.

"God's justice is upon you!"

The agent released Thomas before turning to fire on the heretic doomsayer. As swift and cunning as a fox, Thomas made his escape. He worked his way through the maze of bodies. Medics were treating the injuries of the fallen. The secret building looked to be in shambles. A part of his humanity beckoned him to stop and help those around him. But he knew the worst was still coming. The wrath of time would take no prisoners. The flames of hate could not be so easily extinguished. Letting everything around him pass by him like a horrific nightmare, he kept moving. He had to get to the white room. He wasn't sure why, but he felt as if he was being drawn there; as if his insatiable desire for justice had plotted the course on its own. Back to the beginning to most likely meet his untimely end.

Arriving at the high security room after narrowly avoiding capture, death, or worse, he paused. Something was different. The door was malfunctioning. Its heightened level of security was fractured by mechanical failure. All of its components appeared damaged, as if someone had forced their way inside. Feeling lost, he shook his head hoping to rattle himself back to reality. That's when he saw that the door was ajar just enough to pry his fingers into it. Mustering every ounce of energy he had, he yanked on the door fervently. With a groan and a moan it slid open. He sprinted inside, feeling his heart beginning pound madly. What would he find?

Running out to the middle of the floor, he immediately felt the presence of another. The lights in the room flickered off and on. Sparks shot out from the fixtures, creating a surreal effect. Standing in the darkness were two men. Seeing their silhouettes shook Thomas to his core. One he quickly recognized as Roslin; or at least what was left of him. He had been brutally assaulted, tortured, and looked well on his way down the slippery slope towards death. Holding him tightly was Thomas' nightmare incarnate; his allusive prey. The killer stood firm, fixed, and resolute, holding a gun to Roslin's head. A gun that Thomas knew well, as it was his. His heart sank. How had he been so stupid? Leaving something so critical behind to become a trophy for his evil adversary. It suddenly all became crystal clear. He was being framed for the murders and hell that had been unleashed. He had been but a pawn in the master's hands. The mere thought of it sickened him. He could only conjure a few words in response.

"Why? Why make us all suffer?"

The dark, empty eyes in the mask gazed back. They were burning holes right through Thomas. Although unseen, the hatred, hurt, and pain in the room was palpable. Both men had reached the end of their emotional road. A moment passed like an eternity in time's vortex. The anticipation was insufferable. The harrowing response from the killer made him go cold.

"Justice!"

Thomas' eyes widened. Frame-by-frame the scene unfolded. In an almost supernatural way, his brilliant mind had almost altered time itself. Every detail of what was happening came flooding into the safe harbor of his cerebral memory. The dark, soulless eyes—the dark mask and gloves—the finger pressing slowly to release the hammer on the pistol. In seconds, Roslin's life would be taken. Then the man would promptly deal with him, leaving the rest to whatever his sinister plan called for. He had one chance. Glancing down at his watch, he turned it on and plugged in the one date and time he could think of. It was beyond comprehension that he could get it right, but he had to. His memory had put the pieces together utilizing sticky pieces of emotion, the likes of which he'd never known before. He had changed; the game had changed. As the bullet left the chamber to smash its way through Roslin's skull, shards of light consumed him. Whatever lay in the past was now his only hope for a future. Should he fail, his life and the present he knew would be gone. Only time would tell.

32

LOVE AND DEMONS

Collapsing on the ground, Thomas shrieked in pain. His head was exploding. He had put everything he had, every detail, every clue, every shred of human emotion he could muster, into one daredevil move. He had to be right; he *must* be right. Getting onto his feet he looked at the world around him, frozen in time. A better place, a happier place, maybe at some time, to someone, but to him it was nothing but the spawning pool of a demon. He had chosen this place for many reasons, but one above all; being human. Even the most brilliant, the most psychotic, held on to something that still made them human; habits, feelings, a sense of purpose. Even a deranged killer still had molecules of humanity left. He'd realized this about himself. He'd come full circle. Tommy Gun—brilliant detective, prodigy—but still human. Looking up, he saw the sign to the building:

Cupid's Eros

Such a stupid title. Thanks, Barb.

The quirky hotel was adorned with everything one might expect in a place like this. Red velvet furniture and every hopelessly romantic knick-knack conceivable were on display. All placed to set the mood for the right price. But that wasn't why he was here. He had only one purpose, and he needed to act quickly. Glancing at the open guest registry book at the front desk he saw the names he and Barb had found.

June Smith

Johnny Smith

Even now, their sheer arrogance was fully demonstrated; the couple's complete disregard for authority on display. Love—why did so much hate seem to come from what many would call the purest emotion? Love for one's self, for another, or just the idea alone. Love is what had started all this; or at least the loss of it. Looking past the names, he found the corresponding room number—a suite—why not? Taking in a long, drawn out breath to summon whatever courage he had left, he moved on.

The frozen in place world of the past, as always, was awe inspiring; so many details being held firmly in place, ready to be analyzed. As he moved up a set of winding, carefully designed stairs towards the top level of suites, he took it all in. But for the first time, none of it seemed to be entering the whirlwind of thoughts in his mind. Was it possible that somehow, someway, his emotions were blocking out his logic? If so, what had he become?

You can do this, Tommy.

Arriving at the top of the stairs, he moved forward towards the suite of choice. He was briefly shocked to see the door held open by a chair, just enough to squeeze a body through. Shocking, and yet expected. It appeared he was on the right track. Pushing himself through the narrow opening, he entered the room. It was filled with all of the romantic charm one would expect. The lights had been properly adjusted to further ensure the passion driven aura meant to lower inhibitions. His thoughts turned to Jena. In another life, they could have shared this picturesque, if not overbearingly charming, moment together. Perhaps they'd laugh at how ridiculous it all was before letting loose their caged emotion under ever dimming candle light. But it would never be. Suddenly, he stopped. His mouth fell open and a lump formed in his chest the size of a softball. It was her. The woman from the mountain. She was dressed in an alluring ensemble of lace and satin, her complexion superbly warm. Attire meant to bring any man falling to his knees in desire. She sat, back pressed to the headboard, waiting, smiling, inviting. The contrast between this and her future lifeless frozen body was remarkable. She almost appeared to be an entirely different person. She wasn't alone; standing just a few feet away was a man. He stood over her casting a shadow across the bed that was slipping ever closer to her. His back was turned to Thomas, his identity still shielded. Stepping a few feet closer to the man, Thomas smelled a heavy dose of cologne. Its liberal use had loudly pronounced its presence.

I know this.

Thomas froze in place. The smell was generic cologne. He had smelled it many times on many people. But this was different. The aroma was generic, but not its connections to all of the details he had collected. The bed with the woman from his first glimpse, the shipyard, and now here. It made all the difference. He knew this man. But the thought of it being real, that his brilliant mind had connected enough dots to be judge, jury, and executioner was staggering. How could it be? His heart ached with an incredible pain. He felt both betrayed and let down, as if someone in his own family had been hiding a terrible secret from him. Tears welled up in his eyes. But it was too late now, for both of them.

Taking a few steps closer to the bed, he let himself be seen. He could feel him, his cold, dark eyes watching his every move, anticipating his next intent. It seemed pointless now, to speak to the man who had mastered the brilliant game of time. He undoubtedly already knew what Thomas' presence there meant. And yet he remained silent, watching.

"I can't believe I didn't see it before. All this time . . . you've been showing me all along. I was just too blinded by my own pride. Blinded by my own logic. All those people, all that death, there never really was a true direction or purpose—only revenge—blind, selfish, revenge. That's why you killed them all; so many people that didn't deserve to die. Isn't that right *Johnny*? Isn't that what she called you? We've all got nicknames around here, don't we? Damned if Jo hadn't told me from the start. *Man in Black*, I've always hated that music."

He suddenly felt movement in the shadows behind him. For a moment, the image of the dark, masked horror came front and center to Thomas' mind. But there would be no masks here. Not anymore. Here the killer was his very human self. Wallowing in self-pity and carefully cultivated hate. Hate that had driven his gifted mind mad. Mad enough to forgo all allegiances and promises he had once made.

"They all deserved their fate. Each chose their path."

All shrouds of mystery had been slashed open. He knew this voice.

It was no longer the warped voice of evil he had received from the dark mask. This was human, and belonged to someone he had grown to know well. Banks stepped from the shadows of the room. He looked longingly at the beautiful woman on the bed. He had tears in his eyes and was shaking slightly. A combination of both regret and hate appeared to be fueling his thoughts. The sting in Thomas' heart was now amplified tenfold. Banks had done it all.

"What are you saying? No one reserves that right! You killed those men at the docks, those agents, *Barb*; you even tried to kill me!"

Banks pursed his lips as he fought back his emotions. His inner turmoil was seeping out rapidly.

"I did what I had to! Those men at the docks were the same men I wasted my life chasing! The agents, those men professing allegiance to Roslin and that damned organization, brought this on themselves!"

"Those agents were your partners! They were your friends!"

"Don't you think I know that!" said Banks, tears streaming down his face.

"I see their faces every single minute of every single day. But I had to do it. I had to! They'd understand. I regret it but I did what was necessary."

Thomas watched as Banks's composure crumbled with inner conflict. He felt the pain and remorse for what he had done, and yet still believed that the ends outweighed the means.

"They had nothing to do with her!"

Banks's behavior quickly shifted. His eyes narrowed into two barely visible slits.

"Don't you ever mention her again. Do you have any idea how long I looked? How long it took me to finally find her? I spent a thousand lifetimes retracing her steps throughout time, only to find her abandoned, dead! Her sacrifice meant nothing! She was ripped right out of my hands. The only true thing I ever had! Taken! By them!"

Thomas wanted to say something but knew that his silence would beckon more of the dark tale.

"I told them she had survived! I knew she couldn't have been lost so easily. But Roslin, that damned Roslin, gave up. He gave up on her! He left her to die! On a mission she never should have been on! But did anyone do anything? Did anyone in the organization step in? No, because there's rules. Rules, protocol, and *lies*. It was then I knew what I had to do. If I couldn't have that little scrap of humanity, then none of them would—especially not *him!*"

Banks's absolute hatred for Roslin was in full swing. Now it was clear. All the times that Thomas had seen the fire in Banks's eyes when he looked at Roslin, had been a pure hatred restrained. How many years had he contained his inner demons, waiting for just the right time? How many years had he spent meticulously planning? His lost love had created a monstrosity of a man. It was all making more and more sense. Banks had reprogrammed his watch when he had taken it from Thomas early on. That was how they kept finding each other. Banks knew how to disappear without being traced. He had left the bread crumbs behind. He had been watching Thomas since day one. Whenever Banks was missing was when the calamities reached their zenith. He was a true master of manipulation.

"Don't you see? I had to make him suffer. Make him feel the loss that I felt when the only world he knew burned to the ground. Make him feel my pain. Then, and only then, could I finally take his life— once I saw the same fear and pain in him I once saw in myself—only *then* could I let him die. In his ashes, I'll start anew. I thought you'd understand. I thought you of all people could see what I was trying to do. I thought you'd understand my loss. But I was wrong. You're just like them. Blinded by the pretense of justice in a broken system. Being led around by the devil himself."

Thomas felt his soul sink. All the times he had nearly tasted death were resurrected in full clarity in his mind. The loss of those closest to him. The loss of Jena, and now, Barb. Banks's psychotic breakdown had cost him everything. He had nothing left to lose.

"To hell with your sick sense of justice! You've killed countless innocent people! Because of you, there'll be no world left after it's all said and done! You're sick!"

Banks's body began to tremble. He pressed his hands hard into the sides of his head and screamed.

"I had to do it! I had to make them pay! I hate all of them! I hate this world that robbed me of her!"

Banks's demonic voice of reason divulged the absolute truth. He had completely lost himself to his hate. No matter the consequences, he would destroy the lives of anyone he saw fit to in an attempt to soothe his infinitely tortured soul. But Thomas knew this could never happen. In his own loss he had discovered something. That one can never truly be healed; the scars never go away. But in them he had found strength and purpose. It had taken him this long to finally forget himself. Forget his selfish desires and aspirations. He was no longer fighting for his own personal gain. He was fighting to preserve the chance for others to feel what he had been so shamelessly robbed of—*love*.

"How many times have I come back here? How many times have I tried to save her? But as soon as I return to my present, she's gone again."

Thomas stepped closer to Banks before responding.

"No one can rob death, not even you."

"You're wrong. I'll find a way. Even if I have to destroy time itself, I'll get her back!"

Thomas clenched his fists tightly. He knew that sooner or later the world around him would be shredded to bits, ripping him back to his horrific future. His adrenaline was flooding through his beat-up body. What little energy he had left had to redeem whatever future he had left. He wasn't sure what the consequences would be, but someone was going to die. He knew what he had to do.

"Don't make me do this, Banks! Please don't make me do this!"

Banks's eyes narrowed. His trembling ceased for just a moment. In a deep, inhuman voice he responded.

"But you already have."

In a burst of desperation, Thomas lunged at Banks, who went for his revolver. He caught Banks's hand and smashed it into the nearby wall. Banks howled an agonizing scream as his revolver clacked to the floor. He responded quickly by smashing an elbow across Thomas' face. Drops of blood exploded into the air from the impact. Banks dashed for his gun. Thomas followed on his heels. Spitting out a pool of crimson blood onto the floor, he watched as Banks leaned over to snatch up his revolver. With cat-like reflexes, he threw his body into Banks's back. The two men collapsed to the floor.

"If you don't stop there won't be a future left!" screamed Thomas.

"Without her, it doesn't matter!"

They rolled around on the ground, desperately trying to win control of the revolver. Banks slid an arm around Thomas and caught him in a choke hold. Thomas coughed out a blood soaked wheeze as he struggled to breathe. He appeared to be losing ground in his weakened state. His mind quickly locked onto the revolver. Recalling all the rules of time, he swung one of his feet wildly about, inching it ever closer to the gun. Reaching it, he kicked it across the room. It slid under the bed.

"Stop getting in my way!" screamed Banks.

His grip on Thomas' throat lessened, his attention moving to the revolver. Thomas managed to land a furious punch to Banks's face. The impact sent Banks sprawling to one side. Thomas clumsily tried to stand back on his feet. He could feel his aching body throbbing in misery. He had to fight through it. Taking a few more steps, he suddenly felt weightless as he plummeted to the ground. Banks had swept his feet out from under him. With a juicy crunch, his body hit the unforgiving floor. Thomas let out a painful moan. He frantically rolled to one side and saw Banks struggling to his feet.

"We could have changed it. We could have saved them!"

Thomas shook his head.

"How can you save them when you can't even save yourself?"

Banks let out a roar of anger as he jumped up and sprinted for the bed.

"Then I'll kill *you*. I'll kill all of you!"

Thomas huffed and puffed feeling slightly light-headed. He painfully pushed himself to his feet and chased after Banks, who was already looking under the bed, trying to spot his missing revolver. Banks felt his presence and slowly arose. They were both bloodied and battered and both knew it was the end. For a moment they stood silent, chests heaving in unison. It was Thomas who broke the silence.

"I thought you were my friend! I thought I could trust you!"

Banks's body shook violently. His eyes were bloodshot, filled with a mixture of sadness and rage.

"I was. I tried to show you. I tried to give you a chance! Now you've made me do this! One of us has to die!"

Thomas flinched at the comment.

"I'm already dead."

At Thomas' comment, they leapt at each other as if rehearsed. They threw a frenzy of punches, each trying to subdue the other. Blood was splattered all over the room. And still the fight continued. The struggle spilled onto the bed as the time frozen world sustained them in the most surprising ways. Thomas found himself wedged between Banks's lost wife and his former self. He grabbed onto one of the old Banks's arms to pull himself out of the way of an enraged fist heading in his direction. The punch narrowly missed its mark and instead plummeted into Banks's time frozen self. His knuckles crunched and buckled against his own face, locked in time, years ago. He let out a howl of pain.

Thomas dropped to the floor looking frantically for the revolver. He saw it. To his great frustration, it was on the far side, just out of reach. He quickly rose, just in time to catch a well-placed kick to his stomach. He felt his insides shift around as a stream of blood spewed from his mouth. Through sweat soaked eyes that stung madly, he saw Banks leap across the bed. He was going for the gun. Unsure of how much more he could take, he pursued.

Come on, Tommy, you've got to beat this!

Thrusting forward, he latched onto one of Banks's heels and pulled on it with all his might. The unexpected grab stalled Banks's progress, who responded by throwing a whirlwind of kicks. A few found their mark to bone crunching effect on Thomas' face. Banks snatched up the revolver and spun to face his old friend.

Thomas could barely see. The world was fuzzy; his body was shutting down. He could see the hazy outline of Banks bringing something up in front of him. He knew it was the revolver. With almost no direction or fight left in him, he made a purely instinctive move, falling across the bed and grabbing onto Banks's arms. Banks fought him off. Thomas put every ounce of strength he had into his hands. He needed to make one last move. As Banks continued to ward off the attack, one of Thomas' hands grabbed Banks's free arm. The sudden momentum sent Banks's arm crashing into the nearby nightstand. Then, with a monstrous backhand, Banks sent Thomas sprawling backwards over the top of the bed and onto the floor.

Thomas watched as everything seemed to be fading to black. His physical self was completely diminished. He tried to raise himself up slowly. He at least wanted to see his end standing. Through streams of crimson haze he stood as firm and tall as he could. He watched Banks take aim with resignation.

"It's funny that you and I would finally come full circle like this. In the very place where it really all started for me, it all ends for you. But the world will never know."

Thomas glanced at Banks's hand that was free of the revolver and smiled. Banks followed his eyes and his eyes immediately widened in horror.

"You of all people should know, Banks. It's all about the set up; keeping someone's attention where you want it."

Banks's watch had been smashed to pieces. The prodigious piece of technology that was the brink was no more.

"I agree. It's funny. Time ruined our lives and now it's time that's going to rip us apart. I'm sorry, Banks, I'm so sorry."

Banks's shaking heightened to a new level. His eyes darted around madly.

"You couldn't! You *wouldn't*!"

"I have!"

As if a self-fulfilling prophecy had finally been hastened, the world around Thomas and Banks suddenly began spinning wildly out of control. Brilliant shards of light thrashed their way through the air in the usual maelstrom of energy. In complete terror, Thomas watched as Banks was rapidly being ripped apart. Waves of energy riddled his body with holes. A mortifying howl erupted from Banks that shook the very foundations of Thomas' being.

"I'm so sorry, Banks. For all of this."

At the precipice of destruction, Banks's last labor came with a resounding blast from his revolver. Through space and time the bullet pierced Thomas' chest.

Banks screamed one last time.

His hateful life was finally laid to rest. A massive burst of light arrived with a deafening roar that blotted out the world. As it did, Thomas felt himself fading quickly. His end was neigh. With only moments left to live, he pulled out his watch and put in the only date that mattered to him. Everything went silent and fell into a sudden darkness. Had he been too late?

33

TIMED MERCY

The tornado of light came to a mind-numbing stop. It spewed out a bloodied, battered, barely alive Thomas. He rolled onto the floor and gazed aimlessly up at the ceiling. Every facet of his being had been taken to its limits. Glancing down, he saw his hand firmly pressed into his side. A river of blood oozed its way between his fingers, assuring him that his time was coming to a close. Looking across from him, he saw his hat. The singed red feather, the worn-out details; it had been through hell and back. He reached out for it. His shaky fingers grasped the edge, feeling along its now rough surface. Miraculously, it had made the journey. As to how, he had no idea. Clutching it tightly, he slowly rose to his feet. The effort took an insane amount of concentration. His life essence was draining away.

Just one last time . . . Just one last time . . .

Turning his head, he saw her. Jena. Her face was filled with pure terror. He saw himself trying to shield her from the bullet that had been fired from the would-be killer. His brilliant mind had put him at the absolute precipice of Jena's untimely end. There, floating in midair, was the bullet. It had taken everything from him that day. But now it seemed so harmless, stuck in time here.

Approaching Jena, his heart swelled with pure emotion. It was almost too much to bear. Their potential life together could never be; he knew that. And yet he had returned. Why? He felt himself begin to shake. His body was shutting down. Perhaps this was meant to be, both murdered, side-by-side. It was poetic, if not appropriate. In death they would finally be together again. He looked down at his wounds. Blood soaked hands stared back at him. .

Suddenly, even in his weakened state, something hit him that had eluded him thus far. Time was an incredibly powerful force. One that dictated the ultimatums of everything it touched. And yet, in some intimate sense, it was his. Apart from the universe, he had *his* time. His choices and decisions dictated *his* time. Until now, his sole purpose had been to return to Jena's side. But he couldn't change *her* time; only *his*. The idea came so forcefully that it blotted out all other aspects of his mind. He knew what he needed to do.

Walking to his former self he could see the fear in his eyes. Only it wasn't fear for his self, but for Jena. In that acute moment, he had shed all of his concerns for anything else. It was an act as pure and powerful as any. His love had made him a willing sacrifice, though he had been narrowly spared that day. Instead, she had been taken. His intent had been to save her then, as it was now. Looking himself in the eyes, his heart pounded like a war drum. He was going to finish the job. Grabbing onto his past self's shoulders, he began to scream aloud.

"She's gone and you can never have her back! We can never have her back! But that doesn't mean we can't save her!"

With every fiber of his being he began pushing on his frozen body. He let out a wail of excruciating pain as he leaned in. But his efforts weren't to move him away from the danger, but rather into it. He was trying like mad to put his old self into the path of destruction that had changed his world forever.

"Come on, Tommy! You've got to help me! We can save her!" he screamed aloud.

Tears streamed down his face, mixing with blood and filth. His heart was aching with pain and realization. No matter what the result, she would never be with him again. But his intent was as powerful as ever. His love for her transcended both time and space. It was love that had brought him here, and it was love that he was willing to give everything up for; even his own life. Screaming from the very depths of his soul, he gave one last herculean effort to displace his past self the few inches he needed to put it into the path of the bullet. Just as it seemed that his efforts were in vain, and that the last of his life force had left him, a massive burst of light enveloped the room.

Tommy! Keep going!

The light began to spin uncontrollably around, fragmenting the room into a million pieces. But at the center of the commotion remained Thomas. His efforts continued as he pressed on valiantly. He would not be deterred. With a mind-shattering blast of energy and force, his froze body slid to the side just enough to take its intended place. A tornado consumed the room whole, including him. In a flash of light, it all disappeared.

34

TO DIE ANEW

Thomas looked down just in time to see the bullet enter his chest. Jena's screams filled the air. The searing pain of the heated lead pushing its way through his flesh was all he could feel. He fell to the ground. He watched as the man that had consumed his nightmares forever ran away, diamond ring in hand. He could see everything now, even their old apartment. Everything was just where they had left it that day—each item in its place—every detail, accounted for. He had come back. By some miracle he had altered the course of time; *his* time.

"Thomas! Thomas!"

Looking up as the world was fading away, he saw her angelic face. Jena looked as beautiful and pristine as ever. His heart overflowed with love for her. So much so, that the fear of his imminent death seemed inconsequential now. Using the little life he had left, he put up his hand to her trembling face. Their eyes met and he could feel her energy, her love. So many memories together, so many dreams. In the last moments of his life, he professed everything that meant anything to him.

"Jena, I love you and always will, no matter what."

Her tears pelted his body as his last breathe was drawn. His heart took one last thunderous beat before falling deathly still. Jena's sobs were all that remained.

Thomas felt himself suddenly feel peaceful and free. His tortured soul seemed to be a distant memory. He could sense himself floating through both time and space. The world was dark and yet there seemed to be a ray of light that pierced through the blackness. The light grew and grew until its intense ray had all but removed the darkness completely. He looked on in awe as his paralyzed self could only watch. As the light's intensity grew to blinding white, he found himself being sucked into a spiraling vortex of energy. It jerked his essence around in its tumultuous sea before coming to a complete stop. Suddenly, the feeling of weightlessness was amplified; he was falling.

Thrashing around wildly in the air, he felt a brisk chill rush over him. He opened his eyes just in time to see himself plunge into ice cold water. His lungs immediately burst wide open in shock. The impact rang in his ears as he desperately tried to swim to stay alive. His efforts were rewarded as soon his head popped out of the water. He gasped for breath, his eyes the size of beach balls. What had just happened? Where was he? Looking around frantically, he could finally see where he had ultimately landed.

The river, the bridge, and the location that he had at one time carefully picked out lay before him. This was the exact location where he had once upon a time tried to commit suicide. But that was an age ago, wasn't it? His head spun out of control as his memory became convoluted with so many different details, from so many different times. Forgoing his mental dilemma, he swam to shore. Reaching the shallows, he rolled onto the ground utterly exhausted. Without thinking, he reached for his chest. The bullet hole was gone. But that was impossible. He had felt it blast through him. He had been within inches of death.

What's going on, Tommy? What's happening?

Sprawling out on his back, he suddenly felt the warm embrace of a towel on his face, and a voice that he instantly recognized.

"You'd better dry off. That was quite the plunge. To be honest, I didn't think you could do it. Guess I was wrong. But that fall, must've made a deal with the devil. Would've killed any other man I know."

The voice belonged to Roslin, who stood proudly just a few feet away. He, as always, was adorned in his favorite dark suit. He looked over Thomas carefully, inspecting every detail.

"What are you doing here? What is this? What happened?"

Roslin put on a childlike smile.

"I told you things like this tend to get messy. But you're not much of a listener are you, Tommy?"

Thomas gathered himself, wrapping the towel around his shaking body. He looked at Roslin head on. He could see the small pendant he wore; three triangles locked in the center; once Banks's calling card, still shrouded in mystery. But that would have to wait for another time. A fluster of emotions filled his head, but he disregarded them for his curiosity

"Where are they? Where's Barb, where's Jena?"

Roslin sucked in a deep breath of air. He let his eyes gaze at the freezing river.

"Your lady friend, Barb, is fine, and I'm sure she, as does everyone else, thanks you. Jena, however, is a bit more complicated. But I'm sure you've already figured that out. Love sure is a tricky thing. Two separate lives in two separate places, and yet still so very much connected."

Thomas let his mind dwell on Roslin's words. He recalled it all at lightning speed. That's when he realized that he'd been right. He couldn't save both Jena and himself. But he had, through the grace and power of love, sacrificed *his* time and life to save *hers*. She would go on living in an alternate future, one without him. The ultimate goodbye and gift that he could give her.

"A paradox, I believe, is what Mr. Orson might call it. But that's none of my business. Never quite been my cup of tea. Besides, due to your actions, our entire program has been blown to smithereens. So it's the least of our concerns now."

Roslin then began walking away, disappearing into the darkness. Thomas sprang to his feet, tossing the towel aside.

"What about Banks? What about all of those agents? He killed them . . . *all* of them."

Roslin paused. He puckered his lips and whistled a catchy tune that made him smile.

"Mr. Mathers is taken care of, again, thanks to you. And those agents owe you their lives."

Thomas shook his head. The horrific future that he had once

known had been thwarted. Someway, somehow, he had done it. He had beaten back time itself and one of its most deviant manipulators.

"Now, I'd go play some catch up if I were you. Probably help you to see some familiar faces."

Thomas was overcome with joy but with a tinge of sorrow. The few meaningful lives he had, had been saved. Although he could never see Jena again, it comforted him in some way to know that she was still living her life somewhere else.

Roslin took a few more steps before he came to an abrupt stop. He pulled something out of his trench coat pocket and tossed it at Thomas' feet.

"Here, picked this up on the way over. I've got to admit, it's kind of grown on you."

Thomas watched with disbelief as a peculiar hat he knew well was plopped at his feet. Only this hat was untainted, in its original condition. The red feather looked as vivid as new. It was amazing. As Roslin was now almost completely out of sight, he yelled one last question.

"What now? Where are you going?"

From the shadows came the response.

"Around, Mr. Ghune. I'm always around."

Thomas looked on as Roslin disappeared without a trace. Only his off-key whistling remained for a moment longer.

"Seriously, who is that guy?"

Thomas picked up the hat and looked it over. It had represented so many different things. It had been through the very furnaces of hell with him, in a cat and mouse chase throughout time. So much had changed. *He* had changed. He was no longer the man he used to be. Instinctively, he reached for his badge in his pocket only to find it empty. But he knew it would be; it was just an old habit. His hand landed on something else though, a piece of paper, neatly folded. He brought it out and opened it. In the dim evening's light, he read what had been carefully inscribed there. His heart raced, and his mind was spinning wildly. He looked back at the hat. He picked it up and slowly put it on top of his head. Through all the losses and trials, he had become something more. He now had a direction and a choice to make. Breathing deeply and steadily, he began walking. He was Thomas *Tommy Gun* Ghune; washed-out detective, fugitive on the run, and rogue time traveler. With only the future now ahead, time would only tell what would come next. Adjusting his hat precisely, he spoke aloud, affirming his choice.

"Alright, Tommy. Let's do this."

THE END

Enjoy this excerpt from a thrilling new book by Mikel Parry:

PEDIROL

Chapter 1- Crash Test Dummies

The massive fuselage rumbled with the intense pressure. Violent vibrational waves pulsated as it rattled wildly out of control. The chaos in the brief moment in space and time was all consuming for those trapped inside.

"Cat, what's going on? Give me a read!"

A frantic look of despondency took over the normally stoic man's face. He was aged, yet looked surprisingly young. A few streaks of grey were woven through his thick, dark hair. His eyes were a blazing hazel that beamed like two headlights showing the way. Although average sized, he carried a swagger that made him seem twice as large. He was weathered, but not tarnished; he was someone that had stared directly into the eye of the storm many times, just out of pure curiosity driven indulgence. This man was obviously in charge—and unhappy. His name was Commander Max Colburn, or as his indentured crewmates fastidiously called him, Mack—a clever combination of his first and last name—a name that many had obviously dwelt upon for many, many hours. Continuing on with his demand, he gazed over the chaos.

"Cat, give me something! This whole ship's about to go down!"

The man he was talking to was slender with a luminous set of light blue eyes. Atop his head sat a well-groomed plop of brown hair. His movements were calculated, agile, and purposeful, thus giving him the nickname Cat. As he responded to the Commander, he mashed himself against a seemingly never ending board of lights. Sweat poured down his face like a leaky pipe under pressure, spewing out his anxiety. He was one of the mission specialists, a talented young

crew member with hopes of reaching the stars. His real name was
Phillip Gatti.

"Stone, what's going on? I'm completely drowning over here!"
Phillip yelled, slamming a fist against the flashing board.

Sitting to his side was a beautiful woman also hammering against
the impressive array of technology. Her hair was a deep, almost rusty
red. Her skin was a flawless yet pale shade, divulging her obvious
commitment to her mental escapades taking place indoors. Her
face was as hard-nosed as a diving fighter jet, exposing her unbroken
resolve to stay focused on succeeding in the mission. She was an
unbreakable rock. For her, there could be no failure. She was known
by her peers as Stone, but on paper she went by Stephanie Stendahl,
Mission Specialist.

"I'm losing stability! We've had a fracture to the rear booster! What
the hell is going on out there?" asked another man.

The man unhooked himself from his seat and stood up quickly.
He paced over to the flashing board of lights that both Stephanie
and Phillip were madly trying to tame. He was a taller, well-built
man with finely trimmed blond hair. His blue eyes scanned back and
forth, scrutinizing every detail of the ongoing disaster. His stance and
composure drew a very clear picture of his prominently dominating
attitude amongst the group, the self-appointed alpha of the shuttle
team who went by Sheldon Walker, Mission Specialist. Despite his
inflated self-image, the group had come to know him as Guppy—
degrading stabs to try and slow his all-consuming ego's growth.

Sheldon shoved Phillip to the side as his probing eyes looked for any
appearance of reason among the collection of baffling information.

"Hey, that's not your job! Get back in your seat!"
Phillip slapped Sheldon's hands away from the control board.

"You're obviously not doing your job, so let me fix this!"
Just then the rumbling within the fuselage intensified. The
immense vibrational force sent Sheldon to his knees. He let out a
gruff, grumbling roar in frustration.

"Guppy, get back in your seat! We don't have time for this!"
screamed Max.

"Scotty, can you please help me pull out of this?"

Max glanced over the side of his shoulder to see his trusted co-pilot scrambling like a mad man to keep control of the reeling ship. He had a skillfully trimmed mustache and grey beard that ran directly into his perfectly matching hair. He too, much like Max, had a young, yet also aged look about him. His eyes were a lightened shade of green that made them appear almost grey. He had only a couple splotches of color left in his hair, which gave off a dirty blonde-like tinge. His name was Scott Taylor, Mission Co-Pilot. His behavior divulged the fact that both he and Max had some real, hard-won experience behind the wheel. They moved like a set of twins, recognizing each other's body language and reactions.

"There is no out! This whole section is blotted out like an oil spill on here. There's nowhere to steer clear! We're in an asteroid field!"

Scott's eyes looked deeply worried as he peered into the monitor in front of him. There, the universe around him was passing by in bursts of light, dark, and freely orbiting matter. He tried desperately to keep the ship clear of all of the massive pieces of potentially deathly matter. They had already been grazed, but a full on impact would eviscerate them, molecule by molecule. Prospects for survival were looking more and more unlikely by the second. They needed to do something—and fast.

Max swung a blazing look of anger at Sheldon, who was now just getting back to his seat.

"You didn't see this coming? What were you scoping all this time?"

Sheldon gave him a belligerent look in return. He practically snarled like a dog in response.

"I took the best calculated path! Don't put this on me! Those things came through another orbital path we didn't foresee! How was I supposed to know we'd run dead straight into this?"

Max shook his head before returning his focus to the flashing emergency lights across his own monitor.

"Incoming!" screamed Scott, throwing his arms up in the air.

A massive blast sent the crew into a state of complete weightlessness for just a moment. They were slammed back into their chairs with frightening force. Sparks erupted from the ceiling, along with spewing jets of steam. The ship was falling apart.

"My panel is blacking out, along with our life support systems!

Pedirol Excerpt

We've got to jettison through the escape pod now!" pleaded Stephanie as she rattled around helplessly in her seat.

"Negative—there's no time. We'd already be toast before we reached it. Our only hope is to reroute some power back to the thrusters and burst. We can recalibrate the system once we're outside of this field where we'll be safe!" shouted Phillip loudly over the now deafening noise.

"There is no power! Didn't you listen? I'm blacking out!"

"Mack, you've got to make the call. If we don't do something quickly we're all dead!" yelled Phillip urgently.

Max thought over their options at lightning speed. They only had a few minutes before they would lose control of the ship, impact an asteroid, and be shattered into smithereens. The time for action was now.

"Cat, reroute the power from all adjunct systems. Stone, make it happen! And Guppy, would you keep your eye on that damn radar? We can't fall out of the pot into the fire! Scott, prepare to angle this thing out of here, even if we've got to plow our way through!"

Stephanie shook her head but did as she was told, as they all did. On this ship, the Commander's words reigned supreme, and Max was it. Despite the ill-favored logic that had woven their escape plan together, other options were unraveling rapidly. Scott turned to Max, moving his headset out of range of his whispering voice.

"Max, this is suicide. This mission is a scrap. There's no way we're pulling through this."

Max looked Scott sternly in the eyes. His heart was racing up into his throat, screaming to have it all come to an end. Now the only thing that stood between the crew and ultimate failure was an ungodly amount of tax spent dollars, sheltering them from the cruel reality of the inevitable. Max searched for the words to say, but just couldn't find them. He was freezing up. Throughout his life, he'd always been the one with an answer, a plan, some quick, witty scheme to escape any scenario. But now, stuck in the chaos, he could think of nothing to say.

"Reroute successful! Brace for auxiliary thrusters!" Phillip's voice brought Max back to full awareness.

The crew braced for the colossal force that was about to hit them. Each stared at the wave after wave of battering asteroids that loomed at every path forward.

"Thrusters now firing!" screamed Stephanie emphatically.

The ship suddenly jutted forward, pressing the crew forcefully into their seats. Both Max and Scott were now working in overdrive. The seemingly unbreakable maze of orbiting rock stood between them and salvation.

"It's going too fast!" bellowed Scott, ripping his hands free from the controls. "I can't see anything!"

Max glanced over to see Scott's monitor clouding up with blurred images of the massive rocks they were narrowly skirting by. There was no light at the end of the tunnel. Max hung his head, also releasing his manual controls. He had failed them, failed them all; his crew and his team. He looked up just in time to see the ship heading straight toward an assured impact with another humongous piece of matter. He shook his head with furrowed brows.

Not again; not like this.

The impact rang through the ship, creating a screeching roar. The crew instinctually covered their ears. Suddenly, all went dark. The mission and its crew disappeared into the infinite fathoms of space. A brief silence was interrupted by a discouraged decree.

"That's the fifth time!" yelled someone from the darkness.

Suddenly, the lights burst back on inside of the fuselage. The disoriented crew members were slumped down in their chairs, but slowly began unharnessing themselves. Without warning, and with a steam-filled eruption, a door flew open and even more light flooded the ship's hull. One by one each member of the crew exited, hanging their heads in disappointment while belting out streams of profanity, ripened by frustration.

Once outside, they entered into a cavernous white room. Large cables wound this way and that, like vines in a jungle. Above them sat a massive control room, situated almost directly over the ship's fuselage. The ship, however, wasn't really a ship at all. In fact, the whole purpose of it was to act as a simulator; a space shuttle flight simulator of the highest order. The cutting edge technology used had cost untold amounts of money to build, manufacture, and maintain. It had been painstakingly developed with intricate programs to test crews at the highest standards. It was the closest thing to reality that money could buy. At the base of the massive apparatus stood a wide-set woman carrying a flat piece of electronics. She stared at it up and down as her nostrils flared in anger. She was dressed in a business suit that matched perfectly every item that graced her. Her blond hair was obviously colored to hide her increasing age, setting off her dark blue eyes that seemed to see through everything. The crew knew her as the overseer, though they'd never say that to her face, for fear of a sudden rapture. Professionally she was known as Nancy Dubanowski; Director Dubanowski to be precise. She was at the top of the facility's food chain, next to her equally devious partners. The crew was at her mercy.

Nancy approached Max without hesitation, pointing the tiny tablet like a sword at his heart.

"What was that? Just what the hell was that? This is the fifth time, Max! What, do you think this is some sort of video game? Maybe we should crack open some cold ones and just play another round of asteroids?"

It was obvious that their lack of performance had tipped her already unstable self over the edge. Max shrugged as if still lost in the moment. He turned to see his crew already snapping at each other's necks.

"I told you to let me fix it! Why don't you learn to listen once in a while, Gatti? You're trajectory was wrong and needed correction!" Sheldon screamed, pumping out his inner rage.

"Oh, can it, Guppy! You're calculations were the reason we got caught up in an asteroid field in the first place! Don't you dare try to put this on me!"

The remaining crew members joined in the quarrel, keeping it healthy and alive. Max listened, feeling the frozen shards of panic that had imprisoned him in the last moments of the simulation begin to thaw.

"Alright already, shut up! All of you! Just take it down a notch! We all failed—each and every one of us. There was something we were supposed to do that we just didn't do, okay? It happens. We've got to fix it, so let's stop the whining."

Sheldon shot Phillip another stinging look, clenching his fist into a tight ball. Scott put a hand on Sheldon's shoulder, whispering something into his ear in an attempt to cool this overflowing, boiling pot of a man.

"Can I speak with you for a minute, Max . . . alone?" asked Nancy, putting her face directly next to his.

He could smell her perfume, mixed with the minty freshness of her chewing gum. He could hear her jaw mashing up and down on the gum with a juicy plop each time she spoke.

"Whatever you have to say, you can say in front of my team," declared Max defiantly.

Nancy shook her head and grimaced, pursing her lips tightly together.

"Max, follow me. Now!" Nancy sneered in a gruff, almost man-like voice.

Max turned and made a gesture of sincere disapproval before following her out and away from the group. As he strode after her, his guts squirmed like a bag of bait. How had he come so far, done so much, just to still end up following another suit around like a dog on a leash? He had been a phenomenal pilot, one of the best, always top of his class. He had led countless missions with great success. Never once had anyone questioned his ability or leadership. Yet in the program he was in now, it was an almost daily occurrence. He had spent countless hours on simulators that seemed to be adding up to a big nothing. He wanted to fly. That's where he belonged; in the sky, or even higher. But for now, his space wings had to remain tucked away somewhere inside. If he wanted to follow his dream, he had to accept that it came with all the bureaucracy and paperwork one would imagine.

Nancy stopped on a dime once satisfied that they were far enough away from the group to be heard, and began her premeditated onslaught.

"You just don't get it do you? You really don't. It's like another world for you here, isn't it? This isn't the Wild West that you're used to, Max, where you can shoot now and ask later. You should know better. How many times have I asked—no . . . pleaded—that you get your team working together? We've been at this for months, Max. Months!"

Max nodded his head grudgingly.

"I know we've had some minor hiccups, but these guys are the best at what they do. I feel like we're making good progress and should be on schedule for the launch."

Nancy looked disgusted at the very mention of the word launch. She poked her tablet into Max like a cattle prod.

"That's if there is a launch."

"Wait, what? What do you mean, if there's a launch?'"

Nancy rolled her eyes.

"Again, you just don't get it. This world isn't run by good ideas, new discoveries, or warm feelings of accomplishment. It's run by money. And to be frank, there's none left! This whole program is being bled dry. You have any idea how much it costs just to run these simulations and have you all bunked up here? Well, don't bother trying to guess. I'll tell you. It's utterly ridiculous. Might as well put a waterpark on the moon for what we're spending. And every day that we don't give the board and the public something to sink their teeth into, is another round of funding burned up! People are bored, Max; bored of the whole idea of space travel to the great beyond. People don't care about some planet they can't get to in their car. People don't care about finding new answers to questions. People care about entertainment. And we're not giving it to them."

Max curled his upper lip, feeling the small ember of passion smoldering inside him suddenly burst into a wildfire.

"People will care! We just have to show them how amazing this stuff really is. I mean, we're traveling to Mars and beyond! Isn't that enough? We're doing things our ancestors couldn't even dream of, and yet you want to pull the plug and watch it all go down the drain? You can't be serious."

"As a heart attack. Why do you think I'm riding you like this? We need results, we need success stories. Otherwise, people will just turn back to watching the newest waste of life's five minute claim to fame. You're biggest challenge isn't going to Mars and beyond, Max. It's getting those people to care enough that the gods who sit on high decide to shower their coveted money down on us. Without their funding, this is just a boy scout project."

Max hung his head. How he despised what he had just heard. Had the general public truly degraded to such a numb state of mind?

He didn't want to think about it. For him, getting to see the known galaxy up close and personal was worth all the pain he could fathom.

"Look at me, Max; look at these wrinkles. I didn't used to have these, you know. I was a Dallas Cowboys' cheerleader once. This place is going to be the end of me."

Nancy waived her hand in the air, a flake of nostalgic regret breaking free from her protective, crusty layer.

"Commander Colburn! It's good to see you!"

Max looked up to see the tall man who had greeted him so warmly coming down the stairs. He had the appearance of an ancient tree, strong and tenacious. He, too, was dressed with the utmost professionalism. His name was John Stonebrook. Along with Nancy, he was a towering addition to the overwhelming authority drowning Max's hopes. As John approached, his warmness began to dampen on seeing Nancy's countenance.

"How are you, John? How are things?" asked Nancy sincerely.

John ran his long fingers over his chin. He was assessing the situation before answering, using his experience to do so.

"They're good . . . pretty good . . . well, honestly, they could be better. I hope you've all made progress?"

Max fumbled around his mind looking for a good excuse, but came up short, as always.

"These simulations are ludicrous. I mean, has anyone actually piloted these missions? They're insane! We've put so many hours into that machine, I swear I've lost track of reality. Tensions are a little high right now, and the crew is feeling the frustration, which brings me to some questions. What exactly are we being trained for here? The apocalypse? I thought this was about getting to Mars and beyond? What is it you're expecting from us?"

John closed his eyes and took a deep breath.

"Max, we expect the best. That's what you're supposed to be; that's what it says on paper. We aren't going to fund a billion dollar cruise for you and your crew that ends up like the Titanic. We are taking no risks with a program as delicate as this one."

A retort came promptly from Max.

"I just want to get my boys up there and get the job done, but I can't when you guys keep handcuffing me to bureaucratic BS. What's with all the smoke and mirrors? We know what we need to do on our end, so let's just make it happen!"

"Max, that's the problem. You're not making it happen. The board doesn't like to hear about failed simulations and a dysfunctional crew. What do you think that will do to our PR if your lack of success leaks out?"

Max folded his arms, looking like a scolded child. Although he chose to keep himself quiet and reserved, on the inside he was a flurry of frustrated anger.

"Fine, have it your way. We'll step up the training and burn the already burned out candle just a bit more. But I promise you, we will make that deadline and launch the mission! What more could you possibly ask for?"

John's warm complexion returned as he spoke, calmly walking back the way he had come.

"The best commander; we are asking for the best!"

Max watched him go until Nancy took front and center in his view.

"John can be a real prick sometimes, but he's right. We've got to clean things up around here before the board sweeps it away. You think you can cover that, Max? Did we choose the right person for this?"

The speculative tone in Nancy's voice upset him. Why would she question him at this point in his training? Was she out of her mind? The amount of effort he had put into the program thus far was herculean. Yet another slimy innuendo Nancy was trying to get to stick.

"Just give me my space. I don't like being under a microscope all the time."

Nancy gnashed intently on her gum while shaking her head in disapproval.

"Max, you work for us. Let's just not have another critical failure like today. I suggest you and your little space tribe have a pow-wow and get things lined up. I'd hate to see anyone get replaced."

Crossing her arms with authority, Nancy smirked and walked away. She felt content that the verbal poison she had wanted to inject had found its mark and was now pulsating through Max's veins. As she left, Max closed his eyes and tried to maintain his composure. In his head, he wanted to pop Nancy's bobbly head off her neck like a plastic doll, a bittersweet moment of childish fantasy. He was so tired of having to answer to every mess-up that happened, large or small. Luckily, he had the perfect target at which to vent his steaming furnace of frustration. Walking back to the still bickering group, he honed in on his prey and prepared to fire.

"Alright everybody, let's quiet down! Please, just shut up for five seconds!"

The squabbling group reluctantly obliged and turned their attention slowly toward Max.

"First off, Guppy—what have I told you about getting out of your seat during crap storms like that? What if we hit something, ricocheted, and lost control? What would you have done then? If we lose one of our team, the rest of us have to pick up their work load. A work load, mind you, that we don't have the capability of picking up! You've got to start listening to me!"

Sheldon looked away, trying to avoid the situation.

"Did you hear me, Guppy? Sheldon?"

Still refusing to look Max in the eyes, Sheldon gave a squeamish nod of his head.

"Good. And as for the rest of us, we've got to get this nailed down. The higher ups are frustrated and looking to pull the program."

"What! You can't be serious? We've put months into this thing!" howled Phillip angrily.

"They honestly wouldn't do that to us, would they? This was their program, their idea! How could they be so arrogant!" joined in Stephanie.

Max shrugged, also feeling the sting.

"Honestly, I don't think it was ever about the program. If they can't get something out of this they can use, monetize and slap a sticker on, they have no real reason to stick around. This is what I was worried about when we decided to privatize this industry—money, money, money, but no vision. It is what it is. Until we get off this rock, we have to behave like good little monkeys in our cages."

Scott stepped into the center of the group, looking troubled.

"Guys, we can't let that happen. We're the best this country's got to offer, and this is a once in a lifetime opportunity. All power tripping and titles aside, we've got to pull this together."

The group acknowledged Scott's comment with a grumbling accord.

"I'll polish up my trajectory calculations and figure out how to optimize flight paths to evade the ridiculous asteroids they keep throwing at us," offered Phillip.

"And I'll go back over the system specs to find some more Hail Mary options for the unthinkable," added Stephanie.

Max then gazed at Sheldon who was belligerently keeping silent. The group joined Max and waited, silently pressing in on Sheldon like a vice to squeeze out at least one drop of humility.

"Sheldon?" probed Scott.

"Fine, fine, I'll stay in my chair! I'll sit back and watch Gatti screw things up!"

Max grabbed Sheldon by the collar, forcing him to look Max directly in the eye. Like two caged tigers fighting for territory, they glared at each other fiercely.

"Look Sheldon—you've got a serious attitude problem. I don't care how good you are at what you do. We are a team. Get that through your thick skull!"

Sheldon relaxed his stance slightly, slumping back and away from the enraged Max.

"Alright, I guess I've been a little too hot-headed lately. I'm sorry. We've just been training a lot, and maybe that's got me a little messed up."

Max shook his head, but quickly returned to his composed, in-charge self.

"We're a team, a team! I know it's been said a thousand times, but we're not acting like it. We've got some real talent here, but that doesn't mean jack if we can't work together. We're no better than a bunch of stupidly expensive crash test dummies. Now, let's take some time to think about that, regroup, and meet back fresh in the morning."

The group was dismissed, each robotically heading off in their own direction. They had done this so many times before it was now almost instinctual. As Max walked towards his own locker, his brain was racing through the details of their most recent failure. Although they had failed the simulation, a part of him felt a deep bitterness towards it all. Every time they conquered another mountainous obstacle, they would be forcefully placed at the base of yet another one, twice as tall.

What are they doing to us?

Back at his apartment, Max showered and then sat looking at himself in the foggy mirror. He saw the bags under his eyes from all the lost hours of sleep, dwelling on how to overcome so many unforeseen problems. His dedication, his focus, had cost him what most would call a normal life. He dated, but only enough to fill the void in his life. He had friends, friends that showed up every single day to train. Those were the best kind of friends to have. That's all he needed; he didn't need a so called normal life; not since that had been taken from him at a very young age.

Splashing cold water on his face from the sink faucet, he let out a moan and headed for bed. Before making it there, he heard a quiet tapping at his door. Glancing at the clock he sighed.

Nine o'clock at night? Who wants me now?

Nine might as well have been three in the morning considering the schedule he was on. Fighting the desire to scream, he threw on a towel and answered the door. Standing there in a spaghetti strap top and workout pants was Stephanie. It was obvious that she had just finished a vigorous run. Beads of sweat ran down her face, dripping onto her well-kept frame. Max readjusted his head, realizing he had let his eyes wander just a bit too far down from her face. It was extremely difficult to keep a commanding, professional persona when in her presence. He often wondered why a woman so beautiful would forsake an easy, fulfilling life on the outside for this. But at the same time, it made him even more strangely attracted to her.

"Sorry, Max . . . I know it's late . . . it's just, oh, I don't know . . . I can't get my head on straight. Do you have a towel?"

Without waiting for his answer, Stephanie pushed the door all the way open and entered. Once inside, she headed directly to the bathroom, emerging with a small towel she then used to wipe herself off. Max looked away, again realizing that she was putting him in a weird trance that was taking his focus away from their conversation.

"It's just with all the training, stress, and unbelievable amounts of pressure, I haven't felt like myself. I mean, I like the challenge—don't get me wrong—but it's the method. You know what I mean. The stupid opinions of how we're performing. They don't know what it's like to actually man these missions. I don't know . . . I just felt like getting that off my chest."

As Stephanie continued, she plopped down onto the floor and began to stretch. Her lean muscles flexed beneath her purposeful tension. She was the embodiment of a driven machine. Max began to say something, but found himself completely muted by a sudden rush of hormones.

"You don't really think they'd kick this can down the road, do you? I mean, somebody out there's got to want a mission like this to succeed. Historically, we've done stupider things, don't you think?"

Stephanie flung her arms to her other side, stretching her leg out forcefully.

"Well I . . . I agree. I just don't know what to say, really. You know me; you know that doing something like this has been the most driving force in my life. But, at the end of the day, it's about money and egos. Whose pockets we're filling and whose egos we're building. It's human really, to be like this; castles, weaponry, skyscrapers, rockets; bigger, faster, more and more. It only makes sense that this would be no different. I'm just happy that nobody's brought up marketing yet."

The comment made Stephanie smile. She got back to her feet, keeping her eyes locked on Max.

"So, what have you heard? I know this is completely unprofessional, my being here and asking, but I don't care. We're pretty much family as far as I'm concerned. You can discipline me later."

Max was taken aback by the teasingly forward tone of Stephanie's voice. He paused, wondering if there was more actually happening, but was quick to remind himself of the stone cold woman he was dealing with. She would never waste her time and effort having an impetuous fling after just suffering such a massive failure.

"Money, like I was saying. The investors feel like they're trying to hold water in a strainer at this point. The public just isn't empathetic to our cause. The people in charge say it's not entertaining enough. I say they're out of their minds. What isn't entertaining about furthering the reach of humankind? Do we need a celebrity on board, or maybe stage the whole thing like a reality show? Honestly, this brain dead culture we're cultivating is really starting to piss me off."

Stephanie smiled a mischievous smile that divulged the fact that she had enjoyed his comments on many levels.

"Well, I don't care what they say. We've got the best of the best here. Entertaining or not, we're going to succeed, especially when we've got our overly qualified commander at the wheel. What could possibly go wrong?"

Max also let out a small sliver of a smile. Stephanie had worked her magic on his otherwise impervious armor of duty. Maybe he could be weak just this once? For all he knew, the whole mission was on queue to be defunded, debunked, and tossed anyway. But Stephanie somehow assured him that they wouldn't be derailed.

"Okay, I'll let you be now. You've got a lot to think about and it's late; well, at least late for people like us. I appreciate you lending me your ears for the sake of humanity. Nobody likes a whiner."

"You're not whining. You've got some real concerns, and I appreciate that. Let's just say we're discussing mission issues and keep it professional. Or at least keep the appearance of professionalism."

Stephanie shot him a teasing look and winked.

"Whatever you say, Commander . . ."

Max watched as Stephanie walked away, keeping his door cracked just enough to get a glimpse of her feminine body sway. He needed to take another shower—a cold one.

That woman is going to be the death of me.

Chapter 2- Nightmare Black

The unrelenting screech of an alarm blared off and on. His sheets moved like waves of melted wax as Max slowly rolled over and pried one eye open. It was time to get up, move his ass after sleeping for what seemed like only minutes. An unbelievable fatigue coursed through his body like a seismic tremor. But he had no choice. He was the commander and commanders were never late. Slumping out of bed, he began his tedious morning ritual. After reminding his reflection in the mirror a couple of hundred times why he was doing what he was doing, he headed towards the door. He stopped short of grabbing the doorknob—something was peculiar—slid carefully through the crack under the door was a small slip of paper. He warily bent over and picked it up, reading the short message silently. His morning fatigue morphed into a thick cloud of anger. With an indignant mashing of his hands, he crushed the paper into a ball and tossed it furiously behind him.

Somebody's going to answer for this!

Abruptly leaving his room, he slammed the door purposefully and immediately began searching the facility for the only person he could think of to find—Nancy. This had to be coming from her; this kind of thing almost always did. But he wasn't about to let her win; not this time. Taking long strides, he was shedding the layers of his normally professional, put-together self like a snake slithering out of its old skin. He was poised to strike. Then, his focused rage finally found what it was looking for. Nancy was standing with a small group of very well-dressed men, all actively debating....

Purchase the full book of Pedirol through MikelParry.com

ABOUT THE AUTHOR

Mikel Parry is an engineer, father, husband and author. A storyteller since boyhood, he cultivated his imagination as he grew up with the hope of one day writing the stories he so loved to envision. Born in a small town in Southern Utah, he dreamed of far off places, fascinating worlds, and unconventional ideas that entertained him during his childhood. Over time his dedication and persistent efforts to realize his dream of being a writer gave him the courage to finally decide that he was ready to bring his talent out into the open.

As an author Mikel Parry looks to entertain, inspire and twist your mind into creative gnarls. There's nothing more rewarding to him than to hear that somebody has enjoyed one of his stories.

Check out Mikel's blog, his latest projects and contact him at:

www.MikelParry.com

www.ingramcontent.com/pod-product-compliance
Lightning Source LLC
Chambersburg PA
CBHW061015120726
47910CB00006B/1952